The Ghost of Rataskaevu Street

INDREK HARGLA is one of Estonia's best-known and most prolific crime writers. Hargla's *Apothecary Melchior Mysteries*, set in fifteenth-century Tallinn and starring a detective pharmacist named Melchior Wakenstede, have been translated into five languages, adapted for stage and were the basis for a popular Estonian film trilogy. *The Secret of Saint Olaf's Church*, the first in the Apothecary Melchior Mysteries, is also available from Pushkin Vertigo.

CHRISTOPHER MOSELEY is a translator from Estonian, Latvian, Finnish and the Scandinavian languages. After nineteen years' service at the BBC, he became a freelance translator and editor in 2005. He has translated novels from Estonian by Andrus Kivirähk, Ilmar Taska, and most recently A.H. Tammsaare.

The Ghost of Rataskaevu Street

Indrek Hargla

Translated from the Estonian
by Christopher Moseley

Pushkin Press
Somerset House, Strand
London WC2R 1LA

The Ghost of Rataskaevu Street was first published as *Apteeker Melchior ja Rataskaevu Viirastus* by Varrak in Estonia, 2010

First published in English by Peter Owen Publishers in 2016
First published by Pushkin Press in 2026

ISBN 13: 978-1-80533-576-4

A CIP catalogue record for this title is available from the British Library

The authorised representative in the EEA is eucomply OÜ, Pärnu mnt. 139b-14, 11317, Tallinn, Estonia, hello@eucompliancepartner.com, +33757690241

Designed and typeset by Tetragon, London
Printed and bound in the United Kingdom by Clays Ltd, Elcograf S.p.A.

MIX
Paper | Supporting responsible forestry
FSC® C018072

www.pushkinpress.com

1 3 5 7 9 8 6 4 2

The Ghost of Rataskaevu Street

FOREWORD

Tallinn
AD 1419

The year of Our Lord 1419 saw somewhat more peaceful times in Livonia. The Victual Brothers had been expelled from the Baltic Sea, but long-distance trade was still fraught with danger, as the vogts and vassals of the maritime strongholds had got into the habit of impounding ships close to shallow coastal waters. Letters were exchanged between these towns demanding that marauders be punished and their goods given back. Livonia had been gripped by famine in recent years; the arid summers had caused the crops to fail. This had driven more of the peasantry than ever before to seek work and bread within the town's walls. There were years of famine in the succeeding decades, too; hunger was a serious and very real danger during the Middle Ages.

The greater building boom in Tallinn was over by 1419, but the enlargement of the churches and the strengthening of the town walls continued apace. The grand new Guildhall of the Great Guild of merchants had recently been completed, a symbol of the power and significance of the trading community. Extensive building work had begun at St Nicholas's; a new choir and apse were being constructed on the eastern side of the church. The Dominicans had begun the extension of St Catherine's Church. The town walls, which had to be made thicker and higher all the time to keep pace with developments in weaponry, now needed even more reinforcement around St Michael's Convent. Just at the boundary where the town's land met that of the Teutonic Order, at Pirita – which in those days was called Maarjaorg in Estonian and Mariendal in Swedish – work had finally begun in 1417 on the construction of St Bridget's Convent. But the Master of the Livonian Order himself – the branch of the Teutonic Order based in Toompea – had to intervene to encourage the town to permit stones to be brought from the limestone quarry at Lasnamäe. The first buildings had appeared at Pirita in 1400; the construction of the convent was advocated by the Order, the Order's vassals, the local Swedes and several merchants of Tallinn and Toompea; the town fathers, however, rejected it. It had taken nearly twenty years to overcome the opposition and negotiate diplomatically. One of the nine townsmen who had applied for the construction of the convent had been a certain Laurentz Bruys, 'a miserable and pious merchant', who, however, died just as the major construction work was beginning.

There was constant quarrelling over territory between the Prussian branch of the Teutonic Order, Poland and Lithuania, but, after the defeat at Tannenberg, the influence of the Order was considerably reduced. In 1419 stormy negotiations continued over the Treaty of Thorn, which, despite being discussed before the papal legate and the Council of Constance, had so far not led anywhere. Peacetime in the Order's lands was brief, for as early as 1419 the Hussite War broke out near its borders, and in 1422 yet another war with Poland–Lithuania. Whether Tallinn, too, sent its own troops is not known for sure. As early as 1348 the Master of Livonia had given the town privileges so that they would not have to fight against the Lithuanians and Russians, but this did not exempt it from fighting against Poland. It is certainly known that in one later war – of which there were many between Poland and the Order – Tallinn sent the town's musicians to the battlefield. The Livonian branch of the Order was striving for greater independence and kept increasing distance from the wars going on to the south. Erik of Pomerania, King of the Northern Lands, formed an alliance with Poland against the Order in the summer of 1419, but through the intervention of Emperor Sigismund it was never put into effect. Sigismund did not agree to the plan to liquidate the Order – and, incidentally, Estonia would have had to submit to the Danish crown if that had taken place. In February 1419 the Archbishop of Riga invited representatives of towns in the region to appear before a meeting of the Livonian Diet for the first time, and from that year on envoys from Tallinn did take part in those councils.

In the Tallinn records for March 1419 is to be found an entry recording the death at the harbour bulwark of a certain Gils de Wredte – he who 'painted the walls at the Church of the Holy Ghost' – followed by an intriguing comment which might be interpreted from the Middle Low German text to mean 'he who saw the ghost'.

The material in this novel has also been inspired by one document of Tallinn Town Council dated 1404. The Council warns its colleagues in Magdeburg about a certain citizen of Tallinn, Unterrainer, who was said to have killed several people and who 'thrashes with a whip'. The Tallinn Council recommends that Unterrainer be hanged. Whether there is any connection between this Unterrainer and the Cristian Unterrainer who was executed as a heretic at Fürstenwald in 1413 it has not been possible to establish.

Rataskaevu Street seems to have been notorious since ancient times. The Baltic German historian Johannes von Werensdorff wrote in 1876 that there was known to be a house from the Middle Ages where several women were walled into the cellar alive. Werensdorff does not name his source; he might simply have been passing on a folk tradition. One of the most widespread legends concerning Rataskaevu Street tells of a house where the devil held a wedding and struck up a dance, and since then the house was said to have been haunted. A later legend is known of some evil spirit that lived in the well (the *kaev* of the name Rataskaev, literally wheel well or windlass well) and who would flood the town if sacrifices were not made to him.

The mentality of a medieval person differed greatly from that of someone today – maybe because the spirit of man was younger and more unstable. In those days God was loved more fervently and one's enemy was hated more fiercely. People could be overcome by inexplicable mass hysteria, such as when flagellants went around in procession whipping themselves into semi-consciousness in a religious-sexual ecstasy, thinking that they were saving the world, or when, during the Children's Crusades, thousands of youngsters died from exhaustion and hunger.

Life in a Hanseatic town proceeded according to a fixed rhythm. The Catholic calendar reflects a logical economic life that stems from the rules of nature. From about April to October the Baltic Sea was navigable, and the main trading activity took place in the summer when people were freer from religious obligations. Holy days and the longer fasts were in the first half of the year, and that was also the time when stored foods started to perish or run out. The forty-day fast before Easter enforced austerity and economy; it made one think about one's resources and avoiding extravagance.

In the winter and early spring people could and did take more care of their souls. At the end of spring the town awoke from its piety and began working, which brought bread to the table and made it possible to survive through the next winter.

1

The Quad Dack Tower at St Michael's Convent

2 August, Late Evening

DEATH SMELLED of sweet putrefying blight, of something old and mouldy. Death reeked just like a dead dog wrapped in yeasty dough, and it was nearby. It greeted Tobias Grote, tenderly, invitingly, even alluringly.

They had met before, many times. Tobias Grote was a soldier, and he calculated that at least nine men and one woman had died by his hand. But this Death which was now calling to him was … unjust. Yes, he thought he should not die yet, not because of a ghost, not like that. He saw something like a white shape clad in a death shroud approaching him, and he knew the stench of its stale mouldiness, its insipid rotting stink, and he felt its pain, which was more than one human could bear.

Pain can probably kill you, Tobias Grote, Master of the Quad Dack Tower, was thinking now. It is pain, after all, that kills a man, when he takes so much of it that the body and soul can no longer endure it, and it is simpler to give in to the pain, simpler to die.

And then? What happens next? Will I find out whether everything the Church tells us is really true? Will the Redeemer be waiting for me, and will he tell me why he sent that stinking apparition after me, why he marked me out in that way, why my pathfinder to the heavenly kingdom was this revelation which had, after all, once been human?

Yes, Master Grote was sure of that. That the one chosen as his angel of death had once been a person of flesh and blood, and he had no idea why he was being punished in this way at the last moment of his life, why he had been sent for. The ghost had appeared to him yesterday for the first time, wanting to announce something – but what? He had not understood it then, but now he understood, at his own last moment, why it seemed so tall and at the same time so short. Now he understood. The ghost had come to call him away, to tell him that his time had come. From some corner of his memory Tobias Grote recalled an old hymn; he thought of his brothers, who must be waiting for him in death, his three younger brothers, who had all died in the days of the sea battles.

> Come, pitiless death, enfold me,
> Tell my brothers I am on my way,
> Let them wait for me in the icy silence,
> Let those who remain alive mourn.

He could not remember where or when he had heard that verse – in the tavern, in church, from his brothers in arms or somewhere else – and it did not seem important. The only thing that made him wonder, the only thing throbbing in his head as he awaited his last breath in inhuman pain, was the question of why had this ghost, this apparition with its rotten stench, come to beckon him and not his brothers, not his father or mother.

Only yesterday, yes, it had been only yesterday when the ghost risen from the dead appeared to him for the first time, for one brief moment, and then it had vanished and left Master Grote dismayed and puzzled. Tobias Grote was not yet fifty, and his health was robust, thank God, although his old sword wounds made him ill in bad weather and he was half-blind in the left eye. Nevertheless, he was in full vigour, a strong man, who could hold a battleaxe in his hand, knew how to load and shoot a firearm, and he knew what loyalty and an oath of fidelity were. He had sworn loyalty to the town of Tallinn, and he was proud that the simple son of a tailor from near the town of Travemünde had become the master of a tower in the walls of one of the finest fortresses of the Teutonic Order. And the master of no ordinary or out-of-the-way tower but one of the biggest and strongest towers, almost the foundation of the Order's fortifications, defending the town and the holy sisters.

Tobias Grote had found himself in Tallinn over twenty years ago, when he had been serving as a soldier on a ship from Lübeck. He had found a wife here and stayed. Every soldier on a ship was allowed to do a little dealing on his own, so as to give better service and have more incentive in the fight against pirates. Over the years Grote had acquired a small fortune from such trading, which he had then brought to Tallinn and given the town his loyalty and courage; he had been conspicuous for his service as a town guard and for his diligence until, finally, he had been promoted to Master of the Quad Dack Tower, next to the convent, a post that gave him a permanent and secure income. His wife had already died and his two sons were sailing the seas, conducting trade and, when necessary, using their swords. Formerly the tower had been named in honour of Hunemann, the councillor who erected it, but when, after it had been made taller, the roof began to cave in and the nuns had not taken sufficient care over the repairs, the name Quad Dack began to stick – 'the tower with the shabby roof'.

Grote was, by his own estimation, a God-fearing man, as far as that was possible in his post. He donated as much as he could to the Guild of the Holy Body and diligently attended the convent to hear sermons when they were preached to the townspeople there, and sometimes he worked free of charge for the good of the nunnery, chopping firewood, making the odd repair and teaching the young members of the guilds and the town's defence force how to cut down an enemy with a battleaxe or how to defend the convent better if an enemy should attack the town. The three-storeyed Quad Dack Tower was in the grounds of the convent, and the old town wall surrounding the convent was built into it. Entry to the tower was from the middle floor, to which steps climbed from the courtyard, and between the new and the old town wall was a patch of gravel which stretched to the nearby Louenschede Tower and from there to the stables. The Quad Dack Tower and this narrow patch of ground were both under Tobias Grote's supervision, and it was his responsibility to defend it in the event of an attack. In his own view he had managed this job well, and he had never offended against a single saint and had lived a life pleasing to God, so now, at the last moment of his life, he thought this death meted out to him was unjust.

It had been late yesterday evening, as he was heading home from the nuns' tavern to the little house facing the yard on the corner of Lai Street, when, as if from another world, the spectre had appeared before him from Rataskaevu Street – the shade of a person once alive, which had stretched out its hand to him and wanted to say something, admonish him, warn him or announce some holy act. Grote had seen it only for a moment by torchlight and had been frozen into a pillar of salt from fright before some dim shadows had swallowed up the ghost on the spot or taken it back to the land of shadows. Grote had stopped at the door of his home to pray and to think. Had he drunk too much of the nuns' spicy ale, or had he really been confronted by a ghost risen from the dead? But he knew that it *was* real, not a dream, because he had been drinking beer a couple of times a week at the nuns' tavern, and he had been blind drunk thousands of times in his life, but he had never seen devils. No, no, yesterday he had not been so drunk that he would see something that wasn't there, so he really had seen a ghost. That was his conclusion.

And the following morning, after he had cautiously told his housekeeper about it, it all seemed even clearer, and the image of the ghost was more sharp in his mind than any ordinary everyday thing. So that morning he had gone to the shrewd Melchior, the apothecary, who always had some good medicinal potion for over-indulgence in beer, and after that he had gone, on his housekeeper's recommendation, to the Dominicans, because one of the brothers, Hinric, was said to know everything about evil spirits and even, if necessary, how to drive them out.

But Grote hadn't been able to, just couldn't, explain to Hinric exactly what it was that had brought him to the monastery, and in the end Hinric, who always had plenty to be getting on with, concluded that if the Master of the Tower would drink less ale and sweet medicinal potions he might see fewer demons – and maybe a proper steam-bath might drive them out of his head for ever.

But now death had come to visit him, in the ghostly hours, when Grote's head had been swimming with beer, and it was beginning to seem to him that that previous time the ghost had really been a mere phantom. And then he had heard his name being called quietly.

Throughout the day it had been raining torrentially in Tallinn, as the townspeople had long been expecting, draining the filth from the streets, and, after the rain in the early evening, the wind dropped and the fog set in. Into that fog the Tower-Master had stepped; he came out of the door on the second floor of the tower on to the wooden walkway above the arched alcoves. He remembered no more, for at that very moment he fell. And now he lay on the ground where he had landed, between the nunnery and the town wall. Most likely no bone or joint remained intact. His body was racked with pain, and through the mist he saw the ghost approaching him, shrouded in a white cloak. He smelled the stench of rotting putrefaction and mould. The ghost approached, and suddenly a hot light flared up all around.

He saw the face of the ghost leaning closer to him in the light, and he wanted to scream because what he saw was …

It wasn't possible. It couldn't be. This was madness.

He refused to believe it, and yet he knew that what was looking at him was his own death. The ghost had let him know who or what it was, and death now seemed even more unjust to him, even more senseless.

In the last moment of his life he thought of his own sons and begged God that their deaths be more merciful.

2

Melchior's Pharmacy, Rataskaevu Street

3 August, Morning

For the Tallinn apothecary, Melchior Wakenstede, this day began and ended with death. That was too many deaths for one beautiful fresh sunny August day. People die every day, regardless of the weather, but still this was too many for one day, especially when you have known two of the three deceased very well and you are very sorry for their demise.

That day began with Melchior standing on the threshold of his pharmacy in the morning, greeting the passers-by cheerily and inviting them inside the shop to sweeten their mouths or taste a sip of a medicinal potion. Thus he spent most of his days, and thus he would – God willing – spend the rest. He was forty years old, and he believed that he was as necessary to Tallinn as Tallinn was to him. At that age a man tends to look back on his life and decide whether he has done anything with his days that will be pleasing to God, and Melchior believed he had. Since his father had died – when Melchior was scarcely out of his apprenticeship – he had kept the apothecary's shop on Rataskaevu Street in Tallinn, carefully and devotedly following his father's teachings and the orders of the Council and the town physician. He had been mixing remedies for decades and curing the townspeople's ills, and had been preparing confections and selling several kinds of intoxicating drinks, being especially proud of his strong, sweet 'apothecary's dram', which he sometimes referred to as his elixir. As far as he could, Melchior also dealt in all sorts of other things, from ink to a bitter essence made of marinated wolf's intestines and mummified human remains. And although he might sometimes think himself that such miraculous cures didn't always ease people's illnesses, the trade in these helped to maintain his reputation as a scholarly apothecary and ensure the respect of the town. As an educated man, the apothecary was part trader, part scholar; people often came to ask his advice – and not only about their painful organs.

Melchior had heard it said about himself that he was a perspicacious man, a clever man, a shrewd man. He had his eye on people; he could see what others didn't see. The background to such stories was evidently down to the fact that that several times he had accused someone in front of the Magistrates' Court of killing someone else, and later the court had indeed found that man or woman guilty. Melchior did not think of himself as an informer, but he probably saw more of the people in Tallinn than any other living person. And for the town to flourish, for everyone to have a good life here, sores could not be allowed to fester. People who had assumed the right to kill others secretly and by stealth and then pretend to be innocent did not have the right to live here. If someone kills, they will do it again. It starts to seem simple and convenient; their fear of God becomes a sham, and, worst of all, killing becomes a habit. Melchior feared a town where a murderer goes unpunished, and all those he had accused had killed out of greed, viciousness or avarice and had taken upon themselves the divine right to make decisions over the life and death of others.

The town had gathered within the shadow of its walls people who wanted to live there safely, to breathe, think and strive for their own happiness without anyone snuffing out the candle of their lives through malice. Those people had agreed to respect each other's lives and rights, and the Council was in place to see to it that no one regarded their own rights as greater than those of others.

Melchior's father, who was now buried in the graveyard of St Barbara's Chapel behind the Seppade Gate, taught him this, and Melchior always did everything as his father had taught. 'Poison lurks in the soul of a murderer. A murderer is a person who has stepped over a boundary set by God. Fear the murderer and regard him as your own and God's enemy, and may all the saints give you aid.' Those had been Melchior's father's words, and he had lived by that teaching. He had never accused the innocent or the weak or the poor who had killed only to defend the rights God had given them. He had not accused women who had killed a rapist to defend their honour; he had not accused those who had killed robbers to protect their property; and he had not accused those who had had to kill in revenge for injustice. As well as the human court there is also the court of the forces of Heaven, and before that we will all appear one day.

On this fresh August morning Melchior learned with distress that the soul of the merchant Laurentz Bruys had departed from his body the day before at Marienthal and was probably flying with the angels to God. This had been announced to Rataskaevu Street by Michel – the apprentice gunsmith of the *marstall*, the town stables – who had just heard the news. The stables housed the town's horses, but the foals were taken to an estate on the edge of the town lands, and it was near there that the building of St Bridget's Convent had recently commenced. It was at the convent that the respected merchant Bruys had died yesterday. The news was brought early in the morning by the stablehand, who had been leading two foals from the manor to the stables.

Melchior should not have been surprised, because if any revered townsman had time on earth to gather all the signs around him it was Laurentz Bruys. Still, he felt it was sad. He made the sign of the cross and muttered to himself, 'May the saints bless him, now that he stands at the threshold of Heaven. God will see that this man has suffered much injustice in this life.'

Laurentz Bruys had been old, very old. He was so old that he could no longer walk properly on his own legs and often let himself be carried by servants through the town on a sedan chair. And speech had deserted him a few months before, which Melchior knew to be a sure sign of approaching death. But that was not why this man was so well known in the town. Several scoffingly referred to him sometimes as Saint Laurentius behind his back, and other members of his trading fraternity in Lübeck were said to be downright angry with him, because his business methods were ruining them.

But Melchior's train of thought was interrupted by the arrival of the Magistrate, Court Vogt Wentzel Dorn, who was walking from St Nicholas's to the Apothecary's pharmacy and responding to the respectful greetings of the passers-by with a surly nod. With his greying hair, Dorn was, in many people's eyes, the symbol of justice in Tallinn, for he had been in that post body and soul, loyally and faithfully carrying out his duties to Tallinn, for over a dozen years. He was a serious man who rarely laughed and thus a worthy foil to his friend the Apothecary who, despite his age, could giggle like a child – and, what is more, did so often. Sometimes Melchior wondered whether it was the job that made Wentzel Dorn bad-tempered. Year after year of dealing with thieves, rapists, robbers and murderers, bringing them to court, having them tortured and put to death – isn't that too much for one man's spirit? For instance, the previous week Dorn had had a Swedish thief from a coastal village shackled to the pillory in Town Hall Square and horsewhipped, but after the beating the man had gone to meet his Maker. Melchior knew that his friend Dorn was very annoyed about this because, had he survived, as a punishment he had been going to have a couple of the man's fingers chopped off. The court had not sentenced the thief to death, and such things could hardly make life easier for the court official.

But now Dorn had again turned up at Melchior's pharmacy – as usual when some matter was bothering him, for there is no better cure for melancholy than a few words with a friend and no better restorative than a stoup or two of Melchior's sweet dram. Some things in this world, Melchior knew, never changed. So he was all the more surprised when Dorn motioned with his hand indifferently to his sly wink and greeting, and when Melchior, without asking further, reached for the bottle of spirits Dorn said, 'No, thanks, my friend, I don't think I will today.'

'Oh-ho,' exclaimed Melchior. 'No pains in any of your limbs today? Or have you found some other means of doctoring yourself in this town?'

'I'm just not in the mood,' answered Dorn cautiously. And, as if by way of excuse, he added, 'At my age I suppose a man should be used to death notices, but, you see, they still upset me. And that's why I'm not in the mood.'

'Oh yes,' replied Melchior, nodding. 'I heard that news this morning, too. It does make you sad when such an upstanding and God-fearing citizen leaves our midst.'

'So it does,' said Dorn, 'and so suddenly and unexpectedly, too, that you don't understand any more who or what directs a man's life. Is it God and his saints, or ...?' He sighed and sat down on a chair in the corner of the shop.

'Our pastor at St Nicholas's can surely tell us more about it,' said Melchior. 'But, well, I wouldn't call this death unexpected. Hasn't there been a lot of talk about Master Bruys's will at the Guildhall of the Great Guild and how some merchants have called it excessively magnanimous?'

'Hold on,' interjected Dorn. 'You said Master Bruys? You mean he's dead?'

Melchior stared at Dorn in astonishment. He blinked quickly and grew serious.

'Good heavens. So someone else then?'

'Grote, the Master of the Tower,' said Dorn. 'He fell from his tower last night and died right there between the walls.'

'Fell from the tower?' exclaimed Melchior.

'Well, over the parapet, apparently from the defence walkway above those stone arches. He must have been drunk because the corpse stank of beer and in the tower chamber he had a fair-sized keg. He went out on the walkway while sloshed and stumbled, what else ...?'

Melchior eyed his friend attentively. He knew he had something on his mind, but he didn't push him.

Dorn carried on. 'The guards found him there this morning; at first they thought he might have been beaten to death or something, that there was something on the back of his head, but there were no signs of a beating on his body at all, only his forehead, which was bleeding and broken. He was lying there on his back staring at the sky, a few bones sticking out as you'd expect when somebody falls from a height, I suppose, but …' He was silent for a moment, licked his lips, and Melchior waited. 'It's as if … as if he had been terrified. As if he had been beside himself with fear. I've never seen a dead face like it. Usually they look peaceful, frozen in place, so to speak, but Grote … As if he'd seen a ghost.'

'A ghost?' asked Melchior, animated. 'What ghost?'

'Well, that's what I said. It's as if he'd seen spirits or demons. His face was sort of stiff with fear and not with pain, that I *do* know. After a fall like that the pain is so great that a man can't bear it, but he had a face like … his mouth was open and his eyes wide with terror – horrible to think of. Lord have mercy.'

'Very interesting,' said Melchior. 'Incredible.' He poured himself a dram and drank it in one go. Dorn stared at him and finally muttered, 'Pour one for me, too. A bigger one, full.'

Melchior did as he was asked and told Dorn, 'Yesterday, Master Grote came by here, as he sometimes does. He wasn't feeling too good, and I guessed he must have been drinking beer the evening before because he stank of it even then. He bought a couple of stoups of this drink, but there seemed to be something on his mind. I wouldn't say that we were friends, but sometimes we did meet up here and there, sometimes in the taproom at the nuns' tavern, and one autumn he recommended a good Estonian bricklayer to me who worked in the courtyard of the nunnery and who made a very good job of my back wall. But, anyway, yesterday he really did have something on his mind; he didn't talk much, but he seemed to want to ask me something. I suppose I was just chattering away, asking about his sons' health and so on, because there was nobody else in the shop at the time. And then …' Melchior blinked rapidly and shook his head. 'It sounds incredible, but that's just how it was – that, although he was always quiet when he came here, I must have said, "Master Grote, you have a look on your face as if you'd seen a ghost." And he was very frightened at that.'

'Frightened?' asked Dorn.

'Just that. By St Victor. He was startled and almost knocked his stoup over. He looked at me with fearful eyes, mumbling something I didn't understand, and then he quickly drank up his dram and said he had something to do at the Dominicans and took his leave.'

'What do you mean?' asked Dorn.

'That he looked like a man who'd seen a ghost, and I, like a fool, said that, and he was terribly shocked, as if he really had seen a ghost. And now you come and tell me that he's fallen to his death off the walkway and he had a face on him like one who's seen a ghost.'

Dorn sighed. 'Don't hold on to my every word. That man drank pretty hard, and if he thought he saw something he might have been seeing demons conjured up by his heavy drinking. As they said in that sermon at the Dominicans, about what happened to the man at Dünamunde, the one who just drank and drank and gave up going to church ...'

Melchior smiled. 'That was a very instructive sermon. Prior Moninger admonished Christians to drink less, but I think he also wanted to say that you shouldn't drink alone but with friends, and in a way that there is time left over in a man's life for the word of God. But since you've brought it up, it makes me wonder what business Master Grote – may the saints protect him – had with the Dominicans. My recollection is that he always went to the Church of the Holy Ghost to take the sacrament, and I don't think I ever remember seeing him at a sermon at St Catherine's.'

Melchior was deep in thought while Dorn drank his sweet dram and turned the subject to Master Bruys, for his death was news to him. He knew Bruys the merchant well, as the latter had once been a councillor, and Dorn remembered a very bitter dispute at the Guildhall of the Great Guild when the merchant lords were almost tearing each other's hair out over the building of a new convent.

'Yes, yes,' said Melchior in reply, but his thoughts were elsewhere. 'He died at Marienthal. He'd gone there on a pilgrimage – or had himself taken there. Soon the whole town will know about it, I suppose.'

Laurentz Bruys had been an old and very respected man and must have been one of the richest men in Tallinn. He was said to have donated the most money to his church and the almshouses, and, because he had no children, his will left very large sums to St Nicholas's, the Dominican Monastery and the new Convent of St Bridget.

Master Bruys had fathered seven children, of whom only three survived childhood. One son had unfortunately perished in a fire that raged in Tallinn, one had fallen into the hands of the Victual Brothers and been hanged, one had gone back to Germany under confusing circumstances, and his father had disowned him, and the only daughter who grew to adulthood married a man in Riga but there died in some epidemic. The merchant's wife had also died, and he had lived alone in his house on Lai Street with his servants. Melchior also knew that while many people regarded Master Bruys almost as a saint – because of his exceeding religious reverence and fear of God – others could not stand him because he was one of those who strongly favoured the building of a new convent by the Order. And Melchior also remembered that there had been deep enmity between Master Bruys and another Tallinn merchant, Arend Goswin, that went back several decades, but in the end they had made up. That story was not spoken of much; it was ancient history and should be forgotten. Rumours could spread with terrific speed and just as mysteriously they could die down and disappear. In recent years only good had been spoken of Bruys the merchant – as long as it didn't concern the plans to build a new convent.

'That will of his,' the Magistrate continued (the drink had put him in a talkative mood), 'he made no secret of it. He came to the Town Hall one day, read it out in the presence of two councillors and let a notary sign it.'

'Yes, I remember,' Melchior remarked. 'He allows his house to be sold and some of the proceeds to go to his business in Lübeck, but much more of it will go to the Sisters of St Bridget and churches in Tallinn.'

'Well, he has no living children, and the one son who is supposed to have become a soldier – Thyl was his name – was disowned. Nor does he have any living siblings, so everything is in his will. Oh, I remember well how there were large sums for both almshouses and a small amount for the Dominicans and then some for road building, in particular for the one to Marienthal. Well, and then for intercession to the churches and donations to St Nicholas's and the Church of the Holy Ghost and the other brothers of the Great Guild who are making the pilgrimage in his name to Compostela ...'

'Wasn't there some grim tale connected with Thyl?' Melchior asked suddenly.

The Magistrate frowned. 'Yes, there was, now that you mention it. So many years have passed since then that I've forgotten. Or, well, just between ourselves, I think the Council wanted it hushed up quickly ... in any case it didn't get to the Magistrates' Court.'

'That's how it was, I suppose,' murmured Melchior.

'But so what?' sighed Dorn. 'It's such an old story, and nobody blames Master Bruys, may the Lord have mercy on him. By the way, not even the Town Council was forgotten in his will – with his own money he had two pounds of wax candles bought for the Council and left fifty marks separately for the law court so that justice would always be done according to God's will and the laws of Lübeck – that was what he had written down. And I can't recall all the smaller bequests. Now, didn't he even leave an instruction that any new landlord would not be allowed to drive his servants out of his house and that they should be allowed to stay there? He left money to them, too. Yes, he was a generous man with a noble heart. If only there were more like him. And St Bridget was merciful to him, too, it seems. She allowed him to die while on a pilgrimage to the very place for which he'd fought so many battles – if you can say that about a sacred establishment.'

'You can,' Melchior said with a smile. 'You can certainly say that about St Bridget's Convent. They nearly came to blows with guns and swords over it. Sometimes – forgive me, friend – but sometimes it seems to me that our aldermen look at things a bit too narrowly, and their thinking is stuck in a time when they were still young. I think Tallinn is now such a big, rich town that three monasteries are a good thing for it.'

'That may be so,' opined Dorn. 'No one has done badly yet out of any monastery. Not that I go along with St Bridget's rules or even understand them exactly, but if more pilgrims start flocking to Tallinn instead of scoundrels and murderers that can only be a good thing.'

'I suppose so,' agreed Melchior.

'By the way, Melchior, have you heard the news?' cried Dorn suddenly. 'Pretty good news for once. At the Council they're talking about that pirate, that rascal – who I'd like to have drawn on the wheel – that Clawes Döck who's been robbing merchants around Tallinn, the one we wrote to the gentlemen in Raseborg and Lübeck about, the one that Visby Council is defending strongly … That murderer has now been caught at Abfors and put in chains.'

'That's good then,' mumbled Melchior.

'So far, so good. The only thing now is that Erik of Gotland has got to agree to have that robber chopped into pieces. But I suppose the Council knows how to fix matters in Visby. It's not like the old days …'

At that moment the wife of the butcher from Assauwe Tower entered the pharmacy. Dorn nodded politely to her, and Melchior was interested to know whether the wormwood oil had helped against her esteemed husband's vertigo, and the wife shrieked that it helped so much that it was as if the Virgin Mary herself had blessed him and could the Apothecary give her more, instantly.

'It does seem to help if the wormwood juice and the oil mixture have a bit of powder from pounded mares' hooves added,' declared Melchior, stepping over to the pestle. 'I don't have much of it, but there's always some for Madam Butcher.'

So Dorn bid his friend goodbye, saying it was now time to go to the town guards and find out whether any crimes had been committed in the town.

3

The Courtyard of the Unterrainer House, Rataskaevu Street

3 August, Late Evening

URSULA, THE MERCHANT'S DAUGHTER, was fourteen, and Simon, the goldsmith's son, was fifteen. They were told that they were no longer children, and they must almost have believed it. They had known each other their whole lives, were born in Tallinn and had grown up in adjoining houses at the junction of Karja Street and Kuninga Street. They had walked the path to school up on Toompea together and to hear sermons in church and to Christmas mass.

Simon was a tall, strong-boned, lanky young man with slightly squinting eyes and a nice low voice, which seemed to Ursula to be getting lower every day. Just a few years ago Simon had been singing in the choir of the Church of the Holy Ghost in a very high voice, and Ursula had always gone to hear him sing.

Ursula was a redhead, and, as Simon's voice grew deeper, her hair grew redder. Simon said she was the most red-headed girl in town. Simon had said that several times now, and Ursula had taken to wondering whether the boy actually meant something else by it. Especially the way Simon said, 'I believe that you, Ursula, are the most red-headed girl in town', and then looking deeply into her green eyes, forcing the girl to turn her gaze away and carry on wondering what Simon actually meant.

Talking didn't come easily to Simon. He never actually said anything much. He rarely told stories, and when he did he would get it over within a couple of sentences, as if the only important thing were to find out what had happened and not how it had happened, what people thought and said about it. Yes, Simon spoke little and said only the essential things that he himself believed or knew or was sure of or that he thought very important. And if he said something repeatedly about Ursula's red hair then the girl knew that it was very important to the boy.

That she, Ursula, was very important to him.

In what way important was only now starting to become clear, after it emerged that her father had received a letter from his trading partner in Lübeck, and in it was a marriage proposal for Ursula. It came as no surprise to Ursula that the time for marriage was approaching. Her mother had started talking about it a year ago, at first obliquely but then more directly. Just as noble lords, all sorts of kings and dukes arrange marriages for their sons and daughters, so important merchants do it, too – all in order to secure good relations through the sacrament of holy matrimony, form new alliances and promote mutual family bonds, because nobody wants bad fortune for their own relative, especially one to whom one has betrothed one's own daughter in the flesh. So Ursula awaited the same fate as had befallen her elder sisters – one of them lived in Danzig and the other in Rostock, and in this way her father had built up support for his business. And so, gradually, her mother had started talking to Ursula about matrimonial matters – how a good woman must always be virtuous and bear her husband children, and if she does this diligently she will be highly respected and honoured and have good care taken of her even when she starts to turn feeble and ill.

Simon was an apprentice at the house of the Tallinn goldsmith named Casendorpe, but now his apprenticeship was nearly over and he had to become a journeyman, as agreed, in faraway Münster with an old friend of his father's. There he would learn to make high-quality gold and silver, as they do in Lübeck, and when he was experienced enough he could choose a town where he would work as a master, join the craft guild and become a citizen of that town. There he would also take a wife and remain in the town as its goldsmith, because that was the fate prescribed for Simon. Of course, he *could* come back to Tallinn, but there were already enough goldsmiths here, and he had an elder brother who would soon be coming back from Riga after his journeyman years, and his father wanted to leave the business to him.

So this was Ursula's and Simon's last summer together in Tallinn – such seemed to be the will of Heaven.

They had become friends in childhood, grown up and played together, run together along the moat behind the town wall and gone to the pond to fish. Together they made merry in Town Hall Square among the townspeople, when tournaments or fairs were held there and jesters and musicians and jugglers and wise men from the East came, wearing colourful clothes and exhibiting the black arts of Egypt, blowing fire from their mouths or making bears dance. They were in among the people when the Brotherhood of Blackheads put on their suits of armour and jousted on horseback; they would debate who was the strongest knight and who would stay in the saddle, and when Ursula squealed with excitement at every skirmish, Simon would only grunt something in acknowledgement. On those occasions Ursula always felt somehow very secure, *protected*, because Simon had also been taught to fight with a spear and shield. Every citizen of the town was supposed to be able to defend their own town, defend the people, defend the womenfolk and the weak. Together they had run beyond the Seaward Gate to the parrot competition and put bets on their own favourite birds; together they had hopped up and down among the people when the newly chosen May King rode through the town with his sweetheart, and that spring Ursula had again asked Simon if, when *he* got to be May King, he would choose her as his maiden.

Ursula had asked that every spring for a number of years now, and Simon had always said that, yes, he would choose Ursula and he wouldn't choose anyone else, because Ursula had the reddest hair in all Tallinn.

But this year – Ursula remembered it well – Simon had delayed with his answer; maybe because Ursula had asked in a slightly different tone, but she only understood that later. And Simon, too, had answered differently, had looked at Ursula differently and answered hesitantly – not that he was not certain of it, but it was harder for him to express it, as if he wanted to say more than usual but didn't actually dare. And he probably did say more than Ursula had asked.

They were no longer children. So they were told, and they believed it and knew, although they didn't say it, that it was no longer appropriate for them to appear in front of the townspeople together *so much*. Now they had to behave in a more decent and restrained fashion, and they started to seek out places to be together where they were less in the public eye – behind the town wall along the edge of the field, in the town's gardens or behind the churches. Nothing else needed to change – they were still friends, talking, chatting, playing – yet they were less inclined to play together now. They didn't make games up any more. They talked about adult things, they talked – in so far as Simon talked at all – about *themselves*.

Ursula had noticed this change only a couple of months ago. Much to her surprise she had realized that now they spoke more about themselves, their ideas, their wishes, the future; and perhaps about feelings, too, but in a somehow concealed way. They no longer confessed secrets to one another, and they kept things back.

And when they played, they played a different game to the ones a year earlier. Ursula didn't know what the game was called.

Ursula had found a hidden corner in the courtyard of the so-called Unterrainer house. One could climb into it along the wall of the old stables from the garden that lay between the houses of the merchants Goswin and Wolze. It was the sort of place that didn't seem to belong to anyone, not to Master Goswin nor to Pastor Gottschalk Witte, who lived in the Unterrainer house. A large bush grew there, and the corner was overshadowed by the wooden shed of the Unterrainer house. There, between the houses on a narrow path leading from the shed, where the ventilating windows of the salt-cellars opened, was the courtyard of the Unterrainer house and the exit to Rataskaevu Street. At some point there must have been a gate there, but by this time it had rotted away, and one could quickly get to the street. If either of them needed to avoid detection, one could escape along the wall of the old stables and over a patch of garden and turn up all innocent by the well before heading off towards St Nicholas's. Meanwhile the other could, looking equally innocent, go through the Unterrainer yard to Rataskaevu Street and out through the gate on Pikk Hill.

This was a safe place, somewhere they could talk undisturbed and play the game they now seemed to be playing. Today Ursula believed that it was possible to win this game and that the winner would get a reward.

They were sitting close together on a block of wood, and Simon said that Münster is a beautiful big town, there are many fine castles and fortresses and kings around there, and everyone wants splendid gold jewellery, and there would be no lack of work for a good goldsmith.

'If it's a big town, there should be plenty of red-headed girls, shouldn't there?' asked Ursula, and Simon replied that, yes, there probably would be.

'Interesting. So when you choose a wife for yourself, you'll choose a red-headed girl?' Ursula suggested casually, loading her voice with indifference.

Some time passed before the boy replied. His voice, too, attempted to show indifference. 'But I don't want to be with you just because of your red hair,' he said finally, 'and I'm not thinking about getting married at all just yet.'

'Oh, you must be,' laughed Ursula. 'All boys think about what it will be like to be married to a woman, sleeping in the same bed with her and having children with her.'

Simon stayed awkwardly silent. Ursula's shoulders shivered, and she shifted a little closer to him. The dimmer the light became, the sadder the Unterrainer house seemed. People said the house was haunted – not that Ursula knew anyone who had seen the ghost.

'I don't think about any of those things at all,' ventured the boy.

'Do you know what they say about this house?' the girl asked suddenly. 'About the merchant, Unterrainer, who brought his young wife here?'

'Ah, those are just empty and ungodly tales.'

‘I was listening in once when people were talking about this house. They thought I couldn’t hear, you see. You know, they said that Unterrainer didn’t want to sleep with his wife in the same bed, and he tortured that woman terribly, and she became very unhappy because her heart was yearning for some man to love her. She was a very unhappy woman. And then a monk came to comfort her. But the husband caught his wife with the monk … kissing.’

That was not exactly what Ursula had heard, but she didn’t dare repeat the actual word. When it came to it, she was a decent young lady. The boy mumbled something unclear.

‘Exactly,’ Ursula continued. ‘They were kissing, and not like relatives or good friends but like husband and wife, like that, long and …’

He remained silent because he didn’t really know how they might have been kissing.

‘How then?’ the boy asked quietly.

‘Well, not the way *we* would ever kiss,’ said Ursula. ‘Anyway, the husband caught them at it and chopped them dead with a sword and buried them, and ever since then they’ve been haunting the house here.’

‘Merchants don’t carry swords,’ said the boy dully, and Ursula sighed and thought how she couldn’t tell him any more clearly what she meant. But just as she was thinking this she suddenly felt the boy’s arms around her, and a wet kiss was pressed on her cheek. She felt his teeth and his soft downy hair and … and nothing more. The arms were pulled away suddenly, as the boy shifted away from her.

‘Simon,’ whispered Ursula, and in that whisper there was a note of real reproach.

‘I’m sorry,’ said Simon quickly.

'Simon, oh, Simon,' whispered the girl again. She didn't know exactly either how the kissing should be done but certainly in a different way from that.

At that moment they heard a screech. It might have been an old door, or some chain, or something, but in any case it came from close by, and it sounded somehow ominous. Ursula was startled, but before she could say anything she felt a light gust of wind, which brought a stale musty stench to them.

And then they saw a movement in front of them. Something white flashed for a moment through the dusk, something strange, odd and ghostly, some pale form that departed in a trice.

And suddenly they heard a voice. It was a voice from beyond the grave, a low drone, a long howl of lament, echoing off the wall of the Unterrainer house and moving terrifyingly through the soft summer evening. It was not the voice of a living person; it was ghastly and full of hatred, enmity and complaint.

They took to their heels, together, as they had always done as children when something frightened them. They ran, climbed, rushed, stumbled into each other, and the boy's strong hands grasped the girl's waist and helped her as they fled through the narrow passage from the edge of the wall of the old stables on to the patch of garden, on past the well, stopping only when they had reached the shade of the big linden tree in St Nicholas's Churchyard. Here, on sanctified ground, the ghost would not be allowed to touch them.

They were panting, their bodies pressed together. Simon's tough body and long arms now offered Ursula protection, of a kind she had never felt in her life before. The girl didn't have to say anything. The boy's lips found hers. Now they kissed.

Properly, like a man and a woman.

4

Melchior's Pharmacy, Rataskaevu Street
3 August, Late Evening

MELCHIOR HAD HAD so much to do that day in the pharmacy that he didn't make it to the evening sermon at the Dominican church. Plenty of people came to the shop, which was good for business, but his thoughts kept returning to the death of Master Bruys. Not that he saw anything especially odd in it, no. Master Bruys's time had come, and no one would know that better than him, since he had had the book *Ars Moriendi* copied by the Dominicans. This was the book on the art of dying, which had just recently been approved by the Council of Constance; those who followed the teachings in the book were growing in number all the time. It spoke of the virtues of a God-fearing life and how a Christian should prepare himself for death. Everyone must be ready for death, must accept it with joy and enthusiasm, for the best preparation for a good death is a righteous and God-fearing life. Melchior had once talked about this with the Dominican Brother Hinric, and Hinric had greatly praised Master Bruys's piety and how that merchant had followed the letter and spirit of it and was getting ready for death. And, coming from Hinric, these words meant a lot, because he – unlike Melchior – did not approve of the building of a new convent in Tallinn. But at this point Melchior's thoughts went back to the unfortunate Tower-Master, who had also met his end in the night, but it was Hinric he had wanted to talk to. This seemed a little strange to Melchior, because he knew Hinric well and regarded the Dominican as his friend. And he did not recall Hinric ever mentioning Master Grote.

Evening had come, and Melchior was sitting at his accounts book, making calculations, and was just coming to the numbers that would show whether he could write down a profit on the medicines ordered by the merchants in the spring. Business had gone well this year.

Later his wife Keterlyn came into the shop with the twins – Melchior, the son of Apothecary Melchior Wakenstede, his heir, a five-year-old lad, and Agatha, the lass who was born with him. Melchior kissed his wife on the lips and placed the children on his lap. It was important that they didn't start playing with his apothecary's apparatus and that they treat their father's work with respect from an early age. An apothecary's pharmacy was no place for play, but, when the time came, his son would learn the trade alongside his father.

Just as Melchior had learned from his father.

It had not been easy, and it had never been easy for any Wakenstede to reach a firm decision that he wanted a son. There had been a curse on the Wakenstede line for centuries, and no matter how much Melchior hoped he would, he had not overcome it. It was always present, as a punishment from God or the demons, and he had had no escape from it. Not every Wakenstede boy was burdened, but it could be passed from grandfather to grandson. Melchior's father had not had the curse, but the knowledge was all the worse that his only son would live in its grasp. But every

Wakenstede comes to the point when he has to decide whether he wants to fulfil the directive from on high to have descendants and carry his line forward and hope that his heir is free of the curse. Or, if he isn't, then maybe he will be the one who will find, with the help of the saints, a cure for it.

For hundreds of years the eldest Wakenstede son became an apothecary, took the name of Melchior, studied medicine and the arts of healing people, sought herbs for them that God has placed on the earth for man's use and to ease their distress and called on the help and blessings of the saints for that purpose. In this way, perhaps one day, he or his successor would come to understand a way to cure the Wakenstedes' terrible affliction. All the elder Wakenstede sons must pass on the apothecary's wisdom and hope. As far as Melchior knew, he was now the only Wakenstede in Tallinn because all the rest of the direct line had died out. But the curse lived on in the secondary lines, and nothing and nobody could cure it.

'Listen to the saints,' his father had taught him, 'they know. God is one, and it seems to us that sometimes he is too far away. Christ the Redeemer and his teaching will help us towards Heaven in the next world, but the saints are the only ones who can help our family line in this earthly life. Learn, follow their instruction, know as much of them as one man can know, such is the Wakenstede command, and so it should be.'

And Melchior read the lives of the saints, listened to sermons about them, spoke with men who had studied at the university and the monastery, because perhaps some saint might really help, perhaps some saint knew a cure for his family's terrible curse. He didn't know whence came his father's rock-solid belief in it, he didn't know by whom, why and when the Wakenstedes were forced to become apothecaries and assiduously worship the saints, but he was not a man to question the ways of his family line. He knew just one thing – the curse was with him, kept its fangs deep inside him and would not let go, torturing and oppressing him, exhausting him. The only thing that could ease the curse was a woman, the right woman, who steadfastly stands beside him, loves and supports him. But that was only alleviation. Just as a leech helps to suck poison out of a human body, a woman can be an alleviator of the Wakenstede curse. But just as a leech doesn't help a bodily organ that is already condemned to die and can only bring temporary relief, so a woman can't remove the curse.

And the Wakenstede women didn't live long. The more support they give to their husbands the shorter their lives. Keterlyn knew this.

Loneliness was what broke a Wakenstede most readily. His family tree was full of men who, troubled by the curse of solitude, had bitten themselves to death in mental confusion, bashed their heads to pieces against walls, drowned themselves, just to get away from the mental torture that had seized them when the curse took them over.

Five years before, when Melchior thanked God for the gift of twins, he hoped, oh how he hoped, that the curse had left him. For some years it had not affected him, and in Keterlyn's eyes that same inflamed little fire had appeared as when Melchior had proposed marriage to that non-German stonemason's daughter. But, just a couple of months after the twins were born, one hot summer's evening, the curse had struck again.

Melchior was still young, his wife was still young; together they could find the strength to stand against it. But soon they would no longer be able to. Soon it would be too late, and Melchior had still not found a drug that would free his family line from this horror.

He monitored his son carefully, every day looking for signs, evidently the same way as his father had once done, and praying to God. He prayed to the saints, and he hoped. Maybe young Melchior was free of this terrible fate? But several times it had seemed to the Apothecary that in his son's eyes there flashed an odd spark, something endlessly distant, some emptiness and terror. Had it been the same with him? He knew that the curse did not attack until the boy had become a man, but the signs and omens could be seen earlier. In a few years the time would come when he would have to start telling his son about things that fathers do not usually discuss with their sons at that age.

He looked at his children and his wife and felt in his heart again a sharp radiant spark, glowing and getting hotter. As in church, during the sermon, when suddenly you feel within yourself a hot, overwhelming and eternal love towards the Redeemer and the Lord God, you feel an irresistible desire to love, because that is the right way, and the radiant spark in your heart summons you to it even when your reason does not exactly comprehend what the priest is saying. Now he felt the same spark in his heart as he looked at the two red-cheeked youngsters in the shop, studying their surroundings curiously and cautiously. And he felt it even more when he looked at his wife, who was still beautiful; her form was pretty to behold, and the curves of her hips outlined under her dress provoked in Melchior a desire to strip her naked on the spot. Around his wife's eyes you could already make out dark lines; her face was paler than in earlier years, her eyes were deeper, wider and more sorrowful. Melchior was not sure if that was caused by the twins' difficult birth or by life as a Wakenstede.

'They're talking about the same things,' said Keterlyn tenderly. 'Today they saw the beer-carrier's barrow in front of the house again, and now they won't talk about anything else other than wanting a ride in it. And then young Melchior has learned to throw stones in puddles, so now Agatha doesn't want to do anything except throw stones, too.'

'I suppose she'll start wanting other things when she starts playing with other girls more,' said Melchior. 'They've been together all their lives.'

'I suppose so,' agreed his wife.

Melchior lifted the twins up, one under each arm. The children laughed and screamed and pulled their father's hair.

So happy, so innocent, so unaware of all the world's dangers – and of death, thought Melchior.

'You look very serious,' said Keterlyn. 'Is something wrong?'

'Oh, everything is in the best shape with the shop. With the blessing of St Cosmas our business is going well. In a year or two I'll surely be stepping up again before the Council and addressing them as my father wished.'

'For a man of your age you're wanting to follow in your father's footsteps rather too much,' remarked his wife. 'Not that I disapprove, but time is marching on ...'

'Time is marching on, but some things always stay the same. The town needs a pharmacy, and it's best if it has the Council's seal of approval. That's what they've done in several places in Germany. The local council buys a house and rents it to an apothecary, gives him instructions, and the town's notary seals the agreement.'

'But the Council didn't agree to that.'

'The Council *wasn't sure*,' corrected Melchior. 'The Council hesitated about whether it was in the best interests of the town because, in spite of said apothecary's excellence and his services to the town, they found that this same apothecary was too poor to properly maintain a *town apothecary's shop*. But the Council is looking at its decision again when he appears before it once more and gives a better account of his assets. That was their decision. Those skinflints were worried that I'm too poor and want to get rich at the Council's expense. Well, maybe they'll think differently now – or so I must hope and believe.'

'But still you look too serious today.'

Melchior put the children down. They ran squealing to their mother, and Keterlyn told them not to knock anything over.

'Too much bad news,' said Melchior. 'Master Bruys died yesterday on his pilgrimage to the Convent of St Bridget.'

'Oh, I heard that,' nodded Keterlyn. 'It really makes you sad. I've never before seen such a pious merchant in this town. They say that too much money makes people mean, but Master Bruys was more God-fearing than some bishops.' Keterlyn thought for a bit and added, 'I mean, he was certainly more God-fearing than the Bishop of Tallinn, everyone knows that. But you said there was *too much* bad news. What else then?'

'You mean *who* else then,' said Melchior. 'Last night Master Tobias Grote fell to his death from the walkway on the town wall over beyond the convent.'

'Oh, heavens,' cried his wife. 'That excellent man. He was just here in the shop ... No, wait, wasn't he here yesterday?'

'Yes, he was. He came in here during the day and must have been drinking a lot of ale the night before.'

'He does too much of that. His housekeeper – I know her well – tells me sometimes that old Tobias wasn't such a hard drinker in his younger days. But now he sits in the daytime in the tavern beyond the wall or down by the harbour or else in the nuns' tavern, and it wouldn't be long before he didn't have enough money to buy clothes or wood for the winter …' His wife stopped. She put her hand to her mouth. 'Oh, may the Blessed Virgin forgive me. I shouldn't talk like that about the dead.'

'It will be all the same to him now,' opined Melchior.

'And so what happened? He fell, just like that? A healthy, strong man who climbed that wall every blessed day? Never mind being drunk, but that walkway isn't like a roof where your foot might slip and …'

'I don't know,' admitted Melchior. 'The Magistrate didn't know either. The town guards found him and …'

Melchior thought for a moment, looked at the children and kept his counsel.

'Speak,' suggested his wife. 'It must be the thing that's on your mind.'

'Ah,' muttered Melchior. 'It's just a little thing. So sometimes Satan has to pull a person by the tongue … You see, yesterday, when Master Grote came here he was in a blue funk and something seemed to be haunting him. He was sighing, and his eyes were full of fear. So I asked him what was the trouble and said he looked as if he'd seen a ghost. And he was startled at that, really shocked. I could see that these words really put the wind up him. So now, in comes Magistrate Dorn and says that Grote, who'd fallen to his death, had a face on him as if he'd seen a ghost. Not a peaceful face and not a face full of pain but a face full of fear. I think I understand very well what he had in his eyes.'

'For God's sake,' said Keterlyn, shuddering. 'Not in front of the children.'

'Well, you did ask,' replied Melchior awkwardly.

'Such things shouldn't be discussed,' said his wife. 'The Unterrainer house is just down our street. Last spring when the women were gossiping about that poor prostitute, Magdalena, who drowned in the well, I said to myself then that they ought to keep their dirty mouths shut and not talk about that ghost. The twins are playing right here in front of us. Do they need to hear all this about ghosts? They don't even know what life and death are, and who knows what Magdalena might have thought she saw –'

'Wait now, woman, stop there.' Melchior interrupted her. 'You're talking too fast for my slow understanding. Yes, I know about the Unterrainer house, there next to the Goswin house, and there have been horror stories for ages about spirits and phantoms. Yes, Magdalena did drown in the well, I remember that. But what exactly are you trying to say? I don't understand.'

'Just as well, too, because with the children listening I'm not going to talk about such things at all.'

'Then go and put the children to bed and come back down and talk to me.'

Melchior's tone was strangely quiet and resolute, in a way that his wife had very rarely heard him speak before. The hour was late, and she would have liked Melchior to come to bed, too, but she knew her husband's moods. If some story interested him he had to hear it to the end, even if there was a plague or an enemy at the gates. So Keterlyn shrugged and did as her husband asked.

When she came back into the pharmacy Melchior was sitting in the candlelight at the table and seemed to be scribbling something in his accounts book. But he appeared even more serious than before she had gone up, and looking over his shoulder Keterlyn saw that he hadn't made any progress with his bookkeeping.

'So,' said Melchior, 'dear wife, to make matters clear, please tell me why you started talking about Magdalena when I was talking about Master Grote and the ghost?'

'Because Grote's story reminded me of Magdalena's – when you said the he had a face as if he'd seen a ghost. Magdalena, too, said in the public baths at the Zeghen Tower that she'd seen a ghost on Rataskaevu Street, and the next day she was dead. Dead, head first into the well, right here in front of our house.'

'I didn't know you went to the *saun* with a woman of pleasure,' smiled Melchior.

'It's not bad – in the *saun* all women are alike,' replied Keterlyn, and when Melchior was silent at this, and remained silent for a while, his wife coughed and added, 'But better if you don't dwell on that thought.'

'No, I wasn't thinking about that,' Melchior quickly assured her. 'But, anyway, I don't recall you talking about this before.'

'I don't think I've ever told you what women discuss among themselves in the *saun*. And actually it's better if men never find out what women talk about in the *saun*. But I will say that I think Magdalena was a nice woman in every way, never mind that she earned her living as a whore, for she was a God-fearing woman with a kind heart. She didn't tell idle tales about anyone, and when she was asked whom she'd been to bed with she always said that what went on between the walls of that room would stay there. If she started talking about her clients she'd be left without any.'

'That I do believe,' mumbled Melchior.

'Everyone has to earn their living as best they can. It wasn't Magdalena's fault that her husband fell into the hands of the Victual Brothers. And no other love came into her life; she used to say sometimes that her heart was given to her to love only one man. And then she became a housekeeper, and at one stage she was the cook in Master Bruys's house, if I remember rightly. But she got rotten pay, and that was when she started whoring, they say, to keep body and soul together. When that came out, Master Bruys threw her out of the house, being a pious man. And nobody would give her work any longer, because who would ever want a whore under their roof? So she had no choice but to carry on as a woman of pleasure. She would always say that there were even whores in the Bible and that it was a job that would never vanish from this world.'

'That might be true, too,' mumbled Melchior. 'But what about the ghost?'

'The ghost?' repeated his wife. 'I just happened to be in the *saun* that time, and I suppose they were talking about what they always talk about – but I'm not saying anything about that – and the word cropped up, and then Magdalena went terribly quiet, which wasn't her way at all. Someone asked her something, and she said to leave her alone. When asked what was wrong she said something like she could no longer see a tomorrow any more because yesterday evening she'd seen Death.'

'Seen Death?' enquired Melchior.

'I don't remember her words exactly now, you see, but she said she'd seen a ghost on Rataskaevu Street and that such things did exist, and now she feared her hour was approaching. Then she left.'

'And the next day she drowned,' noted the Apothecary. 'If I remember rightly, I was away from home that day ...'

'You were with the Magistrate out beyond the limestone quarry looking for that itinerant doctor who was supposed to have poisoned the goldsmith's son.'

'It wasn't an itinerant doctor at all,' said Melchior angrily. 'It was a thief and a bastard who was peddling all sorts of poisonous rubbish as medicines, which he had stolen. And it took two days before we caught him. The Magistrate sent him straight to the gallows. If people like that are allowed to go free the townspeople would have all the honest apothecaries burned at the stake.'

'Anyway, that day Magdalena was found drowned in the well. After that, though, clean water was allowed to flow through it, and Witte, the Pastor of the Church of the Holy Ghost, blessed the well. And, just to be sure, before that a thief from the prison after a flogging on the pillory had been given water from it to drink.'

'But Magdalena said she saw a ghost on Rataskaevu Street?' Melchior asked.

'Yes, she did. And afterwards the women were wondering whether that was the ghost of the Unterrainer house that Magdalena saw, whether it had come to announce her death and whether the death was for her sins. Then I told them to shut up and not to tell their children such tales. If they'd been in Magdalena's place half of them would have been whores, too. But, well, as the Holy Virgin is my witness, I didn't say it to them quite like that.'

'The ghost of the Unterrainer house,' murmured Melchior. There had been talk of its hauntings ever since Melchior was a child, but even though he had spent his whole life on Rataskaevu Street he had never seen nor heard a phantom. But the stories about that house stubbornly persisted – in fact, so stubbornly that the house had stood empty for years, until now, when the new Pastor of the Church of the Holy Ghost, Gottschalk Witte, had bought it and was living there with his sister. On those occasions when she came in to buy medicine for her brother's disturbed sleep Pastor Witte's sister had always caused some unease in Melchior. He sometimes suspected that she wasn't always in her right mind, with her sparkling eyes and strange words.

But this story of a ghost and the Unterrainer house – Melchior had never taken it very seriously. Against demons and ghosts we are protected by our holy faith, the saints and care of the soul, of that he was quite sure.

'It's getting late,' Keterlyn decided then. 'Let's not start talking about ghosts in the middle of the night and call down bad luck on ourselves. Let's blow out the candle now, and you'll come with me to the marriage bed.'

'I've not the slightest objection to that,' replied Melchior, but he knew that some unarticulated thought was slipping through his head at that moment – some recollection, some snatch of a sentence, something connected with the ghost, to death, the sea and beer, but it was so vague that he couldn't catch it. There was something else he had heard about the ghost and about death, but where and when?

As he stretched out his hand to the candle, a shout could be heard outside the window. Then another, and he saw someone running past with a torch.

'Must be the town guards,' guessed Keterlyn when Melchior emerged from his thoughts and looked curiously towards the window.

'I'll just take a peep and see what's going on,' said the Apothecary.

When he opened the door, he almost collided with a town guard carrying a torch.

'Mr Apothecary,' he cried. 'A blessing that you're still up. Have you seen anyone running past here?'

'I don't think so,' replied Melchior. 'Or if I did, it was some man with a torch.'

'That was Joachim, the town guard. Nobody else?'

'No. But what's happened?'

'A person has been struck down, right here. Seems he's still breathing. Mr Apothecary, would you …'

'I'm coming,' shouted Melchior. 'Still breathing, you say?'

All Keterlyn saw was her husband rushing out of the room – even forgetting to take his hat. She sighed, shrugged and went to bed, leaving the candle to burn for her husband.

5

Rataskaevu Street
The Night of 3–4 August

MELCHIOR COULD see that one guard was bent over something lying on the ground in the torchlight. Another guard, who had come in answer to the first guard's call, ran with Melchior and then carried on towards the gate on Pikk Hill. Joachim, the third guard, had rushed towards St Nicholas's.

He recognized the guard bending over the recumbent form as Peter Kylckme, a distant relative of Keterlyn's non-German family. This man had beckoned to him from a distance, and Melchior ran over to him. All the town guards knew that the Apothecary was a favourite of the Magistrate and an authorized town sentry.

'We heard screams,' said Peter to Melchior. 'We came here from Pikk Street and found this here. He still seems to be breathing – may the saints have mercy on him.'

Melchior kneeled down and looked at the human form lying on the ground. The first thing he saw was blood. The man's jacket was soaked with bright-red blood. But he was no longer breathing. This man was dead. He had died just a moment ago, because …

Melchior pulled up his jacket and revealed a scrawny body. Blood still seeped from his wounds. There were three deep wounds on the body, two to the chest and one to the stomach, any one of which could have been fatal, as far as Melchior could see. You could sew such wounds up and apply whatever potions or lotions, but God would still call a man with such injuries. There was nothing left for him on this earth.

'Who is this boy?' asked Peter. 'I don't think I've ever seen him. He's terribly thin.'

'Give me some light,' demanded Melchior. He studied the dead man's face.

'He was alive. I swear, he was still alive when I got here,' said Peter. 'He was breathing and shaking and trembling, and then he breathed really deeply … and then he must have gone. That was the last breath … when the soul leaves the body … it must have been.'

'These wounds are fresh,' said Melchior. 'Good God,' he whispered after taking a closer look at the dead man's face. He had not seen this man before either. Or, rather, this wasn't a man, it was a boyish form. Or a young man, it was hard to say. And he was very, very thin. The boy's head was twisted backwards in his death throes, the chin forced upwards and his chapped, bitten lips might still have been letting out the sigh of death. In the torchlight the spectral-looking face seemed pale and sunken; the cheekbones and jaw could be made out under the fragile skin. This was not a beautiful face – in fact, rather an ugly one, somehow frightening. But what was most astonishing were the boy's eyes. They were bulging but at the same time half closed, as if death had overtaken them in the middle of blinking. But this face was as unfamiliar to him as it was to the town guard. If Melchior had seen such a face before it would certainly have stayed in his mind. There are faces that you never forget, and this was one of them.

Then Melchior examined the boy's frail body. His bones didn't seem to have any flesh on them at all. When he had wiped away the blood he saw an emaciated frame, hardly a man's, so delicate and slender it was, so prominent were the breastbone and other bones.

'This young man has been living in great hunger,' said Peter, and Melchior had to agree. Certainly this boy had not been used to eating every day, and since Livonia had been hit by crop failures for the past couple of years this came as no surprise. And yet … and yet there was something strange about this young man. His face, so delicate and frail, although contorted in its death throes, did not seem to be the face of an Estonian. Melchior could not quite explain the feeling to himself. The boy was of short stature and so lanky and emaciated that it was a wonder that he had remained alive at all. His arms and legs were like whip handles; there was hardly any flesh on them, and the legs were stunted from the knees down. On his arms the dark veins were visible under the delicate skin.

'Some beggar or tramp,' guessed Peter. 'Look, Mr Apothecary, he's had nothing at all to eat. He must have been escaping famine somewhere in the Order's lands by coming into town. If he'd lived nearby he could at least have got hold of some fish and a crust of bread or gone to the almshouse …'

'That might be so,' muttered Melchior. He was now looking at the jacket that covered the body. In fact, it was not a jacket but some sackcloth with holes cut into it. The garment scarcely reached the boy's knees.

By then the other two town guards had returned. They were panting. They had been running, but it was hard to run in the dark while holding a sword and a torch.

'Nobody,' said the guard called Joachim, who had come from St Nicholas's. 'The gate up to Toompea is closed, but if he'd slipped through the churchyard, over to the stables and gardens behind the church, or by the wall between the Estonians' houses …'

'Yes,' said Melchior. Behind St Nicholas's Churchyard and Seppade Street there are many shadowy courtyards and vaulted passages. It would have been easy for the murderer to get away.

'So what happened to this little chap?' asked Joachim.

'Dead,' Melchior affirmed. 'No doctor could have helped him. He suffered some very deep knife wounds.'

'Heaven have mercy. Who is he?' asked the other guard. 'He's still just a boy.'

'I don't know. I've never seen him before. Must be someone from outside town,' Peter answered.

'So he must belong to somebody,' said Joachim. 'Do you have any use for him, Mr Apothecary? A very fresh corpse, too – you might get some medicine or something from it.'

'He's too scrawny,' said Melchior pensively, 'and I don't know how old he is. If he were a young man in his prime and a redhead, you could get some strong medicine out of his thigh muscles. If you cut them to shreds, sprinkle them with myrrh and aloe and marinade them in spirits, dry them when the moon is full ... But he must be too young. And you wouldn't get a good belt for back pain out of the skin either – it is too poor. What are you going to do with him?'

Peter shrugged. 'I guess we should take him to the mortuary at St Barbara's; sure they'll dig a hole there to bury him themselves if no one claims the body. The Council won't allow corpses to be left lying around. But how are we going to get him there now, at night?'

Melchior was thinking. Yes, a young and strong and recently dead man or woman, from a body like that you can extract good medicines, but this boy really was in too poor a shape. Wiser doctors than he always wanted body parts from vigorous men and women for medical purposes. True, this boy had just died, and the life force – such as it was – should still be in his limbs, but you couldn't take out any fat, because there wasn't any. The skull and the brain would yield a good medicine if boiled up, but Melchior had never done that; he didn't know precisely how to do it. Besides, he wouldn't dare to dissect the corpse if he wasn't quite sure that no relative would claim it. But now his nose was assaulted by a faecal smell emanating from the body, and that reminded him that he could boil an elixir for strength from the semen of a freshly killed man. And no relative could have any objection to that if it were collected in a bottle. A couple of vassals from Toompea had paid a very good price for a drink made from the semen of some robbers executed at Võllamägi last year.

'So what's to be done, Mr Apothecary?' enquired Peter. 'Shall we take him to St Nicholas's Churchyard now and lay him under a bush until the morning, or do you want to do a little dissecting?'

'Maybe,' muttered Melchior. This boy couldn't be so young that he wouldn't yield some semen. Melchior pushed the upper body of the corpse out of the sackcloth, revealing the midriff. He was taken aback. Peter, too, leaning in closer, gasped and whispered, 'St Catherine and the hairy devil.'

There, where the man's penis should have been, was just a withered stump. The boy's sex organs had been ripped out, and the remaining flesh had been scorched. The poor boy had been castrated. Melchior noticed that this had been done long ago, because the wound had healed. The scrotum, too, had been chopped off, so there would be no semen at all in the body. This was a ghastly sight, painful for any man to look at.

'Someone has already ripped the poor chap's balls off,' said Peter. 'Who knows for what terrible sins …'

Melchior pulled a knife from his belt, one that he always carried with him, and instead of a body part he cut off a little piece of the boy's sackcloth jacket.

'Mr Apothecary, what on earth are you doing now?' asked Joachim.

'Just in case,' replied Melchior. 'There's nothing left to take from his body. Take him away now.'

'I suppose we should drag him to St Nicholas's then,' said Peter. He got up and looked around. Then he let out a hearty curse.

'What now?' asked Melchior, still examining the corpse closely.

'That damned house,' said the town guard. 'That something like this should happen right outside *that* house.'

Melchior looked up. He hadn't realized that they were standing in front of that selfsame Unterrainer house. The old two-storeyed gabled building raised its ghostly form before them, and its blackened windows were gloomy witnesses to the corpse and the guards.

Peter said that these were just silly old-wives' tales really, that he had never seen a ghost in the town and that this was a house like any other – and, anyway, what they should do is knock on the door and ask whether anyone had seen or heard anything.

Melchior thought this was sound advice, but the whole street here was closely packed with houses, and the respectable townsfolk would hardly be pleased to be woken up in the middle of the night. There was the Unterrainer house, now occupied by Pastor Gottschalk Witte, and right next door was the merchant Arend Goswin. Then there was a patch of garden, where fruit grew, bordered at the rear by the old stables. Further on, in two grand three-storey houses, lived Burgomaster Wolze and Nider, another merchant. Beyond these there was one small house that had stood empty for over a year, followed by the home of the respectable merchant Mertin Tweffell. There were distinguished people living on the other side of the street, too, opposite the hill that led up to Toompea. The house on the corner belonged now to Lübbink, the goldsmith, and opposite was the residence of the Order's vassal for Harju, Kordt von Greyssenhagen, Master of Jackewolde, and then the home of Canon Albrecht.

But Peter had got up and was heading for Goswin's house. He said he knew the merchant's servant Hainz well, and he could speak to him. Hainz would open the door anyway, and Goswin was so old now that he would have been asleep long ago. Besides, a guard always had the right to get even the most respectable townspeople up at night if necessary.

The door was opened, however, by the merchant's old housekeeper Annlin, and even then only after knocking for a long time. The poor woman was full of terror, barefoot and staring perplexedly at the corpse lying in the torchlight. Soon her husband Hainz was also present, a tall strong man who had previously been a porter at the harbour and who was generally thought of as a bit slow. Peter talked to them, and Melchior overheard that no, they hadn't seen anyone, they had been asleep for a long time like good Christians, and what should their Master, a merchant, have to do with the corpses of tramps? Next Peter stood on the other side of the street, in front of the Knight Kordt von Greyssenhagen's house, but he gave up knocking. Strange, thought Melchior. A candle flame had seemed to flicker for a moment behind the window, but he wasn't quite sure.

The guards didn't dare cause any more disturbance. They took the dead body by its arms and legs and started dragging it towards St Nicholas's Churchyard. The boy was very light. Melchior stayed a moment staring at them in silence, the piece of sackcloth between his fingers, then sighed and felt a strong desire to sleep.

6

The Dominican Monastery
4 August, Noon

WAKING EARLY – and how can you sleep any later when the twins raise such a racket at sunrise from hunger – Melchior had that familiar feeling that while he was sleeping at night, as his senses were resting, something had fallen into place. Although his dreams had been haunted by the dead body of that emaciated young man and the dismembered genitals, he realized that what yesterday evening could only be recalled to mind in vague fragments had now come to him of its own accord in the night. His reason had shuffled the disjointed features into place by itself. Something told him that it was all connected with the medicinal herbs he sometimes bought from a farmer's wife at the town market. That old Estonian woman knew her plants well and understood their medicinal properties. She would bring entire bushes to market, and Melchior usually bought a whole armful of them and gave a couple of pennies more than these shrubs, picked from meadows and forests, were really worth. But then he would bring the shrubs to the pharmacy, spread them out on the table and start sorting them. He would put all the different plants in different places and then divide them up again according to what herb would go straight into an infusion and what would go into the attic to dry and later be powdered with a mortar and pestle. Sometimes it is the same with human memory.

As his tired head rested at night, his reason had taken the correct fragments out of the bush and arranged them in their rightful places. His mind had put the snatches of sentences and words – ghost, sea, death, beer – into place. Now he remembered. Oh, of course, it could only be that old inmate of the almshouse, the former ship's captain Rinus Götzer, who had told such a story in some harbourside tavern. Götzer had, as was his wont, been drinking a few tankards of ale bought for him by kind sailors, and Melchior, who had found himself in the harbour on some business one scorching day and had dropped into the tavern to wet his whistle, had, with half an ear, overheard Skipper Götzer's story. He spoke of a man who had talked of a ghost, and after that he had … well, he had met his death. The ghost was said to have come after this man and killed him, and all this happened right here in Tallinn, but when and by whom Melchior had not heard. Or had he dreamed it all up? Either way, he now remembered, and that knowledge gave him no rest.

He went down to the kitchen, and Keterlyn gave him gruel with bacon and peas, and to perk himself up he drank a mug of beer. Then he went and unlocked the door of the pharmacy, brought a jug to the table with some sweets and confections left from the day before and thought, for the umpteenth time, that he ought to take on an apprentice until young Melchior grew up, because Keterlyn was so occupied with the children that she scarcely had any time left these days to help him out.

People came in, telling him the news, buying his sweets and other tasty things, some asking for medicines as prescribed by letter from the town physician. Melchior talked with them, but his thoughts kept returning to those ghost stories. Tallinn was his town, and Rataskaevu Street was his street, and there should be no place for demonic forces here. But no matter how much he rejected these thoughts they kept returning.

Too many deaths, too much talk of ghosts. And the corpse of some unknown young tramp in front of the ghostly Unterrainer house.

The townspeople who visited the Apothecary, though, were mostly talking about the funeral of Laurentz Bruys. His grave was already being dug in St Nicholas's Churchyard because the weather was hot, and the body had been brought to town yesterday from Marienthal. The fellow guildsmen of the deceased had ordered masses to be said at the church and a handsome gravestone from the stonemason. They had sent word to Toompea and the vassals in Harju, as Bruys was a friend of the Order and highly respected among the vassals.

At about noon, when a woman from the *saun* had come to help Keterlyn with the children, Melchior said that he now needed to go into town on business, and may the women manage without him in the meantime. He went along a familiar route, past the magnificent frontage of the Guildhall of the Great Guild, past the Church of the Holy Ghost, down the hill to the Dominican Monastery. At that time the preaching brethren were having their lunch in the refectory; Hinric, the *cellarius*, whom he was seeking, was said to be in the infirmary with a patient. Melchior thought he would wait in the monastery garden. He sat on a little bench, looking at the well-cared-for fruit trees and beds, in which grew various herbs and grasses; Ditmar, the monastery infirmarer, used them for mixing medicines, and the brothers brewed their famous spicy ales with them. Many a time Melchior had done business with Ditmar, bringing his own herbs, which he had bought from merchants or country people, for trade and exchange. He had held heated disputes with Ditmar about the qualities and curative powers of some plant or other and would no doubt continue to do so because, despite his status as a monk, Brother Ditmar was a fierce debater and blindly convinced of what was written in the prescriptive monastic books about the curing of the sick.

Prior Reinhart Moninger passed by. Melchior bowed before him and kissed his hand. They had met a number of times, exchanged a few words; Melchior had listened to his sermons and sat with him in the Guildhall drinking ale. The Prior was a quiet and serious man. Many regarded Prior Moninger as *too* quiet and serious, as he did not want to get involved in worldly affairs, but Melchior saw him as a wise man, a very wise man.

Then along came Brother Hinric, framed by a tousle of light-grey hair. Hinric was a tall man of Estonian origins, whom Melchior had called his good friend for over ten years now. He bowed in greeting to the Apothecary and asked with a doleful smile whether Melchior had come in a spiritual emergency or whether he wanted to discuss the word of God.

'Actually I don't know that myself,' said Melchior cheerily. 'Both, I suppose. Forgive me for interrupting your lunch.'

'It really isn't appropriate to disturb the servants of God during mealtimes,' replied Hinric, 'for that is the only hour of the day when they can refresh themselves so as to resume diligently praying for the welfare of the townspeople. Actually, I'm fasting today, and I was with a young lay brother, Eric. I was praying with him. He's been laid low with a fever for quite a while, and he's already hearing the angels calling him.'

'So I've come at a bad time,' said Melchior.

'That can't be helped. What about your own mealtime?'

'As ever,' replied Melchior, and before he had time to protest Hinric beckoned to one of the brothers and asked him to bring some bread baked with salt herring and a skin of ale.

'I promised the Prior that I'd help him put together some ideas for this evening's sermon,' said Hinric a moment later. 'So don't be offended, friend, if I can't spend long with you. We have to keep Master Bruys's sermon in mind, and tomorrow there will be a mass said in the church in his honour.'

'Yes,' muttered Melchior. 'I suppose he left a big sum to the Dominicans?'

'He was a pious man,' said Hinric, shrugging his shoulders. 'He had great respect for the Dominicans, but I think I understand why he also wanted St Bridget's to be built. We aren't too happy at the prospect of yet another religious community in the town – and, what's more, one with such modern rules – but the Pope has approved it, the Order wants it and … and I understand that if there is one very devout man with plenty of money then it doesn't matter how much he donates to existing churches and monasteries, that won't be talked about in days to come nearly as much as what he caused to be built, how a magnificent convent had been created with his money. He wanted to be the founder of such an establishment.'

'I suppose so,' said Melchior, breaking a piece of bread, putting some dill and parsley on it and taking a man-sized mouthful. The herring bread made by the preaching brothers was, he thought, the best bread in Tallinn, and it tasted all the better with fresh dill and bitter beer. 'Actually, I wanted to ask you about quite a different man, one who has also been called to meet his Maker.'

'Might you be thinking of Master Tobias Grote?' asked Hinric.

'That's the one.'

'And why do you come to ask the Dominicans about him? He was the Master of the Tower on the grounds of the holy sisterhood.'

'Why I've come is because on the day of his own death he visited my pharmacy. He was for some reason very much out of sorts and said that he had to visit the Dominicans. The next morning he was dead.'

'May the angels help him,' murmured Hinric. 'He was a good man. But I understand, Melchior, what you're thinking. So, he told you about the ghost and Master Bruys?'

Melchior now took a proper swig of beer and sighed deeply.

'No,' he said finally, 'actually he didn't. He didn't say a word about a ghost or Master Bruys. And what you're saying now makes me even more curious – you know it's an affliction from which no apothecary is free. Listen, I'll tell you what happened.'

Hinric listened with interest, nodding, and when Melchior finished, he said, 'So that makes two men who are very curious. Grote, the Master of Quad Dack Tower, came to our monastery and asked to speak to me. I asked if he wanted to be shriven, and why didn't he confess at the Holy Spirit, but he said no, he didn't want to confess, he wanted instead to ask advice about ghosts and get some guidance. Melchior, you know I'm a man of great patience, and I heard him out. At first I also thought he must have drunk too much beer and started seeing devilish visions, and when he spoke I thought I'd recommend that he go on a long fast, to say the Lord's Prayer ten times a day and to go on a pilgrimage and think a bit more about his own soul. But as he carried on – and his story was confused, I have to say – I started to feel that he wasn't talking about demons caused by too much drink at all. These demons are different.'

'So what had he seen?' Melchior enquired.

'His story was confused, but he said something like "Holy Father, help a sinner and tell him what he must do when he has seen spirits. Does it mean his death? Should he be afraid?"'

'Does it mean his death?' repeated Melchior thoughtfully. 'Evidently it *did* mean his death.'

'I wasn't able to say. I asked why he came to me, and he told me they were saying in town that Brother Hinric knows how to drive evil spirits out.'

Yes, thought Melchior, they do say that. They said that Hinric had been summoned four or five years ago by the Bishop of Tartu, where he was supposed to have carried out a rite, as prescribed by the Pope, to drive a demon out of a person's soul. That Canon of Tartu was still alive and well today. Hinric never spoke of such things, because the holy rite of exorcism has the same secrecy as that of the confessional, but still the word had spread. So who else would the poor Tower-Master turn to if he genuinely believed he had seen a ghost?

'His story was confused,' Hinric repeated thoughtfully. 'He asked for advice and guidance and he was really afraid. He said, "It came to me, there at the end of Rataskaevu Street. It came from the realm of the dead to bring a message. It was the voice of Death", and would I please tell him what to do now and how he could defend himself.'

'And Master Bruys,' insisted Melchior, 'what did he say about Master Bruys?'

'Something cryptic,' replied Hinric. 'He sort of mentioned Master Bruys in passing – and you understand that he was also drunk at the time and must have had a few beers on top of your apothecary's dram – and I know from experience that that on its own can make a man pretty groggy. I recall that he mumbled something along the lines of "May Heaven have mercy on Bruys; may the angels be merciful to him."'

'May Heaven have mercy on Master Bruys?'

'Yes, I think so. And then he said he had to go, yes, he had to go and talk … Forgive me, I didn't understand him exactly, but he said, "I saw the face of Death, and the shadows swallowed it", and then again said something about Bruys, but I don't remember what exactly. I told him what I really thought was true, that people talk too much about ghosts and see them where they really are not. There is only one man who has risen from the dead, but he did it through the Holy Spirit.'

'And yet the saints can appear to people,' said Melchior.

'Yes, the church investigates all these apparitions in great detail, because you cannot be careless about them. Saints are people marked out by God, who were born through His will to announce His word, and he has given them the power to work miracles. The appearance of a saint and a miracle are thus things that really may happen, but only a few of them have happened. Some people are inclined to be too keen to see saints and angels, and the church cannot allow that … But death, Melchior, death is final. One does not come back from death.' But something in the monk's words forced Melchior to look straight at him seriously and to ask him to explain further. 'My people believe – still now, even after they have heard the word of God – that the spirits of their ancestors can come back,' explained Hinric, speaking in a measured voice, but Melchior perceived irritation behind his words. 'As a learned man and a servant of God I must consider it to be empty superstition. The death of the body is also the death of the soul on earth, and the soul lives on in God's realm. The soul of a sinner dies completely in hell.'

'But a soul is not a ghost,' observed Melchior. 'Tobias Grote said he *saw* a ghost.'

'He believed what he had seen,' said Hinric with certainty. 'He believed he had seen a spirit, and my words didn't make him think differently. I remember that in the village where I was born and lived, before Brother Arnulf took me away with him to bring me to the Dominicans, there in the village, Melchior, they believed firmly in ghosts haunting the living. There was a man living there who died – and he was a Christian – and his wife came to complain to the village elder that the man was haunting the house after his death. I saw and overheard how the wise men of our village cast spells and curses like the heathens do on the house and the wife. I heard their incantations, and I saw what they did and how they cast spells. And I saw how that woman fretted and cried out in terrible pain because her husband was holding on to her as the only thread connecting him to his earthly life. And the wise men visited this woman and cast spells on her and drove the evil spirit back. They made her drink potions boiled up from roots and chanted heretical words. That must definitely have been more than twenty years ago, but I remember it still, and I saw ...'

'Did you see the ghost?'

'I ... I don't know *what* I saw, but if I had then been able to, I would have prayed and cried to the Virgin Mary and St Catherine for help and put my hope in their power and blessing. I remember I was afraid, but my parents forced me to look because they had recognized in me that power which might have made a sorcerer out of me, too. And when Brother Arnulf came visiting they let me go with him because, according to those people's understanding, monks were men with the same power as their wise men had. But, Melchior, their charms helped, and that woman was freed from her tormentor. They said that after death some people don't get the correct guidance and remain stranded between two worlds, trying to get back home. I've always wanted to think that that can only happen with people who have not accepted God's love into their own souls, but ... but sometimes I even think that the heathens, too, will get to know the difference between the Kingdom of Heaven and hell, and they will know what God's guidance really is, but they don't know how to find the right path to get there. Demons, though, can torment both Christians and heathens, only the heathen's soul is an easier catch for them. That woman regained her health, but otherwise, without the wise men's help, she would have died at the hands of her persecutor.'

'And Tobias Grote died shortly after complaining that he'd seen a ghost,' said Melchior. 'Yet I don't want to believe that ghosts can kill.'

Tobias Grote fell to his death from his tower,' replied Hinric. 'He'd had too much to drink and didn't know where to draw the line.'

'He might have been so frightened by the apparition that ...' said Melchior with a sigh, and didn't finish the sentence. They both drank a decent draught of ale. Hinric would soon have to start the lunchtime prayers, and Melchior didn't want to detain him long. Yet he still had something to ask.

'When I came here,' he said, 'I couldn't have guessed that there could be any connection between the death of Grote and pious Master Bruys. Now I'm confused. Friend, surely you can guess my question without my asking it. Master Bruys went on a pilgrimage to the future convent, and on the same day Tobias Grote saw a ghost – on Rataskaevu Street, he said. Some sort of ghost that made him say the words "May Heaven have mercy on Bruys; may the angels be merciful to him." The next day Master Bruys died at Marienthal, and Tobias Grote died that same night, his face distorted with horror as if at the moment of death he'd seen … what?'

Hinric closed his eyes and rapidly uttered a prayer.

'You want to ask,' said the monk finally, 'whether it is possible that Grote saw the ghost of Master Bruys? That he saw his angel of death?'

'I have heard of such things,' said Melchior gravely. 'Before death, a person's death-double has been seen, their soul shadow. I know that the Scriptures and the canonical books don't speak of such things, and even the saints don't protect us from such demons, but still …'

Hinric was silent, his gaze far away, as if he were wondering whether, as a holy man, he should say aloud the words he wished to. 'I have also heard that a person can foresee the death of someone close, even when that other person is far away. Didn't that happen with one woman who lived with the holy sisters at the Convent of Esswein, and she went there when her husband died and all their sons were spread around the world. She hadn't seen her youngest for over ten years when, one morning, she started weeping and praying to St Michael to defend and bless her youngest son. She prayed until she lost consciousness, and when she recovered, she didn't eat a single morsel for several days, spending all her days fasting and praying in the chapel, until word reached the convent that her son Michel had been killed by an arrow during the siege of a fortress. That woman herself died a few days later, and the night she died they say that tears flowed from the eyes of a wooden image of St Michael.'

They were silent for a few moments, until finally Melchior blinked rapidly and asked, 'You said that a person can foresee the death of someone close. Were Grote and Bruys friends then? Bruys was about twenty years older than Grote.'

'They had become close,' said the monk. 'Someone was talking about that today, and I'm sure I'd heard it before. That was when Grote was a simple soldier travelling the seas. He was on the ship that carried Bruys's goods, and on that ship was Bruys's youngest son, the one who later perished in the fire, as well as his wife. The son was still just a boy, and their ship was attacked by the Victual Brothers. Thanks to Grote's bravery the attack was repelled and Bruys's wife and son spared. The Victual Brothers might not have killed them, but they certainly would have abused them and demanded a ransom.'

'Not that God would have spared their lives anyway,' muttered Melchior to himself.

Probably everyone in Tallinn knew the story of Laurentz Bruys. He was thought to have been from somewhere near Bremen, but he had come to Tallinn when still a young man. His business prospered, he became powerful, a respected citizen of the town, a distinguished patron of St Nicholas's Church and, of course, a guildsman of the Great Guild. Out of an old house on Lai Street he built a new and bigger one. At one stage he was bookkeeper to the Council, and everyone praised his upright nature and moderation. He required law and order to be maintained by himself as well as others – in fact, he was severe, that you could say of him. His wife was also a respected and virtuous lady, who bore her husband seven children, but three of them died in their infancy.

Melchior recalled that Master Bruys had not been lucky in his children. The story that somehow involved Arend Goswin, the merchant, had taken place when Melchior must have been about fifteen, when he was an apprentice apothecary in Riga. He had heard it later through rumours, but he did know that Bruys was very angry with his eldest son Thyl, had disowned him and sent him off to Germany. That had been a reckless and impetuous decision, because at that time Bruys still didn't have an heir. True, Melchior had once heard someone whispering something about Bruys's bastard child, but that must have been just a wicked rumour. But when Bruys had driven his son away, it seemed that God had approved of his decision because the following year Bruys had a son, who was given the name Johan. Melchior calculated that the merchant himself must have been forty-five years old and his wife a little younger. But no further children were born into the Bruys family, and the patience of the heavenly powers came to an end.

A dozen or so years ago Master Bruys's barn caught fire, and even the nunnery suffered a little damage. Several houses burned, but the townspeople managed to contain the fire. By that time most of the houses in that part of town were already built of stone, the wells were full of water and people were alerted early. All the same, a number of sheds and barns fell victim to the fire, and several people were lost in the ruins. One of the victims was Johan Bruys, who was one of the last to be found under the burned-out ruins of Master Bruys's barn. That was a blow from which Laurentz Bruys's wife never recovered; she was overcome by grief and depression and some time later took her own life.

Bruys was left alone in the world. This fateful blow changed the man drastically. The respected, yet in every sense ordinary, merchant became an extremely pious merchant who regarded the destiny he had been dealt as a punishment from God for his excessive meanness and selfishness, although he could hardly have been accused of that. Since then Laurentz Bruys had become a saintly man who cared for his own soul more than anything in the world.

He donated generously to the church altars and for the poor, he ordered masses to be said, he had prayers read, he even set off on a pilgrimage to Rome, although he did not get very far. On the way he was struck down by an illness. He was said by then to have reached far into the Habsburg lands, as far as the Monastery of Mariazell, which made him the only man from Tallinn who had been a pilgrim there. He was nursed for several months at the monastery, and when he recovered he returned to Tallinn to devote himself to more pious works, supporting churches and monasteries with the income from his trading. And he became one of those who, with the approval of the Order, began advocating the foundation of a new religious community. This made him plenty of secret enemies, because several men spoke openly of their opposition to the plans, but few dared to say anything bad about Laurentz Bruys.

In recent years his health had again become poor, and he moved around little on his own legs. The Lord had deprived him of the power of speech as well. Three days ago Bruys had had himself carried in a cart to Marienthal, where work had begun on the new convent. He wanted to go on a final pilgrimage, and this was the final excursion of his life, for Laurentz Bruys came back in a funeral carriage.

And Melchior now felt compelled to ask Hinric, 'Tell me, friend, do you know how Master Bruys died?'

'No, Melchior, no,' the monk replied rapidly. 'I know what you're getting at. You see murderers everywhere, I know. But, no, Master Bruys died of old age. God was calling him to himself, for his time had come. He knew long before that he was dying. He went to the convent and once more read to himself the book on the art of dying because he wanted to die in accordance with those wise teachings.'

'I know,' Melchior nodded. 'No doubt it is a wise book and contains lessons on how a dying man can console himself and prepare for transition to the next world.'

'Yes, it is a very good book, and Master Bruys hoped that he could die in his own home and that he would spend his last energies on the prayer *Profiscere anima Cristiana*, which he wished to say with the Pastor of St Nicholas's, turning to all the saints that he held dear. Sometimes he visited the monastery to ask advice on how to keep himself from the five temptations of the devil in his last days. But God ordained otherwise, and he died on his pilgrimage at Marienthal. His servant and the new Abbess of St Bridget's were beside him in his final moments. I know. They brought me word from Marienthal.'

'Nevertheless,' said Melchior, 'we know how he *wanted* to die, and we know that he was old and feeble, but we don't know *how* he died.'

Hinric shook his head with regret, as if his friend's doubts pained him. 'What sows the seeds of doubt in your mind and sets you looking for a murderer once more?' he asked.

'May St Cosmas assist me if I'm mistaken. I can't answer your question. There are so many evils in the world which people can cover up so well. But, look, there are several facts that seemed to me to be connected. Grote and Bruys die at almost the same time, Bruys in the daytime and Grote at night – although Grote wasn't to know that. Grote says that the previous night he'd seen the Ghost of Rataskaevu Street, and he asks God to bless Master Bruys. And people in Tallinn have talked of the Ghost of Rataskaevu Street for years. There was a woman, Magdalena, a prostitute – you might have heard of her – who had once served Master Bruys and who also said that she'd seen the ghost, and the next day she drowned in the well. Those ghost stories, for their part, are connected with the Unterrainer house, which is next door to that of Master Goswin, with whom Bruys had once, maybe about twenty-five years ago, had a major quarrel. And last night, in front of the Unterrainer house, the town guards found the corpse of some young beggar or tramp whose genitals had been cut off and whom neither I nor the guards had ever seen before.' Hinric crossed himself and quickly recited a prayer. 'As I recall,' continued Melchior, 'that ghost story about the Unterrainer house goes back a very long way and is somehow connected with the Dominicans.'

'Yes, it is,' said Hinric at length. 'But it really goes back a *very* long way. Let the dead lie in peace, Melchior. Let the Lord God and his angels take care of them. Let the spirits of the dead be in peace.'

Melchior sighed, took a sip of ale and said, 'But do the spirits of the dead leave the living in peace?'

7

The Red Convent
4 August, Noon

WHAT WAS KNOWN as the Red Convent in Tallinn was a modest-looking two-storey house in a street running along the wall east of the Seppade Gate, where, with the Council's approval and to the pleasure of some men of the town, a number of single women accommodatingly offered their charms. There is not a single town of any size or importance that has got by without such an establishment, and neither had Tallinn; it was a necessary evil, and it had even been acknowledged by a number of holy men that if there were no public women all undertakings would be overrun by the desires of the flesh.

When Cornelis de Wrede, a merchant from Antwerp, once again found himself striding towards the Red Convent on this August day, he was thinking that he was doing two things in Tallinn about which his mother, father and uncles had most sternly warned him: he was placing the family business in jeopardy, and he was falling in love with a whore.

The first thing was actually simpler, because Cornelis believed that what he was doing was right and proper – and wasn't that why he had been sent here to faraway Tallinn? If you're alone, you must decide alone and take responsibility for your decisions, and

Cornelis was not afraid of responsibility; he was prepared for it if things were to turn bad.

The second was harder. His father had sought out a bride for him from a decent family, a well-mannered and virtuous lass and pretty good-looking as well. She was the daughter of a rich merchant in the town of Antwerp and a seventh child, which meant that the women in that family tree were as fertile as needed and their broad hips and swelling bosoms promised de Wrede the abundant continuation of the line.

This summer, however, Cornelis had discovered here in Tallinn that he did not want to share his bed with any woman other than a whore named Hilde, who slept with men at the house they called the Red Convent and had agreed readily to Cornelis's proposal that she leave behind her whoring, make a pilgrimage to the town of Aachen – just in case – and wear penitent's clothes so as to appear, redeemed, before Cornelis's parents and ...

And Cornelis de Wrede knew no more beyond that. Beyond that it was more complicated because his father was a stern man and would certainly not agree to such a marriage, at least not at first. Beyond that things would depend on how Cornelis got on with his most important task in Tallinn. Maybe then his father would close his eyes to the fact that his middle son wanted to marry a former prostitute.

As a merchant abroad Cornelis had had to join the Brotherhood of Blackheads. This made it easier to get on and much more straightforward when arranging business deals and communicating with the townsfolk. The Blackheads were a peculiar society. Some of their young men had, like him, come from abroad, from German towns and from Burgundy, but there were also some from Sweden and from Riga. Most of them, however, were the sons of local merchants as well as those who were not yet married, had not become citizens or had set up in business independently. The Blackheads got on well with the Dominicans and kept an altar at their Church of St Catherine. They organized extravagant drinking feasts and tournaments. They kept a tavern at their guildhall and were the most lively company in the town. They were respected, they were honoured, they had good relations with the Great Guild, the Council and with the ruling Order itself – as long as the Order was not at war with the bishops. There was some old secret connected with the Blackheads, something very unsavoury, which none of them wanted to talk about and about which most of them knew only rumours. At the beer table Cornelis had, however, managed to extract a few details from the guildsmen. It had happened about ten years ago, when the Blackheads were still a young guild, and at their head was a certain Clawes Freisinger from Cologne. Freisinger had breathed some life into the Blackheads, joining the brotherhood, which at the time existed in name only, and made them what they were today. But then he had vanished from the town, and no one seemed to know exactly where he had gone or why he left. Some said he would return to Tallinn because he had bills to settle. And so there was some old secret about which the current Blackheads had not the faintest notion but for which Freisinger had almost paid with his life. And implicated in all this was Melchior, the Tallinn apothecary, because he had solved some crime. It was said of the Apothecary that he was a clever man and especially resourceful when it came to tracking down killers.

I need to keep an eye on him, Cornelis had decided.

Now Cornelis was standing again in front of the Red Convent, his heart beating painfully and his palms sweating. He had not even eaten properly today. Milling around were all kinds of farmhands, peasants, sack-makers and other ordinary people; a few of them sneered at him. The door opened unexpectedly, and out of it stepped a nobleman with a magnificent red hat who cast a mistrustful sidelong glance at Cornelis. That hat was a very fine piece of handiwork. There were few in Tallinn who wore such things, although in Flanders it was the height of fashion, and the richer townsfolk were already wearing them. That man must be one of the kinsmen of the vassal, one Greyssenhagen, recalled de Wrede. He was a little surprised that such a noble gentleman would be visiting a whorehouse – but we all have our own little pleasures, he figured. The Council did not recommend that married men or the clergy from the town go to brothels, but, as for the subjects of the Order, Cornelis knew of no prohibition. The Knight cast one more suspicious look at the Fleming and disappeared towards the Seppade Gate.

In fact, at this very moment Cornelis should have been somewhere else, at an actual convent – that of the Holy Sisters of St Michael – looking around and listening out to see what he could make of the rumours being spread there from the tavern behind Seppade Gate since yesterday when Dorn had been chatting about the death of the Tower-Master.

'He had a face on him like he'd seen a ghost. And, from what I hear from Melchior, poor Grote had been to visit the Apothecary, and when Melchior happened to ask whether he had seen a ghost he was terribly frightened, as if he'd really seen something from beyond the grave, may the Holy Virgin have mercy on us …' Those had been Dorn's words, and Cornelis's blood had run cold as he heard them. He ought to investigate; he ought to go to the spot where the Tower-Master had died.

It was because of a ghost that Cornelis had for the first time come to *this* convent, too. He had come looking for the prostitute Magdalena who had seen a ghost and then fallen into the well. That had been in the spring; it had been the first time he had stepped over the threshold of the Red Convent, paid his money and been allowed to choose from among the girls brought to him, and that was when his gaze had fallen for the first time on the flaxen-haired Hilde.

There was a playful glint in the woman's eyes; she was amusing, she was kind and inviting, and although at first Cornelis didn't even want to go to bed with any of these whores – or at least, so he assured himself – at that moment he no longer doubted or speculated about fidelity to his future spouse. He probably hadn't been thinking of anything, not even the task his father had sent him to Tallinn to undertake. He had paid and allowed himself to be led by Hilde into a chamber where there was just a stuffed straw mat. Hilde had slowly let her cloak fall away from her and stood in her nakedness before him, her straight white hair falling on to her delicate shoulders, her small, pert breasts begging for tenderness, her broad hips anticipating his embraces and her bare-shaven vulva demanding kisses. She was a woman of small build, a good head shorter than Cornelis, and she was everything a man could want from a woman. Even her teeth were beautiful, glistening and snow white, not like those of ordinary prostitutes.

Cornelis was not quite sure how Hilde had ended up in a brothel. Hilde herself had told him three different stories, the only common thread being that bad people were to blame, people who wished her ill and left her with no inheritance, so perhaps Hilde was the daughter of some rich foreign count. But revenge and redress for injustice – weren't these matters close to Cornelis's heart?

From that day on Cornelis was bewitched; every week he found time to step into the Red Convent, and he never took any other woman. He made connections in Tallinn, he sought merchants who took grain from the countryside to the town, which he would then buy to export to Flanders. He sought out Russian merchants who knew the cheapest sources of bearskins and those who wanted Flemish cloth, glass and spices from him. He was a diligent man, and he had much work to do, but there was never a week when he forgot to visit Hilde, bringing her some gift – maybe a hairclip or a dainty morsel of food. Gradually they started talking about the future. Cornelis wanted to take the girl with him to Antwerp as his secret bride, and Hilde asked whether she could then start to wear jewellery and bearskins, which she would not be allowed to do in Tallinn, not even if they were given to her. And they *were* given to her with the promise that she could wear them in Flanders.

The previous week Cornelis de Wrede had made a deal with the Red Convent that he would buy Hilde's freedom and pay for her board and lodging if she no longer slept with other men. As soon as Cornelis had arranged his affairs in Tallinn he would take her away as his wife. That was a dream that would not be easy to realize, but have people not realized the most important things in their lives based on dreams? A lot of money was required for Hilde, and that money was not Cornelis's own – it was money from his father's and uncles' trading company – but he had promised to pay it.

He stepped over the threshold of the house, and the old woman who kept the place greeted him with a sly sneer. 'Sir is coming so early today,' she uttered in a screeching voice, smirking repulsively. 'We weren't expecting sir.'

'Where is Hilde?' demanded Cornelis.

'But little Hildekins has visitors,' replied the old hag, giggling obscenely. 'Russian merchants. They wanted to pick out one girl, and one of them had been with Hildekins before, and now he's brought his friends with him. There are quite a few of them in Tallinn and they have –'

A blood-red fog rose before Cornelis's eyes. His arms flew into a spasm and were almost reaching for the old crone's throat. His voice was hoarse and breathless.

'We made a deal,' he finally blurted out. 'And I forbade – forbade, do you hear, you old bitch – I *forbade* her to sleep with other men.'

'Oh, sir, don't upset yourself,' exclaimed the crone, waving her arms about. 'No need for sir to be afraid. You'll still get a good price for her in Flanders. She'll be just as beautiful for ten more years, so even bishops would go for her – of course – and sir will get good money for her.'

'I *forbade* it,' shouted Cornelis shrilly.

'Ah, how can sir ever forbid it here, when Hildekins herself wanted it? She has to earn a living, too. These Russian merchants pay well, and we're not going to start peeping at what they're all up to in there ...'

Cornelis shoved the old woman out of the way. He wanted to storm into Hilde's room, but then he realized – even at the height of jealousy and rage he had enough cool common sense – that he didn't want to see what some hairy, uncouth Russian traders were doing with Hilde. At that moment he seemed to sense his father appearing to wag his finger at him and saying, 'In the name of all the saints, son, didn't I warn you? A whore is always a whore. She only wants your money and nothing else.'

So he remained standing in the middle of the hallway of the whorehouse, understanding that he had been miserably duped. He had not been sent to Tallinn to turn whores into gentlewomen; he had been sent for other things.

'You pay me back every penny,' he hissed at the shocked old woman, 'otherwise I'll tell the Council that you allow Russians to practise sodomy under your roof.'

'Oh Lord, protect us,' screeched the crone.

'Exactly,' Cornelis affirmed, adding a couple of choice Flemish words. He spat on the floor and left with a slam of the door. In one moment all his love for Hilde seemed to have evaporated as if it had never been. He had other things to do in Tallinn.

He had to go to the nunnery and then meet with that witch who could summon ghosts risen from the dead.

8

St Michael's Convent
4 August, Afternoon

MELCHIOR DID NOT go straight home from the Dominican Monastery but turned his steps uphill and walked between the narrow lanes to the nuns of St Michael. This path was very familiar to him, for he had for many years loved to sit in the courtyard of the convent, in the tavern of their brewhouse, and savour their mint-flavoured beer while having a chat. The tavern was almost straight in front of the Quad Dack Tower, the master of which, Grote, had so unfortunately met his end.

In Tallinn the nuns owned vast lands, and they had been there even before the Order had taken the town and most of Livonia back under its control. As far as Melchior knew, the Cistercians had been established in Tallinn even before there was a town wall. And when it was being built, a couple of hundred years ago, the nuns' extensive pastures and paddocks, their convent house and church remained outside it. Later, however, when the convent house was extended and the church made bigger, the nuns were also enclosed within the town wall, for whose construction they themselves had had to pay. Even now the Cistercians had large gardens and graveyards to the south and east of the church, green patches in the midst of a sea of grey stones, and these properties were enclosed by a low wall along Lai Street. Outside the wall lay the nuns' pastures and gardens, extending as far as the suburb of Süstermaye where the poorer people lived and where there were plenty of taverns.

The town's land and the convent's land had been a source of constant discord between the Council, the convent and the Order, especially when there was a need to extend the town wall or build the tower higher or stronger. The nuns sometimes evaded the issue by saying that they had no money, and if the wall belonged to the town then let the town build it. The Council said, in turn, that the land to which the wall extended now belonged to the town as well as the land beyond the wall. To this the nuns protested strongly, producing a document saying that the King of Denmark himself had decreed the land was theirs. And this brought the vassals of Harju and Viru into the dispute, asking by what right the Council should take away the convent's lands and assets. A mediator had been called in by the Order, and now the Order was in a difficult position, since most of the nuns in the convent were from families of the Harju and Viru vassals and the manorial lords and other loyal subjects of the Order, with privileges confirmed by the Order as well as the town. So the Commander of the Order always had to employ stratagems and diplomacy to conciliate the parties in a Christian spirit, as was the way.

Yet, despite the wrangling, the nuns of St Michael were a part of the town, and the townsfolk loved the convent. In recent years the desire of the Order and of a few merchants to build another religious community in Tallinn had further exercised the Council and the nuns and thus slightly distanced them from the Order. The Council and the nunnery were of one mind on this point, that the town did not need a third religious community because then all three would suffer for it.

Now Melchior was walking along Lai Street towards the oaken back gate set low in the wall. The nuns led a less austere life than the Dominicans. Their lands were expansive, and there was constant building work taking place, as in all of Tallinn. Just a few years ago they had started building a new refectory, and the work was ongoing, although it had stopped for now because the town promised to pay the master builders more if they built the Seaward Gate and carried out work to enlarge the harbour.

Approaching the nunnery's lands from the west the visitor would see before him the beautiful inner side of the town wall and the towers, in front of which lay the towerless St Michael's Church and, beside it, in a square, several other monastic buildings, the chapter house and the Abbess's house. First the visitor had to walk through extensive gardens, an orchard and a paddock. Entering through the gates from the cobbled street, which was noisy and none too clean, the visitor encountered a marvellous sense of peace as if, at one step from the town, he had gone into the countryside, to beautiful meadows, sheep pastures, amid apple trees and birdsong. Monastic air, thought Melchior, monastic air is always distinctive, just as town air is always distinctive.

He kept going along the path, bowing to the lay sisters working in the garden, and arrived at the church. Then he walked through the new refectory building and the apple orchard until he finally arrived at the Louenschede Tower. The old town wall ended about here, having been demolished to the north. The convent's gardens continued to the stables and houses of Köismägi. He stopped and thought for a moment.

Tobias Grote had fallen between the walls, as Dorn had said. Just here, where the old town wall ended, one could access the strip of land between the walls. This was a sort of no-man's land, a simple, sandy, shingled and weedy patch of earth. The old town wall enclosed the convent's inner courtyard, which contained all kinds of outbuildings, including the nuns' bathhouse, the brewhouse, the tavern, the laundry, the storehouses, the woodshed and the smithy. The old wall was built on to the convent building, so that from where the Apothecary was now standing there was no access to the courtyard. From the area between the walls, however, it was easy to get through the apple orchard and reach the Köismägi stables, where the convent's land was enclosed by a low wall and in which there was a small gate. At night it was closed, but it would not be hard to scale the wall. From this no-man's-land there was no access to the town wall or to the Quad Dack Tower because the only entrance was from the convent's courtyard.

Melchior stood and thought. What could the Tower-Master have seen here that terrified him so? A ghost? Why should the ghost of the Unterrainer house – if it existed at all – haunt Grote at the sisterhood? But since Melchior was now here, he went to the area between the walls and took a look around.

It really was very quiet here; the air hardly moved. The afternoon sultriness was heating the stones of the wall. All that could be heard was a gust of wind in the treetops and the chirruping of the grasshoppers from the gardens. The town wall was supported on the inside by arched niches, and on these a defensive walkway with wooden parapets was built; it was from here that Grote had fallen. The walkway was not very high, Melchior noticed, but if you were to fall, head first or onto the stones, you might indeed be killed. Access to this walkway was from both the Quad Dack Tower and the next tower along, the Nunnadetagune, the 'tower behind the nunnery', which was between the Louenschede and Quad Dack Towers.

Melchior shrugged and examined the ground. Grote had fallen somewhere here. The soil was uneven, lumpy, full of gravel, puddles, weeds and goat droppings; over by the wall lay the stinking carcass of a cat. Melchior recalled Wentzel Dorn's words and frowned. Grote's corpse had been lying on his back, his face skywards and contorted with horror. His head had been bloody and his bones broken. As he fell he must have smashed his head against a stone. Melchior looked for some such stone and finally found one, at the edge of the old wall. No matter how carefully he looked that seemed to be the only largish stone here on this stretch of ground – an oblong chunk about the size of a couple of clenched fists, the tip of which did indeed seem to be covered in blood. What bothered Melchior, though, was that Grote could not have fallen on it when he fell. And, what was more, how could a person strike his forehead if he landed on his back?

He considered it a little and decided to try to climb up to the wall. From this side he couldn't manage it because there was no access to the Nunnadetagune Tower from the town side, and the lower gate of the Louenschede Tower was locked, which was as it should be. Melchior hummed to himself as he marched back and around all the convent buildings to the church door, but when he heard the sound of the nuns' singing from within he changed his mind, went back through the gardens around from the direction of Lai Street and a short while later was stepping again into the courtyard from the main gate of the convent. He knew this route well because his beloved brewhouse tavern was right there, and that was where Melchior now aimed his steps.

The tavern was kept by a lay sister, Gude, a plump middle-aged woman whose arms were like oak beams and her face as round as a pumpkin. Gude hailed from the Order's lands somewhere to the east of Tallinn, where she and her husband had been servants on the vassal's estate. When her husband died Gude sold all her worldly possessions and came, with the estate owner's permission, into town to St Michael's Convent. Here she cooked meals for the nuns and did some gardening, but mostly she sold beer in the tavern. It would be hard to find a more suitable woman for this job because, if required, Gude could lay several men flat with her bare hands and her voice was so powerful that when she screamed everyone started with fright. In the convent's tavern there was regularly a need for this skill because the nuns sold beer for more hours in a day than the Council thought decent. Sometimes it might be that the men's chatter at night became too loud, and there was no woman more capable than Gude to quieten them down. The convent got a good income from beer sales, however, and sometimes, when the Council found itself at odds with the nuns over something, Wentzel Dorn had to come to the convent to impose a fine for staying open for too long and disturbing the nocturnal peace of the town. Naturally, Dorn did this reluctantly because he also liked to sit in the brewhouse tavern on occasion, but he had to undertake the wishes of the Council. Certainly there was no one better than Gude to give Melchior the lowdown on all the gossip and rumours from the convent.

So this afternoon Melchior was boldly stepping over the threshold of the tavern, calling out a loud greeting to Gude and asking for a stoup of the nuns' best mint-flavoured ale. There were not many people here – a few weavers from Köismägi, a couple of apprentice cobblers and saddle-makers. At a table in the back Melchior noticed a foreign merchant, whom he must have met at some drinking session in the Blackheads' Guildhall. If he remembered rightly, he was from Antwerp and his name was de Wrede.

'Good God, it's Mr Apothecary,' shouted Gude in shrill greeting. 'Haven't seen sir around here for a good week or so. Is your throat dry? I know just the medicine for that – one much better than a stoup of mint ale.'

'I don't know … What could that be?' asked Melchior.

'*Two* stoups of mint ale, brewed with the blessing of St Michael himself,' replied Gude as she filled the cups from the keg and placed the foaming beer in front of the Apothecary.

'I can't say no to that,' laughed Melchior.

Gude immediately asked him his news – how the children were growing, how was Mistress Keterlyn's health and what was going on around Rataskaevu way. When Melchior had told her everything and assured her that the twins were growing well and Keterlyn was in the best of spirits and good health, he, in turn, enquired about the nuns' news and asked her what she knew about the tragic event of Master Tobias Grote falling to his death.

'I was weeping about that yesterday morning,' replied the lay sister sadly. 'Yes, he fell to his death, and a fine intelligent man he was. He wasn't old, not one whose time had come, not at all. A terrible story – why should anyone die in such a senseless way?'

'That I can't say,' grunted Melchior. 'But you know what I heard? The Magistrate himself told me – and maybe the sisters who found him saw it, too – that he had a horribly contorted face, as if he'd seen a ghost.'

'Oh, yes,' Gude shrieked. 'The nuns were horribly frightened when they saw him.'

'And, what's more,' said Melchior, 'before he died Master Grote had mentioned to a few people that he'd seen the Rataskaevu Street Ghost. Tell me what I'm supposed to make of that. I've lived most of my life on Rataskaevu Street and never seen a single ghost or spirit there.'

'Mr Apothecary must be thinking about the ghost of that filthy woman, eh? Oh, yes, I've heard of it, but I haven't seen it – may the holy angels protect me.'

'The very same, I suppose,' Melchior confirmed, although he didn't remember exactly which ghost was supposed to be haunting the Unterrainer house, as he'd heard any number of conflicting stories about it.

'And nobody's able to say what sort of death they'll die,' said Gude with a sigh.

Melchior turned his head, and his gaze crossed that of the Flemish merchant's. Melchior flinched. The Fleming, who had been concentrating on his jug of ale when the Apothecary stepped in, had now raised his head and was looking at Melchior. Or, rather, he was observing him furtively and with great interest, his body taut as a bowstring. He was tense like a person trying very hard to overhear what others are saying. But when Melchior turned towards him de Wrede quickly looked away, but not so quickly that Melchior didn't spot it. De Wrede – Melchior now remembered that his name was Cornelis, Cornelis de Wrede – had been straining to eavesdrop on their conversation. Melchior bowed in his direction, but the Blackhead pretended not to notice. His attention seemed to be diverted to something outside the window. He drained his jug and left.

'Does that Blackhead come here often?' Melchior asked Gude.

'Oh, that gentleman who speaks such beautiful German, as if he had doves nesting in his throat? No, I'd never seen him here before yesterday – then he just hung around. He sat here and tried chatting to a couple of people, but who'd want to talk to someone who can't speak the language properly?'

‘He was hanging around?’ asked Melchior with interest. ‘Why would he hang around here?’

‘I don’t know. He just walked around the convent and then stepped into the tavern and asked whether we sold beer. What fool would ask whether ale is sold in a tavern? I don’t know what we’re supposed to sell here – pork or what? The idiot. But all Flemings are like that, I guess. And then – yes, word of honour – he asked about the poor Tower-Master.’

‘You don’t say. Did he and Grote know one another?’

‘I don’t know. Grote had never mentioned him.’

‘And what did he ask about Grote?’

‘How he came to fall off that tower, and so on …’

‘And how *did* he come to fall off that tower?’ asked Melchior. ‘I’d like to know that, too.’

‘Good gracious – do you think I saw it happen?’ shrieked Gude. ‘It must have been long after the evening service when the tavern was shut and all the sisters were asleep.’

Gude told him that Grote used to come to the nunnery’s tavern quite regularly, but occasionally he went to other places so that the Abbess wouldn’t think he was drinking too often when he was supposed to be working in the convent’s courtyard. But Gude had never seen him chatting to that Flemish Blackhead – in fact, had never seen that man before yesterday. Melchior tried to steer the conversation around to the ghost, but the saddle-makers were starting to demand more ale. He asked whether Grote had said anything to Gude about a ghost, and the woman looked at him as if he were mad. Melchior assured her quickly that he was just asking, for no reason. Gude was known as a bit of a chatterbox. Sometimes that was useful to him, but it wouldn’t be if she started to spread all kinds of stories about him.

He left the tavern and decided to have a look around the Quad Dack Tower before going home. Looked at from the yard, behind the old town wall, the walkway didn't look particularly high, but he knew how misleading it could be to judge height from below. You could get to the Quad Dack Tower only from the convent yard. Melchior climbed up the steps and rattled the big heavy door. As he suspected, it was locked, and a couple of carpenters who were working in the convent's woodshed watched him with unfeigned curiosity. It wasn't an everyday occurrence for the town's apothecary to wish to climb the town wall. But Melchior went on along behind the nuns' bathhouse to the next tower, the Saun Tower, the lower door of which looked ajar. It was less robust than the Quad Dack Tower, but wasn't that as it should be? From what the Apothecary knew of military matters, the cannons were located in both the Quad Dack Tower and the next one on from the Saun Tower, the Nunnadetagune Tower. It would not make sense to site the two strongest cannon-towers too close together.

There were a couple of shacks and the nuns' *saun* next to the Saun Tower. Melchior recalled that the Council had wanted to pull the *saun* down so the town wall could be strengthened, but, of course, the nuns had firmly resisted this. Their gardens ran beyond the bathhouse, under the slope of Toompea as far as the Nuns' Gate. Melchior went boldly up to the Saun Tower, opened the door slightly and called to see if anyone might be in. An old sentry limped over, grumbling about strangers bothering him when he was having lunch, but then he recognized the Apothecary. Melchior asked him whether he might have a look at the walkway, and the man told him he had better be off. But when Melchior recommended a good cheap salve for a painful leg the guard became more cordial. Melchior chatted with him a while longer and discovered that the keys to the tower supervised by Tobias Grote were now with the nuns until the Council found a new tower-master and that when Grote was in the tower he didn't usually lock the lower door. From this side you could get to the walkway between the Quad Dack Tower and the Nunnadetagune Tower only from inside the Quad Dack Tower.

When Melchior promised to send some salve for the sentry's aching bones the next day – but only if he didn't breathe a word to the Council's doctor about it and didn't tell anyone about letting him on to the walkway – the man shook his hand and said the Apothecary could inspect whatever he liked. Melchior climbed the steps and passed along the walkway, which at this point was at the same height as at Quad Dack. The parapet was the same height, too, reaching up above Melchior's waist.

'How could he fall from here?' wondered Melchior, and the sentry replied that anything was possible when one was very drunk.

'But it's never happened to anyone before,' he continued, 'and I can't work out how he was so unlucky. It had been raining heavily and it was foggy.'

Melchior made himself trip and stumble on to the parapet, but there was no danger of falling. True, if the Tower-Master had wanted to climb on to the parapet and reach out to look at something hidden by the eastern flank of the Quad Dack Tower, something in the convent yard, then maybe …

'Any number of accidents can happen, can't they?' said the captain of the tower. 'A person doesn't appreciate that he might lose his footing or something. It was foggy and slippery. Maybe he dropped his torch and –'

'Torch?' asked Melchior quickly. 'But, of course, he must have had a torch. It isn't wise to walk along the town wall in the dark. But was there a torch down there where the body was found?'

'I don't know. I can't see between the two walls from here.'

'That's true.'

'The town wants to build the wall higher and stronger here, you see,' the man explained. 'All sorts of builders have been here measuring, and even that Knight of the Order, Greyssenhagen himself, came here. Apparently he's quite an expert on walls and cannons. The Council asked him, so he came. He explained something to Grote.'

'Interesting. What was that?' asked Melchior cautiously. He had heard that the Master of Jackewolde was something of an expert when it came to fortifications. Hadn't he even assisted in the building of the Order's fortresses somewhere down south? And if he were doing something for the town, it would surely be for a lot of money.

'I didn't hear that,' the man replied petulantly. 'He criticized poor Grote angrily, waved his arms about – he must have thought that the tower was badly defended or something. Why don't you ask the Council?'

Melchior nodded and looked up, but as he did so he saw the Flemish merchant de Wrede again. The man had stepped out from behind the nuns' bathhouse and stopped unexpectedly when he saw the Apothecary on the town wall. He quickly turned around and vanished behind the *saun* again.

But the man carried on chatting, about how human life is strange, you can survive battles, you can be jabbed with spears and lances, you can be chopped with a hatchet, but in your own home your foot can slip, you fall down and that's that, may the Lord have mercy on your soul.

Melchior agreed. It was more than remarkable – and stranger still was the grimace of horror on the face of the dead Tower-Master.

9

Melchior's Pharmacy, Rataskaevu Street

4 August, Evening

On arriving home Melchior discovered Keterlyn gossiping intensely at the counter with an old woman. The hour was late, and usually at this time there would be no more customers, just a few thirsty for a restorative dram while on their way past. Melchior stopped on the threshold, for Keterlyn threw him a confidential glance. But the old woman also sensed that someone had entered the pharmacy, and she turned around. Melchior recognized Annlin, the housekeeper at the merchant Goswin's house on Rataskaevu Street, now of advanced years, and near whose dwelling they had found the corpse yesterday. Last night she had been quivering and goggle-eyed with horror as the town guards examined the dead body, but now the woman's curiosity had presumably got the better of her and she had come to ask the Apothecary what had happened the previous night. Perhaps Goswin had sent her.

Seeing Melchior, the old woman curtseyed to him and said she really must be going; the Master had only sent her out for some wax, but she'd stayed on grinding away like an old mill.

'Not at all,' Keterlyn assured her. 'I was the one doing the asking, and neighbours should catch up now and again, otherwise life would get very dull.'

'And which salve may I give Master Goswin?' asked Melchior. He did indeed recall that over the autumn and winter he had sold the merchant several medicines – potions compounded of juniper berries, caraway, camomile, celery and buck's blood, which must have been for pain in the legs, and also his famous paste made of salvia, marjoram, dill and plenty of peppermint oil that was an effective remedy for headaches.

'Oh, Mistress Keterlyn has already found it,' responded Annlin. 'It's the same one, I think, that took away the Master's leg pain last winter.'

'That's an excellent mixture,' chuckled Melchior. 'It's good for several ailments. It heals wounds and, if you make it into a liquid and drink it, helps in cases of poisoning. And, of course, for leg pain you have to boil oat gruel as well. But how is Master Goswin doing?' Actually, there should have been more to the question – how is Master Goswin doing now that his former arch-enemy Bruys is dead? But Annlin didn't catch – or didn't want to catch – that, so she simply told him that her Master had plenty to do and was eating very frugally, that he didn't have much appetite in the heat, he just wanted light food, but old Annlin didn't know what light food was and cooked as she had learned to cook so that a person would have strength and his soul would stay whole within him.

Annlin was not actually all that old, probably less than sixty, but some women look older than their age. Her dark hair had gone grey long ago, and she walked with a slight stoop, although she seemed quite brisk and nimble otherwise. She had long bony arms and fingers. Once she might have been quite good-looking, and she had lived at Master Goswin's house on Rataskaevu Street for as long as

Melchior could remember … at Master Goswin's house next door to the Unterrainer house. Which reminded him that Annlin must know that old ghost story or would at least have heard of it. When he was about to ask about it in a polite way he saw that Keterlyn was glancing at him again slyly. Melchior shrugged – evidently his wife had already taken care of that question.

But Annlin, who was fumbling in her efforts to get going, had in her tale of Master Goswin's eating habits skilfully swung around to the previous night, to the effect that her Master was old now and had to sleep a lot and eat frugally, but how could he get any sleep with people being stabbed and with screaming in the street at night?

'Did he hear screaming yesterday?' asked Melchior, and Annlin replied that her Master – thank Heaven – had been asleep and didn't really wake up, but in the morning he had asked his servants what the commotion had been on the street in the night. Annlin could respond only that someone had been killed and the town guards had been making a noise outside. 'So you don't know who it was that was killed?' ventured the old woman.

'Some stranger,' replied Melchior. 'The town guards had never seen him before. He seemed to be some young man or even a boy. Must have been someone from the outskirts.'

'I suppose so,' agreed Annlin. 'But, forgive me, Mr Apothecary, for staying here chatting for so long. Really, my Master was expecting me back ages ago. Good health to your family, and may St Agnes bless your happy children.'

'Thanks for your good wishes, neighbour,' Keterlyn responded politely. 'And may the saints' blessings continue for your family, too.'

'Oh, my family is just me and old Hainz,' sighed Annlin, 'and sometimes Mr Goswin, too, because he's very sickly now. My only son left home years ago, and he's a stablehand with the Bishop of Tartu.' There was a tinge of pride in that last sentence, Melchior noticed. Annlin fumbled a little more and was gone. Melchior went straight up to his wife, took her in his arms and kissed her on the mouth.

'You have a nice way of greeting your wife,' Keterlyn said at length when she was free of her husband's embrace, 'as if you hadn't seen her for years.'

'Actually I've been visiting a few religious establishments,' chuckled Melchior. 'But when a woman gives you such a sly look she's only got one thing on her mind – that's what I learned when I was an apprentice in Riga.'

'I don't want to hear about all that debauchery. But I was winking at you because Annlin and I were having a chat about the very thing that we discussed yesterday evening – the ghost at the Unterrainer house.'

'Interesting,' said Melchior. 'How did that come up?'

'It didn't actually come up, but today I've been bringing it up with all the women on our street, as you would have asked me to if you hadn't rushed straight off into town this morning.'

'I might very well have asked you,' admitted Melchior. 'You're a very perspicacious wife.'

'The wife of an apothecary, especially one like you, has to be perspicacious,' replied Keterlyn with a smile. 'Yesterday evening you seemed curious about the ghost at the Unterrainer house –'

'And then an unknown tramp was killed in front of that very house. It does look like the work of the devil, doesn't it?'

Keterlyn uttered something rapidly in Estonian meant to keep evil spirits away. She then told Melchior that she had discussed the Unterrainer house with everyone who had been into the shop and then she had been to the *saun* and on various errands to the baker's and the butcher's and brought up the subject of the ghost everywhere. It was known that some stranger had been knifed to death in the street the previous night, and some said that it portended no good for the Unterrainer house.

'It happened there so long ago,' said Keterlyn. 'Some people say a hundred, some say fifty years ago, but most of them agree that it happened since the Order's been in power.'

'So it certainly can't have been a hundred years ago then,' said Melchior quietly. 'And what do people say?'

'Well, everybody's heard a slightly different version of the story, from their grandmother or some old town guard or whoever. But generally the tale is much the same, only differing in a few details.'

'Every rumour has a grain of truth in it, they say – never mind that every bit of gossip and every gossiper distorts it slightly. But go on, woman.'

And Keterlyn told him. The house was said to have been built long ago by a rich merchant, Cristian Unterrainer by name. Some said that he was already an elderly man but some maintained that he wasn't that old. He came to Tallinn accompanied by his wife. One version of the story is that she was a beautiful and virtuous woman, younger than her husband, a caring and fine wife who wanted to be loyal to him, love him truly and deeply and bear him many children. The husband, though, treated her badly. The man took his wife only occasionally, and from behind, not as a woman wants her husband to do. This man is said to have drunk a lot of ale, and that made him very cruel. He beat his wife with a whip and wanted sex with her only by force, standing up and beating her at the same time and making her sick, because that was the only way he could become aroused.

'Bizarre tales,' remarked Melchior. 'Do you know who witnessed these goings-on or who knew about them?'

'Just people talking,' said Keterlyn with a smile. 'And don't you know that there hasn't been a rumour unless there's been a witness?'

'All right, tell me more.'

'They go on to say that this virtuous woman was terribly unhappy and cried bitter tears when she thought no one was looking. They say she went to church and prayed to the saints and the Virgin Mary to change her husband's ways so that she wouldn't have to suffer. One monk, though, happened to overhear her prayers ...'

'A Dominican?' asked Melchior.

'Just so, and a couple of older women even knew his name – it was Abelard or Adelbert or something like that. And this mendicant brother was a young – so some say – charming and handsome man, who had not joined the Dominicans of his own free will. He was the fifth son in his family, and he'd been given over to the Dominicans more or less by force to make a servant of God out of him. And when he heard this young lady's complaints and prayers he was overcome with pity, and he addressed her. So they started talking until they became friends, and from friends they became lovers.'

'Oh, good heavens,' sighed Melchior. 'I think I've heard this one. A bit differently, though.'

'So when the young monk went around town with his alms-basket and he reached Rataskaevu Street he would always go to that nice woman's place, and – so people say – they'd take their clothes off in front of the inglenook and start making love under the crucifix on the wall, so that one was breaking his monk's vow and the other her holy sacrament of marriage.'

'You often hear stories like that,' opined Melchior. 'Which means that they happen often, too – not that I want to condemn anybody.'

'This tale is a bit different,' Keterlyn went on, 'although there are stories that are similar in some ways but different in others. But it's getting late, and I'd rather continue with this some other time.'

No matter how Melchior pleaded, Keterlyn remained firm. The children had to be washed and put to bed, Melchior had to close the pharmacy, so there was no time for chatting just then. Only hours later, as the tender dusk of an August evening descended over Tallinn and Melchior and Keterlyn were heading for bed, did his wife take up the story again.

'Another version of the story is that the wife of Unterrainer the merchant wasn't so young and virtuous at all. Rather, she was a mature woman who hadn't borne her husband any children because that blessing had not been granted by God –'

'At this point I would say, my dear,' remarked Melchior, 'that people don't always know the facts about such matters. Quite a few physicians have written that it isn't always the woman's fault, but it might also depend on the man.'

'Well, whatever, I'm only telling you the gossip. Anyway, Unterrainer didn't want to sleep with his wife any more, but the wife was of the age when she doesn't think of much else but getting together with a man because she feels a tickling between her legs and she's like a cat on heat ... You understand, of course, dear husband, that I'm only telling you what –'

'What the gossip says. Yes, of course. Carry on,' interrupted Melchior.

The twins were asleep in their cradle, and he lifted the candelabra and a jug of water on to a little table beside the marriage bed.

Keterlyn sat on the edge of the bed and shook her hair free from under its coif.

'I heard that when the woman saw the young monk in the street with his alms-box she remembered some rumour about him being particularly well endowed …'

'Oh, my dear, do women really talk about things like that among themselves?' said Melchior, suppressing laughter.

'I told you yesterday you wouldn't want to know what women talk about in the *saun*. I was chatting in the bathhouse, and it doesn't take much to get women started on ghosts and suchlike – or anything a bit indecent.'

'*A bit* indecent,' exclaimed Melchior with a sigh. 'But carry on, I won't interrupt you any more.'

'It's better if you don't interrupt, otherwise I won't go on,' she replied and then continued. 'So, young Abelard or Adelbert turned up with his alms-basket in Mäealune Street – as it was called before the well was dug – and our cunning and shameless Mrs Unterrainer had kindly invited him inside, because she had a very generous donation to make to the young monk, but all the while she was wondering whether young Abelard had as big a tool under his cassock as she'd heard. And so the woman poured the monk some sweet wine and opened up her dress a little in a suggestive way, like this …'

'That was a very suggestive thing to do,' agreed Melchior.

Keterlyn loosened the ribbon that held her dress together at the breast, sat closer to her husband and pulled her dress up above the knees.

'Very,' nodded his wife. 'She drove that monk wild in every way, hoping that the rumour was true, that young Abelard hadn't gone into the monastery of his own free will and that he wouldn't hold tenaciously to his monkish vows. So then, to lure the monk, she casually let the hem of her dress ride up and shamelessly showed her legs, so the young man gasped for air. And then she said that what she wanted to donate to Abelard was the joy of sex because it wasn't a sin when a man and a woman both want it together and they get pleasure from it. And then she said that while she might be older than the monk her womb was like a young virgin's, narrow and smooth, because as she hadn't borne any fruit she had never given birth. And when she'd enticed the monk in that way and revealed her body from under her clothes Abelard couldn't control himself any longer, and from beneath his habit the reason she had lured him inside in the first place appeared to be stirring. So then, they say, what the woman saw really pleased her because those tales about him all turned out to be true. Under the monk's habit a big strong tree was growing, and when she saw it the woman grabbed it in her hands, and Abelard couldn't find the strength to resist because the pleasures of love probably weren't unknown to him. And what do I see, Melchior? It seems that your resistance isn't any stronger than Abelard's was, not at all.' Keterlyn blew out the candle, and in the last glimmer of light Melchior saw her taking off her dress.

'Something tells me that young Abelard started visiting that house,' he persisted.

'Oh, they do say that. That lustful, disreputable woman caught him in her snare so that every day, when the merchant Unterrainer wasn't at home, Abelard just happened to come by with his alms-basket and into the house, and they did all sorts of immoral things, standing up and lying down, and got a lot of pleasure out of it. And something that is called love grew between them, for what else is it when a man and a woman get happiness from touching each other?'

'You don't seem to condemn what they did.'

'Who am I to have the right to do that?'

'You have the right because this story didn't come to a good end, and God punished them for their sin,' opined Melchior.

'They really do say that. Their immorality didn't go unnoticed by the townsfolk, and somebody must have whispered something to the husband, and so one day Unterrainer came home when his wife and Abelard were stark naked. Apparently she was in the monk's lap like a rider on a horse, and he was sitting on the chair where the merchant usually took his breakfast.'

Keterlyn turned her husband, who was also already undressed, on to his back and sat facing him to ride him.

'Go on,' ordered Melchior.

'If you really want me to,' responded his wife. 'This story has a horrible ending. When the merchant saw what his wife was doing with the monk, they say he pulled the woman off the monk, grabbed a sword and chopped the monk's big dick off right there and then. And then he tied them both to the chair and stuffed the man's prick into the woman's mouth. Then he left them there to die, one to bleed to death and the other to waste away from hunger. And he went into town and carried on doing his business as if nothing had happened. If anyone asked, he'd say that his wife had gone on a pilgrimage to the lands of the Bishop of Riga, and he didn't have to say anything about the young monk because no one ever asked him. But he enjoyed every moment he was at home, watching his wife and the monk getting weaker and weaker every hour, every day, the life ebbing out of them. And when the time finally came, he walled them both in the cellar, sold his house and left Tallinn for good. But those souls who died in sin and who were buried alive stayed on to haunt the house.'

They didn't talk any more about ghosts that night.

And as Keterlyn moaned with ecstasy at her husband's touch her voice flew out the open window and on to Rataskaevu Street, passing from house to house and delicately drifting even into the Unterrainer house before finally dying away.

10

The House of the Merchant Arend Goswin, Rataskaevu Street

5 August, Morning

TODAY IS THE FUNERAL of Laurentz Bruys. Laurentz Bruys is dead. I did not have a chance to talk to him before he died. Those three sentences were the first and only ones to enter Arend Goswin's head on waking. He lay in bed under the covers and thought over those three statements and felt his soul filled with torment, pain and untameable anguish. Bruys's death had been a very painful blow to him. It had come too soon and should not have happened that way. Bruys should not have died like that. Good Lord, it wasn't fair.

He had not slept well – in fact, he had been tossed between dozing and a half-waking state the whole night, his dreams and his waking thoughts entangled. His spirit pained him and wouldn't let him rest.

The following winter Arend Goswin would be seventy years old, and the past few decades had been haunted by his relationship with Laurentz Bruys. All this time – and how time flies much faster when you're getting old – not a day had passed when Arend Goswin hadn't thought of Bruys and said prayers that the man would not die yet, that they would have time to talk face to face over old sins, that Goswin would be able to face his own death with a peaceful heart.

But, no, that time had not been granted to them.

In the eyes of the townspeople and the Great Guild they had been reconciled – oh, of course. At feasts, at Christmas and on Council business they would exchange a couple of sentences; they were polite, and no one would say they were mortal enemies. But they were both stubborn old men; they had exchanged the gestures and statements that were publicly expected of them, but both knew that there had been no full reconciliation and there never would be if they did not sit and talk sincerely about what had happened twenty-five years before.

It felt like yesterday, thought Arend Goswin, stretching out in the bed, and his heart was tugged by a painful spasm. Dorothea. He was sure that Dorothea had never left, that the girl's soul was still hovering over the house, that she approved all her father's thoughts and deeds. And when he thought of his daughter he imagined her talking and watching what happened in the house. The girl had been seventeen then, and she did not grow older in death. Dorothea would be eternally seventeen, even though Annlin, who sometimes chatted with the old non-German women at the market and elsewhere, would say that if children die – and if they stay to haunt the house – then they, too, live through a human lifespan and grow old. No. Arend Goswin did not believe that. If Dorothea was still present in the house, then she was seventeen years old and no older.

These were painful thoughts, but Goswin had grown accustomed to them. He forced himself upright in the bed, fumbled for the wooden hammer beside the night-table and struck the wall hard with it a couple of times. He waited a moment until the faithful Annlin appeared at the door.

'You called, sir?' she asked obediently.

'Oh, woman, since when has my knocking meant anything else?' grumbled Goswin. 'Did you go to the market?'

'You want to hear the news, sir?' ventured the woman. 'What people are saying about the killing?'

'First of all, sir wants a warm foot bath. Did you buy oats? I have a long day today, a lot of walking and a lot of things to do.'

Annlin nodded. Yes, she knew. The funeral. For some years now her Master's feet had been hurting him, and, as Melchior had recommended, they needed to be soaked in boiled oat water. Since cock-crow this morning she had been boiling the oats, and the warm water now awaited her Master.

A little later Goswin was sitting in the kitchen, his feet in a bucket full of warm water, and Annlin was kneeling before him and rubbing her Master's spindly, hairy leg in the liquid. This time of the morning was Goswin's best time for thinking. Annlin's soft hands and the warm oat water stimulated his thinking processes, and he had known for years that if you need to come out of some complex situation, if you want good advice, you should let yourself have a good steam-bath or get Annlin to bathe your legs.

As Annlin bent over his legs the front of her dress fell open, and Goswin saw the woman's old breasts dangling. Now they were long, narrow and pendulous, although old Hainz – despite his age and dull wits – still touched them at night and took his wife as was proper and dutiful. Goswin could hear it clearly in his own bedroom; he had very good hearing. Hainz's understanding was feeble, but he still had bodily energy. Once he had been a porter at the harbour and the weighing-house, toiling with the bags, and from there Goswin had taken him on as a servant. And looking at Annlin's old breasts he thought again of those years when Annlin was younger – and she had been quite a beautiful woman – and he had felt a wild temptation to see them. He even remembered that day when he had taken Annlin and Hainz into service with him, and maybe even then he had secretly thought that the pretty servant girl might once in a while be disposed to favour her Master – of course, when the mistress wouldn't find out, but ... but it had all gone quite differently. Arend Goswin had never touched Annlin's breasts or hips or any other part, and he had got over his temptations decades ago, although – may the saints be his witness – he had seen Annlin's breasts close up and naked several times when they were beautiful, large and full, but that was when everything had changed, everything became different. Suddenly everything had taken on a different meaning, although he still loved Annlin and her breasts. Still, and in his own way. Fidelity. Yes, I have been a faithful husband, thought Goswin. In life and in death.

'So what are they saying at the market and in town?' he asked.

'Might sir be thinking about the killing that happened the night before last on Rataskaevu Street?'

'That is just what sir is thinking of,' snapped Goswin impatiently. 'What else do you suppose? Did you go to the Apothecary's?'

'I did. And I brought that salve of juniper berries and cumin to smear on sir's feet.'

'And what did the Apothecary know? Melchior arrived on the spot, and he's a sharp man. So what does he know?'

'The Apothecary said that he had never seen that boy – that's what he said – ever before, and the town guards hadn't either. He said he must have been someone from outside town. At the market I heard that the guards took the corpse to St Barbara's Chapel, and if no one comes to bury it and blame someone for the killing, then it will probably be placed in a hole in St Barbara's Churchyard.

And what else would people say about it – whoever is interested in the killing of some strange tramp? Any number of beggars and tramps are piling up in the town waiting to be buried – who would care about one of them?'

From the hallway Goswin heard some pattering and knocking then voices, then the grey shaggy mop of hair of Hainz, his servant, appeared in the doorway.

'To say, my lord, the selfsame, that the servant of that Gentleman Knight is here. His Master has sent him to ask you, my lord, whether my lord has the time, the selfsame, to ...' Hainz was somewhat dim-witted, and clearly talking had never been his strong suit. He may have been stupid, but he was loyal, and that was why Goswin had kept him for decades – and, of course, Annlin, too.

'Speak more clearly,' demanded Goswin, and with Annlin's help Hainz was finally able to say that the neighbour from across Rataskaevu Street, the Knight Kordt von Greyssenhagen, had sent his henchman to ask if Master Goswin could spare a little time for him before the funeral.

This was peculiar. Of course, Goswin knew this liegeman of the Order, and he knew vaguely that somehow this Greyssenhagen was involved in the building of the new convent at Marienthal – and why would he not know, as the convent was very close to his Jackewolde lands? And had it not been at the wishes of the Order that Greyssenhagen had been recommended as one of the patrons of the new convent? At any rate the merchant was surprised at this visit, but he let the servant know that he would, naturally, be glad to receive the Knight and, if needs be, before the funeral.

Greyssenhagen had bought the fiefdom of Jackewolde, or Jägala, about ten years before, and it included several estates and one village quite close to Marienthal. He was from somewhere in the Order's southern lands. Greyssenhagen had acquired the house on Rataskaevu Street just five years before, however, since he was one of the few vassals from around Tallinn who had had no grand residence in the town – although Greyssenhagen's house could hardly be called grand, and it was also a little strange that while the richest and most important vassals' houses were on Toompea Hill the Lord of Jackewolde had bought his house in the Lower Town.

Greyssenhagen came as soon as his liegeman had brought the message back. It was evident that the Knight was in a hurry. Goswin recalled that he was seen very rarely in town – mainly when the commander had summoned the vassals together, whether attending the chapter or convening the court or discussing the vassals' service or estate matters, but if other vassals were seen more often in town, Greyssenhagen always came for the business. He was quite a bit younger than Goswin, a man of about forty perhaps, who had buried two wives and had recently been courting the widow of the liegeman down Tartu way, had sold that man's estates to the Bishop of Tartu and earned a tidy sum from it. Three years ago the Council at Viborg had complained that the coastal dwellers near Jägala had taken over a ship with the liegeman's certain knowledge if not his actual encouragement. But Greyssenhagen had sworn on Toompea that *he* knew nothing of the affair, and *his* tenant farmers had not plundered any ship, and that was how the matters remained, as there were no witnesses.

Greyssenhagen was a fine fellow, Goswin decided, as he got his clothes on with Hainz's help and hung a chain around his neck in order to show off his worth and wealth and look decent for the funeral. He could detect a cunning merchant from several hundred versts; Greyssenhagen got steadily richer and knew which way the wind blew.

He received the Knight in the *dörnse*, the living-room area at the back of the house, and got Hainz to bring a jug of the best beer and gingerbread with honey and pepper. When the Knight arrived they embraced and kissed cheeks and exchanged other common pleasantries. Greyssenhagen had a squint and walked with a slight limp in his left leg. He was wearing an austere black coat, but his hat was magnificent and striking. There was only one hatter in Tallinn, on Toompea, who made those. In truth, instead of a hat he could have worn a red kerchief wound around his head, with one end hanging down the right-hand side. That was said to be the fashion overseas now.

The Knight didn't waste any time – he drank a jug of beer but politely declined any bread and came straight to the point of his visit. 'Master Goswin, as you perhaps know, I and several others of the Harju vassals have been asked by the Order to become patrons of the new Convent of St Bridget. Together and separately we have to fulfil the duty of defending the interests of the convent, promoting its cause, giving advice and representing the convent in Tallinn and elsewhere. Everything we say must be taken as if coming from the Abbess's own mouth.'

'Yes, I know that,' murmured Goswin.

'And that esteemed merchant Bruys was a citizen of Tallinn who was one of the few people from the Lower Town to also be a patron of the convent and defend it before the Tallinn Council and, when necessary, to promote and press issues which quite a few other respectable men in this town did not dare to do.'

'That's how it was,' agreed Goswin.

'And now he's dead,' continued the Knight, and Goswin had to agree to that, too, although, the saints be his witness, he wished it were not so.

'It's necessary, it's absolutely essential, that someone takes the flag from the dead merchant's hands and carries it forward. We vassals from Harju have been thinking among ourselves that we want to make such a proposal to some respected, rich and honourable Tallinn merchant whose word will count before the Council and who would be prepared, body and soul, to support the St Bridget enterprise. Master Goswin, we wish to make that proposal to you.'

Master Arend Goswin was very surprised, but he promised to think over the proposal.

'Why are you making the proposal just to me?' he asked. Apart from the fact – as you said – that I'm rich and I don't have heirs.' Becoming a patron of the convent would mean handing over a large part of his assets to the convent. True, it was an exchange, but everything that the Convent of St Bridget could give back would only come to Goswin after his death.

'I did tell you, didn't I, that you are respected and honoured?' asked Greyssenhagen, with what seemed to be the flicker of a smile.

'It goes with wealth,' conceded Goswin, 'but you must have had some other reason.'

'Yes,' said the Knight, 'we had. At the convent we know very well what is going on in the town, who has a grudge against whom and who is friends with whom. Master Bruys had many enemies just because of support for the Bridgettine Convent.'

'If you know these things so well, then you've obviously heard that Bruys and I … that we …' he stumbled, looking for a word, 'that we were hardly regarded as friends by many.'

'I know,' nodded Greyssenhagen, 'but I also know that you were reconciled, and I know that you are one of the few – perhaps even the only – merchant in Tallinn who has not come out strongly against St Bridget's Convent in the Council or the Great Guild.' He leaned closer to the merchant. 'I know people well, Master Goswin,' he added softly, 'and I know that if anyone wanted to avenge Laurentz Bruys's death or promote his cause it would be you.'

Goswin was taken aback. 'Avenge his death?' he asked, shocked. 'Laurentz died … he simply died. He was old, he was ill, he died in his own prayer room and –'

'And he had many enemies,' the Knight interrupted him. 'He was hated because he wanted a new convent and the Council did not. I have seen a lot of this world. My family has not always had a coat of arms, and I know that always, when some rich person dies, hated by many, you have to ask *who did it?*'

'Merciful heavens,' cried Goswin, alarmed. 'You don't mean to say that someone killed Laurentz?'

'I didn't say that, but I have wondered. I don't know the answer, but if the question has an answer then I will make a bet on my own blessed soul that you would want to know that very much and would want to punish the man who killed him.'

Goswin was silent for a while, but then he conceded, through gritted teeth, 'I'd strangle him with my own hands.'

'So would I,' agreed the Knight, getting up. 'So you'll think over my proposal?'

'Certainly, but I don't believe for a moment that anyone would kill Laurentz – it wouldn't have been possible. He died in his own prayer room. The Abbess was there, everyone saw him die –'

'Oh, let me tell you how it is possible. That man could neither walk nor talk, he was constantly in someone's care, and it would have been very simple to put some poison into his food or drink. Someone could buy off his servant or nurse. Someone only had to get to him for a moment to put a drop of poison in his cup, which might not kill immediately but certainly would kill, and no one would suspect a thing because the man was dying anyway. And at the convent they also gave him communion, and he was anointed, and some very cunning man could easily have slipped some poison in.'

'But why, for Heaven's sake?' Goswin almost shouted. 'Why kill a man who has one foot in the grave? Who could be so cruel?'

'He had many enemies,' repeated Greyssenhagen as he departed, 'and as long as he still breathed he could revise his will.'

When Greyssenhagen had left, Goswin realized that he had lied to the Knight. No, he would not strangle the man who might have killed Bruys with his own hands.

No, definitely not with his own hands.

11

The Unterrainer House, Rataskaevu Street
5 August, Morning

GOTTSCHALK WITTE, Pastor of the Church of the Holy Ghost, sat with a surly expression in his bed in the bedroom for which he had converted the loft of the old house. He had been living in Tallinn for over two years by this time and had adapted as best he could to this northerly country, putting up with countless discomforts and oddities.

It was raining, and it looked as if the long dry spell was over, and Witte should have been glad about the rain because it meant that this year he wouldn't have to fear crop failure and the stunted plants would be revived and bear fruit. And yet he could feel no special pleasure this morning. He was troubled by a dream. He had recently turned fifty, and he thought that a man of his age should not be troubled and oppressed by dreams. But this one did oppress him, so much so that Witte was not sure whether he would find peace and consolation, as he usually did, from serving at the altar, praying, preaching and undergoing profuse penitence. He was a man of God, spiritual, and he loved God and loved his work. When anyone in spiritual difficulty came to ask his advice he would always recommend prayer, confession and penitence because they ease the troubled soul and cleanse the person. From the Kingdom of God there is consolation for all manner of things.

This dream, which had started off so sweetly, had later turned into a nightmare, as if demons had come in the night to torment him and brought back painful memories of distant times, so distant that they rarely came to mind during the day. But at night, yes, at night they were present, pressing on his soul. Old sins cast long shadows, Witte had sometimes heard people say, but had he not been repenting his sins for decades, mortifying himself, diligently fasting and even going on a pilgrimage to Compostela? So did this nightmare have any right to come back to torture him, reminding him of things of which – as far as is possible for any mortal – he had thought himself redeemed? And if anyone had the right to reproach him it was himself and no one else.

And yet the nightmare came as he slept, bridging the decades: that old man, the Master, his inspiring words – they were *hot* words – how their blood was now admixed with the blood of Jesus Christ and how pain is born from sin and joy is born from pain and closeness to God from joy. Oh, Witte recalled the pain, the joy and the ecstasy, in which the joy had suddenly vanished and been replaced by knowledge. Cold and eternal knowledge. And Witte's joy at the same moment turned into sin.

Margelin arrived carrying Witte's washed clothes. She put them on a chair by the man's bed and remained staring askance at him,

'You're not feeling well, dear brother?' she asked.

Witte sighed. 'I didn't sleep well at all,' he replied shortly.

'Again?' asked the woman, looking at Witte with concern. 'Last time I went to the Apothecary to get medicine and he recommended a mixture of dill and yarrow to put on your face, but that didn't work, I suppose?'

'I think it helped once, but today …' He didn't dare to tell Margelin about his dreams. Never mind that Margelin was also present in the dreams, never mind that they were both young then. Margelin need not think that it was troubling him still.

'I know,' she said. 'It's this house. Because of this house I, too, sometimes don't get any sleep.'

'The house?' muttered Witte, feigning surprise. 'Why should I not sleep because of the house?'

'Don't deny it. You've heard it, too, I know.'

'Heard what?'

'The ghost, that penitent. You know it is moving around here, begging forgiveness for its sins, dear brother. You know because it's true. The Master himself talked about it because the Master knew, the Master himself –'

'Quiet, woman,' demanded Gottschalk Witte harshly. That *name again, that man again*. 'We were young, we believed too many things we shouldn't have believed.'

'Don't deny it,' she said again, and more severely. 'You know what the Master said about this house is true. You've heard them, too, the voices. I've read it in your face sometimes in the mornings, and over the years I've learned to read your face and those feelings that you try so hard to hide.'

'The Master couldn't have known that the spirit can't find rest. This is all just idle talk and nothing more.'

'It's not idle talk. You want to make yourself deaf to those voices, but you *must* know that the Master never lied.'

'Sister,' exclaimed Witte. 'Are *you* reproaching me? You?'

'What's done is done, and you can't undo it, dear brother. And that applies to this house as well. A horrible and obscene sin was committed here, and since then the souls of the sinners have been wandering this house, and *you have heard them*. It is the Master himself who is oppressing those penitents. You, too, have woken up at night, and you, too, have sensed that debauchery that once took place. The Master is flogging those sinners from beyond the grave, and they are repenting.'

Yes, Margelin was right. Witte had heard that howling or sighing – a yelping, the moaning of a person in the grip of terrible pain … No, not of a person, because in this house there was no one but Margelin and him, and such sounds could not belong to any living soul. He had heard those sounds, perhaps even a few nights ago, and before, and he had prayed in order to keep away those thoughts which shook his faith in God. And on several occasions he had woken in the night and stared in horror at the door and feared that the Ghost of Rataskaevu Street would now step from it, sent by the demons to punish him.

But he had to be strong and believe, and if he were destined to suffer then he must face his ordeals proudly and in an upright manner. He had known what a house this was, and that was why he had hoped for escape, redemption and salvation from it. Surely they were not denied to him? Even when he let his heart be warmed occasionally by little pleasures. For he knew of one certainty: there is no redemption before repentance – but even penitence can be joyful.

He pulled the coverlet aside and stood up straight out of bed. He now stood stark naked before Margelin and said, 'You know how a person must behave and think in order to keep evil away.'

'Yes, I know, dear brother,' said the woman with a prolonged stare at Witte. 'The Holy Virgin shows us the way if we diligently pray to her and keep our thoughts pure.'

'Exactly so,' said Witte, 'always according to her guidance, and no doubt our sins will be forgiven.'

'Sins? Have you sinned, dear brother?' The woman kept looking at the man. His breath was faster and his hands starting to tremble.

'Yes, I am a poor sinner, and I want to confess. I have to confess straight away.'

'And for your sins you have to be punished.'

'Very severely punished. Please punish me, mistress.' *The Master – he had once asked that of the Master.*

'On your knees then,' commanded the woman. Her voice had changed. A heap of clothes tumbled to the floor, and her hand now held only a whip, which she had kept under her brother's washed and ironed habit.

'How long is it since your last confession?'

12

The Precincts of St Nicholas's Church
5 August, Morning

MELCHIOR WOKE UP earlier than usual that morning. It had started to rain, and it pattered hard against the roof tiles. A wind had risen from the sea and was rattling the windows. Autumn was gradually beginning to make itself felt, the northern autumn of chilly winds, storms and showers.

He turned on his back while pulling the coverlet over Keterlyn's curved body, entwined his hands behind his head and thought about the women's gossip concerning the events that had once occurred at the Unterrainer house. There was certainly some truth there. Gossip is able to join and separate different stories, cook up a casserole of half-truths out of the truth and borrowed legends, and if Melchior was sure of anything it was that that monk's name was not Abelard. It might, however, have been Adelbert, and, if so, there should be some note about him in the records at the Dominican Monastery. But how did those ancient events have anything to do with Master Bruys, Tobias Grote and the killing of that strange little man in front of the Unterrainer house? Melchior was not sure, but he felt he ought to be. Life had taught him to see links, and he felt he would get no peace until he could be sure that there were no such links.

Later, down in the kitchen – where Melchior's father before him had set up a laboratory and in which he boiled, pressed, mixed and pounded herbs – Melchior once again took up the subject of the Unterrainer house with Keterlyn.

'If I remember rightly, last night something stopped us from talking this through,' Melchior told his wife.

'Oh, I suppose you could say that,' replied the woman cheerfully.

'So then, when you were chatting with people about the ghost, did anyone say that they'd actually seen the phantom of the Unterrainer house? And who is it who is supposed to be haunting the place?'

Keterlyn thought for a moment. 'No,' she replied, and her tone of voice became surer. 'No, I don't remember anyone saying they'd seen anything *themselves*. Many could say that those two unhappy spirits – or maybe one of them – are haunting the house. But the only person who, as far as I remember, ever said she had seen a ghost there was Magdalena.'

'And she died a while back,' said Melchior.

Keterlyn turned around and looked at her husband with concern. 'Surely you shouldn't be worrying so much about the spirits of the dead. Aren't you bringing bad fortune on yourself? What if – may St Catherine preserve me – what if the ghost really exists and ...'

'I want to know that, too. What if?' said Melchior with assurance. 'And I can't recall anyone saying they'd seen a ghost with their own eyes either. They keep talking about a haunted house, though. That's interesting.'

'Perhaps you could ask Pastor Witte or his sister. They should know – assuming they'd want to talk about such things.'

'I think I shall do that,' reflected the Apothecary. 'But, still, it is astonishing. People say that the house is haunted and terrible deeds have been done there, but who has seen or heard it? No one can say.'

'That's how the stories go,' said Keterlyn. 'Long, long ago some man saw the ghost of a bloody monk at the Unterrainer house, either that or they saw the merchant's wife … But, really, the stories are all about how someone heard from someone who heard from someone else who was supposed long ago to have seen …' She stopped short. 'No, wait. Now that I think about it, yesterday somebody did say that someone's daughter had *heard* the ghost. Yes, that's right.'

'*Heard*? And recently? Who, dear wife, whose daughter heard the ghost?'

'I'll have to try to remember. I'll be able to tell you this evening.'

'Evening then,' sighed Melchior. 'I have plenty to be getting on with. It wouldn't be right to open the pharmacy, I suppose, because they're burying Master Bruys today. I think I'll put my other hat on and go and take a closer look at the funeral. But if someone does come by wanting a sweet dram or some confections, I reckon you can sell them. And – most important – I have to have one more sweet kiss for the road.'

'Well, that didn't take long,' smiled Keterlyn.

And Melchior did get that kiss for the road.

Tallinn was today, four days before the feast of St Lawrence, burying Laurentz Bruys, the merchant. In his will Bruys had asked to be buried in St Nicholas's Churchyard and nowhere else, not inside any church. To be buried in a church under a gravestone he would have had to pay the church a hefty sum, and his grave would have been grand and majestic. But Bruys had preferred to be buried cheaply so that more money could be donated to the poor, the needy and to his sacred undertaking, the foundation of St Bridget's Convent. Hallowed ground under the young linden trees of St Nicholas's Churchyard was good enough for him, and for that the church could not demand money – and anyway the church had received more than enough in donations and fees for masses during Bruys's lifetime.

A stately funeral – paid for, naturally, by the Great Guild – had enticed plenty of people into town from beyond the town walls and further afield. As Melchior trudged from Rataskaevu Street towards Town Hall Square he saw an ugly brawl between alms-people and beggars and a dozen or so vagrants from out of town who were coming into Tallinn from the direction of the Nuns' Gate. The town guards had just arrived to separate the two groups, but one man's head had already been split open. The local beggars slipped away into cellars and dens at the approach of the guards, and the guards did not take the trouble to pursue them. But coming from beyond the town wall through the gates were not only beggars but fishermen, herdsmen, millers, train-oil-boilers, tanners, their wives and children and even peasants from further away. Everyone knew that a magnificent funeral would take place today, the Great Guild and the Kanuti Guilds would be distributing alms to the poor, and food and clothing would be laid out. Among them there must have been some serious mourners, those who had done business with Master Bruys or come into contact with him in other ways.

Around midday the corpse of Master Bruys, in his coffin and wrapped in a shroud, was carried out of his house on Lai Street. A fine little assembly of people had already gathered in front of it, paupers and beggars among them. The coffin was borne by members of the Great Guild, somewhat younger ones who had enough strength to carry a coffin of heavy oak with a canopy.

Leading them was the Bishop of Tallinn in his white cassock and carrying a cross, followed by the Pastor of St Nicholas's and then the Ministers and Pastors of St Olaf's and the Dome Church and, of course, Melchior's neighbour, Gottschalk Witte, Pastor of the Church of the Holy Ghost. In the merchant's lifetime they may have had their several differences on the question of favouring the Convent of St Bridget, but now they were all decently serious, their faces full of sorrow and the pain of loss. Walking behind the clerics were the Commander of the Order from Toompea, the two canons, Albrecht and Bolck, and a few vassals, among whom Melchior recognized the Knight Kordt von Greyssenhagen from Rataskaevu Street. Coming after the coffin were the burgomasters, councillors and other members of the Great Guild, aldermen in front, and behind them the other guilds – the brothers and sisters of Kanuti, St Olaf's, the Blackheads, the Sacred Heart and Rochus. On the heels of the guilds came three brothers from the Dominicans and the Abbess of St Michael's. Melchior also noticed Brother Hinric and waved to him. The ordinary townsfolk walked behind them, Master Bruys's household retainers and his servant Mathyes among them, and right at the back the Council's musicians, one beating a drum and two playing a very sad and doleful melody on pipes.

Melchior mingled with the funeral-goers at the rear, and as they went towards Town Hall Square – Master Bruys's corpse had to be borne with dignity across the town's principal public area – the procession became more mixed up, and then he pushed forward, ending up beside Brother Hinric. The monk greeted him with a nod.

The funeral procession made its first stop in front of the gate tower on Pikk Hill, where the guilds distributed bread and ale to the paupers and beggars. It was the custom to make three stops on the way to the burial place, and since there is not much distance between Lai Street and St Nicholas's Church the coffin was carried onwards to the front of the Town Hall, where a second stop was planned with a third after that at the Seppade Gate. During the stop the pallbearers were supposed to change over, alms were to be distributed, strong ale would be drunk and the musicians would play such sad songs that this day would long remain in everyone's minds.

In Town Hall Square the funeral procession was besieged by a huge number of beggars and paupers, and while the Bishop exhorted them to virtue and decency and the guildsmen handed out bread and the ale-bearers poured ale, Melchior found a suitable moment to tug at the front of Hinric's habit.

'This isn't the only burial in Tallinn today, is it?' he asked the monk, and when he raised his eyebrows in surprise Melchior added, 'I don't suppose Master Grote is being buried so grandly?'

'I hear he was laid to rest at dawn,' replied Hinric. 'And the reaper of death has brought his scythe to our monastery as well in the night. Eric, our young lay brother, died – of a chill, we think. He had been in poor health and suffering from a fever for a long time. Poor boy.'

'May St Catherine bless his soul,' replied Melchior. He had seen Lay Brother Eric a couple of times – a thin, lanky boy who was always coughing and who had not been helped by any cure in the infirmary.

'But, to tell you the truth, I'm surprised to see you here among the funeral-goers,' said Hinric.

'I wanted a bit of fresh air and to take a breather,' Melchior responded nonchalantly. 'And there are a few things that just won't leave me in peace. Among the mourners I can see a few patrons of St Bridget's Convent.'

'Generally they're not very welcome in Tallinn – at least, not yet. But people have a way of getting used to everything.'

'Isn't that so,' sighed Melchior. 'Friend, if I were to ask you whether anyone named Adelbert or Abelard has ever been on the list of preaching brethren, what would you answer me?'

'I'd answer that you don't seem to be able to leave the dead in peace,' said Hinric sullenly.

'So you know what I'm talking about?'

'You're talking about a very old story, which, God willing, is long forgotten and which it would not do anyone any good to dig up again. It's a sad and painful story, Melchior.'

'It is. But I hear so many different versions of it that – inquisitive man that I am – I really want to know the truth. So what happened at the Unterrainer house, and are the horrible deeds that were done still haunting the living?'

A couple of beggars had broken through the crowd to come up to them, throwing themselves on their knees in front of Hinric and asking for a blessing. He hurriedly said a prayer and made the sign of the cross over them.

'Do you think it's possible to find out the truth about that old story at this remove?' the monk asked Melchior.

'That's what I'm asking you. Is there anyone who knows what actually happened and what your monastery daybook says about Adelbert.'

'His body is resting in the monastery graveyard,' replied Hinric.

'So there is no way he could be haunting Rataskaevu Street. Is that what you mean?'

The monk shook his head impatiently. 'It's a very old story, Melchior.'

'And old sins cast long shadows. Let me tell you something. Rumour has it that it was a Dominican monk called Abelard or Adelbert, but I think it was definitely Adelbert, because there was a famous Abelard to whom a similar thing happened, and maybe those two stories have got mixed up.'

'Are you thinking of the learned Abelard of Paris?' asked Hinric.

'Yes, that's the one. It's a famous story, and I've heard it told and even read it in a book, how Abelard the philosopher was in love with his pupil Heloïse. If you recall, it ended with Abelard being castrated and both lovers entering a monastery. Basically it's the same story – forbidden love and castration, and that's why the rumours have mixed up the two names. So the name of that unfortunate Dominican – who was also castrated by his lover's husband – is more likely to be Adelbert. Am I right?'

'On his gravestone it says Adelbert,' nodded Hinric. 'But I don't know that story. I will listen, friend, and watch to see if I can help you, but I'd advise you to leave that old story in peace.'

Finally the funeral procession passed from the Seppade Gate back to St Nicholas's. The mourners went into the church where the Bishop of Tallinn, along with the Pastor of St Nicholas's and the canons, said a brief mass. St Nicholas's was being enlarged, so the mourners occupied just one aisle to avoid the scaffolding. Work had been broken off for the funeral. As the members of the Great Guild stepped up one by one to Bruys's wooden casket and bid the deceased farewell – for which purpose a hole had been cut in it above the face – Melchior's eye was caught by Master Goswin. The old merchant was having trouble holding back the tears; his face was screwed up with pain and a hopeless despair overshadowed his expression. His hands were trembling, and his face twitched. Master Goswin's grief seemed different from that of the other Great

Guildsmen – it seemed he felt real pain at the loss, and his presence was more than just a dignified leave-taking. The bearded old man leaned over the corpse lying in the wooden casket, touched his face once and said something, some last words. Only the deceased and the mourner could know them. It was pain, it was mourning, it was genuine unbearable loss that afflicted Goswin's face.

What really happened between them? wondered Melchior. That I have to find out.

Afterwards the coffin was carried to the grave, where the Bishop sprinkled holy water into it and dropped in some incense and some coal. The Bishop of Tallinn, an elderly and God-fearing man, kept very closely to that custom, although pastors did not often conduct funerals that way any longer. The holy water was meant to keep demons away from the grave, so that they would not attack a Christian and do what they could not do in his lifetime. The incense, though, was so that the corpse would stink less in the hot weather. The coal, which does not change its form and appearance underground, is a sign to future generations of gravediggers that they may no longer touch this ground, for a blessed soul is resting here. Then the Bishop laid some ivy and evergreen laurel in the coffin, saying that those who die keeping Christ the Lord in their thoughts and loving Him may have died to the earthly world but their souls lived on in God.

The ordinary people who had accompanied the funeral procession did not come into the graveyard. Melchior, however, noticed among the other mourners an old woman who, to judge from her dress, was certainly not a merchant's wife, more likely the wife of a farmer or publican. She was old, in a soiled grey dress, and Melchior thought he had seen her before on the town's streets among the lower orders of people. Or was she maybe one of the beggars who asked for alms? Melchior couldn't recall. At any rate, the woman caught his eye because she didn't belong here. Her face had a sadness – and something else. She was at a funeral, and she wasn't begging; she had come to say farewell. Who was she? Some former servant of Master Bruys? A housekeeper perhaps? One of the poor people for whom this holy man had done good?

Master Bruys's body was laid to rest in the grave in the casket, his head facing west and his feet to the east so that on the Day of Judgement Christ the Lord will appear on the earth to the east, and so Bruys will be able to see the last sunrise and the Redeemer coming towards him. His face was covered with a handkerchief, and then there was singing. Among the other merchants of the Great Guild Master Goswin again caught Melchior's eye. He was not singing. Tears were streaming down his old bearded visage, and he closed his eyes to hold them back.

People of higher rank – Church fathers, knights, members of the chapter and other noble gentlemen – then departed for the Guildhall of the Great Guild, where a mourning wake was held in memory of Master Bruys. The Apothecary, of course, was not invited to that.

13

Frückner's Tavern, Kalamaja
5 August, Afternoon

As the thunderclouds gathered once again over the town, the air growing thicker and threatening rain, Melchior hurried through the Coast Gate and set his steps towards that part of town to the east of the harbour that was covered in wooden shacks. Estonian and Swedish fishermen lived here, and there were plenty of taverns. In one of those, he was sure, he would find the honourable Rinus Götzer, inmate of the almshouse, a one-armed beggar and former skipper.

Decades before Master Götzer had been a captain on Tallinn ships and later even on one Hanseatic 'peace ship', which had pursued the Victual Brothers and cleared the seas of those pirates. He had lost an arm in battle, and he had lost all his property and had been living on the charity of the Church of the Holy Ghost for many years. Almost all his hair had fallen out, and he had difficulty walking, but his mind was intact. Melchior occasionally prepared him a gift of some medicine for a cough or pains in the limbs. Rinus Götzer was an honoured and respected man in Tallinn. That he was as poor as a church mouse must therefore be God's will, as was the fact that the townspeople did not forget him, because Götzer never went hungry in the almshouse, and his clothes were clean and of good cloth because all the good that he had done for Tallinn in the past was now being paid back to him by the town – albeit not in abundance, because is not poverty bestowed on some people just as wealth is bestowed on others, so that the wealthy may distribute their assets to the poor? And perhaps not just out of piety, but because of another thing, something which Melchior had been reading about for ten years and which he privately called 'the mystery of St Olaf's Church'.

Actually, Master Götzer had one more merit, of which not every inmate could boast. He knew many stories about the Victual Brothers and earlier wars at sea. He had seen Gödeke Michels with his own eyes and had taken part in battles with the Victual Brothers, and when he spoke of these events in harbourside taverns there were always people who would drop him a penny or two or buy him a stoup of ale. And since Master Götzer visited these taverns often and knew all the seamen he also heard all kinds of tales. No one was afraid to tell their own stories in front of the old skipper, and when Götzer asked, by way of continuing the story, what the situation was in Visby or Stralsund harbour there was always someone to tell him.

In short, Master Götzer was a mine of information about what went on around Tallinn harbour, who was carrying what sort of goods where and taking what in exchange, the state of the ships, who their captains and crew were, where crew were needed, who was talking behind whose back, who was not satisfied with what, who was looking for what, and who had what. They were valuable bits of information, and they were paid for. Sometimes some merchant would slip old Götzer a penny to put his ear to the ground and listen as to how things were aboard his rival's ships, who was seeking a better company, and so on. Now and then a seaman would be dissatisfied because there was too little room for his goods in the hold, and this reduced his enthusiasm for picking up an axe or a knife when pirates attacked the ship. Most ships belonged to more than one shareholder as well as to trading companies, and the Order had shares in nearly every vessel. The captain, too, always owned a small hypothetical share. Of course, this gave rise to disputes between owners. Shareholders paid well for gossip, for what the men were saying onboard ships and what the actual situation was at sea. So Götzer had his own source of income, but since there was no special need to buy clothes and food in the poorhouse he spent it in the taverns, investing his money in enterprises that promised even greater dividends. Master Götzer was thus something of an eavesdropper and knew everything about the affairs of the harbour – or almost everything.

And a little while ago – as Melchior well remembered – he had heard Master Götzer in a tavern chatting about a man who had spoken of some ghost that had pursued him, and that man had later died. Who this man was and how he met his end Melchior did not recall, and the story had faded from his mind, either that or he had considered it too unimportant to remember.

Melchior strode along the hedge-lined road and saw before him the first houses of the suburb they called Kalamaja, shacks thrown together out of beams, planks and anything else that was to hand, inhabited by fishermen, bargemen, their families and other harbour people. The harbour was to the north-east, and one could see the harbour tower and the landing-bridge, alongside which were moored ships with shallower draughts. The masts of the bigger *kogge* ships could be seen out at sea, where they sat at anchor. Wagons rolled past Melchior, and the commoner people were milling around. Melchior stepped into several taverns and asked after Master Götzer, and in a few he had indeed been seen that day. Here and there the old skipper had had a stoup of ale and then stumbled off to places where there were more receptive ears for his stories and more generous people. The local seamen had heard all Götzer's tales before, so he would be looking for some place where there would be sailors from foreign ships who did not know his yarns. Melchior had heard these narratives from Master Götzer many times, and on each occasion the battles would get bloodier and the boldness of Tallinn's seamen greater. That is the way with war stories. Melchior remembered times when Master Götzer spoke merely of doing battle against Gödeke Michels, but over the years the old skipper had heard tell of others, so now he was relating how he had been in combat with Arend Stycke, Ulrich Bernevur and Egbert Kale, depending on where his hearers were from. Melchior recognized this gambit – for every party you had to find something to engage their interest.

He found Master Götzer at a tumbledown tavern by the stony shore that led to the pier. A few boats were tied up alongside it. The sea was whipping up a storm, and a light rain was pattering. Rinus Götzer was hanging around in front of the tavern and was half-asleep. Melchior tapped him on the shoulder and asked if the Honourable Skipper wished to remain lying in the rain because there were threatening dark-blue clouds over the sea, and – as far as Melchior knew of weather signs – a heavy thunderstorm was brewing over the town.

'That's God's truth,' stammered the skipper, aroused from his doze. 'There'll be thunder here, my word there will, and a terrible storm over the sea. But what brings you here, Apothecary? I haven't seen you for a few months.'

'That's what brings me,' replied Melchior. 'It's been a few months since I chatted with Master Götzer and heard his news. If I remember rightly, it was in the spring when I last saw you.'

'I suppose it was,' said Götzer.

'But it wasn't here in this tavern,' Melchior continued. 'I think it was somewhere near the harbour, in that place with holes in the roof.'

'Exactly, yes. It was at Frückner's, the boarding-house belonging to the grim-looking Swede whose wife died last spring of the breathing disease. That was it.'

'People die,' replied Melchior, 'that's true. Oh, I'd be pleased to come along and listen to you telling your best stories, but, unfortunately, the fact is that I was looking for you to ask about someone else's death.'

'Were you just looking for me, Apothecary?' the poor man exclaimed.

'I was indeed. Just you. And how would it be if we went to Frückner's Tavern now, and I'll buy you a couple of best ales, and you'll tell me the same story you told last time – only then I didn't have the sense to listen.'

And they walked along the muddy, faecal street, among the wooden shacks where nearly every household smelled of fish. The fishermen were just coming in from the sea, the threatening weather having driven them back early into harbour. They walked almost as far as the harbour, where, to protect the ships, a strong stone bulwark had been built against the west wind. Melchior recalled that it had just been completed when he and his father first arrived in Tallinn, and to him it had then seemed like the greatest of stone bastions rising up out of the sea. True, there were already complaints that the old bulwark no longer withstood the autumn storms and was greatly in need of rebuilding. From what Dorn had told him, Melchior knew that the harbour guard was constantly going to the Council cadging money to build it bigger. Tallinn harbour was defenceless against the northerly winds, and a storm had already smashed some ships to pieces while at anchor. Jutting out from the bulwark were two wharves on log piles rammed into the sea bed, alongside which the last boats and small ships were just arriving back. Between the bulwark and the boathouses stood the three-storey port tower that marked the site of the harbour to friendly ships and from which approaching enemy ships could be seen while still far out at sea.

The bargemen had already finished today's runs. The goods had been unloaded from the ships into their boats, everything had been carefully logged in the port and the boatmen were drifting off to the taverns to relieve themselves of a small part of the day's earnings. They were a different sort of people from the townsfolk. They spoke a different language and about different things. Life here was seedier and crueller than within the walls of the town, and it smelled different, too. Quite a few taverns doubled as dosshouses, where foreign sailors and other wanderers could take shelter, and thus there were plenty of whores around, often living in the taverns. Of course, the whores were older, more slovenly and more hideous than those offering company within the town walls to rich knights and merchants.

Frückner's Tavern was miserable-looking on the outside and no better inside. They sat in a back corner on blocks behind an old herring barrel, and Melchior ordered the Swede to bring the best ale available in this hovel. And when they discovered that Frückner's finest was much better than one would have guessed from the appearance of the place they wished each other good health and long life, and the old alms-taker's curiosity grew about what need of him, a poor beggar, the noble Sire Apothecary could have. Melchior knew that this was just a ruse, for noble masters do sometimes need the services of Götzer, so he told him that he was seeking information concerning a death.

'Is that so?' said Götzer. 'Time passes, yet you keep on chasing your murderers. It's a dangerous thing, Master Melchior. I've seen a fair bit of hatred in my life, hatred that drives people to kill, and if someone gets in their way ...'

Melchior smiled sadly and shook his head reassuringly. 'No, no, Master Götzer, it's not as bad as all that. At least not like ten years ago when I was looking for one particular murderer.'

'Ah, that Master Wigbold,' cried Götzer, but Melchior raised his hand to his mouth in warning. What had happened ten years ago was a dismal and repulsive affair, one that brought into the light of day much that should have been left buried. On the initiative of Councillor Bockhorst the interested parties in the case reached an agreement that the almshouse of the Church of the Holy Ghost would support Rinus Götzer for as long as he lived, to buy fine woollen cloth and ten marks' worth of herring and bread every year – on condition that Rinus Götzer did not tell anyone what he knew of the fate of Master Wigbold.

'Let that matter rest,' Melchior now admonished the pauper. 'It isn't proper for either of us to recall that name, and I was looking for you about quite a different matter.'

'I'm listening, and, with the support of St Joost, I want to be of help,' Götzer assured him eagerly. The Apothecary had never left him unpaid. He had always slipped him a penny or two for a good yarn.

'What interests me,' Melchior went on, 'is a story that you told here in this same tavern around springtime, from which I remember only a couple of snatches. But in the meantime that story has become very interesting to me. You were talking about a man who had seen a ghost in Tallinn, and a little while later that man died.'

'Oh, yes, I did tell that one right here, yes, and that story is probably known by every bargeman and that glum-looking publican, too, because it was right here that the man fell to his death, hitting his head on a rock as he was waiting for the morning ship and – '

'Please tell it in the right order now, Master Götzer, and as exactly as you can recall. When did it happen, and who was the man?'

The pauper rolled his eyes for a moment and grabbed his stoup and took a manly draught.

'It was none other than that Flemish painter who was invited here by the Council and painted pictures in the churches and then at some rich councillor's house, too, What was his name now?' Melchior waited patiently. 'Gils or Gillis, some name like that it was – surely you should know it, Apothecary. Painted something at some churches. And his other name was something like Schwartz, but said the way the Flemings say it, I suppose. Ah, so it's him you've come to ask about? That was a funny story that.'

'Has anyone else come to ask?'

'Well, they did come – those Flemings and Hollanders are wandering around the harbour here and in town all the time – but only about a week ago a Blackhead came here snooping around and asking one or two people –'

Again Melchior had to ask the pauper to tell everything in the correct order. But now the man's name came to his mind. Of course, he had heard of him, but, as it always is with things that don't concern you directly, it had gone in one ear and out the other. It might have passed Melchior's memory by in the summer when there was talk in the town about a Flemish painter called Gillis de Zwarte, who had been working in Riga when Tallinn Council invited him here to paint pictures of saints. Apparently he had finished several paintings and then St Nicholas's or the Church of the Holy Ghost disputed the price, saying the work was bad. Or perhaps they said it because the fee for an overseas painter was too high. At any rate, de Zwarte was then said to have painted some councillors' portraits, and then ... well, what happened after that Melchior didn't know.

'He fell to his death when he'd had a skinful,' Rinus Götzer refreshed his memory. 'Right behind this very tavern, against a big rock left over from building the bulwark.'

And gradually, with occasional promptings to Master Götzer, putting questions and directing the tale back on track – because the man really was very old now and his train of thought tended to get confused regularly – Melchior finally got to grips with the story.

Gillis de Zwarte had done a spell of work in Tallinn, painted portraits and been in quarters at the home of some Blackhead and come into direct contact with the Brotherhood of Blackheads, although he was not a merchant but an artist. And then his work and livelihood in Tallinn had come to an end, and the man wanted to sail back to Flanders before the rough autumn storms came and the ships were no longer plying. This must have been the previous October or so, when he had had his boxes brought here to Frückner's boarding-house and started doing a deal in the harbour to find a suitable conveyance. So one evening Master Götzer happened to be here in this tavern, and de Zwarte was, too, boasting about his big purse and lapping up the beer that loosened his tongue. But while some men get merry from beer de Zwarte had become doleful, and with every tankard the melancholy took a greater hold on him. Then Götzer heard him talking about a ghost that he had seen with his own eyes.

'Now I don't remember his exact words any more,' Götzer went on, 'but roughly what he said was that Tallinn is a frightful town and he would thank his guardian saint when he finally got out of here – and that was supposed to happen the next day at dawn, you see, because he had a deal with a ship owner – and then he would also be free of the ghost that was now haunting him day and night. And he also said that the whole town be damned and that Rataskaevu Street and those people and –'

'Rataskaevu Street?' Melchior asked with interest.

'Yes, that's what he said, and he reckoned he'd seen that Rataskaevu Street Ghost, but I don't know any more about that. And, well, here in the tavern there were all sorts of other townsfolk as always, servants and rope-makers and porters and boatmen, and no one was pleased, what with him cursing our town like that and rambling on about some ghost. But he didn't say any more about it, and then I went off back to the almshouse because they were about to close the town gate. The next morning, though, I heard that the same evening the painter had fallen to his death behind this very tavern, and, instead of a living person, they put his coffin on the ship, and that was how he sailed back to Flanders.'

'So that was the story you told in the tavern when I was here? Now I recall it. A man who had seen a ghost and then died.'

'I suppose so,' agreed Götzer. 'Wasn't it strange? It's not every day you hear someone saying that a ghost has been chasing them. But he was dead, banged his head against a rock, and there was no sign of a ghost when he was found. His head was split open. The Flemish ship owner was a generous man, and the harbour guard Granlund thought that it would be right that the money paid for a living man to be carried should now be used to carry a coffin, and he was taken onboard.'

'A thousand thanks to you, Master Götzer, but now, who else has come asking you about this death?'

'Hah, who? It must have been that Flemish Blackhead with the name that ties your tongue in knots, that de Wrede or whatever. He was in a few taverns, just asking around – from me, too – but he bought only half a stoup of flat ale and went on demanding what ghost and how and so on, but I didn't chat to him for long.'

'Cornelis de Wrede,' muttered Melchior to himself. 'Cornelis de Wrede yet again. That's interesting.'

He thanked Master Götzer once more, bought him two stoups of ale and left a couple of pennies and suggested he come by the pharmacy if he had any aches or pains. Next he quizzed Frückner the publican, the Swede with the glum face, but that left him none the wiser. Yes, there had been a Fleming who had arranged a passage for himself last autumn, drunk, who had then fallen to his death behind the tavern. He had paid in advance for board, and he had probably moaned about some ghost, but what man doesn't talk nonsense when he's drunk? The harbour guard had come to look at the corpse, and then he must have informed the Town Hall that the foreigner had fallen to his death while sloshed, and that's how things had stayed.

That's how things had stayed, Melchior mused to himself as he made his way back to town. That's how things had stayed with Magdalena, too. And that's how things would stay with Grote the Tower-Master. And who knows with how many others …?

14

St Barbara's Chapel
5 August, Evening

THE STORM HELD OFF. Although deep black clouds had been piling up in the vault of the sky since noon, and somewhere out at sea lightning flashed and thunder rumbled, not a drop had yet fallen on Tallinn. Melchior was walking through the storm-threatened town in the evening light, his head full of strange thoughts. He wanted to talk to Dorn, to ask him any number of questions, but the Magistrate was not in his office. So Melchior had a better idea. He hurried towards the Seppade Gate, went through the magnificent arches and under the gateway and came out at the start of the highway that led south, bordered by the lattice-fenced garden-plots of the townsmen and, further off, the cemetery of St Barbara's Chapel. Melchior's own garden, on land which his father had bought from the city, was also nearby, but today he would not have an opportunity to go there. The recent rain had watered the plants well, and in a couple of weeks he and Keterlyn would probably be faced with a lot of work, harvesting the fruits and plants, putting them out to dry and starting to prepare for the long winter. Yes, autumn was on its way, and that meant a lot of work for Melchior. In the autumn the last ships came, and the merchants would bring the potions, spices and oils he had ordered.

The firewood needed storing in preparation for the tough northern winter, which brought with it many new diseases and epidemics. But for a few days all those things could wait.

He passed the pond by the watermill in front of the gate and carried on along the gravelled road, beside which stood a few taverns and a boarding-house for travellers who arrived too late at night to be allowed through the gate. Then he hurried through the cemetery of St Barbara's Chapel where his father rested under a modest cross. Maybe he should have slowed his pace here, as he usually did, to say a few prayers over his father's grave, recall his words of instruction, but not today. This evening he had something else to do.

St Barbara's was by no means a large chapel; although it was sometimes referred to as a church it was nothing like either St Nicholas's or St Olaf's but was a modest structure with limestone walls, a low tower and a vault, a similar size to one of the smaller townhouses. People came there to pray, and there were two meagre altars, the responsibility of the town's poorer artisans. The graveyard around the chapel was large, however. On one side it extended from the mill by the Seppade Gate to the edge of town and of Toompea, on St Anthony's Hill, over which the Toompea gallows towered, and the boundary of the lands was marked by a stone cross; on the other side it ran along the edge of the highway as far as the western sand dunes, where the town's great gallows stood. The humbler people were buried in St Barbara's because a burial there was inexpensive, and the artisans' guilds would order a simple service of mourning in the chapel. The remainder were laid to rest without even that, and very plainly. If the relatives of the deceased had a coin or two for the churchwarden's assistant and the parish clerk, a brief service was conducted at the graveside, but if there was not even that, or the deceased did not have any kin, the corpse was lowered into the hole in ragged swaddling clothes paid for by the Council. This was best for everyone, as the bodies did not then lie around and cause disease.

The chapel was separated from the cemetery by a low stone enclosure, and at the back of the chapel was a shed where corpses were laid until burial. When an epidemic was visited upon the town, or the corpses had accumulated for some other reason, they were stacked end to end until the gravediggers had prepared a large common grave.

St Barbara's was the largest cemetery in the town, and hundreds of nameless people rested here, those for whom no one could be found to pay for a Christian burial.

Melchior sought out the churchwarden's assistant at the chapel and asked him whether the town guards had brought a corpse here the night before last and, if so, what had become of it. It transpired that nothing had become of it yet; it was lying in the chamber. No relative had appeared, and the next morning he would have to lay it in a hole together with a peasant family from beyond the dunes with two malnourished children who had died from poisoning – they must have eaten forest mushrooms, may the Virgin have mercy on them.

'But, yes, that tramp is lying here – indeed, someone got here before you, Apothecary,' muttered the man as he hurried back to the altar, leaving Melchior to wonder who had got there before him and why.

A little later he was standing in the bleak and chilly charnel-house, which smelled of decay and putrefaction, with the morbid, sweet stench of corpses. Again he examined the body of the strange young man who had died of his wounds on Rataskaevu Street. If he closed his eyes for a moment the events of that night appeared before him again. He had seen a number of corpses in his lifetime but rarely one that had departed this life just moments before. This body had still been warm, and his spirit would not have been far away. Someone had stabbed him three times with a knife in the chest and belly, three times and very deeply, in a rage, with a desire to kill, the blood running from the wounds in a veritable cascade and not yet congealed.

Melchior shook his head and pushed those memories away. He would examine the corpse because a body can tell you a great deal about a person; even a body that awaits burial and whose breath has long since departed.

The young man's corpse was wrapped in a tattered shroud. Melchior untied it. The body had been washed but not very carefully – the assistant had apparently simply tipped a couple of bucketfuls of slops over it, so that there were still traces of faeces and blood clinging to it. But there he lay, strangely thin, skeletal and pale, with that face of indeterminate age that might have belonged either to an adult or to a youth.

First Melchior examined the face and tried to remember. But he was already sure that, no, he had never seen him before. And if neither he nor the town guards had seen that face, then the youth was not from the town. The face now looked even thinner and odder, with sunken eyes, and somehow despairing and pleading in the composure of death. With his fingers Melchior felt the boy's cheeks, but he felt no beard growth at all. Shouldn't there have been some, even if he had been castrated? Melchior did not know. At the same time something about the skull and the bone structure led him to suspect that he was not so young that no beard would have grown. The teeth? Teeth could tell a lot about a person's age, and Melchior did not recall looking at the teeth of the deceased before in the torchlight. He prised the corpse's lips open. Yes, the teeth, those that were left – maybe half of them – were not those of a child; they were yellow and broken, and from this one could deduce that he had eaten very poorly and probably mainly spoiled food. Now Melchior caught the foul stench coming from the dead mouth that mixed with the stink of the corpse.

But then something in the dead man's mouth caught his attention. He bent closer and forced the teeth apart. The poor man had no tongue. Just like his genitals, his tongue had been cut out, and long ago; evidently the wound had been cauterized with a hot iron.

Melchior's eye now caught many more wounds on the dead man's chest than he had spotted in the dark. There were scratches, abrasions, wheals from lashings, incisions. It seemed that in some places even festering wounds had been cauterized, and when he looked closer at some of them he could see that they were yellow around the outside. Melchior examined the wounds with special interest – it was as if someone had been treating them or rubbing them with ointment – and when he breathed in he thought he caught the faint whiff of mint. On the corpse's thin arms were circular abrasions; the skin on them had been rubbed away, in places even to the point of festering.

Melchior shook his head. The corpse disturbed him. It spoke of suffering and pain, hatred and misery. This unfortunate creature had a painful story to tell, a story of a life full of suffering that had ended two days ago on Rataskaevu Street in front of the Unterrainer house, a few hundred paces from Melchior's own home.

Now he pushed the shroud aside from the corpse's feet and stiffened with surprise.

He racked his memory to recall how the feet of the dead man had looked, and he was sure that they were *ordinary* feet. The corpse was now naked, of course, but in Rataskaevu Street the unfortunate fellow had been covered with a knee-length hessian cape, and Melchior had cut a piece of it off. Under the cape it had been revealed that the penis had been cut off, but his feet ... Yes, Melchior had not examined the feet at the time, but he was sure that the man had had something on his feet, some ragged leather sandals perhaps; if not he would have noticed, he would surely have noticed ... But now the corpse's left foot was missing. The right leg was also chafed at the shinbone. The nails were long, dark yellow, curling and in-growing in places, but there was no left foot at all; just a stump was visible, with flaps of skin where it had been hacked off.

How stupid of me, thought Melchior. Of course, the left foot had been in place that night. If it had been chopped off at the time the legs would have been bloody all over – and, what is more, the foot had been removed after death, of that he was sure. He had flayed enough corpses in his time to know what a wound on a dead body looks like. Someone has got here before me and removed the tramp's left foot, he thought, but why he couldn't understand. He knew of no prescription that would require the left foot of a scrawny, wretched boy, nor the flesh, nor the bone, nor the nails. Usually the parts of a person that had curative properties were taken from a healthy person, not a wreck such as this. True, there were a few special prescriptions that required a dead body at a particular time, a certain kind of death – a person hanged under the full moon or a virgin who had died from lily-of-the-valley poisoning or a man with joined eyebrows whose throat had been cut with a silver knife – but there was no prescription involving the left foot of a wretched, castrated youth. At least, no prescription used by any doctors or apothecaries, but they were not the only ones who cut up corpses.

There are medicines and potions known to all medical people, age-old knowledge written down in Johannes Platearius' *Curea*, described by Copho and Ferrarius, by Trota in his *Practica Secundam Trota*, mentioned by the women of Salerno and Hildegard of Bingen. But there are also other kinds of teachings, dark teachings, those that are called black magic. There are sciences and practices about which wise men have warned that they poison a man's soul; these are squalid and contemptuous of God, heretical doctrines, and they are called witchcraft. His father had warned Melchior about such teachings, as he knew something of them himself, but he chose not to share them with his son, either that or he regarded them as too dangerous for him.

Melchior felt that he should leave now. His head was starting to swim from the stench of the corpse, and it was hard to breathe. He cast one last look over the poor young man's body, and more and more questions came flooding into his head. Were those three knife-wounds supposed to ease the suffering of the poor man and send his soul where earthly pain no longer has any power? Or were they meant as the final blow in his sufferings? Who could hate such a pitiful creature so?

He staggered out of the mortuary and felt his legs becoming numb. He was no longer sure whether it was from the corpse's stench or whether the dead man had bewitched him. The fresh air just increased his giddiness. All that suffering, pain and torture – suddenly all this was too much for him. He felt that he wanted to scream and cry; he wanted to rail against the world's spiritual agonies and pains; he felt that he was no longer able to control his own mind; demons had come from somewhere, tearing his soul apart and filling it with a frenzy, with madness and rage. He tried to hurry, but his legs wouldn't obey him; he reeled along the path towards the wall of St Barbara's Chapel, and before him spread the cemetery, full of the graves of poor sinners. How much pain and suffering, how many lost souls and shattered hopes. His father was resting here, and his face in its death throes appeared once again before Melchior. And then his father's last, enigmatic words, 'Saint, remember, fear'. Melchior had not understood those words. Who was this saint that he had to keep in mind and fear? But his father was granted no more time, and he expired with those words on his lips.

The curse of the Wakenstedes was taking over Melchior's faculties. He could get no help from anywhere. A wave struck him right there at the chapel gate. There was no Keterlyn, and he had none of his medicinal drink, which sometimes helped him a little. Melchior had no choice. A moment before turning into a screaming madman he was able to collect himself enough to strike his head hard against the wall of the chapel's enclosure. He felt an extreme pain but a relief, too, that his reason carried on into that twilight hidden behind the black veil.

Apothecary Melchior Wakenstede collapsed with a bloody head wound in front of the wall of St Barbara's Chapel.

15

Melchior's Pharmacy, Rataskaevu Street
6 August, Mid-Morning

MAGISTRATE WENTZEL DORN apprehensively eyed his friend, whose head was bandaged and who was walking as if every step caused him the tortures of hell – but who, despite this, kept busy in the pharmacy preparing medicines, although on this occasion for himself. Dorn knew that Melchior was from time to time overcome by an attack, which Dorn believed to be epilepsy but he was not sure, and the Apothecary did not deign to talk about it much. If Melchior wished he would tell him; if he didn't, then it was none of the Magistrate's business. The message the previous evening, though, that the Apothecary had been found at St Barbara's Chapel with his head split open, had worried Dorn greatly. Melchior was inquisitive, Melchior was on the trail of murderers, but murderers could be cunning and cruel, and when Melchior was pursuing someone he might become the quarry himself. So Dorn had hurried straight to Rataskaevu Street, taking the Council's barber with him, but Keterlyn had reassured them – her voice calm, grateful and cheerful but her eyes tearful and deeply sad – no, Melchior was quite all right, St Nicholas be praised; he had simply stumbled and fallen. His head was indeed cut, but it was nothing serious. At Dorn's insistence the barber had nevertheless looked at the wound and applied a new bandage. Melchior, however, had assured them in a feeble voice that he was not yet going to meet his Maker, and if the Magistrate would come back the next day there would be much to talk about.

So here was Dorn now, full of questions and a little concerned as well. The pharmacy was closed today, when no one was mortally ill. There were such times when the Apothecary had to heal himself. Melchior stumbled around the shop and explained to his friend that sometimes, when too many humours, such as phlegm, accumulate in a man's head the head becomes drowsy and the person may collapse and become ill. Now his head was bursting with pain, although the wound was no longer a concern, and he was making his famous salve, which was supposed to take away pain, for himself. He rubbed various salves, marjoram and fennel into a juice, added a larger amount of peppermint and mixed it with butter to make a greenish-yellow ointment. When the mixture was ready it was allowed to stand for a while to draw and then smeared on the wound. And while the salve was drawing Melchior smeared rose oil on his temples, because that was supposed to help, too.

'And what led you to the chapel?' asked Dorn, drawing the pleasant scent of the rose oil into his nose.

'The corpse of that poor man your guards found three days ago on Rataskaevu Street.'

Dorn cleared his throat. 'Well now, I could have taken poison on it that you wouldn't leave *that* case alone – all the more so since the men said you were called straight away.'

'Don't take poison,' recommended Melchior cheerfully then screwed his face up because the smile had so stretched his muscles that the pain flared up again. 'Poison is no joke. But you're right, though. If someone's killed on my street, where my wife lives and where my children play, I'm likely to be just a little interested in both the victim and the killer. All the more so if it happens in front of the Unterrainer house and other deaths and events seem to be mixed up in it somehow.'

'I see. So once again you've got several deaths all mixed up together.'

'And in a very odd way. Three people have said they'd seen a ghost on this street, and all three died very soon afterwards.'

'Three?' exclaimed Dorn, amazed. 'What ghost? The Ghost of Rataskaevu Street?'

Melchior shrugged warily. 'First of all, the unfortunate Master Grote. You said that when he died he had a face that looked as if he'd seen a ghost. *He had*. I visited the Dominicans and talked to Brother Hinric. On the day he died Grote had come to him asking for advice about ghosts. He had told Hinric that at the end of Rataskaevu Street a ghost had come to him, bringing a message from the realm of the dead with the voice of Death. Those were his words, and he was very afraid.'

'May Holy Mary and God the Father have mercy,' murmured Dorn. 'And the next morning he was dead.'

'Exactly. And he also told Hinric something about Master Laurentz Bruys. Hinric didn't remember what exactly, but he's supposed to have invoked a blessing on Bruys from the angels or something. Hinric had put that story down to too much beer because Grote was very confused, but the late Tower-Master had mentioned that he had to go and talk – he must have meant he had to talk to Master Bruys.'

'But Bruys was by then already … dead?'

'Pay attention, this is very important,' said Melchior. 'At the time Grote visited the monastery Master Bruys *may* have been dead already because he did die on that day, but that happened at Marienthal, and the news only reached town the following morning. So Grote didn't know it at the time. He fell from the tower that same night, and by that time Bruys definitely was dead.'

'That is a bit strange,' conceded Dorn, 'but I don't see any crime in it. Tobias Grote really did drink a lot, and he and Master Bruys were old friends. They say that Grote had once saved the lives of his son Johan and his wife when he was a trooper on a ship.'

'Yes,' said Melchior, sinking into thought for a moment, 'that they do.'

'You said that three people had seen the ghost ...' Dorn pressed.

'Yes, three,' said Melchior, roused from his thoughts. 'Three that I have heard of. The first was a woman, Magdalena. You remember how we pursued that wandering quack down near the limestone quarry last spring.'

'I think I do,' muttered Dorn. He remembered very well all those he had caused to be tortured, beaten or led to the gallows under the laws of Lübeck. He remembered all those faces, and sometimes he dreamed of them, and in the morning he would always wonder where, when and how the kings and the masters of the Order and the councils had been granted the power of life and death over anyone. But this mood would quickly pass, because robbers and murderers needed to be punished.

'While we were away a prostitute, Magdalena, fell into the well on this very street. The day before she had told the women in the *saun* at the Zeghen Tower that she had seen a terrifying ghost on Rataskaevu Street and that she feared her end was near.'

'Ha! Women's chatter,' snorted Dorn.

'*Keterlyn* told me. She heard it with her own ears.'

'Well, that's all right then,' said Dorn quickly.

'And what's interesting is that Magdalena had previously been a housekeeper at Master Bruys's house but had become a whore to earn more, and Master Bruys was very angry about this – pious man that he was – and had driven Magdalena out on to the street. After that she'd entertained men at the Red Convent until one day she saw the ghost and the next she was dead.'

Dorn could say no more to this than that it was indeed strange.

'Again, this story is bound up with Master Bruys, isn't it?' remarked Melchior. 'But, listen, there's more. Now I'm talking about a third person, a foreigner named Gillis de Zwarte, a painter from Flanders. You must have heard of him.'

Dorn nodded, and Melchior carried on, 'He painted pictures of saints in churches and probably portraits for councillors, too. On his last night here, as he was about to board a ship and sail away, he was heard at Frückner's Tavern saying that Tallinn was a terrible town and that it was good that he would finally be free of the Rataskaevu Street Ghost which had been pursuing him day and night. But he didn't get away because the next morning he was found by the bulwark, his head smashed, dead as a doornail.'

Dorn smacked his lips for a while and admitted that he knew the story. The harbour guard had come to the Council the following morning to announce that such a man had fallen to his death in a drunken state. The Council Clerk noted it down, but the corpse was already bound for Antwerp. Such things happen often.

'But they don't simply happen like that,' said Melchior gravely. 'Women of pleasure don't simply dive into a well. Tower-masters don't simply fall out of towers. Drunken painters don't simply break their heads open by themselves and die on the spot. Human life is tenacious, and it doesn't simply desert a person. You must know that, surely. And what is even harder to believe is that on three occasions there were these bizarre deaths of people who had seen a ghost right here on Rataskaevu Street. Stranger still is that two of those people were closely connected to the blessed Master Bruys. About that painter I can't say, but I almost believe that he had also come into some sort of contact with Laurentz Bruys when he was painting holy pictures in the town.'

For a moment Dorn stared straight at Melchior and shook his head in wonder. 'I knew that painter,' he declared. 'Yes, he came to the Council to complain that the Pastor of the Church of the Holy Ghost didn't want to pay him as much as had been agreed –'

'Gottschalk Witte? The man who lives in the Unterrainer house?'

'The very same, but I don't know whether de Zwarte would have known Bruys. *And yet*,' he continued meaningfully, 'de Zwarte *did* visit the merchant Arend Goswin on Rataskaevu Street to paint *his* portrait. And Goswin and Bruys have – or rather had, I suppose – a grudge, or –'

'De Zwarte went to paint Goswin's portrait?' Melchior asked slowly. 'I didn't know that.'

'Not only his but the Knight Kordt von Greyssenhagen's, too, because it became fashionable on Toompea for every person of importance to have his picture painted in the manner of a saint – like St Victor with his sword and so forth.'

'Greyssenhagen . . .' muttered Melchior. 'That knight with a *not very important* pedigree, as they say?'

'Seems his father was an ordinary squire on Teutonic Order lands somewhere down Colberg way,' Dorn answered, 'but for his bravery he was given a larger fiefdom. Young Kordt was able to increase the family's riches with his smart deals, and in the end he bought himself the Jackewolde Estate.'

Yes, Melchior had heard something of the sort about his neighbour. Relations between the governing Order and the noblemen, though, were something outside of Tallinn, far from his everyday activities and concerns. He did know, however, that these days an old and worthy family tree didn't count for much. Money was what counted and the qualities of the man himself. Some noblemen with an old and fine lineage kept a low profile, while others with a lower title might be diligent and zealous, making themselves useful to the greater masters and thus gaining favour. And that must have been what happened with Kordt von Greyssenhagen, because now he, with his little fiefdom of Jackewolde, seemed to be a great confidant and favourite of the Order. And if the great and good have their portraits painted then their favourite underlings must be painted, too.

'Greyssenhagen is supposed to have squabbled with Master Grote about the wall,' said Melchior. 'A few days ago, by Quad Dack Tower.'

'Pah! The Commander of the Order recommended him to the Council as some great expert on positioning cannons and defensive towers, and the Council got him to look at the wall by the nunnery where it's at its weakest.'

But he got into an argument with Grote, thought Melchior, and that tramp died right in front of his door.

Dorn continued, 'About that painting at the Holy Ghost, Witte said that he certainly wouldn't pay such a price for a bad wall painting. They were squabbling in front of the Council, but in the end it was decreed that what had been agreed had to be paid, and Witte paid up.'

Melchior lapsed back into thought. His eyes glazed over. Dorn knew that look. It happened when Melchior's mind was following all sorts of trains of thought, where he often divined things that wouldn't occur to a regular person. But the Magistrate had to admit that things had taken a strange turn when several people had seen a ghost, talked about it and then met unfortunate ends. And he said so to his friend.

'What did you say?' Melchior asked with a start. 'What?'

'I said it's a queer business when three people see a ghost and then die,' Dorn repeated.

'No, that's not what you said,' stammered Melchior, excited. 'You said that it was odd that several people saw a ghost, *talked about it* and then met unfortunate ends. Three people *talked* about it. They said they had seen the Rataskaevu Street Ghost and died. One talked in a bathhouse, one in a tavern and one in a monastery, although God alone knows where else they might have mentioned it. But do you know what Keterlyn told me? There are supposed to be people who have *heard* the ghost, but they are still alive. And, strangest of all, there has been talk of a ghost at the Unterrainer house for decades now, but I still haven't found out whose ghost it's supposed to be. One says it's a monk, another a woman ... some say both. Terrible things once happened in that house, but who killed whom, and whose ghost is supposed to be haunting it? That's a mystery to me.'

'And to me,' admitted Dorn. 'It's been called an accursed house, but as for anyone becoming a ghost after death and anyone seeing a haunting there, that I've never heard. There is talk, but people are always talking.'

'Somebody did die,' Melchior reminded the Magistrate. 'Three days ago an unfortunate tramp was killed in front of that house.

This was no ordinary score-settling between beggars. He was stabbed three times with a knife, hard and deep, killed in a rage. As the deaths connected with Rataskaevu Street happened one after another, that makes me suspect there is some sort of connection between them.'

'I know. I saw that corpse, too. Odd little chap. His prick cut off and as thin as a rake. Amazing that he stayed alive at all.'

'Who was he?' asked Melchior. His salve now seemed to be drawing. He took some of the yellow-green ointment on his finger and smeared it on his forehead. If it was working, he didn't show it; he simply screwed up his face.

'I don't know,' replied Dorn. 'No one knows. I had the men investigate and ask around, but not a single town guard or tower-master had seen such a fellow coming through the gates. Simply no one has seen him before. My men even brought a couple of beggars and people from the almshouse to look at him, but none knew anything. He must be from somewhere in the country-side, come to the town to beg. Or ... Do you know what?' The Magistrate's face came alive. 'Didn't a lot of cripples and tramps come into town for Master Bruys's funeral? He might have been one of them.'

'The word about Bruys's death reached the town that same morning,' Melchior pointed out. 'This chap was murdered that night. If he came for the funeral he must have moved quickly, but a cripple like that can't move quickly.'

Dorn shrugged. 'Well, we asked the beggars, but none knew anything. My first thought was that some Tallinn beggars might have bumped him off, as a stranger coming to muscle in on their patch. There have been a few scuffles between town beggars and those from elsewhere in the past couple of days.'

'I saw one of those,' said Melchior. 'But when have Tallinn beggars killed anyone before – and, what's more, murdered with a knife and with such ferocity?'

'That's what I was thinking, too. They squabble and fight, they even fight in the almshouse sometimes, but not with knives, at night, secretly and to the death ... That's never happened before. Of course, there's always a first time. Maybe that little chap had something valuable or had some long-standing grudge hanging over him.'

'Indeed, anything is possible,' agreed Melchior, 'but it is very strange. First, the poor man had his tongue cut out – and a long time ago. Second, there were many wounds and wheals on his body, his arms were chafed and his legs, too, as if he'd been kept in chains. His teeth were very poor and half of them had fallen out, which means that he was very badly fed. The wretch was barely alive, Dorn. He was so feeble that he would certainly have died if no one had taken care of him. Why kill such a man? Who could be so enraged about such a pitiful creature? As for him having anything valuable on him, that is hard to believe. For him the thing of greatest value – at the same time his greatest misfortune – was that he was alive.'

The Magistrate silently assented to the Apothecary and smacked his lips. 'Ah, so you went to St Barbara's Chapel to examine him?' he asked at length.

Melchior nodded. 'And what's strangest of all, someone had cut his left foot off. That was done when the poor man was lying in the mortuary. In the name of St Nicholas, can you imagine someone coming to him, to him of all people, although there were other corpses there waiting for burial, and sawing off his left foot? As if he hadn't been tortured enough by having his organs ripped off while he was alive. But *someone*, Magistrate, sought out that corpse and cut off his left foot.'

'Someone tampered with him even after death,' muttered Dorn. 'That someone must have known who he was.'

'That is possible, and I think, yes, that someone did know. But what if it was just some heretic who just wanted to perform a blasphemous act of witchcraft and was looking for an unknown corpse who wouldn't be buried by his kinfolk?'

'There are no witches in Tallinn,' exclaimed Dorn.

'And may all the saints preserve us from them ever coming,' declared Melchior. 'And yet someone had a use for his foot, and I can't think why.'

They fell silent. In the town of Tallinn there was a murderer who knifed poor cripples and a madman who sawed their feet off.

'I asked you who he was,' said Melchior at length. 'I still can't answer that question, but, as St Nicholas is my witness, I will find out. I've been wondering whether it was some peasant who had been punished for some terrible crime by his overlord who had finally managed to escape to the town to take advantage of the Lübeck law that states that the air of the town sets a man free. If that were the case then mightn't his master's servants pursue him and kill him in revenge? And then I thought about it again, how he was killed right opposite the Knight Greyssenhagen's house, but I don't want to think about that any more now, because sixty shillings is still sixty shillings, and I don't have that kind of money to spare.' He smiled bitterly.

'I suppose so,' murmured Dorn, 'and I would be duty bound to charge you that sum under the law.' And then keep one-third for the court hearing, one-third for the Council and one-third to the Knight Greyssenhagen. For Lübeck law requires that if someone accuses someone else of robbery, murder or a crime and cannot prove it he has to pay sixty shillings in silver as a fine. Melchior would never in his life name someone as a criminal if he couldn't prove it.

'What is more, Greyssenhagen is in every way a God-fearing and pious man and, furthermore, a patron of the new Convent of St Bridget at Marienthal, and it would never occur to me to think of anything criminal of him,' continued Melchior. 'So what if there's the odd rumour about him and that he isn't from a very old lineage? I have heard that landlords do punish their peasants by torturing them and keeping them in chains. If someone commits a crime they go to court according to the law of the land; they are hanged from the gallows or have their hands chopped off or have to pay a fine in grain, but before that they can be kept in chains, can't they? But what I don't understand is how someone like that could come to Tallinn by foot from somewhere far away.'

'Maybe he was brought,' surmised Dorn. 'But why would a landlord saw the foot off a dead man?'

Melchior nodded. 'And another odd thing, Magistrate. The poor man was wearing a hessian cape. I cut a piece of it off and compared it with the sacks from the Tallinn weavers I have at home. It's the same weave, the same fine cloth. So this chap can't have come from any great distance.'

'That's quite true,' agreed Dorn, coughing. 'But the truth must be somewhere. I was wondering who goes around in hessian capes and looks pretty feeble and miserable, and I thought maybe he was a pilgrim …'

At this Melchior's eyes lit up with excitement, and he nodded approvingly at Dorn's words. 'By St Catherine, that's quite an interesting idea.'

'Isn't it,' enthused Dorn, basking in the glow of Melchior's obvious encouragement. 'Could it have been someone who was punished for some sins and sentenced to go on a pilgrimage, or was he punishing himself and so came to Tallinn? They're always coming to the Dominican Monastery. And now pilgrims from the Order's lands have already started going to Marienthal, because news of the new convent has spread right across Livonia, and, although there are no hospitals and poorhouses there yet, they still keep coming, especially Swedes from the coast.'

Melchior became animated. 'That really is good thinking. I've also heard that pilgrims have been going to Marienthal and then sometimes carrying on to the Dominicans, and although they'd usually have a haversack on their shoulders and a cross, a testimonial or be carrying some other sign of their pilgrim status ... Didn't the Magistrates' Court sentence some wrongdoers to go on pilgrimages to atone for their sins? Which means that somebody had to feed this poor man on his way. He must have found shelter somewhere, so some innkeeper around Tallinn ought to remember him.'

'And even Master Bruys died on a pilgrimage,' Dorn pointed out.

'On a pilgrimage to the convent that was so dear to his heart,' said Melchior, snapping his fingers. 'Damn it, Dorn, there has to be some link between these things, but just now I can't quite see it. If he had been a pilgrim then couldn't he have come from Marienthal? Maybe he knew something about Bruys's death and was hurrying into town. He was followed and ...' Melchior fell silent and looked intensely at Dorn. The latter merely shrugged. 'Something's afoot. Something evil has got out. I can feel in the air that things are not right.'

Dorn shook his head doubtfully. For him a crime was something that had been done, as when someone cheated in the market, wounded or strangled someone. Then the Council authorities had to impose a punishment.

'Don't just keep shaking your head, friend,' the Apothecary admonished him. 'This murderer, who knifes poor cripples to death, has to be caught, and if no one demands justice then I'll do it myself because, as the old saying goes, "If there's no accuser, there's no judge either." But I'd recommend you to think a little about Master Grote's death. I went to visit the spot at the holy sisterhood, and I also went on the walkway. It's not at all easy to fall from there because the railing is pretty high. You said his forehead was bloody, but, tell me, how does a man strike his forehead if he lands on his back? I found only one rock there on which he could have struck his head – and it was a little bloody, too – but that rock was several steps away from him. So did the nuns or the town guards move the rock or ...?'

'Or what?' asked Dorn.

'Or Grote fell down, groped around, found the rock, bashed himself in the forehead with it, threw the rock away and fell down dead. Of course, it's not impossible that someone else did all that.'

'They would have had to find themselves in the right place at the right time of night, just when he was there, just when he fell.'

'Which would be very unlikely,' said Melchior. 'By the way, was there a torch near Grote's corpse?'

'I didn't see one.'

'So why would he go out on to the town wall at night without a torch and fall off? I think that's strange.'

'Sometimes I think you simply want things to appear strange.'

'Not at all, dear friend, not at all,' Melchior assured him. 'But now, may I ask you two favours? I've got a strong urge to head off to Marienthal soon. At the manor house there's a farmer who collects plants and from whom I get my wormwood, thistle, pepper, yarrow and other plants when I'm short of –'

'You want to go to check out where Bruys died,' Dorn interrupted. 'By the dear Virgin, Melchior, he just died of old age.'

Melchior shrugged innocently. 'I thought it would do no harm to take a look. It's no secret that he had many enemies. By the day after tomorrow my head will have healed, so it will be able to stand a little excursion.'

'It's on the Order's lands. I have no authority there.'

'I know that. But I still wanted to ask you if you had a horse you could lend me.'

Dorn grumbled, but he promised that if Melchior went to the stables and found Hartmann the stablehand and told him that the Magistrate ordered him to hand over one of the Council's horses Melchior would get one, and if Hartmann queried this the Magistrate would put him in irons in the marketplace for two days.

'A thousand thanks,' replied Melchior. 'My second request concerns an old story about which I've only heard hints because it happened when I was still a boy and an apprentice in Riga, but about which I'd very much like to find out more.'

'So what sort of story would that be?' asked Dorn with a sigh.

'What the feud was between those two respectable merchants Bruys and Goswin.'

Dorn sighed deeply. 'It's an old, sad and painful story.'

'Which means that you'll be needing a sweet strong dram to wet your tongue and tell it,' decided Melchior, pouring out the drink.

Dorn downed it, bit into the accompanying biscuit and made a calculation on his fingers. 'It would be twenty-five years ago now,' he said at length. 'I was a junior partner then in the merchant Dyneaur's company, but our business was starting to go downhill, probably because the Victual Brothers were gathering around Abfors and harassing all the ships, making havens for themselves on the Finnish coast and lying in wait there like spiders in a web. But enough about that. The story was that Laurentz Bruys had a son whose name was Thyl, and he was his only heir because his daughter had died in Riga, another son had fallen prey to the Victual Brothers and three children had died in infancy. Thyl was a wayward lad, full of pride, getting into fights with the sons of others in the Great Guild and scaring the older merchants away. He had an impatient nature, and he was a bit of a thug, full of himself, relying on his father's wealth, thinking he was entitled to what others weren't.'

'That would have been the year of Our Lord 1394,' ventured Melchior.

'Must have been,' agreed Dorn. 'Dear Jesus, how quickly time flies, eh? But, in a nutshell, it so happened that Thyl's eye was caught by the prettiest girl in town, none other than Dorothea, daughter of the merchant Arend Goswin.'

'Oh, God bless us,' whispered Melchior.

And Dorn told the story, one he knew very well because Dyneaur had a joint company with Arend Goswin, and at that time Dorn's uncle was Harbourmaster of the Council. Arend Goswin had four children, three sons and one daughter, but all his sons died in infancy and his wife Elsebet died in an unfortunate way, giving birth to their fourth child, the daughter, who was given the name Dorothea. Arend Goswin was destroyed by his wife's death, and his disturbance of mind was very great, so great that he couldn't find it in himself to look for a new spouse and produce more heirs. Melchior nodded at this tale; the same thing had happened with his own father. So Master Goswin remained a widower and lived by himself with his housekeeper Annlin and his servant Hainz, raising his daughter, who grew into an inexpressibly beautiful girl.

'Half the boys in Tallinn must have been out of their minds about her because a girl as beautiful as that isn't God's blessing to every town,' Dorn went on. 'But she was a very pious and virtuous maiden. She was under her father's control, and she received a good education and upbringing under the holy sisterhood. She went to church diligently. All this should have been very good for Master Goswin because for such a pretty and virtuous maiden he would have found a very rich and noble bridegroom, and his household and assets would have gone into the right hands – except that the lovely Dorothea had one fault.'

'Was she crippled?' asked Melchior in surprise.

No, said Dorn, physically Dorothea was not a cripple. She had ebony-coloured fluffy, curly hair and cherry-red juicy lips, and her graceful rounded body would make a man's heart fairly melt to look at her. She had sky-blue eyes and delicate white skin. She was as beautiful as St Ursula and as virtuous as St Bridget. She was modest and submissive and more of a dream or an angel than a girl of flesh and blood. But she did have one flaw, and the more she grew in years the more evident it became. For in a young child it isn't usually understood; children can often be wilful and stubborn, behave strangely or ridiculously. But Dorothea was insane. So much beauty God had given her, but the Creator had not given her the mind of an adult, and this became clearer with every year. Dorothea appeared to be very pious because she attended church frequently and prayed with the holy sisters, but she was silent, she hardly said a word, and as the years passed the more silent she became. In the middle of the day she would go out of the house and wander alone in town, and if she was asked where she was going or what she was doing she wouldn't utter a word. She would fall down in the mud and start praying, but not a syllable, not a word, would come from her mouth. Her eyes were beautiful and deep, but anyone who looked into them saw no understanding of the world's affairs or even Heaven's, for in there reigned emptiness and madness, indifference and incomprehension. Even the Sisters of St Michael's said that Dorothea did indeed pray but in silence, and she was doing it because others did, but to whom she was praying and why she did not understand.

'I think I know that sort of insanity,' said Melchior. 'In the human body there are four humours, and they have to be in balance. But if phlegm gets the ascendancy – in a person's head, for example – then that person becomes pale, very peaceful, inward-looking, restrained and inert. But if the phlegm repels the other humours from a person's head he remains shut in himself; the whole world is just in his head, and no one else knows what goes on there.'

'That might well be,' agreed Dorn. 'You're a learned man and you know these things. But with Dorothea, since she was believed to be insane, Master Goswin had no hope of marrying her off. The holy sacrament of marriage would have been meaningless to her, and although she was told about it she showed no sign of understanding it. And if she didn't understand it, there was no assurance that she agreed, and no one should be paired off by force. And, well, no one wants a madwoman in the marriage bed or as the mother of his children.'

'Maybe not the marriage bed, but when the girl's body is so pretty …' murmured Melchior pensively.

'Exactly,' sighed Dorn. 'As they say, that kind of thing has happened in the world before and will happen again, and there's nothing new under the sun. Laurentz Bruys's son Thyl wanted to have the beautiful Dorothea, to quench his strong desire, which wasn't put off at all by the girl's madness. Melchior, no one knows when or how it happened, but one day Thyl tricked Dorothea. Whether he lured her into the meadow beyond the town wall or into the bushes behind the stables none can say. A person's head may indeed be mentally insane, but their passions think in their own way, and desire got the upper hand. Thyl led that blissful girl into temptation and violated her honour. He often talked to other people about Dorothea at the storehouses, praising her beauty and saying that the girl was so mad in the head that she didn't understand a thing, and one day, his eyes full of guile, he boasted that he had made the most beautiful girl in Tallinn his own.'

'Did it happen by force?' Melchior wanted to know.

Dorn shrugged. 'They say that Goswin asked the holy sisters to look her over, because the girl had become even odder, and the rumours going around the town reached the father's ears, too. But the sisters at the convent didn't find signs of violence, although they did say that the girl was no longer a virgin.'

'Good heavens,' whispered Melchior. 'Surely she didn't ...'

'No, probably *not that*, but the stories spread, wicked and spiteful stories, but Master Goswin did not – maybe he couldn't – go before the Council and accuse Thyl of taking his daughter by force, because who would want such shame and misery ever to fall on their own head? Besides, there was no way he could prove it, because Dorothea wouldn't speak and there wasn't a single honest citizen present as a witness. It would have been his word against Thyl's, or he would have had to demand from the Council that Thyl must stand before the Judgement of God, but not a single swordsman could have been found to champion Dorothea's honour. To say nothing of the fact that permission for such a duel would have had to have been given by the Commander or even the Bishop, and, again, who would want to appear before the people with such shame and dishonour?'

'So there was no court case?'

'None, and nor could there have been, because Dorothea was seen one day arriving at the mill at the Cattle Gate, and they say she said some words to the miller's wife – but what those words were no one knows – then she took her dress off right there and then, and, before anyone had time to stop her, she stepped slowly into the pond and drowned herself.'

'Merciful heavens,' cried Melchior.

'She was only seventeen years old. Again, what exactly went on between Goswin and Bruys no one knows, but from that time onwards they were no longer friends. Much to Master Bruys's credit, I must say, he drove Thyl, his only heir, out of his house, sent him to Germany and disowned him.'

'The rest I know,' said Melchior. 'God blessed Master Bruys, and the next year his wife bore him one more son, Johan, when she and her husband were both over forty. But this blessing was fickle, for Johan died and the wife died of sorrow. Master Bruys became an extremely pious man.'

'Well, haven't some people said that Goswin also went off his head after that fire?' remarked Dorn. 'He became increasingly peculiar, started going to the Guildhall rather less often – he wasn't even always seen there at Christmas festivities. Then he stopped trading in salt, which some thought quite foolish, because salt turns a good profit, but ...'

Yes, salt was what some merchants called white gold, Melchior knew. It was cheap to buy from Holland, France and Lüneburg because there was plenty of it there, a surplus indeed. Merchants would buy it by the pound on the last ships of the autumn, keep it over the autumn and winter in their salt-cellars and then sell it on to Russia as the price rose. Salt kept food fresh, and without salt it was hard to survive the winter.

'Does anyone know what happened to Thyl?' asked Melchior.

'Some say he became a mercenary and died in battle, others that he was hanged for robbery in Magdeburg. Who knows? Bruys didn't mention him in his will.'

'It must be a painful decision for any father to disown his son and leave him without an inheritance,' said Melchior thoughtfully. 'And Master Bruys was rich, very rich.'

'Now the Convent of St Bridget – and the town, too – are that much richer for having inherited his wealth. According to Lübeck law Thyl would not be able to inherit anything, even if he were alive, because he is no longer his father's lawful child – although in court you can try to twist the law any which way, so, if he had a good lawyer, who knows what might come out of such a case? But now, Melchior, it's time for me to go. And you'd better recuperate in peace, too.'

'A little nap wouldn't do any harm. But, before you go, what can you tell me about a certain Flemish merchant, Cornelis de Wrede?'

Dorn raised his eyebrows in surprise. 'Nothing much. One of the Blackheads, isn't he? Said to hang around the Red Convent a lot.'

'Around the Red Convent? Very interesting.'

'Why do you ask?'

'I'm not the only person in Tallinn who's very interested in the Rataskaevu Street Ghost and about those who spoke about it and died. De Wrede was snooping around after the deaths of both Master Grote and the other Fleming, de Zwarte. I think you and

I should go along to the Blackheads one evening and have a chat with that man over a tankard.'

'Those Flemings are all misers, cheats and cheeseparers,' grunted Dorn, getting up. 'I'd keep away from them. But, if you want to, then all right, one evening we'll go along to the Blackheads.'

16

Melchior's Pharmacy, Rataskaevu Street

7 August, Morning

When Keterlyn opened the pharmacy door in the morning, to her surprise and evident astonishment she found a very old Dominican waiting for her, a mendicant's basket in his hand, who asked whether the Apothecary was up.

'He is indeed,' replied Keterlyn. 'Heavens, it's already broad daylight outside. He's working in the loft on his medicinal plants. But what's happened? Do they need some remedy at the monastery?'

Instead of a reply the monk pointed to his basket and asked whether he could step inside for a moment to rest his feet.

Keterlyn headed upstairs to tell her husband that an odd visitor had arrived, some monk who looked so ancient that he might have dragged himself out of the mortuary. When Melchior came down he found the monk by the counter sitting on a chair and sniffing a plate of biscuits with evident interest. He reckoned that he might have met the man a couple of times at the monastery, but he was so old that he probably didn't work any longer and presumably spent his time going between the infirmary and the dormitory. And he was certainly not the brother who usually went through town with a mendicant's basket.

'What brings you to my pharmacy, Brother?' asked Melchior kindly. 'And what would be your esteemed name?'

'They call me Brother Lodevic,' replied the old man. 'And what brings me to your pharmacy is simply that, as our *cellarius* was saying after morning prayers, a certain apothecary bitterly regrets that he has not been donating recently to St Catherine's Church as diligently as a Christian should.'

That isn't quite true, thought Melchior, but he got the point. It was characteristic of Brother Hinric to stand first and foremost for the interests of the monastery, even when a friend had asked him for help. He nodded and went to close the shop door. Service would have to wait a little while today.

'Ah, so Brother Hinric sent you,' said Melchior. 'May St Catherine be thanked in that case, because yesterday evening it occurred to me to go to the monastery to put a little silver coin in the donation box. But now, since the monks' donation basket has arrived here ...'

'A little silver artig for St Catherine,' cried the old monk in a high voice. 'May all the saints bless you for such generosity. That more than makes up for the pain in my feet.'

'Maybe you'd like a sweet biscuit, Brother?' asked Melchior. 'And, of course, you can stay and sit and chat, for where would a holy brother be going in a hurry in the morning?'

'A biscuit, gladly,' chuckled the old man. 'But I don't have time to stay much longer because times are hard now, and all the brothers at the monastery, whether they're old and feeble or young and weak, have to toil through the day by the sweat of their brows to please the Lord God and praise St Catherine.'

Melchior sighed and cursed Brother Hinric under his breath. A sly holy brother was that old fox, his friend the *cellarius*.

'Brother Lodevic, perhaps you will still do an apothecary the favour, if another six pennies are put in the basket as well as an artig, of staying a little longer to rest your feet?' asked Melchior. 'At the moment I don't have too much to do, so if you, Brother, would like to tell me a few old stories I'd be interested to hear them.'

'An artig and a half?' hummed the old man thoughtfully, glancing at the basket of biscuits and licking his lips. 'An artig and a half will be a very great help to our monastery, it surely will. And a biscuit would be permitted, too?'

'Baked with the blessing of St Nicholas himself and the consent of the Council,' said Melchior. 'These are very good biscuits, and they have spices in them, notably ginger and cardamom, which are good for the health.' He took the basket of biscuits and held it in front of the old monk. 'Please, take one, Brother.'

'The rules of our monastery do not approve of eating sweet things,' responded the decrepit monk, extending his sere and bony arm towards the basket. 'And I fear that a biscuit like that might leave too many crumbs in the throat and make one's voice hoarse, which wouldn't be good for telling tales. Apothecary, do you happen to have anything that might make the vocal cords smooth again?'

'Hmm, and what might that be?' wondered Melchior. 'Maybe a little stoup of my sweet elixir? It's freshly made, so it's strong, warms up your insides and helps you breathe.'

'I could certainly try that. Lately we've had a great fast, and apart from thin beer, black bread and salt herring they don't give us anything to eat because we live in the proper Dominican way in piety and austerity.'

'And praising the Lord,' remarked Melchior. He knew well that the Dominicans do not live austerely, and their fasting period had been quite some time ago. Under Hinric's practical arrangements the Dominicans ran a good business, and it was rare for them to eat only black bread and salt herring. And their bread was the best in town, sweet and chewy, full of rye flour with no chaff at all.

'I suppose we're a storytelling brotherhood,' stated old Lodevic after he had turned a couple of biscuits to mush in the drink and knocked it back. 'And it is our custom that if we're fed well somewhere we tell a pious tale by way of thanks. The thing is, we are now on Rataskaevu Street, aren't we, and so it occurs to me that I once heard a very instructive tale connected with this street … Now, how did it go …?'

Melchior would have guessed Lodevic to be about ninety years old. The monastic air was clear, and the men in the monastery generally lived to quite a good age if they weren't broken by some nasty ailment like young Lay Brother Eric. There were many wise practices in a monastery that allow the brothers to live to a great age – they kept clean and ate fresh ingredients, they drank diluted drinks and they had infirmaries to care for the sick. A religious community is able to keep epidemics at bay. Brother Lodevic no longer had any teeth, his face was dry and wrinkled, but there was considerable intelligence and cunning written on it. From his manner of talking and his oblong head and brown eyes Melchior surmised that maybe he wasn't German but from one of the lands of the empire further south. Men of many breeds had lived among the Dominicans of Tallinn, he knew – brothers from Burgundy, Castile, Portugal, Lombardy … The Dominicans were a peripatetic order. They came from one monastery and went to another, they begged and preached, spread the word of God and stood firm against heresy, which was once more spreading through

Christian lands. But when they got too old they stopped moving and remained in one place. Brother Hinric had said that he would have plenty of time to move on and go to live somewhere else – in the Rhineland, perhaps – and spread the Word there, but his heart kept him in Livonia where his own people lived, who were still far from versed in the meaning of the gospel and often went to church just for a change of scene and without understanding that Christ the Lord was true joy and peace.

'If I now poured for you, Brother, another sweet dram, maybe you'll recall what the story was that you wanted to tell me concerning Rataskaevu Street,' Melchior said.

'If this drink is also brewed with the blessing of St Nicholas then my heart may not refuse it,' replied the monk joyfully. 'So let's have another stoup.'

Some time passed before Brother Lodevic got around to telling his tale after the biscuit and the drink, but he eventually embarked on his narrative.

'In the cemetery of our monastery there rests a brother whose name was Adelbert and who came to Tallinn from the town of Nordhausen. It is written in the daybook that he died when he was just twenty-five years old. Perhaps you don't know, Apothecary, that this is my second time in Tallinn, and the first time I was here was only a couple of months after Adelbert's funeral, and he was still the subject of much conversation among the monks – although the Prior didn't approve because Adelbert was not the sort of brother to set an example to the others. He was something of a reluctant Dominican, and his behaviour had instigated a lot of gossip about the preaching brothers. The year was reckoned to be one thousand three hundred and forty-nine years since the death and resurrection of Our Saviour, and Tallinn had just passed back from the Danish King to the power of the Order, may the Lord be praised for it.'

'That's my firm opinion, too,' remarked Melchior. 'May he be praised for it. So Brother Adelbert was buried seventy years ago?'

'If that's what you calculate, then he was,' replied the monk. 'At that time I was just twenty, and Tallinn was my second monastery. I'd entered the order in the town of Palermo, where I was born, in the *ballei* administered by the General Preceptor of the Teutonic Order in Sicily and Calabria.'

Melchior had to spur the old monk on a bit – and there was no better stimulus for that than Melchior's dram – so that he wouldn't spend too much time chatting about his youth in Sicily, which was under the Teutonic Order and where he had seen bitter days, for he was the son of a servant in one of the Order's manor houses and the local nobles were fighting against the Order, and his father was hanged on the manor's gates, while his mother was delivered to the Dominicans in her son's donkey cart, taking with her the only silver coin they had; at the Dominican Monastery, under the guardianship of the Order, the coin was given back to her, and young Lodevic was taken anyway as a novice for no money, for they had seen how the love of God in his heart radiated like a flame ...

But a couple of sips of the sweet drink forced the monk back to Tallinn, and he continued, 'In charge of the Tallinn monastery at the time was Prior Helmich, a very God-fearing man. Times were hard because war had recently been raging across the land, monks had been killed, the heathens had risen up, washed off their baptismal water and torn up all the agreements that bound them to the power of the Danish King and the Order. All of Livonia was drenched in blood – and Tallinn did not escape. Brother Adelbert had been buried in the Dominican cemetery, and one day Prior

Helmich led me to his grave on which the grass had not even begun to sprout. That was to be a lesson to me, a novice, about whose determination the Prior was not yet fully convinced. He told me there how Satan had amassed temptations for Adelbert, for he was very greedy for the souls of monks, and in the end Adelbert had given in to the temptations of the flesh. And all this had happened on the street that is now called Rataskaevu Street.'

Melchior listened, and Lodevic related. Brother Adelbert was the son of a pious town clerk in Nordhausen. When he was young his father had started setting money aside to send him to the preaching brethren because as a child he had displayed a remarkable aptitude in reading the Scriptures and had a retentive memory. As Adelbert got older, however, he developed a taste for various kinds of worldly pleasures, and the company of women was one of them. And women, for their part, liked him and wanted to lead him into temptation at every opportunity. In the end, however, Adelbert was sent to the monastery anyway and then to Tallinn to keep him away from his old temptations. At first it seemed to the Tallinn brothers that young Adelbert was truly dedicated to the monkish life and bitterly regretted his sinful youth. He confessed assiduously, and, as is the Dominican custom, he confessed to his brethren as well and not just in the confessional. So the word about his old sins was spread among the brothers, and those stories must have been corroborated when the brothers saw, when they visited the *saun*, that young Adelbert's organ was really long and thick, one that would be very appealing to women, so all the brothers who saw it looked away and mentally said prayers of thanks that they didn't have one like that, one that would always lead them into temptation. Young Adelbert was sent out to collect donations, as is the custom with all preaching brethren, and he began to enjoy this work, so much so that he asked to be released from his other monastic duties and be allowed to go into town more often with his basket. Some days Adelbert did not even make it back to the monastery in time for vespers, and for this he was roundly rebuked by the brothers. The Prior, though, was mostly satisfied with him because his donation basket always contained plenty of money, and in those hard times, when Tallinn was smaller and the monastery half the size that it is now, that was a great help.

Stories started to get around, said Brother Lodevic, vicious and spiteful stories about how Brother Adelbert, in preaching the gospel, was not only collecting a lot of money in his basket but that there were some wives in the town who lured him into their chambers to see his long sex organ and generously donated money for the pleasure. And they didn't just want to take a look. Some of them wanted to take it in their hands, play with it, stroke it, lick it with their tongues and even put it in their mouths to see how large it might get.

Melchior noticed that at this point a strange lustre came into the old monk's eyes. He licked his dry lips with his tongue, and his hands, groping for the bottle of spirits, trembled slightly.

'But stories are stories,' Lodevic continued, 'and no doubt it's happened before that they are driven by sheer malice. So one day the Prior invited Brother Adelbert into the scriptorium and demanded of him to swear in the name of God that the stories were false and that he was not going around the town shaming the name of the Dominicans. Adelbert burst into tears, kissed the cross and confessed that on one occasion he had been led into such temptation and that he found the determination to resist the sins of the flesh, that the woman had taken his tool only into her mouth and he had allowed this to continue for the sole reason that he knew that if he did she would be very generous when it came to making a donation. But she had demanded that he come back to her house again when her husband was busy at the weighing-house and in the storehouses. Prior Helmich believed his story and commanded that Adelbert now pray more diligently and do more work around the monastery and not go into town where he had so easily been led into temptation. And so it was that Adelbert worked industriously around the monastery, even taking on those simple tasks that are the lot of the lay brothers, chopping firewood, watering the plants, harvesting the crops, washing the other brothers' clothes and digging the cellar. He often went to confession and repented that he had dishonoured his monastic robes in that way.'

'But what did he die of?' asked Melchior.

'I was coming to that,' replied the monk. 'Prior Helmich led me to his grave and said that here lay a brother who had died from the weight of his sins. That God had decided to call him to Him so young as a lesson to the other brothers who do not find the determination to resist temptation. One sin leads to another, a little one to a bigger one. Brother Adelbert bitterly repented of his sins, and the Prior had confidence in him, so a few months later he sent the young man back into town to collect alms but swore to him that if any evil rumour reached the Prior's ears he would be thrown out of the monastery in disgrace. That day Adelbert left for good. He didn't come back for evening prayers. Nor did he come the next morning or the morning after.'

Melchior shook his head. He didn't understand. 'Didn't you just say he was buried in the monastery graveyard?' he asked.

'You're rushing me, Apothecary,' replied the monk. 'I'm an old man now, and I have to take my time in order to keep things clear. And this biscuit is sweet indeed. Could I have another tot of something to drink with it?'

'A jug of cold water from the well?' asked Melchior. 'Or perhaps you'd like another dram, Brother?' What the devil! The old monk is ruining me, he thought to himself.

'A sip of water would be good for a teetotal and frugal old man like me,' declared Brother Lodevic.

Thank God, thought Melchior, but as he poured water from the tub into the jug the old monk suddenly croaked, 'A little sip of water and then perhaps a mouthful of that sweet dram, too, since you're offering. The one made with the blessing of St Nicholas. You can't let things approved by the saints go to waste, can you now?'

'Of course you can't,' grumbled Melchior, topping up his cup. 'You got to the point where Adelbert disappeared – and yet he's buried in the Dominican cemetery.'

Lodevic sucked on the biscuit and gulped down his drink, breathed out and crumbled the sopping biscuit on the table, saying, 'Yes, that's how it was. He vanished, and Helmich guessed that he had fled from Tallinn, because that had happened before when young monks struggle to keep their vows and the lay world calls them back so forcefully that they run away from their duties. Helmich thought he must have lost his head over some young woman and eloped with her, or something like that. The brothers went around town asking whether anyone had seen him, but no one had, and that's how things would have stayed had Adelbert not come back to the monastery one evening on the verge of madness.'

'Heavens, so he hadn't run away then?' exclaimed Melchior. 'Where had he been?'

'They thought he had been in a brothel somewhere. At first they couldn't get a sensible word out of him. He only had prayers and the saints' names on his lips, and he couldn't speak properly. When they got him to perk up and let his blood he lost consciousness altogether and collapsed in an apoplexy and was sick for several days. He had a fever and was rambling. He was treated to get his reason back so as to be able to confess his sins, because he did have a few lucid moments during which he begged Helmich to take him for confession, and Helmich treated him so he would be fit to confess, because a person can only do so when sound of mind.'

'So what happened then?'

'Nothing more happened because, as Helmich told me, Adelbert never recovered and died on his sickbed in agony, in terrible spiritual suffering. Before he died, though, his mind was sound enough to be able to confess, but Helmich didn't tell me what sins he had to forgive. And now I come to the point in my story where I began – why this is all connected with Rataskaevu Street.'

Thank heavens, sighed Melchior to himself.

'The well had not been dug yet,' said the monk, suddenly becoming pensive. He was thinking intently, and Melchior waited patiently. 'What did they call this street then? Nothing comes to mind. It must have had some name, but ... It's all the same ...'

'I think so, too,' replied Melchior, bored.

'But, yes, that's how it was. Gossip gets around, and where there are acts there are witnesses,' the monk eventually continued. 'This is what our esteemed Prior told me at Adelbert's grave, "Behold, here lies a sinner who could not manage to keep his monastic vows and heaped shame on the monastery, and to wash that away the brothers now have to serve God more diligently and pray for the welfare of this town." And then he told me that a while after Adelbert had died in his agonies a rumour started that there had been a merchant by the name of Cristian Unterrainer who lived on this very street, here, in the house that still stands today, and that man had left Tallinn. At some point a wall had collapsed on to the house, and the Council sent masons to shore it up again, and then they had to demolish another wall and ... and in a chamber of the cellar in the Unterrainer house a recently walled-in section was discovered, and it had to be demolished, and there they found ...' The monk paused and slurped the last drop from his cup, but since Melchior was looking at him expectantly and not offering anything more he continued, 'Yes, so it was, they discovered the dried-up corpse of a woman, who was stark naked and bound to a chair. The body was so well preserved that people recognized her as Ermegunde, wife of Unterrainer, whom her husband had said had long before gone on a pilgrimage to Germany.'

'The woman was immured alive in the cellar?'

'So she was, and so then the story got about town, and this person and that person had seen how Brother Adelbert often visited the Unterrainer house, and, what's more, when the husband was away on a ship or out of town and the wife Ermegunde was home alone. And they went on to say that this Ermegunde was a really bad woman and she had told other women and she knew who had the longest and thickest dick in all Tallinn, and that she had made that man her own and now she knew what real heavenly love was like. That's the kind of shameless woman she was.'

'So Adelbert visited Ermegunde to lie with her?'

'Oh, that's what I heard later. The Prior didn't tell me that, but he did say that Adelbert did go in and out of the house. So one day Unterrainer happened upon them and ...' The monk lowered his voice, and again an odd lustre came into his eyes. He licked his lips and carried on, but with a rather soft tongue and fumbling for words. 'When Unterrainer saw what kind of whoring Adelbert was up to with his wife, he tied his wife up and ordered Adelbert to put on his wife's clothes, and then he threatened to cut off his dick if he didn't have sex with his wife again while he himself looked on, constantly beating Adelbert with a whip …'

'Did Adelbert have wheals from the whip when he died?' asked Melchior quickly.

'The Prior didn't tell me that, or if he did … Lord bless us, it was seventy years ago. Adelbert didn't die of his wounds but of repentance for his sins, and this instructive story I've kept in mind all my life, even though no one in the monastery has talked about it for a long time and everyone apart from me to whom Helmich spoke has long ago gone to meet his Maker and is sitting at the right hand of the Virgin Mary in Heaven.'

'And have you heard anything, Brother, anything about the Unterrainer house being haunted?' asked Melchior.

'The spirit of that shameless woman,' whispered Lodevic, leaning closer to the Apothecary, 'who died in terrible agony and unshriven and who, after her death, was cast into a pit beyond the town as a worthless woman and an adulteress and whose grave is unmarked by any dedication … The soul of this sinner flew out of her body when she was immured alive there in the Unterrainer house, and there that spirit has remained, oh yes. There she appears as a warning to all adulterers and temptresses off the monastic path.'

Before Brother Lodevic made ready to go he asked whether he could take a few small biscuits with him for the other brothers, since they didn't receive such things very often and after long hours at prayer they taste pleasantly sweet in the mouth and are beneficial to one's health as well, since they contain ginger and cardamom. Melchior agreed, of course, and watched dolefully as Lodevic emptied almost the whole tray into his alms-basket, explaining that there were many brothers, they had everything in common and it wouldn't be right for only one of them to get to taste them.

'Perhaps you know, Brother Lodevic, when young Lay Brother Eric is to be buried?' asked Melchior as the monk was departing.

'Tomorrow. The ceremony should take place right after the chapter meeting,' replied the monk. 'The grave is being dug today, as there's hope that the rain will wet the soil.'

'If you'll wait a moment longer, Brother, I'll send a little message with you to your *cellarius*.' And without waiting for an answer Melchior grabbed a quill.

When Keterlyn appeared in the shop, the twins running behind her, she found the street door still shut and Melchior at his desk, deep in thought.

'Are you fasting from work today, Mr Apothecary?' asked his wife. 'How many times a day do I have to open up, or are these ancient monks buying so many medicines that there's no need to serve anyone else? Oh, look, you've sold out of biscuits.'

Melchior was jolted out of his meditations. 'The biscuit dough can be made to rise again, so it can. But instead of serving customers we're the poorer by a few artig. You see, that monk remembered the prior who once buried Brother Adelbert, the very man responsible for the haunting of the Unterrainer house today.'

'Then I'll pray to St Catherine that those old horror stories will help us get a few pennies back. Perhaps you don't remember, but you have two children to raise.'

'Don't scold me, woman,' responded Melchior. 'If nothing else, then at least now I know who is haunting the Unterrainer house. Only ...'

Agatha and young Melchior came screaming to their father, demanding to be taken on to his lap, one on each arm, and then rocked.

'Only what?' asked Keterlyn, her hands on her hips, watching as her husband picked the children up.

'Only things still don't fit together,' said Melchior. 'There are too many gaps in the story. I think Prior Helmich didn't tell the young Lodevic the whole truth, not by any stretch. That house is full of secrets, and I think we might be helped in solving them by Lay Brother Eric who died at the monastery the day before yesterday.'

Keterlyn shook her head and went to the kitchen to mix up some more biscuit dough. Sometimes her husband's thoughts followed strange paths, and it was best not to ask anything more because when asked he got even more peculiar. To earn a few pennies from the biscuits and buy bread for the children, right now that was much more important to Keterlyn.

17

The House of the Merchant Arend Goswin, Rataskaevu Street
7 August, Towards Evening

HEAVY RAIN HAD visited the town during the day, and the cobbled streets were trickling with rivulets of water, in which floated faeces and mud, despite which the streets still smelled fresher than earlier. The townsfolk were pleased that there would be no need to fear drought as they had last year; there was more rainfall now, and the turnips would be growing nicely and would make a welcome supplement to the winter diet. The summer had been hot, and the crops had been abundant; the mills were working hard, and there would be no shortage of bread or any of the other staples this winter.

And the ground was wet. This was the best time for digging, thought Melchior – for grave-digging, indeed. May the Almighty give Hinric the goodness to listen to my request. The request that he had sent Hinric was certainly unusual, but surely he would understand that everything Melchior did was not for himself and his own peculiar whim but for the good of the town?

Towards evening, after the rains, Melchior set off for the stables to examine the dapple-grey mare, but in the street he met Annlin, Master Goswin's housekeeper, and couldn't help but ask how the

Merchant was feeling, whether he was still ailing and eating little or whether the ointment of salvia and marjoram was helping with his pains.

'May the Master's angels thank you that you know my poor Master's failing health so well,' replied Annlin. 'But I suppose he'll always be infirm, for he has many years on his head. Today he hasn't complained of any pains but he's had no appetite. For the second day on the trot he sat in his room all day. He didn't even go to the weighing-house to trade. He just sat and didn't say a word or eat a mouthful. And I'm afraid he probably didn't sleep a wink last night, because this morning he looked terribly troubled.'

'Deep sleep is very important at his age,' said Melchior with concern. 'A person must sleep because that's when the marrow grows. But if a person doesn't sleep properly the marrow does not increase, and the body cannot rest because the marrow is lacking. I'm sure the murder a few nights ago will also be keeping Master Goswin up at night – when a person is suddenly woken up it is very damaging to the marrow. Do you know what, neighbour? Since I don't have anything very pressing at the moment I'd like to come and prescribe a remedy for your Master, one that is sure to help against sleeplessness.'

'Oh Lord, that's so kind of you, Mr Apothecary,' said Annlin, clapping her hands together.

'Just one thing, though, it's best not to mention this to the Council's doctor, because I'm not supposed to treat patients without his permission. But I know how much money he would charge to recommend what I already know anyway. So would you ask your Master whether I could call on him in a little while and bring him a brew that will definitely help him to sleep better?'

Annlin promised to do that, and an hour later, while Melchior was waiting impatiently by the boiled herbs and the dill pot, Annlin came to say that Master Goswin would be very grateful if the Apothecary would be able to treat his sleeplessness. On the contrary, it's I who am grateful, thought Melchior. He was only on nodding terms with Arend Goswin, and now he had skilfully managed to engineer an opportunity to talk to him. He was terribly interested in what the old man thought of the story of the Rataskaevu Street Ghost, and even more interested in why Master Goswin had shed tears as he had at the funeral of his once-sworn enemy. He and Annlin hurried along past a couple of houses, past Mertin Tweffell's house and the garden, rejoicing in the rain and the freshness it brought to the ground, and then they were at the notorious Unterrainer house and the place where the town guards had found the corpse that night. Annlin stumbled up the steps to her house, opened the parlour door, and immediately the grey-haired head of Hainz appeared before them, his eyes bulging and his mouth drooling.

'To the Master?' enquired the servant.

'To the Master, of course, you booby. Do you think that Mr Apothecary has come to doctor a blockhead like you?' Annlin lashed out, pushing her husband out of the way.

'To me?' asked Hainz stupidly. 'Nothing wrong with me.'

'No, there's never anything wrong with *you*,' scolded Annlin, 'only that your head is warm like a boiled cabbage.' And then, by way of apology to Melchior, 'Take no notice, Mr Apothecary. I'm saddled with a dolt, but he's got a good heart.'

'Good evening, Hainz,' said Melchior, intending to follow the woman's wishes and pay no attention to the half-witted servant. 'I have business with your Master, but if your health is in any trouble then please call into my pharmacy.'

'Ah, to the Master? I'll lead the way,' grunted Hainz. 'That's what I thought … to the Master.'

'Out of the way, and don't dawdle,' Annlin cut in. 'Go and chop wood or something, and mind your own business. He's come to apply some salve to the Master. Useless, you are.'

Hainz was a big-boned man with long arms and legs, a good two heads taller than his wife and evidently stronger and hardier than Goswin. Reasoning power had not been given to him, and the whole town knew that. From between the two tousled tuffs of his grey hair his watery, empty eyes stared out, and whenever Melchior had met him the man was smacking his lips with dribble. He had once been a salt-carrier, evidently, and he had taken the citizen's oath because all carriers were required to do that.

'Chop wood, chop wood …' repeated Hainz to himself now, as if trying to keep in mind a complex order, and he pushed past Melchior and Annlin as he went into the yard.

'In his younger days that one was a bit more alert,' noted Annlin regretfully. 'But what's the point of talking about it? Not everybody's faults are obvious when they're young. As a girl I was looking at his strength and how tall he was and his beautiful wavy hair. And he loved children – he was always dandling our Hanns on his knee and teaching him things. In his old age, though, he's got a bit dense.'

'Hanns,' enquired Melchior, without interest. 'That was your son, yes, the one who's now a stablehand in Tartu?'

'Oh, stablehand, yes,' chirped Annlin. 'He'll be forty-one this year, and he's in charge of the Bishop of Tartu's very own stable of horses.'

'Good man,' said Melchior absently.

'But what are we chattering on about? The Master is waiting for the Apothecary in the *dörnse*. I'll show you the way.'

They walked through a large vestibule, at the back of which was a kitchen where Annlin evidently had soup cooking on the fire, since Melchior could smell parsley, onion and lamb shanks. There were large boxes lying around, and there was a writing-desk, too, with papers scattered over it; maybe this was where Goswin sealed his trade deals. From visits to the homes of other important merchants Melchior had noted that they tended to be decorated with large carved ashlars; the richer ones had had a few holy icons placed in the entrance hall, the *diele*, and an altar, and now the latest fashion was to order grand paintings of biblical figures. Melchior looked around inquisitively, but no painting caught his eye. Interesting if this old fogy got de Zwarte to paint his portrait, he thought. The vestibule of Master Goswin's house was bleak. He had not had it beautified or ordered paintings or decorative stonework to make it less austere.

Annlin opened the door of the *dörnse*. It was dim at this time of day because its wide windows opened on to a side courtyard of the Unterrainer house, and in the late afternoon the sun shone on the south-east corner. However, it was warm in the room – Melchior thought it might even be heated by an oven in the cellar below. Since no one else lived there Master Goswin's broad curtained bed was also in this room. On a chair in front of the bed sat the old merchant himself. It was not easy to see his face.

'And that's how he's been since this morning,' whispered Annlin in Melchior's ear. 'He just mopes around and doesn't eat anything.'

Melchior screwed up his eyes to get used to the crepuscular light. He noticed that the *dörnse* was somewhat more luxuriously decorated than the vestibule – there was a stone carving between the windows, on the soffit of which were coloured clay plates; the red curtains were drawn on to the walls. At the back of the room there seemed to be an entrance to a cellar, and there was something painted on the stone lintel. But Melchior's eye was not caught by any portrait.

'Mr Goswin, my respects to you. I am Melchior Wakenstede, the apothecary from your street,' said Melchior, bowing.

'I know who you are,' said Master Goswin quietly. 'Woman, bring Mr Apothecary a chair and something to drink.'

'As you wish, sir,' replied the woman meekly, shifting a chair from near the wall to Melchior and disappearing towards the *diele*.

'I don't need anything to drink,' said Melchior quickly. 'I've just brought the gentleman some medicine that will help him to sleep better. Looking at you, sir, I can see that you haven't slept well.'

Arend Goswin was sitting in an armchair into which he was sunk deeply. He seemed never to have been a strong-boned man, but old age had shrivelled him further. He was gaunt, with great sunken blue eyes, and his great greyish sideburns emphasized how thin he was. Stepping closer, Melchior saw that the man had been weeping. His beard and his big sad eyes reminded him of a dog. That's it. He has the face of a faithful old dog.

'So what medicine do you recommend, Apothecary?' asked Goswin in a hoarse voice.

'It's an old and tested remedy, which will certainly help,' replied Melchior enthusiastically. 'It contains fresh dill, a little salvia and twice that amount of yarrow, which I boiled and squeezed out, and now the mixture should be put on your forehead and bound and kept there. Look, sir, you see, the dill has the property of helping a person sleep, the yarrow and the salvia give warmth to the heart and slow it down so that a person can sleep peacefully.'

'Thank you, Apothecary,' said Goswin. 'Annlin will put it on my forehead then and bind it up. How much does the medicine cost?'

'It doesn't cost anything,' replied Melchior boldly. 'I thought that I took too high a price last autumn for that salve of salvia, marjoram, dill and peppermint, and my mind's been troubled by this. By the way, did it help?'

'Yes, I suppose it did. What was it actually for?'

'Pains, and it helps against injuries, too, by the grace of St Cosmas.'

'Yes, it helped,' admitted Goswin laconically.

'That's good then. Well now, I also thought that we are neighbours, and shouldn't an apothecary always take care that no one in his street is complaining of pains? So I'm not asking a penny for this infusion.'

Arend Goswin raised his head and even managed a slight smile.

'May the saints bless you, Wakenstede, but a businessman will run a pretty poor business if he gives his services away for nothing.'

'That's why I'm not really a businessman,' shrugged Melchior.

'Or you're wanting something in return then,' noted Goswin, blinking quickly. 'Some other motive?'

Melchior licked his lips a little, breathed in, gestured with his hand and said, 'Yes, actually you're right, sir. Why deny it? I do have one little motive in getting to see you, and if you don't throw me out straight away I'll tell you what it is.'

'You talk then, and I'll see whether I throw you out or not,' said Goswin. 'But I don't take anything for free. If you don't want money then I'll have a bottle of Nuremberg malmsey that I just got off the ship sent to you.'

'You're too kind, sir,' replied Melchior, bowing, 'and I shan't say no to a good wine. And if we've agreed on a trade of that nature then I'll come straight to the point. I wanted to ask you about the Rataskaevu Street Ghost. You live right next to the Unterrainer house, which is where there are supposed to have been hauntings.'

'And why do you want to know that?' Was Goswin slightly alarmed, or did it just seem so to the Apothecary?

Melchior told him why. Three people who had said they had seen the ghost had swiftly died in unfortunate ways. One whore, who had previously been a housekeeper for Master Bruys, one Flemish painter, who had painted Master Goswin's own portrait, and, most recently, Grote the Master of the Quad Dack Tower, who before his death had wished to speak to Master Bruys about something.

'And I am perplexed,' declared Melchior. 'This sort of coincidence is hard to regard as just a matter of chance. It seems to me that there's some link between them, and since I myself live on this street, my wife lives here and my children play on this street, I started to wonder what people remember and know about the haunting of the house next door to you. I hear various stories, but one thing seems certain, seventy years ago a terrible sin and a murder were committed at the Unterrainer house, and the shadows of that horror still pursue people today. So, that was my other motive. Do you know anything? Do you remember the Flemish painter de Zwarte mentioning anything about a ghost? Can you raise the veil of secrecy on any of this? And – and I know this is a difficult question – can you guess how this ghost might be connected with Master Bruys?'

Goswin was silent for a long time, looking thoughtfully at Melchior. His face was doleful, and it was as if a shadow of anger passed over it.

'You have many questions, Wakenstede,' he said finally.

'And if you don't wish to answer them, sir, I'll leave immediately with my apologies.'

'No, no, sit down,' demanded Goswin. 'Maybe I can help you, maybe not, but you have many questions, and I don't know where to begin.'

'The house next door,' offered Melchior cautiously, 'which is said to be haunted. Have you perhaps seen or heard something at some time? They say that a woman who had been immured alive was found in the cellar. She had committed a sin with a monk. The monk died among the Dominicans, but the spirit of that woman is supposed to be haunting it to this day.'

'Yes, those stories,' said Goswin slowly. 'Some say that that monk was left to die with the woman … some that he had something chopped off him.'

Melchior nodded. 'Yes, there are various stories – but that monk rests in the Dominican cemetery.'

'Ah, so,' whispered Goswin. He sank into thought and considered for a while then shook his head, saying, 'No, Apothecary, I've never seen any ghost at the house next door. Yes, I've heard talk of it, but … I haven't seen it. I've lived in this house for over forty years, and I don't believe those stories. Maybe a terrible bloodbath did take place there, and people talk of it perhaps, but it's not worth seeing connections where there aren't any.'

'You don't believe in ghosts, sir?' asked Melchior. 'That the spirit of a person who died in horrible agony can stay in a place to haunt it? Men of the Church also say that after death the soul goes either to Heaven or to purgatory, and yet there are cases known where after death … something is seen or heard.'

'That is memory,' said Goswin rapidly and very testily. 'It's the memory of a person, his spirit, which does not leave his home. It's not some evil ghost cursing others to death; it's a happy spirit. It's an angel which watches over its nearest and dearest and whispers at night in their ears that it loves them and praises everything they've taken as advice. The saints also appear to people but not an ordinary person of flesh and blood whom God has called to Himself.'

'I can only agree with you, sir,' nodded Melchior. 'So you do still believe that after death a person can come back to his loved ones? You have witnessed that?'

'I have buried four children and a wife, Wakenstede, and I believe quite firmly that when they have gone on from the threshold to Paradise they have come to look at their father and husband, whispered into his ear in the night that all is now well, Christ the Lord has saved them from earthly travails. But if you want to tell me that that is one and the same thing as the ghost of some whore who can find no peace after death and leads people to their deaths then …' He was agitated. His sad, canine face had become fiery. Foam sprayed from his mouth, and his eyes had turned fierce.

'No, I didn't mean anything like that,' Melchior hurried to assure him. 'And I beg your pardon if my talk has aroused painful memories for you. Magistrate Dorn has told me what happened to your daughter, and I have heard what pain you have had to live through. Perhaps you know, Mr Goswin, that I have children, too, and my heart is torn with anguish when I have to imagine …' He fell silent. He looked meaningfully at Master Goswin's face and saw rage turning to sadness there.

'Yes, you have children,' whispered Goswin. 'Yes, I know.' Then he was silent. His doleful eyes filled with tears.

'Agatha and Melchior,' added Melchior. 'In our family it has been that way for centuries; the eldest son takes the name Melchior from his father. And perhaps you also remember my father, whose name was also Melchior? He was the apothecary here in this town, and he must have been so at the time when …' Melchior ended the sentence abruptly, as if he wanted to say something more but had to stop at the last moment. Those were painful times and things that he wanted to hear about.

'Yes, I remember,' said Arend Goswin very quietly. 'I remember him very well. I bought a medicine from him for Dorothea's fever when she was very small. She was extremely hot and rambling, and she couldn't sleep. The fever was burning the life out of her. It had been a very warm autumn. There was a fetid smell all around, and everyone was sick because the air was thick with disease –'

'That would certainly have been a mixture of bay cooked in wine, aloe juice and liquorice,' interjected Melchior. 'My father taught me that recipe, and nothing works better against fever. A little horehound herb mixed in, and it is bound to help. So my father treated … Dorothea?'

The merchant raised his gaze. There was only pain and sorrow to be seen there.

'Dorothea,' he whispered. '*She is still here*. She has never left here. *This* is her home and not the unmarked grave far away at the back edge of St Barbara's Cemetery where they allowed her to be buried. And no priest came to her funeral to speak. She was buried like a …'

Like a suicide, thought Melchior. A suicide who has taken from herself her immortal soul which the Lord has granted to her. Having taken her hand to the divine gift and therefore deserving of contempt, even in death. Oh, of course.

'I appreciate that it still troubles you deeply,' said Melchior quietly and with compassion. 'Who wouldn't feel that way? I would, too, and I would also believe that my daughter visits her own home at night, and I wouldn't believe either that earthly death can be what permanently separates a young soul from the body.'

'If you believe that then you know that what appears in angelic form cannot make anyone ill,' said Goswin. 'She was sacred, you understand. My Dorothea was sacred. She was chosen by Heaven; she was one of the elect. Many people thought she was insane ...' His sad eyes bored into Melchior's face, and his voice was suddenly louder. 'But I, *I* knew. I brought her up. I knew, and I believed, and I saw that the material world was a mystery to her, but she understood holy things, and she yearned to be near them. And when she spoke to me, and she *spoke*, oh, angels, she spoke with her own father because she only dared to speak with those people whom she trusted and believed in. She was not insane, you understand. She was simply different and marked out by Heaven. She was waiting for St Michael to appear to her and give her a message, and she told me about it clearly, beseeched me to believe her and not regard her as mad ... And she is still here in this house because this is the place where she was happy and where she wanted to return to after her death, and she reassures me that consecrated ground is only a human invention. She is in Heaven with the angels ...'

'I believe that,' said Melchior very quietly. He felt awkward at having steered the conversation in such a painful direction. But people do talk most about what they want to discuss, and about what they don't want to discuss they are mostly silent.

'And then,' continued Goswin in a broken voice, 'one day she changed. She told me that she was now unclean. She was filthy and could no longer be a bride of Christ the Lord ... She went, and I never saw her again until word was brought that ...'

Goswin fell silent and wiped away a tear. Melchior sighed deeply. It was painful, it was moving, and yet the image of Goswin's daughter's visitation to her home in spirit form was not what he wanted to hear about.

Goswin, too, seemed to realize this. He was silent with his gaze for a moment on the ceiling, and then he remarked, 'But you didn't come to ask about my departed daughter. Forgive me. My story didn't concern you.'

'On the contrary, it is I who should be begging your pardon. My questions awakened painful memories for you. I have no right to pry into these agonizing things.'

'Agonizing?' repeated Goswin in a low voice. 'Yes, you're right, it does still … and yet it doesn't. A man learns to be reconciled to his fate and learns to forgive. But you were asking something about Master Bruys?'

'I suppose I was. I was telling you that three people had seen a ghost on Rataskaevu Street and met their deaths. At least two of them were somehow connected to Master Bruys, and you and Master Bruys were …' Melchior left the sentence hanging in the air.

'Master Bruys and I …' said Goswin meditatively. 'Do you want to hear that story? Do you want to hear about two friends who became enemies and regretted it for decades but could not find the words or the acts to reconcile their differences? Well, it was that story you came to hear, so listen.'

He fell silent again and then said so suddenly that Melchior was quite taken aback, 'Thyl Bruys dishonoured my beloved child. Thyl Bruys, that bastard, drove her mad, led her into temptation. Thyl Bruys took her down from Heaven and from me and from herself only to laugh about it and boast about his sinful act around town. Don't tell me that you know what that means to a father, and don't tell me you understand my pain. I didn't understand it myself, and I suppose I still don't understand it. Ten years had to pass to understand that fathers are not answerable for the sins of their sons, that I had no right to hate the innocent and that everything an innocent man can do to punish himself had already been done, and neither I nor God has any right to demand more.'

Goswin's gaze was aimed straight at Melchior's face. His sorrowful eyes begged the whole world for forgiveness, and suddenly he grasped Melchior's hand.

'But I did demand it,' he cried. 'Oh, may the saints bless me. I did demand it. I said words to him that I can never take back. I demanded more of him than one can ask of a man who is himself innocent. He abandoned his son, his only child; he disowned him, left him without an inheritance and sent him packing, as his name had been shamed. And then he asked me, tearfully, what more he could do to put his guilt right. But I? I was so haughty and full of hatred that that was not enough for me. I cursed him – him *and* his family. And then came the time for me to regret it, for God took from him an innocent child who was burned to death. I went to him. I asked forgiveness for the words I had said. I offered him my repentance. I begged his forgiveness. But he? He said that in people's eyes we may be reconciled, but in God's eyes never. I had called down damnation on his family, and I had got it, and now there was nothing left for him but to ask God for the sins of his children to be heaped upon his own neck manifold and that the Lord would find for him a penitent's cell where he could lament for ever in his agony. Those were his words, which he uttered twelve years ago, and since that time we are reconciled in people's eyes, and our old enmity should not have troubled us, but in his own heart he carried a poisonous grudge against me. And I, Wakenstede, have been searching in myself for twelve years for the right words with which to face him and beg forgiveness. For I still clearly remember that moment when the two of us together, two young apprentice merchants, stood in Tallinn harbour and looked at the ship that had brought us here and prayed to the Virgin Mary for a blessing on our enterprise. We swore to each other that, no matter what happened, a friend would help a friend. That ship, Wakenstede, disappeared from Tallinn harbour for ever, and until Laurentz Bruys's last breath I never had the opportunity to dare to recall to him that moment and kneel before him and ask forgiveness for the injustice I had caused. It remains to trouble my old soul, and for that sin I will burn in hell.'

'Sir, you shouldn't be so harsh on yourself,' replied Melchior awkwardly after a long pause. He had not expected such an outpouring. Yet this did explain Goswin's tears and despairing appearance at St Nicholas's Churchyard.

Goswin silently let go of Melchior's hand.

'Yes,' he whispered, 'I'll burn in hell, and I'm happy about that. But you came to ask about a ghost. No, Wakenstede, I haven't seen that ghost, and I haven't heard it. You think that Master Bruys and this ghost are somehow connected?'

'I said that it seemed that way to me, that it was strange.'

'You're labouring under a misconception, Apothecary. Hundreds of people in this town are connected with Bruys in some way, and dozens of people fall to their deaths or drown. You see connections where there are none. Forget it, and don't attach any ghost to that man's soul any longer.'

'You might be right,' mumbled Melchior. 'But, one more question, if I may. Don't you recall de Zwarte talking about a ghost? He did paint your portrait ...'

Goswin shook his head. 'He could only see a ghost in his own drunken head. That man didn't know how to curb his ale-drinking. He didn't say anything to me about a ghost.'

'But that portrait,' ventured Melchior cautiously. 'He must have come to your house quite often … Portrait-painting takes a long time and …'

'No, Apothecary,' said Goswin firmly. 'That portrait was a silly idea anyway. I should have listened to those who said that de Zwarte couldn't paint. I sent him packing halfway through and put him on a ship. And we never talked much. The portrait wasn't finished.'

As Melchior left the room with a bow – while Master Goswin carried on sitting motionless in his chair, staring vacantly out of the window – he bumped into Annlin at the entrance to the *dörnse*. The old woman was a couple of steps away from the door, but Melchior realized that she had been eavesdropping, her ear to the door. And a burning smell seemed to be coming from the kitchen.

18

The Dominican Monastery Graveyard
8 August, the Feast Day of St Dominic, Morning

THE AREA BOUNDED by the wall of the Dominican cemetery, at the western edge of the monastery's land, was by no means large, for the monastery itself had never been that large. It was located between the main gate and the church. Ordinary monks and lay brothers were buried there, the more recent nearer the wall and very tightly packed. The priors and deputy priors, the bishops as well as noblemen from among the vassals and other high-ranking gentlemen, got themselves – if they were rich enough – the best resting places under portentous carved ashlars either in the monastery or within the church itself.

Lay Brother Eric's body was to be buried almost up against the wall of the enclosure, in a narrow little spot between a bush and a thick yew tree.

Apothecary Melchior's message to Hinric yesterday had changed things. Hinric had received it when Brother Lodevic returned to the monastery for horary prayers in a more cheerful mood than the decrepit old man usually was and smelling strongly of spirits and ginger. Melchior has done him in with his magical remedies, Hinric thought crossly. Melchior is otherwise a fine man,

God-fearing and diligent, with more knowledge of the saints than some bishops have, but when some idea, some sniff of a crime, takes hold of him it throws him. His eyes start to blaze, and he rushes around until he has found his murderer. Yes, he does good for the town, but sometimes his methods …

And now he had made a brother drunk.

'How much did you squeeze out of him?' Hinric enquired of Lodevic, who at that moment was trying to whistle along with a song thrush, which sounded like a wheezing demon stuck on a pole.

'One and a half artig in silver,' stated Brother Lodevic proudly, and Hinric softened somewhat. If he was prepared to donate that generously Melchior really must be serious about this ghost business.

'Rest until vespers,' he had recommended to Lodevic, but then the old man had passed him Melchior's message. Hinric read it through and questioned Brother Lodevic at length. He had not understood matters any more clearly, apart from the fact that Melchior had got a good deal for his silver. Hinric thought the matter over for some time, and only just before evening prayers did he go to Prior Moninger and tell him he had received an unusual request from Apothecary Melchior.

Reinhart Moninger had been Prior for about eight years. He had been sent to Tallinn from Lund following the poisoning of Prior Baltazar Eckell ten years earlier, a crime that Melchior had helped to solve, and Reinhart and Melchior had met several times over the years. Reinhart was about fifty, a good-natured and soft person. In the worldly contests of strength that went on between the Council, the Order and the bishops he preferred to remain silent, for he didn't want to understand worldly politics. He was an expert on the Scriptures, and he preferred, instead of managing the monastery's economic affairs, to stand in the scriptorium and read, for which purpose he wore costly reading-glasses. He even loved to copy out books. He was a devout man – maybe *too* devout for a town such as Tallinn in Hinric's opinion. Instead of making sure that the brothers had enough salt herring to last the winter or that the Blackheads weren't being too thrifty in maintaining their altar, or disputing with the Council over the ground rent of the monastery Prior Moninger was much more interested in the interpretation of Gratian's decrees in the light of Pope Gregory IX's decretals or the dogmatics of the doctrine of transubstantiation.

But he was Prior, and it was to him that Hinric went with Melchior's message.

The Prior was – naturally – in the scriptorium with his spectacles on, and reading, to Hinric's surprise, *Der Edelstein*, moral tales by Ulrich Boner of the Berne Dominicans, translated from the Latin.

'This is that same Melchior, eh?' asked the Prior when he had read the letter.

'Yes, *that same* Melchior,' Hinric assured him, mentally adding a curse.

'And this is quite a peculiar request that he asks of the monastery,' said the Prior. 'Why is he doing it?'

Hinric told him. He told him about the corpse in front of the Unterrainer house and Melchior's interest in the deaths, the stories about the ghost.

'So this man is looking for the truth?' The Prior's question cut into Hinric's narrative.

'The truth about the shadows of the past, yes,' agreed Hinric.

'Aren't we all looking for that?' muttered the Prior meditatively.

'If you put it that way, holy Father.'

'Then he must find it. May I refuse him on the day of St Dominic?' Those were the Prior's last words on the subject of Melchior's request, and then he turned back to his manuscript and placed his glasses on to his nose.

And Hinric gave an order that the old grave of Brother Adelbert be dug up for the interment of Lay Brother Eric.

Melchior was at the monastery straight after the chapterhouse meeting, and he arrived on horseback. He arrived, a dapple-grey mare on the end of a halter, tethered it to the monastery's hitching-post – Hinric noticed that the Apothecary wore a proud expression in doing so – and then rushed up to Hinric, who was standing near the main portal.

'Good morrow, holy Brother,' he said. 'What reply did the Prior give to my request?'

Instead of answering Hinric motioned with his head in the direction of the graveyard, towards which the lay brothers were bearing the corpse of Eric, resting on a frame and wrapped in a winding-sheet.

'And the grave,' asked Melchior, agitated. 'Was it dug yesterday?'

'Until they got to Adelbert's corpse,' replied Hinric peevishly. 'Listen, tell me the truth, in the name of St Nicholas. What *are* you up to?'

'And you haven't opened the coffin yet?' Melchior enquired further. 'And it was a coffin, as I thought?'

'Yes, it was a coffin,' replied Hinric laconically.

'Isn't that strange? As far as I was aware, in those days the lesser brothers were simply buried on planks wrapped in a shroud.'

Yes, it was passing strange, Hinric had to admit to himself. A coffin was expensive, and it was far from usual for brothers to be buried in coffins – especially not sinners like Brother Adelbert. Yet this poor wretch had been buried in a casket, even at a time when the monastery's finances were scant.

'No, we didn't open it, but it has been dug out now,' Hinric said.

'So it could be opened now?'

'I won't allow it until the Prior gives his blessing.'

'Well, here he comes,' said Melchior. Hinric turned his head and saw that the Prior was indeed coming from the dormitory and walking towards the freshly dug grave. Hinric and Melchior went after him.

The service at the graveside was brief. Eric had not, after all, taken his vows, and the monastery had many other activities to attend to since they were marking St Dominic's feast day. The brothers had already prayed for the soul of Lay Brother Eric at the vigil and the first mass, so after the precentor had said the words that he was obliged to say everyone remained standing, perplexed and silent. The precentor had a book in one hand and a coal-pan in the other, but he didn't know what to do – whether to have Eric's body placed in the grave on top of the old coffin or do something else. He didn't even know why the grave had been exhumed because there was still space in the graveyard.

Melchior and Hinric stood side by side, both fixing their gaze on the decayed coffin that had been revealed. Without turning his head or changing his expression Melchior asked Hinric very softly, 'The brothers ate my biscuits last night, did they?'

'We didn't have any biscuits,' whispered Hinric in reply, staring straight ahead. 'You know what the times are like – no sweet things.'

At this Melchior hissed something so softly that Hinric didn't hear it, but it was probably a curse.

The precentor, meanwhile, was looking questioningly at the Prior; the Prior's mild eyes bored into Melchior, and he finally nodded to Hinric. The *cellarius* sighed deeply and ordered the lay brothers to jump into the grave and prise open the lid of the old coffin.

A moment later they all leaned over to look.

And then they raised their eyes in astonishment. Only the Prior closed his eyes and nodded to himself. He turned to go.

The casket was half full of sand; there was not a single bone.

'Father,' whispered Hinric, shocked. 'Did you know about this?'

'There is a scroll, the first lines of which were written by Prior Maurice about two hundred years ago,' replied Reinhart Moninger. 'It is passed down from prior to prior, and it contains things that may not be said in the daybook or the account book, but they are things the priors have to know about the monastery. I think this is the time when an old lie is turned into a truth.'

And then, with slow steps, he trudged back to the scriptorium.

'What does this all mean, Melchior?' Hinric now asked him. 'You must have known this.'

'I didn't,' he replied quietly, 'but I guessed that it might be so.'

'So where is Adelbert's corpse?'

Melchior didn't answer, but the shocking realization came quickly. The *cellarius* was breathing very softly and rapidly. Then he closed his eyes and whispered, 'Holy Virgin. Adelbert is still there … in the Unterrainer house.'

19

On the Road from Tallinn to St Bridget's Convent, Marienthal
8 August, Mid-Morning

EARLY THAT MORNING Melchior had done exactly as Dorn had instructed. He had gone to the stables, asked for Hartmann the stablehand and told him that the Magistrate had ordered him to give him a horse to ride to Marienthal, and if Hartmann raised any objection he would be put in irons in the marketplace.

The stablehand did grumble that the Magistrate could go hang himself in the Town Hall tower and then the townsfolk could have a bit of fun, but he brought Melchior a dapple-grey mare saying she was a good, peaceful animal who knew the way to Bridget's well, since she often visited the Varsaallik Estate.

'Bridget's?' asked Melchior. He had not heard of such a place before.

'Isn't that what they call it?' responded Hartmann. 'The new convent? The Swedes used to call it Mariendal, but now people tend to call it Bridget's. On the way you come to Martin's Brook, don't you, and there's a good place to drink that this animal knows, so if she starts pulling that way you'd better let her go there because she drinks her fill and goes straight back on to the right road. You won't need to use your spurs much with her.'

Melchior assured him that he wasn't in any hurry – which was not entirely true – left him two pennies and a sweet confection as a tip and promised to be back by sunset. He had put a bottle of his spirits into his travel pouch as well as a double handful of sweets wrapped in a cloth – after Brother Lodevic's ravaging this was a great sacrifice, but perhaps on this pilgrimage of his he might need to sweeten some mouths into talking.

With Eric's funeral at the monastery now behind him he led the mare through the bustling town with a thoughtful mien and out through the Clay Gate, nodded gratefully to the image of St Victor – which stood at the side of the foregate as a sign to strangers that this town was under the protection of heavenly powers – swung into the saddle and headed westward. The miller at the Clay Gate mill looked on curiously at the passing apothecary, and Melchior waved in greeting to his old friend. Straight after the embankment and the mill the road divided into three. One fork carried on west along the edge of the town wall and the embankment; another turned south-east, past the clay-ponds to St John's Hospital, where the lepers were kept, then through the outskirts and over the sandy hummocks up the hill to the shale quarry and on towards Viru and Tartu. But Melchior had to choose the narrower and rougher fork, leading along the seashore towards Marienthal and the Apenes Peninsula. This was a quieter road, for ahead of it, on the peninsula, lay only the Order's meadows, coastal villages and marshy forests. But this road could become important in the future, once the large and splendid convent had been finished, thought Melchior. Inns and guesthouses were already being built alongside the road and large crosses were being erected for the pilgrims. At present only the old town gallows stood by the Seppade Gate, and they were hardly ever used now, but they served as a sign that Tallinn had the right to exact a price in blood in this land where the town had the right to strike with the sword. Anyone coming to town by this road would get the message that St Victor protected the town and all evildoers would be dealt with.

Just ahead of the bridge over the Härjapea river, where there was an image of the Mother of God and where many beggars usually gathered, another road led off towards the shale pits, and from there on the road was deeply rutted by wagon wheels. Shale from the cliffs was taken into town or to the lime kilns beyond, at Köismäe, and Melchior saw a couple of wagons approaching from afar. He rode the mare over the bridge and followed the road as it went down along the littoral to the meadows by the seashore and the Swedish fishing villages.

The weather was windless and cloudy. Melchior breathed the fresh sea air deeply and settled comfortably in the saddle. He was no great rider, but the road wasn't long. And he needed to think. The morning at the monastery and the opening of the casket, Hinric's words at the graveside – 'Adelbert is still there … in the Unterrainer house' – aroused a vague kind of terror in him. He could not shake the feeling off that he was circling around a riddle, the solution of which was simple and whose clues should already be present but also that he had got himself involved in something very dangerous. He was lost in a false labyrinth; he must escape from it; he ought to be afraid. He asked himself whether forces from beyond the grave could harm the living – his own experience told him that only the hatred of the living could cause suffering to others … and something of that nature had taken place in the Unterrainer house in times past. Or was it so long ago? Adelbert had died seventy years ago. And Cristian Unterrainer might still have been alive when Melchior was born. He was haunted by the thought that Unterrainer was said to have whipped his wife, and that corpse of the unknown tramp had wheals from a whip, and that Unterrainer had castrated Adelbert, as had also happened to that poor wretch who was killed in front of his house. And yet it was as if St Cosmas were whispering in his ear that he was following the wrong path.

His earthly path now, though, was the right one, and there was no fear of getting lost, as he knew this road well. He rode steadily along the shore until the road rose from the Härmapõld pasture lands up to a plateau. To the south-east he could make out the escarpment of the shale quarry; behind him were the beautiful towers of Tallinn. Gentle waves lapped against the shingly shore. Carts loaded with logs were travelling from the direction of Marienthal, and he let the horse go aside to the bank. Out at sea he could see Wulvesøø, the island where the Council had its timber cut and its hay made; for centuries pirates had used the island as a hiding place. The shipping lane to the east went through the Strait of Wulvesøø to avoid the reefs around the island and the shallows of Nargensgrund where ships ran aground every year. Keeping to the correct shipping lane was so important that each spring the Council marked it with a couple of tuns floating in the water that were securely anchored to the sea bed. But the pirates also knew this passage well and were used to lurking around Wulvesøø. It was especially easy for them to try their luck with ships seeking shelter on the island during a storm – although no pirates had been spotted near Tallinn in recent years, as the Council had taken care to send its warships to Wulvesøø and see them off.

Now the road turned a little to the north, on to the Apenes Peninsula, and there, in the distance, was Martin's Brook. The old mare pricked up her ears and started to speed up. Melchior did not rein her in when she stepped off the road down towards the grassy path and the drinking-place. At the brook was one more road leading from the shale pits, and here the cartwheels had created deep ruts in the mud. Stones had been taken from around here to the new convent for over a year by this time and would surely be for years to come until the job was completed.

Ahead, though, lay a straight road along the high shoreline, and the dark line of the forest at beautiful Marienthal was already in view. The quarry lay ever further behind, and the weather grew warmer; the sun came out from behind the clouds, and a light gust of wind blew in from the sea. Melchior was now at the boundary of the town's lands and entering those of the Order. This was marked out with stones and at the road junctions. The last time Melchior had come so far had been the previous summer when he went riding the boundaries. None other than Wentzel Dorn had assigned him this task as an honoured citizen of the town, one who certainly must be one of its luminaries. The town's musicians had woken the townsfolk early in the morning with their bagpipes as they gathered in procession in the main square. Yes, there were aldermen, soldiers, tower-masters, guildsmen, Council officers and plenty of others. In the morning they drank dry the vat of ale donated by the Dominicans, accompanied by singing, and then rode off to shouts of praise from the people towards the town's boundaries. Beggars and tramps came rushing after them; merchants and aldermen showered them with coins. As they passed the town's mansions they were offered ale and food, and the bagpipers kept on piping until some of them fell drunk in a ditch somewhere. Slowly, though, they made it to the boundary stones, and they were all welcomed with great shouts, flags were lowered in their honour and soldiers touched the stones with their swords, symbolically pledging that the town would defend its borders by force of arms. Melchior had been elevated there to the rank of Witness, made to sit on a boundary stone and given a few jocular blows with a stick – which was followed by a feast and more ale – so he would remember the town's limits well and rush to defend them if required. The Dominicans had even loaned the reliquary of the head of St Rochus upon which the townsmen swore that as long as they had strength in their bodies they would stand, with the saints' names on their lips, in defence of the town's borders against all enemies. It had been a merry day, but at the same time it had reminded everyone that they were breathing the free air of the town, and not a single freedom in this town comes of itself by the Lord's grace, and everything has its price. Melchior had then recalled the words of his neighbour Mertin Tweffell, 'Tallinn is for no one to command and forbid. Tallinn is a town by its own grace and for itself.'

Apart from a couple of solitary peasants and farmhands the road was now empty. Melchior was just thinking that he could cautiously hasten the mare's step when a band of riders hove into view up ahead. Even from afar Melchior could make out that they were gentlemen of high degree; there might have been a dozen of them, and he soon directed the horse to the bankside. As the riders approached Melchior recognized some of them. There were a couple of vassals of the Order, among them the Knight Kordt von Greyssenhagen, Hinrich Huxer, the merchant from Toompea, and Guide, Captain of the Guard of the Bishop of Tallinn, accompanied by a number of their men.

They trotted on, not paying attention to Melchior, who nevertheless bowed from the saddle to the noble masters on seeing them. Only when the horsemen, raising the dust from the road, had passed did their leader suddenly stop his horse and turn around.

The man motioned to the others to go on without him and rode back to Melchior. From his peculiar red cap one could recognize this man; he was the Knight Kordt von Greyssenhagen, Lord of Jackewolde, one of the patrons of the new convent and, according to evil tongues, one of those whose manned boats had been guarding the port of Wulvesøø. The Knight was coming over to him, although his horse would have liked to have carried on with the others, and it whinnied and stamped when Greyssenhagen pulled on the bridle and stopped before Melchior's mare.

'Ha!' cried the Knight. 'Apothecary Melchior from Rataskaevu Street.'

Melchior bowed. 'The very same, my esteemed lord.'

Greyssenhagen's horse would not stand still, but the man studied Melchior, pulling on the bridle.

'They say you're hunting a ghost,' the Knight said unexpectedly. 'The one they say is haunting my neighbour's house.'

'You have very good sources, my lord,' replied Melchior. Actually there was nothing puzzling about this. Everything that Dorn knew was known to the whole Council, and if the Council knew then all the lesser people in the town knew as well.

'You must come and tell me about it some day,' said the Knight. 'I like ghost stories.'

'With the greatest pleasure. But which ghost do you want to know about? The monk's or that sinful woman's?'

Greyssenhagen had not expected this question. 'Monk? I don't know about any monk. I've only heard about the woman and her child.'

A lump seemed to rise in Melchior's throat. 'Did that woman have a child?' he asked cautiously. 'You think, sir, that Unterrainer's wife had a *child*?'

Greyssenhagen restrained his recalcitrant horse and cried, 'Damn it, how would I know that? They just say that Unterrainer buried his wife alive with the child that was in her belly. Or else he cut the child out before he beat the woman to death, and now their souls cry out there. That's what I'm asking *you*.'

'At the moment I can't answer that,' replied Melchior.

'Then I'll expect you on Wednesday when I'm in town,' shouted the Knight, 'at the Guildhall of the Great Guild. Consider yourself invited.' And he dug his spurs into the stallion's flanks and hurried off after the others.

Melchior had no idea what would be happening at the Great Guild the following Wednesday, but he decided that he was invited and that he should notify an alderman of that. As for Ermegunde being tortured to death in pregnancy, that made him shiver all over. So he bade his mare to redouble her steps and thought about Greyssenhagen and the convent at Marienthal. His thoughts then turned to St Bridget, who must have died about five years before Melchior was born.

Since Melchior and his father had settled in Tallinn, that is, since he was a child, he had heard the local Swedes talking about St Bridget. There were many people of Swedish origin around Tallinn, and the Bishop had invited increasing numbers of them in. Sometimes there were conflicts with the Estonians of the coastal villages, in which cudgels and forks were used as weapons. Most often these conflicts took place on the Apenes Peninsula, where there were regular squabbles over land between the Swedes, liegemen of the Order, the Council, the Bishop of Tallinn and Estonian villagers, who, according to Keterlyn, had had the use of wasteland there for centuries.

The Swedes were numerous in these parts, and stories had been circulating among them for some time about a certain Swedish noblewoman to whom the Holy Virgin and Christ the Lord had manifested themselves. Bridget had died in Rome, where she had performed miracles of her own and cured poor people; she had called upon the Pope to return to Rome. She had also travelled to the Holy Land. In accordance with a vision of Brigit's, a new convent had been founded at Vadstena in Sweden, an establishment supported evermore enthusiastically by Livonian Swedes. And it was Grand Master Konrad von Jungingen of the Order himself who, a little before his own martyrdom, brought before Tallinn Council a request that a new religious community be built at the boundary of the town's and the Order's lands in the beautiful valley of Marienthal. Disputes over the new convent had been going on for over a decade now – the Order's own permit, received from Rome, coupled with a desire to influence matters with the Kingdom of Sweden on the one hand, and the rights and freedoms of the town of Tallinn on the other. The Council and the Dominicans were opposed to yet another community being built near Tallinn, as it would start to minister to the care of souls and collect donations. Tallinn had managed very well with the two existing establishments. This was actually part of an ongoing power struggle between the town and Toompea. The Order would be very happy to have a large, strong and wealthy convent on its land on the edge of town, which would at first draw pilgrims and country folk to it and might perhaps become a centre that would diminish the importance of the religious communities, churches and clergy in the town. Marienthal had a good place for a harbour. There were forests, villages and fields; there was an estuary. And wouldn't a new town also grow up around it? All the better if this new convent were to be as big as intended, the greatest in all Livonia, with such a church as can be seen from far out at sea and visible in neighbouring regions.

Melchior remembered heated arguments at the Council and in the guilds; he remembered battered faces and angry words. It was an attack on the town's freedom … The Order wanted to oppress Tallinn and create a new town … It was a conspiracy by Swedish robbers against Tallinn … The convent would attract artisans, merchants and taverns around it, and thus Tallinn would die … The Dominicans were afraid that their prestige and significance would dissipate, but they didn't dare articulate this to the Order. The Council feared that the Order would start trading overseas through a new harbour at Marienthal, and the merchants of Tallinn would be forced to become cowherds. There were many alarmists – but there were also citizens of the town who dared to proclaim that with the new convent Tallinn would only benefit and become even more important, and it was now a rich enough town to *need* three monasteries. Building such a large establishment meant that unlettered stonemasons, bricklayers, carpenters and master builders would get work, and until the huge convent was built these dealings would all go through Tallinn. If the town wanted to reject such an opportunity it deserved to die.

According to the Rule of St Bridget three men had to request the convent's establishment, and they were the Toompea merchants Henric Schwalberg, Gerlach Kruse and Hinrich Huxer. To these were added nine citizens, merchants and vassals, one of the most vocal being Laurentz Bruys. They were supposed to donate most of their assets to establish the convent, and that is what they did. Some of these men went to Rome and to the Council of Constance to plead their case. Since a bitter dispute and correspondence arose between Rome, the Order and the Council, the erection of the first buildings had been held up for ten years. But then the first master builder arrived from Sweden, as well as the Abbess of the new convent, who set about explaining the Rules of the Bridgettine Order to the townsfolk. It had been two years since the Master of the Order had found it necessary to lay the law down so that, in the end, the Council allowed stone to be sourced from the town's shale quarry – a concession that pleased the burgomasters. But the naysayers and deniers had not gone away, and the arguments would continue until the work was all finished and the town got used to the convent. So far, though, several Tallinn master builders had been working at Marienthal, and the Bridgettine Chapel had been built along with the first wooden church, residences for the Abbess and the builders, auxiliary buildings and shelters for the pilgrims. Yes, pilgrims had started coming after the Abbess arrived bringing relics with her. Praying to St Bridget helped epileptics, the deaf and the dumb.

At Hirwenoye Bridge Melchior crossed the border of the town's lands, rode through the little grove and then stopped. It had been over a year since he had last passed this way, and in that time the work had progressed far. Between the sea and the road was a thin line of trees, but to the south-east, on the plateau, bounded to the south and east by the river, lay the land for the new complex. It already had a garden enclosure around it, and within he saw a couple of stone houses and a little chapel and another hexagonal chapel by the gate along with a few smaller wooden structures. But, as he rode closer, he was shocked, for he saw countless poles and stones that marked the foundations. They were already digging and laying the foundation walls. The convent was obviously going to be extravagantly large – and when you thought how the Dominican Monastery was constricted by the town walls …

There wasn't much going on at the site just now, as the larger jobs had been by and large completed for the season. Melchior looked for something like a hitching-rail, until a farmhand ran over to him and led the horse to a shady area from where it could be taken to the river to drink. And then he had only to mention Laurentz Bruys's name and some apprentice bricklayer explained to him straight away that Master Bruys's prayer house was there beyond the bend in the river where a path over a ford led into the forest. And that Bruys's servant Mathyes was there at the moment. Melchior walked over the ground where the church would rise but where St Bridget's Chapel now stood. This road led from the building site on towards the river bend where he could see some log houses. As he had heard it, some of the project's supporters had constructed temporary dwellings for themselves until the permanent building had been completed, while Master Bruys and a few others had had their own private houses of prayer built.

It was a simple square building at the very edge of the convent's land, in a shady spot, one side of it facing the bushes. Melchior knocked softly, and the old grey-haired Mathyes opened the door.

20

Master Bruys's Prayer House, Marienthal

8 August, Noon

MELCHIOR HAD NO definite plan – and he didn't know what exactly he was seeking here – he simply wanted to see where Master Bruys had died and find out who had been at his side in his final moments. Mathyes greeted him with surprise, and Melchior told him that he happened to be in these parts looking for medicinal plants and to settle an old debt, and then he had wondered if this was the place where Master Bruys had died – that benefactor of the town of Tallinn and a man whom Melchior had always admired and for whom he had prayed for blessings from his guardian angels.

The prayer house was sparsely furnished, but one could spend the night there. On the back wall of the room was a wooden crucifix, and in front of it a very simple altar with candles, a clay image of St Bridget and a Bible. A rosary and a large seashell were also placed in front of the altar. At the other end was a place to sleep and a little table for eating breakfast. On the walls were a couple of shelves for everyday items – evidently Mathyes had been tidying and cleaning these.

'This is the very place where he died,' affirmed Master Bruys's servant. 'I was at his side, and I saw how his eyes would close no more, and he continued to stare at me, and at that moment I knew that all my sins were redeemed.'

Mathyes was an old man, perhaps around the same age as Bruys himself, and, as far as Melchior recalled, he had been a part of his Master's household for a very long time. Melchior had been selling him medicines for at least ten years, and more and more as time passed and as Master Bruys's health had grown feebler. Melchior prised from his bag the bottle of his sweet dram and asked if he could rest his feet a while and offer old Mathyes some kind of comfort. He could indeed, as it happened, because the servant was not offered such an exquisite drink every day.

Twenty-two years, Mathyes told him, for twenty-two years of his life he had stood beside his Master, helping him and faithfully serving him, until six days ago, in this very building, as a terrible torrent of rain poured down, his Master had breathed his last.

'And it was just the two of you here?' enquired Melchior.

'Oh, a priest came here, but the Master could no longer confess, as he'd lost the power of speech, but the Bridgettine priest gave him communion and anointed him, commending his soul into God's care. And the priest forgave his sins without confession, because when the Master could still speak he had gone to confession very regularly, so the priest let him kiss the cross anyway, and then there was the Abbess here, from the nuns, and a few other masters.'

As time passed, and he sipped from the bottle, Mathyes opened up somewhat. Bruys had ordered him – communicating with his servant by signs, and if you have served someone that long you understand even without words – to take him to Marienthal on 1 August because he felt death approaching. The Master had hoped that he would be granted time to make his last pilgrimage and then die in his own home. He had wanted to live until St Lawrence's Day at least and took with him only a nurse from the Sisters of St Michael and his servant Mathyes, and he had come here in his own cart on his last pilgrimage. The nurse and Mathyes usually spent the night some distance away with other servants in simpler houses designed for pilgrims, and the Master prayed alone here and fasted and several times had himself carried into St Bridget's Chapel where there was a reliquary. He often prayed there together with other supporters of the convent – Mr Schwalberg, Mr Huxer and the Knight Greyssenhagen, and even on the day that the Master died Greyssenhagen had come to the prayer house in the morning and asked Mathyes about his Master's health. His Master's health had not been good because the previous day's travel had worn him out, but by evening his health had got even worse. He could no longer breathe properly, he hadn't the strength to pray, he fainted away, and when the nurse said that his soul was being called Mathyes ran to the Abbess.

'It wasn't granted to him to live to see his own saint's day,' complained Mathyes, his eyes brimming with tears. 'He couldn't even hold the candle the priest gave him. When the priest washed him and anointed him with oil, he looked at the Abbess and me, but his gaze was already on the Kingdom of God, and he must already have been hearing the angels' bells ringing.'

Melchior understood that Bruys had suffered a stroke before his death, and he knew of no cure for it. Mathyes spoke, the Apothecary listened, and nothing in this tale seemed suspicious to him. The old man had died, perhaps a little sooner than he had hoped, but he died among friends and well-wishers; he died after he had received the sacrament, and his soul was ready to meet God. He had quietly expired, dying as old people do die.

'At what time of day did his soul depart to God?' asked Melchior.

'In the afternoon, when it was still raining fearfully. We couldn't even set off for town before dawn. Everything was flooded.'

'It was a powerful rainstorm,' Melchior confirmed. 'It came bucketing down.'

'His death was a blessing from God,' Mathyes affirmed. 'I take it as a holy sign that the Master, who had donated and prayed so much and kept his mind on holy things, was allowed by the Lord to die without pain in front of an altar to St Bridget.'

'Before he died did he, by any chance, mention Tobias Grote, the Tower-Master, his old friend?' Melchior asked suddenly. 'I ask because Master Grote died the very next day, and, from what I've heard, just before he died he had been wanting to tell Master Bruys something.'

'The Master couldn't speak,' Mathyes reminded him, 'oh, and he couldn't walk well either, could he? He left the Tower-Master gentleman twenty marks in his will. I haven't seen the Tower-Master at our house for quite a while, but they were good friends because Grote once saved the lives of Mistress Bruys and Johan, may the Lord bless them both.'

'It's an old, unfortunate story,' said Melchior sadly. 'So you were in your Master's house?'

'As I had been for ten years,' Mathyes reminded him, sipping from the bottle. 'I was previously a sailor on one of the Master's ships, but the Master noticed that I was clever, obedient and skilful and invited me ashore to his house. That was a few years before Johan was born, and I recall that it was a blessing from Heaven, for the Master had no heir ...'

Yes, that was how it was. His wife Gertrud had wanted to bear one more child, and masses were said for this purpose, and churches received donations, and, when the miracle happened, there had been no limit to Master Bruys's joy. But young Johan lived only twelve years, for a terrible and evil fire at the storehouses took his life.

'I remember that fire,' said Melchior. 'It started in the grain stores and –'

'The Master's store burned to the ground, and Johan had just gone down to the granary and must have been trapped among the burning beams. After it had been put out he was found under the rafters, mostly charred, but the Master recognized him – who wouldn't recognize their own son? – but his corpse lay there straight and peaceful as if he were accepting his fate without resisting …'

'And Mistress Gertrud was called by God soon afterwards,' Melchior recalled.

'The Mistress didn't come out of her chamber at all for several days after Johan's death, and when she did emerge she went only to St Nicholas's Church and wouldn't eat a single mouthful. She died of grief. She must have foreseen her end, as she asked the Pastor of St Nicholas's to take her confession, and she sent letters to her relations, and the next morning she didn't rise from her bed.'

These were the events that had led Master Bruys to his path of piety. He sought consolation in monasteries and churches, he visited the Dominicans and the Cistercian abbey at Padise, he wrote to the Church fathers in Lund and Rostock, he sought ways of repenting his sins that were most appealing to God – he even started flagellating himself. But just at that time the Order's vassals and the coastal people were starting to move more insistently for the foundation of a new community. The Toompea merchant Schwalberg was seeking allies and sympathizers, and Master Bruys had decided that his sufferings were the results of too little penitence. He was seized by the idea that by his money and his acts a new convent could be founded in Tallinn. He was in a long correspondence with the Rector of the University of Cologne, who recommended that he make a pilgrimage to Rome. The Master had entrusted his entire business to his associates, said Mathyes, and invited Mathyes along, and they had set off for Rome to pray at the church festivities at the tombs of St Peter and St Paul. They had with them a certificate from the Tallinn Chapter. They dressed in penitents' garb and travelled by ship to Lübeck to set off overland from there.

It had been a long and dreadful journey. They had encountered wars, perils and enemies, seen much suffering and had themselves suffered cold, hunger and every sort of vicissitude, but all this had only made Master Bruys even more determined in his penitence, and they journeyed south with even greater resolve. And when they were in the Habsburg lands, that was when the Master's health started seriously to give way. He had begun coughing terribly, his bodily strength was beginning to desert him and his legs gave him pain. Good people had helped them and led the way to the shrine at Mariazell. They had joined other pilgrims who were on their way there, and they had sung together and told each other their woeful tales. At Mariazell the monks had taken the Master to the infirmary and said that if he carried on with his journey he would die on the way. So Bruys had promised to send the monastery a hundred marks in silver and stayed there for a long time. The infirmary doctor knew that Bruys's feet were aching because of a congenital defect. This was a hereditary disease whereby men grow six toes on their feet, and some even said that it was the mark of Satan, who despoils people in this way, so that after death even the most pious can be spotted. The doctor said that these were all silly rumours. But the sixth toe does not want to remain on the body, as God has not ordained it, and it had started to rot. The doctor cut it off and treated the wound until Master Bruys could get back on his feet. They had diligently prayed before the Mariazell altar, and the Prior gave them both a certificate to show that their sins had been redeemed. By this time they had been too long on their journey, however, and Bruys decided to head for home. He was afraid that he might die on the way to Rome and would no longer be able to assist in the building of St Bridget's Convent or pay his debt to Mariazell. So they travelled back to Tallinn, and since that time there had been no holier man in the town. Without heirs and alone in the world before the face of God Bruys gave most of his assets to St Bridget's and decided to support the convent in word and deed and in every way.

'Without heirs ...' repeated Melchior. 'It is a terrible thing when a man is left in the world without children. But his oldest son, Thyl, whom he drove out, did your Master know whether he was still alive?'

'I never saw Thyl myself,' declared Mathyes. 'He was driven away before I came to serve the Master, but I remember that one day, about four years ago, a foreign merchant visited, bringing the Master messages and a letter. After that the Master told me that even the Lord God cannot give refuge to those who do not want to find refuge, and then he said something about the gallows in Magdeburg.'

'Ah,' noted Melchior, 'I have also heard that Thyl was hanged in Magdeburg.'

'Yes, that may be so. The Master never talked to me about Thyl, but I heard things from people in town – not that I would have gone gossiping about my Master's life and affairs. He strictly forbade that.'

And now Mathyes told Melchior what a faithful servant he had been and that the Master had kept him in mind in his will, allowing him to visit the prayer house to pray for him, and he was to stay for life at the townhouse where he now lived, even after the house was sold.

'That is a proper master, one who looks after his servants even after death,' cried Melchior.

'Yes, he left something to everyone who served him faithfully and took care that they would be provided for.'

'Did he also bequeath something to an old woman who was at his funeral, someone I'd never seen before? Do you remember, good man, that there was a woman in a grey dress who kept apart from the other mourners?'

Mathyes did remember the woman, but he didn't know who she was. 'Quietly and timidly she came among the mourners,' he said, 'and no one drove her away, but I don't know who she could have been.'

'And who is selling Master Bruys's house?' enquired Melchior.

'He entrusted it to Brassenke, the President of the Great Guild. He has distant relatives in Germany, but he didn't know them, and he feared that they might not be God-fearing people, so he didn't dare bequeath his house to them. So the President has to sell it off to the highest bidder and divide the sum into five parts, of which one goes to St Bridget's, one to St Nicholas's, one to be divided equally between several dozen churches in the Tallinn area, one to St John's Almshouse and one to the most direct descendant of the male line in Germany, although the Master didn't know precisely who that might be.'

'And that's why he didn't want to bequeath a bigger share of it,' muttered Melchior.

'Yes, and the Master thought that the Bruys clan had only met with disaster and misery in Tallinn, and he didn't want any more of them to come here to live. If we are destined to die out in Livonia then that is the will of the Almighty, he always said.'

They were drinking the bottle down to the dregs and remembering that holy man who would be talked of in Tallinn for a long time to come. Yes, thought Melchior, the Bruys clan was doomed to die out in Tallinn, but maybe that was as it should be. When the bloodline doesn't last, words and deeds will last longer because if one cannot bequeath one's assets to one's kin then one bequeaths them to the town and its people, each and every one. The Convent of St Bridget was rising and transforming the town, and it would be there for centuries while Laurentz Bruys rested for ever in the soil of St Nicholas's.

On arriving home, a little past the time when the preaching brethren would have finished divine service, Melchior found Dorn in the pharmacy doing three jobs at once – dandling Agatha on his knee, duelling with young Melchior with bits of wood instead of swords and gossiping about Council matters with Keterlyn. Dorn had, of course, been expecting Melchior, and when the Apothecary asked him why he replied that the Blackheads' Guildhall would be open for 'penny drinks' tomorrow, that there would be plenty of people there and that he had heard that the Flemish merchant Cornelis de Wrede should be one of them. Dorn asked where Melchior had been, and Melchior told him what he had heard at the new convent.

Before falling asleep in Keterlyn's arms the Apothecary was thinking again about Master Bruys. He thought about the fleeting time God gives to people to live and of the little that anyone can achieve in their lifetime. He thought that even when Master

Bruys's bones had long since decayed the magnificent Bridgettine Convent would still be standing, proclaiming far and wide that in Tallinn there had once lived a man who thought more about others and about the deprived than of himself. If a man's bloodline is not destined to continue then his works must.

21

Beyond Reppen's Pastures, South of Tallinn
9 August, Late Afternoon

MELCHIOR AND the Magistrate had arranged to go to the Blackheads to taste some beer after the Sunday service, but, as it turned out, they didn't get to the guildhall rooms. As they turned the corner on to the long street that ran to the Coast Gate, Melchior grabbed unexpectedly at Dorn's sleeve and pulled him back into the shade of a house. Dorn asked what the devil was going on, and Melchior indicated with his head across the street where, in front of the Blackheads' Guildhall, a couple of people stood engaged in a lively discussion. One of them was de Wrede and the other a young man in a plain cloak. They seemed to be bargaining or arguing over something but soon reached agreement and started walking together towards the marketplace.

'Who is that boy?' asked Dorn. 'I think I've seen him before.'

'I think I know who he is. He's the gravedigger's son from St Barbara's, Jacop. Estonian, I think. Let's follow them and see what they're up to.'

'Wouldn't it be simpler to grab them by the scruff of their necks and ask straight out?'

‘They’re not being accused of anything, and we might not find out what they’re doing if they don’t want to tell the truth,’ replied the Apothecary.

‘Mm, yes,’ muttered Dorn. ‘And it wouldn’t be hard to guess that they’re heading for St Barbara’s Cemetery.’

His prediction turned out to be correct. From Town Hall Square de Wrede and Jacop proceeded to the Seppade Gate, went through it and straight on to the graveyard, while Dorn and Melchior followed. On arrival Jacop led the Fleming along the narrow tracks among the graves until finally they arrived at the newer plots at the southern edge, which was more open with younger trees, so their followers had to keep a distance and lurk in the shade of the older oaks.

Jacop led de Wrede to three newly dug graves. He called out, and thereupon the head of his father, the gravedigger Tonnis, appeared from out of one of them. Young Jacop ran off, and de Wrede and the gravedigger stayed to chat. It wasn’t hard to see that the bargaining was continuing; de Wrede – merchant and ‘crafty miser’ as Dorn called all Flemings – laughed out loud and shook his head, Tonnis climbed out of the grave, waved his hands and settled it. They seemed finally to be reaching an agreement. The Fleming rummaged in his purse and handed the gravedigger some coins. Tonnis went away for a moment, brought back some tool and handed it to de Wrede.

‘Good God, Melchior, I’d swear that’s a small axe,’ exclaimed Dorn.

‘Yes, and I swear that de Wrede will now climb into the grave with that axe,’ replied the Apothecary.

Melchior was not wrong. Tonnis remained sitting at the edge of the grave as de Wrede worked in the pit. Soon the merchant climbed out of it and jumped into the next one as Tonnis tore at the end of a loaf and started munching on it.

'It seems to me that grave desecration is taking place,' said Dorn sullenly. 'It would be good to know what Lübeck law has to say about this.'

'Interesting,' noted Melchior, 'I wanted to ask you about that.'

Finally de Wrede seemed to have completed his work. He climbed out of the grave with a sack over his shoulder that looked like it must have weighed at least twenty pounds. He said goodbye to Tonnis and started walking towards the edge of the cemetery.

'I'm going after him,' said Melchior. 'I want to see where he's taking that sack.'

'They say,' muttered Dorn, 'that in one English monastery they go through the graveyard cutting bodies up, and that the monks sell the parts as holy relics. I heard it with my own ears. It came up in the Council once.'

'This stinks of something else,' said Melchior gloomily. 'But now I'm going.'

'You're not going anywhere without me. Would I leave you on your own?'

So once more they followed de Wrede who, on reaching the southern gate of the cemetery, turned on to the broad highway. This was the main road, paved with gravel and limestone rubble, that led south from the town and which could take you to a number of different places. Where, with his load of body parts cut from corpses, would the Flemish merchant go from here? Melchior had not the faintest idea.

It was afternoon, and there were plenty of people about. Dorn and Melchior remained several hundred paces behind the man and didn't have to make too much effort to keep themselves hidden.

Along the highway there were plenty of taverns and guesthouses; there was a small market, too. People were leading cattle and pigs, and it was bustling with farmers, artisans from the town, servants, professional people from the outskirts, farmhands from the Order's lands, horsemen, carousers and all manner of other folk, with carriages and carts rolling along.

'Interesting. Which way will he turn at the crossroads?' wondered Dorn.

'Where are his quarters in Tallinn?'

'I hear they're behind the Lysingnicke residence, President of the Blackheads, in a small house somewhere between St Olaf's Church and the Louenschede Tower.'

From here the highway went on to the Order's lands and up St Anthony's Hill, named after the Chapel of St Anthony situated upon it. Down to the west of the hillock lay the great wide pastures of the Toompea Knights. Beyond the rise three roads merged: the great highway that started at the Seppade Gate; the road over the sand dunes that led from St John's Almshouse and along which travellers coming from Marienthal could head south; and the road leading down from the south gate of the Small Castle of Toompea, which, running along the edge of the paddocks and behind St Barbara's Cemetery, led to the main highway near St Anthony's Chapel.

From St Anthony's Hill the highway continued over the sand dunes. To the east stood the gallows of Jerusalem Hill, where Dorn sometimes presided – it was clearly visible from the highway between the trees – and beyond that, past the dunes and the pines, was a swampy lake where the corpses of the executed were thrown. The grove by the roadside was called the Hangman's Garden, and, in times past, the executioner had also lived there. Now there was only a shack where the current incumbent made his preparations for executions and kept his tools. The very worst criminals were, as a very visible warning to travellers, killed by being dragged among the dunes on a wheel.

A little further on from the Hangman's Garden stood a large stone cross by the roadside, indicating where the town's and the Order's domains met. Magistrate Dorn's power did not extend beyond this point, and his word counted for nothing.

De Wrede, however, had gone past St Anthony's Chapel and kept walking, self-assuredly and boldly like a man who knows where he is going and why. He passed the Hangman's Garden and kept on marching. He kept pace with the market traders and farmers who had finished their business in town for the day and were going back home. He walked with a quick and determined step and did not seem to intend to rest his feet or drink a tankard of ale at a roadside tavern – of which there were fewer and fewer in number from here on.

A few market traders turned to the south-east at the next crossroads, but de Wrede kept on marching south. Melchior and Dorn had by now given up trying to guess his destination. The only thing they knew for sure was that he had been this way before and knew exactly where he was going. They had been walking for a good hour by this time, and other wayfarers had become fewer and further between, most of them having turned off into narrow lanes and dispersed into farms; generally those who had further to travel set off earlier in the day so as not to be overtaken by darkness.

After the crossing the road carried on through the pastures. Melchior's memory told him that this land belonged to the Bishop of Tallinn and was called Reppen's Pastures after his estate manager. They had to go at quite a pace to keep up with de Wrede.

Beyond the pastures the land became hilly again; the road went over a sandy, mossy wilderness on which a few sturdy pine trees grew. Ahead of them loomed a thick pine forest. Coming towards them were a few late-riding farmhands from the Order's estates. Between Melchior and Dorn and de Wrede there now walked only the odd ragged tramp, and they had to hang back even further so as not to be too obvious. The weather was cloudy and muggy, and rain seemed imminent, which worried them even more.

Dorn grumbled constantly about what nonsense was driving them on and on and that maybe de Wrede had decided to walk all the way to Antwerp, but without a juicy steak he wouldn't be trudging back to Tallinn, and where could a poor soul get a juicy steak at this hour, because it was still quite a way to the inn on the Weylandt Estate.

But then the forest began, and – for better or worse for them – the Fleming soon turned on to a path heading eastward and disappeared into the trees.

'Where does this road lead?' asked Dorn. 'I suppose to some liegeman's estate?'

Melchior didn't know exactly. Those few occasions when he had wandered this road he hadn't taken the least bit of interest in where all the countless tracks off it led. De Wrede, however, who had been just a short time in Tallinn, seemed to know it well. As far as Melchior knew there were a couple of farms belonging to an estate here by the forest, for every path leads somewhere. They stopped at the edge of the woods and consulted quickly about what to do next.

'I have no power in these lands,' Dorn stated, 'so I am a simple townsman like you. In fact, you are now the leader of our enterprise, so you have to say.'

'One possibility is that we turn right around and eat at the first tavern we come across – eat the juiciest steak they've got on their spit,' said Melchior, 'and never mind the fasting day.'

'That suits me very well,' agreed Dorn, 'exactly so – whatever else Mrs Dorn might think about it.'

'But *another* possibility is that we sneak quietly along behind the Fleming, because otherwise my mind will be distressed that we've been wasting precious time and still won't have found anything out. I'd rather you told me. Have you ever heard anything about the witch Kibutze?'

'Nothing,' replied Dorn.

'Well, I have. Keterlyn told me. Somewhere in the woods to the south live the Kibutze family, Estonians, who belong to some vassal but who are powerful witches and understand black magic. The peasant folk visit them to buy charms and things like that.'

'Holy Virgin, I've never heard of such a thing – and may the saints be praised for that.'

'But that doesn't mean that de Wrede wouldn't have,' said Melchior. 'I will sneak after him, and you can wait for me here or go back to town on your own.'

'And I certainly will not do that, because I'm not leaving you with the Fleming in the forest,' asserted Dorn.

'So, Magistrate, after him,' commanded Melchior.

It was now approaching evening. The wind had calmed, and the trees cast long shadows in the forest. The narrow forest track went first uphill among the pines and then down into a bushy landscape. De Wrede could go nowhere but straight along the path, and Melchior and Dorn went after him, trying not to step on twigs or make any other noise. Finally, beyond the thick undergrowth, the bushes began to thin out, and ahead there was a clearing, and a babbling brook could be heard. Melchior, who was walking in front, raised his hand in warning, and Dorn stopped. Then Melchior crouched and headed for the thick growth at the edge of the clearing. They threw themselves on the ground, pushed branches aside carefully and saw a glade in front of them at the back of which was the bank of a stream and, beside it, a large rock.

De Wrede had settled down to sit on the rock and seemed to be waiting calmly. He opened his sack and examined its contents then he pulled something out of it, examined it and put it back in the bag. Although Melchior already knew what de Wrede was carrying, he was still taken aback.

'That's a human hand,' whispered Dorn. 'That's what he cut off the corpse. Did he come here to peddle them, or what?'

'Who could have been in those graves?' asked Melchior. 'Three graves, all newly dug.'

'God, I don't know. One fisherman died recently, and then the sons of an innkeeper died of some terrible disease.'

'Terrible disease?' muttered Melchior. 'Some witches want the body parts of people who've died of diseases.'

They waited, and de Wrede waited, too. An hour or so passed, and the clearing grew dusky. Night noises began to sound from the forest. The wind had quite died down, but luckily it still wasn't raining. It was with the onset of darkness that a splashing sound came from the brook, as if someone were crossing a ford. De Wrede started and jumped up. The arrival was an older man. He walked with a stout pinewood stick, and he wore a filthy shirt; his beard was grey, and Melchior guessed that he was barefoot.

'A farmer,' whispered Dorn.

The brook and the hooting of night birds drowned out their conversation, but some of it could be heard. Melchior had to strain himself to understand – de Wrede spoke German with a Flemish accent, and the farmer seemed to have trouble with plain simple German.

'Not suitable at all,' said the old man. 'Too old, too wrong. Better must be, you understand, and from a child.'

'It was a right foot,' asserted de Wrede, and Melchior did not understand his next words.

The old man grumbled. They argued. 'Died at the full moon,' said the old man, and then, 'too old, younger … soul doesn't come out … and the hair …'

De Wrede handed his sack to the old man, who rummaged in it. He took something out – it must have been a human body part, but which one Melchior's eyes couldn't exactly make out – sniffed it and threw it over his shoulder towards the stream. He did the same with the next one, but the third seemed to suit him, and he stuffed it in his own sack.

Finally, the old man took out a human head. It seemed to Melchior that it was a girl's head, but he wasn't quite sure. The old man held it by the hair, examined it from a distance, tried it with his tongue and eventually put that in his sack, too. After that they seemed to be arguing about money. There was talk of three pennies and then of 'big silver', but in the end a deal was struck. De Wrede paid the old man, and they both went over the stream and disappeared into the gathering darkness.

Melchior and Dorn, however, wandered back along the road by which they had come. It was a long way, and they didn't stop at any tavern, for Mrs Wakenstede and Mrs Dorn wouldn't have liked that. On the way they cursed all Flemings and all Estonian sorcerers. They didn't even stop at the guesthouse for late wayfarers by the town wall, and Dorn raised hell at the gate, demanding that the portcullis be raised or tomorrow morning all the town guards would be hanging on the gallows.

And so they finally got back into town just before midnight.

22

Melchior's Pharmacy, Rataskaevu Street

10 August, Noon

'IT IS AN EVIL FAMILY,' Keterlyn told Melchior, 'the Kibutze. They're sorcerers. They aren't proper Christians. I have heard of them, but my family has never had any contact with them nor had anything to do with them. They live down that way, in the woods beyond Reppen's Pastures, and if they go to church it's only out of hypocrisy. There are those quacks and witches who help people in need, mix potions and boil up medicines as you do, but there are also those who call forth the spirits of the dead – and not like the Redeemer – to chastise them. They call them out, talk with them about things beyond the grave and command them. I think it is only demons from hell who come out when summoned, and they steal people's souls away.'

'These sorcerers seem to take money, too,' muttered Melchior.

'The Wizard of Iinistagana, who really does know how to help people, only takes money from those who have got better from his treatment. He has no use for human body parts at all. He simply picks plants from the meadow and from the forest floor, boils them up and charms them with spells.'

Keterlyn had mentioned the Wizard of Iinistagana before,

who he was related to and how. As far as Melchior understood it, this man was, in his own world, the same as an apothecary in the town; he mixed cures and boiled potions. But there was another sort of sorcerer, one who wanted to open that gate that has been closed shut by the saints and the laws of the Lord God, and if such a witch got it open it was not human souls that came out but the minions of Satan.

It was Monday, and the noon lunch-hour. Melchior's bones were aching from the previous day's journey. He had closed the shop and was taking a meal in the kitchen. For lunch Keterlyn had cooked him a little piece of pork and two turnips and a carrot. As a side dish Melchior was chewing some dark bread baked the day before yesterday, on which he had rubbed garlic, and sipping some ale. He was sitting in the kitchen and had received a scolding for the previous night's adventure. All the more diligently had he been working in the pharmacy this morning and tied up a largish sum for any possible eventuality. The town's doctor had visited and berated him as to why the mixing of his prescriptions was taking so much time lately, and Melchior had replied that he was a witness of the town's boundaries and had to go and inspect them occasionally. Three times he had sworn the oath of an assistant bailiff before the Town Council, and if the Magistrate demanded it, he had to fulfil it. And then a servant had come from the Great Guild and had invited the Apothecary, by authority of the Knight Greyssenhagen, to the Guildhall of the Great Guild on Wednesday where Master Arend Goswin was being approved as a new patron of St Bridget's, defending the interests of the convent before the town and the Council. That startled many people but not Melchior. He recalled Goswin's tears at Master Bruys's funeral and the anguished heart with which he spoke of his own spiritual torment. Yes, if anyone were to carry on Master Bruys's enterprise it was Arend Goswin and no one else.

And, of course, in the morning Melchior had had to tell Keterlyn where he had been until late last evening and why there was no smell of ale on him like other decent men coming home from the Guildhall rooms after midnight.

'I'd like to get together with your Wizard of Iinistagana some time,' said Melchior, wiping his greasy chin on his sleeve. 'Maybe he has something useful to teach me. Pharmacy, as my father used to say, never ends and is never complete. There's always something new to find. The new becomes old and then the old becomes new again.'

'He never visits the town. And there are several other things he doesn't do – like hunting murderers or ghosts.' As Keterlyn said this rather pointedly Melchior thought it wiser to keep quiet and carry on eating. 'One thing I have to tell you,' Keterlyn continued, 'if you're still hunting that ghost. I heard at the market from the wife of Rosen the Saddler, who is a good friend of the wife of Kogge, the merchant, that it was their daughter Ursula who had been at home crying and talking about a ghost at the Unterrainer house.'

Melchior raised his gaze from his plate with an alarmed expression. 'Ursula? The one who is in love with Simon, Casendorpe's apprentice, and thinks no one knows about it?'

'That's the one,' said his wife. 'A few days ago apparently. Ursula was terribly upset and cried at home and admitted that she'd heard the Ghost of Rataskaevu Street.'

'She must have been with Simon at the time. I should go looking for that boy.'

Afterwards, though, their conversation shifted back to why Melchior couldn't stay at home and get on with his job and earning bread for his family. For instance, what business did he have in going over to Marienthal?

'Even I didn't know what I was looking for, and I don't know whether I found what I wasn't looking for or whether I found out that what I thought was true was false,' replied the Apothecary. Hearing this Keterlyn felt like emptying the pan over her husband's head. But Melchior sipped his ale and told her what he had seen and heard there.

'Very odd,' said Keterlyn, 'very odd and very strange.' And she looked at her husband seriously with astonished eyes.

Melchior put his piece of meat back on the plate and took a big quaff of ale. 'Are you thinking of those words of Master Bruys about the Lord God and refuge?' he asked at length.

'No, I'm thinking of the five strange coincidences between Master Bruys and that unknown tramp's corpse.'

'I don't understand,' muttered Melchior. But soon he did, and soon he cursed himself that it hadn't occurred to him before.

'It occurs to me that someone wanted to make that tramp like Master Bruys,' said Keterlyn. 'Bruys wasn't able to talk before he died, and the tramp had his tongue cut out. Bruys was an old man and couldn't have children any more, and the tramp had also had his manhood cut off. Bruys couldn't walk before he died, and the tramp had a foot sawn off after he died, so it was as if he couldn't have walked. Bruys flagellated himself, and the tramp had been flagellated.'

'That's it. That's it,' Melchior cried. 'Why didn't I see that straight away? But the fifth thing? What was the fifth coincidence?'

'The fifth is that they're both dead, and both died on practically the same day. But one died by himself and the other was killed.'

'One day's difference,' said Melchior. 'The tramp was killed when the town already knew about Bruys's death. Bruys died during a downpour, and ...' He stopped in mid-sentence. 'The rain was bucketing down,' he suddenly whispered. 'It was terribly heavy rain. They couldn't send word from the convent that Bruys had died. Oh, St Cosmas. And those other things, woman, those other things – those other things might mean something quite different.'

Keterlyn shook her head. As usual, her husband's talk was starting to get confusing. 'What's the significance of that downpour?'

Melchior was about to answer, but then a knocking was heard from the shop. Keterlyn rushed to answer and found the bad-tempered joiner Ditman at the door, who grumbled as to whether the Apothecary was going to have too long a lunch-hour because he urgently needed a strong mixture to ease a stomach ache, that one made of bitter herbs.

Melchior returned to the pharmacy, decanted some stomach medicine and extracted the price of three stoups for two of them from the joiner. A little later the next customers arrived – he had to work and mix cures, but his mind was constantly on Keterlyn's words. Five coincidences. Five. And yet, shouldn't one of those be the key? Even if it wasn't precisely what Keterlyn supposed, something that explained everything and announced to him ... something more terrifying than resurrection from the dead.

Among those who came into the pharmacy Melchior's eye was caught by an elderly woman named Margelin Witte, the sister of the Pastor of the Church of the Holy Ghost, from the Unterrainer house. As always when he saw her Melchior was slightly startled. The strangest thing was that, although the Pastor's sister must have been over sixty, she was still an attractive woman, and it was written on her face that decades ago she must have been quite a beauty.

And yet, despite the comeliness, there was something forbidding, something cruel about her. Sometimes Melchior thought the woman was insane, but then he was not quite sure. Margelin looked after her brother; they had no housekeeper or servant. She didn't often go around town, and she was regarded as a stranger because she had come to Tallinn only two years before. But she lived in the Unterrainer house, in front of which that tramp had been killed and in whose cellar there might still be immured the body of the wretched Brother Adelbert.

This time Margelin needed something for wounds, something strong that would stop them festering. Melchior conjured up his most sympathetic face, offered Margelin a sweet – 'free of charge to a neighbour' – and asked for what kind of wounds and who needed this medicine.

'For the Pastor of the Church of the Holy Ghost,' said Margelin. 'Do you have any lily-of-the-valley wine, Apothecary?'

'I do,' said Melchior, 'but the thing is, without the approval of the town doctor I'm not actually allowed to make it. But, you know,' he said more quietly, bending in closer to Margelin, 'if I could have a look at those wounds with my own eyes I dare say I could prescribe that medicine without the approval. Lily-of-the-valley is poisonous; it's dangerous.'

'I know it's poisonous,' replied the woman in a whisper, also leaning closer to Melchior. 'Lily-of-the-valley is *very* poisonous.' And again there flashed in her eyes a sort of cruelty, a kind of madness. *Heavens above, do I really recognize this,* thought Melchior. Does one madman recognize another?

'What wounds does the Pastor have then?' he ventured.

'Mr Gottschalk was severely repenting of his sins, and his blood was united with Jesus Christ's blood,' whispered the woman, 'but the wounds are not closing, and the Pastor sent me after medicine.'

'Then he has been repenting much too hard.'

'Sins have to be repented severely. The Master himself said that.'

'Oh, well, if the Master said it ...' Melchior stepped over to his shelf of medicine bottles, looking for a particular oil, 'the Master's words have to be obeyed.' He had no idea who the Master might be. He put two small bottles in front of Margelin Witte. 'One of these is amber oil and the other lily-of-the-valley wine. They're supposed to be mixed together and then drunk. It stops a wound from festering. But since we don't have the doctor's seal of approval, and I haven't seen those wounds, I don't know how strongly to mix them. Lily-of-the-valley is poisonous – as we've agreed – and I might make it too strong. I have to see the penitent's wounds.'

'Then I will show you the way to them – and, who knows, maybe that way will be the way of your own penitence,' whispered Margelin. 'Come and treat the poor sinner's wounds.'

'I'm coming,' replied Melchior. 'Oh, I'll come with pleasure.'

23

The Unterrainer House, Rataskaevu Street

10 August, Afternoon

FOR THE FIRST TIME in his life Melchior stepped over the threshold of the Unterrainer house. It was very ordinary. The *diele* looked like the *diele* of any other house in Tallinn. It was impersonal. In the summer heat it gave shade from the blazing sun and in winter a warm refuge from the searing cold. And, of course, being the house of a holy man, even the *diele* featured a wooden image of the Redeemer and an altar on the west wall. When the Apothecary arrived the Pastor came downstairs and stood staring in amazement at Melchior.

'Your esteemed sister invited me to treat your wounds,' said Melchior.

'And he knows about the Master,' said Margelin. 'He knows that the Master's word has to be obeyed.'

Pastor Gottschalk Witte was of short stature with a balding head and an unkempt appearance. He did not exude strength and power, only piety and modesty. His congregation loved him, and the Council held him in high esteem. By the wish of the Bishop of Tallinn the Council had invited him from a German university, where he had received his education and previously lived. He looked like a very pious and rather feeble man, and he was in a state of terror, that Melchior could see clearly.

'I was told that you have wounds,' he said and bowed. 'And I came to treat them. If you would show me your injuries, Pastor, then I'll know how strong a solution of lily-of-the valley to mix for them.'

And then, after they had gone into the kitchen, Melchior carried on chatting. He said he had also brought an ointment of salvia, mint, marjoram and dill because maybe he didn't need such a strong drug as lily-of-the-valley, for you had to be very careful with it. Lily-of-the-valley is a good cure, but it is very poisonous, and so on, and he praised the Witte residence, that it was beautiful and clean and one could instantly see that Mistress Margelin was a diligent housekeeper and took good care of the household. That before the Wittes had moved in the house had been empty for a long time, and it was always hard to settle down in a house such as this with so much cleaning and housework to get rid of the dampness and the dirt. But one could see straight away that just as Mr Witte took care of his parishioners so Mistress Margelin took care of the house, and so forth, and that all sorts of tales were told about this house, about who had lived here previously and what terrible things had happened and ...

Meanwhile Margelin was helping Gottschalk Witte remove his coat and shirt, and then Melchior saw the wounds. Yes, they were wounds from flagellation, no doubt about it. His whole back was covered in them, and some of them had started festering and must hurt a great deal.

'I'd rather rub them with ointment,' decided Melchior. 'They're not such terrible wounds as to need lily-of-the-valley. If the lady will bind them up they'll be all right in a couple of days.'

'We're very grateful to you, Apothecary,' said Witte quietly.

'Don't mention it,' said Melchior kindly, 'and don't mention it to the town doctor either. He would prescribe the same sort of ointment and nothing else. But doesn't this say something about your piety, Pastor, that you have beaten yourself so hard to repent of your sins? Not every clergyman has such courage and enthusiasm – at least, not in Tallinn.'

Actually Melchior had not heard of any lay brothers in Tallinn beating themselves and so valiantly seeking penitence. In the monasteries and convents, monks and nuns were sometimes punished by whipping if they had committed some disgraceful act – whipping was said to be a good method for subduing the flesh – but as for lay preachers doing it ... Melchior recalled that wasn't it St Peter Damian who had once written a eulogy on the virtues of flagellating oneself?

'I'm sure that our Pastor does not have any sin on his conscience so great that it would actually merit a whipping,' said Melchior half in jest. Witte, however, was alarmed at this; Melchior could clearly feel that under his fingers as he was rubbing ointment into the man's back. The wounds were caused by a short whip. The wheals were more delicate down below and deepest around the shoulder-blades, ending with a coarser rupture; therefore the end of the whip must have had a knot. Melchior greased the wounds while thinking about what kinds of sins would necessitate such self-abasement.

'Oh, but the Master said that a whip wards off sins, and a virtuous and pious man may find happiness and joy in it even when he hasn't sinned,' Margelin suddenly whispered.

'Shut up, woman,' Witte snapped.

'But Melchior knows about the Master, he said so himself.'

'I'm afraid my knowledge of the Master is quite sketchy,' remarked Melchior with a smile.

'I received a very stern education at Heidelberg,' said Witte. 'Only by cleansing my soul may I stand before my congregation and demand the same virtuous life of them as of myself.'

'One can only respect your fortitude,' said Melchior.

'The Master said that –' Margelin started to say, but Witte interrupted her sharply.

'You have jobs to do in the laundry, sister.'

'Yes, dear brother,' said Margelin meekly and left.

'These wounds will close up quickly,' Melchior continued. 'They aren't deep by any means, and the pus has not got far, but it would not be a good idea, Pastor, to flog yourself again too soon.'

'I'll try to be more gentle with myself in future,' he promised.

'That would certainly be wise. It seems as if you, sir, have been taking all the sins committed in this house on to your own shoulders. All sorts of things have been said about what once happened here. True, it was all of seventy years ago, but a woman was immured in the cellar, and, do you know, sir, that the skeleton of a certain monk might still be lying down there?'

Witte was startled again but didn't answer.

'Sometimes I like to take an interest in the things that go on in my own street, and all sorts of tales are told, indeed,' Melchior prattled on, putting the lotion carefully on the wounds. 'A certain Cristian Unterrainer, who lived here once, had caught his wife in the act of sinning – my tongue can't be brought to say how exactly, but they say it was with a Dominican. And then he walled his wife in, alive, in the cellar, and this was discovered … But, do you know what happened the other day at the Dominican Monastery? On St Dominic's Day they buried a lay brother, and for that purpose they dug open the grave of that same wicked monk, and then, sir, truly, I swear to you, they found that the coffin was empty. There wasn't a single bone or anything in it – not that I mean to say that he's definitely still in the cellar, but, you know, people do start to talk.'

Witte was silent, but his body was tense, and he listened attentively to the story, which he evidently regarded as ordinary apothecary's gossip. Apothecaries are known to be inquisitive chatterboxes, and Witte had come to this town recently and obviously didn't know what many others knew, that when Melchior talked of crimes and corpses he wasn't just doing it to keep his mouth warm.

'And then all those stories about the haunting in this house – you must have heard of those, Pastor? That the spirit of that poor sinner woman still haunts this place and tempts sinners? Of course, *I* don't believe those stories, but, you know, three people have perished recently after telling that story, so, you never know, is there a curse or a scourge or something ...?'

'A Christian should not be telling such stories,' said Witte sternly, 'and an educated man such as yourself, Apothecary, certainly should not.'

'It's not *me* telling them. I'm only reporting what they're saying in town. You know yourself, sir, that all kinds of stories come into an apothecary's shop, some of them pious but some of them a little more ungodly. You must know what is being said about this house, and some say they have seen that ghost here quite recently ...'

'I've never heard it,' said Witte. 'No ghost, no nothing. Are you finished now, Apothecary? How much do I owe you?'

'It might be better, Pastor, if you say a prayer for the medicine at the Church of the Holy Ghost,' opined Melchior.

'I will certainly do that.'

Witte got up, covering his body with the shirt. They said goodbye. Melchior bowed and gathered his medical things together. Witte withdrew and went upstairs. At the street door Melchior bumped into Margelin, who was coming from the washroom in the yard, carrying under her arm a batch of washed clothes and casting a very strange look at him.

'The Pastor will recover,' promised Melchior. 'Madam needn't worry about it at all.'

'Thirty-three and a half days of suffering,' whispered Margelin, looking Melchior steadfastly in the eye, 'and then the whole world will be saved, so the Master said. I suppose you know that yourself, Apothecary.'

'Thirty-three and a half days,' Melchior whispered back. He had no idea what the madwoman was talking about. But he did know that if anyone wants to lie, they never tell a complete lie, and there is always a grain of truth in their story. At the same time, the fact that a person is mad does not mean that their whole story is borne of an evil spirit and excessive phlegm accumulated in the head. Not the *whole* story. 'Thirty-three and a half, so it has to be. Thus it is written,' he repeated.

'Oh, it is, of course. The Holy Virgin herself wrote thus, and the angels brought her message to Rome.'

'The Holy Virgin wrote it, oh yes, of course,' agreed Melchior, although he was quite sure that Brother Hinric would hardly agree with such an interpretation of the Scriptures.

'And the whips will wipe away the whole world's sins,' said the woman. 'Whips will save the world.'

'So it is,' agreed Melchior again. 'But I would also say that too much whipping may bring with it a great bodily scourge. I don't suppose madam will show me the Pastor's whip? If there's old blood on a whip, and it mixes with new blood coming from a wound, then too much poisonous pus gets into the wound, and that's bad, that's very bad. So wrote St Damian.'

'Oh, would you like to see the whip, Apothecary?' Margelin asked. 'It's here, right here.'

The pile of clothes fell from Margelin's hands on to the stairs, and under it she had been holding the whip. It had a short handle and a leather cord about an ell long at the end of which was a coarse knot, one that would deliver the most pain. Margelin's arm was sinewy, and she held the handle so that her knuckles were white. Her hand loved this whip.

Melchior took the whip and smeared it with salve. He said that would stop the poison, and the Pastor need not be afraid. He need not be afraid even of ghost stories because they were just idle gossip.

'It was a terrible sin that was once committed in this house,' said Margelin. 'The Master punished those wanton ones. The Master knew how to punish. But his wife's spirit is still here, yes, we have heard it. But we're not afraid of it. She's afraid of us. She does us no harm because she's afraid. She howls at night because she's repenting her sins. The Master decreed that she should suffer in this way so that she would never see the gates of Paradise.'

'The Master himself?' asked Melchior cautiously.

'Oh, yes, this is the Master's house,' whispered Margelin. 'And the sinner's spirit which can find no peace comes where there is a cold spot …'

'Sister,' boomed the loud voice of Gottschalk Witte suddenly. 'Sister, where are you? I'm waiting for you. My wounds have to be bound up.'

'A sinner is calling me,' said Margelin. 'I have to go.'

'Of course, gracious madam, go,' said Melchior.

Margelin gathered up the washing from the floor, hid the whip under it and left, casting Melchior a strangely inviting and inexplicable look from the threshold. Melchior did not, however, hurry back to the pharmacy. He waited until Margelin had closed the door and then slipped along a passageway to the courtyard alongside the house and straight into the yard of the Unterrainer house. As a little boy he had played here. The old stables were still in use then, and the facility had not yet been completely transferred to Mäealune Street under the slopes of Toompea. These old stables by Town Hall Square were encircled by a low wall from the backyards of the houses on Rataskaevu Street, and there were several dark recesses and exciting lairs where it was fun to play.

Right beside the Unterrainer house was Master Goswin's property, and there had never been a wall between them. Someone must once have built an enclosure out of slats, but that had long ago decayed and been buried under weeds. In the backyard of Witte's house was a washroom, a little wooden shack and, beside it, a woodshed, behind which, against the wall of the stables, grew a large bush. Similar structures belonging to Goswin's house were at the southern edge of the land so that between the two houses were just this garden and a narrow passage. From here the narrow ventilation windows of the salt-cellars opened out on to both houses. Seen from Goswin's house there was just the unused edge of the land; seen from Witte's, on the other hand, there was the principal area for visits and activities. Melchior looked around for a while and found that from behind the bush one passed along a cluttered path to St Nicholas's Church, exactly as it had been during his childhood. From there one could walk along the back edge of Goswin's land to an orchard, located between Goswin's and Tweffell's houses, and onwards to Rataskaevu Street. This could be an ideal escape route for anyone needing, say, to escape from the Unterrainer house on Rataskaevu Street and then creep behind the houses straight to the well and then hotfoot it to St Nicholas's.

Say, for example, if you have dealt somebody three deep wounds, and the town guards have heard it and are now running towards the Unterrainer house.

24

The Council Prison
11 August, Late Morning

A COURT ATTENDANT stepped into the pharmacy just at the point that Melchior noticed the delicious smell of pea-and-ham-hock soup wafting from the kitchen. There was a queue of people in need snaking into the pharmacy, and they wanted their cures before the lunch-hour.

The attendant, however, marched straight in and up to Melchior, and after he'd whispered his message into the Apothecary's ear Melchior decided immediately that pea soup tasted better when it had been standing for a while, and, right now, it was more important to go to the Council than care for the sick.

Dorn's message had been brief and clear. 'Cornelis de Wrede has been summoned to the Council's prison, and it would be worthwhile for Melchior to appear there also, in the name of St Victor.'

Melchior shut the pharmacy and ran down the street towards the Town Hall, turned the corner and stood panting in front of the door of the low stone building into which no townsman would ever go of his own free will. This was the Council's prison, where they kept those whose guilt was still under investigation or whose punishment was restricted to one night spent in the cells. The more vicious criminals were taken from here to the prison in the Bremen Tower – mostly after they had been tortured, according to procedure. Drunks and brandishers of knives, who were not guilty of anything more serious, spent one night in the cell and were then taken to the Magistrate's office. From there their path might lead to the pillory. In the back room of the prison was a torture chamber where, according to Lübeck law, they questioned those who would not confess voluntarily. It was a grim place, but often it was the only place where the truth might rise above lies and silence, and it was under the Magistrate's jurisdiction.

Melchior entered the chilly stonewalled chamber, which had shackles on the wall and one plain chair fixed to the floor. This was the antechamber of the torture room where the prisoner was interrogated – sometimes there was no need to torture them. The air and the walls of the prison, the words and expressions of the officers working here, and sometimes just the sight of the implements of torture, would open quite a few mouths.

When Melchior stepped inside he saw the Flemish merchant de Wrede sitting on the chair with Dorn standing in front of him. He was sitting freely; he was not shackled, and he had not been tortured. Dorn grasped Melchior by the arm and led him over to the narrow window.

'I had this chap brought in here,' he said to Melchior in a low voice.

'So I see. And what does he say?'

'So far nothing much. I ordered him to confess everything, but he says he has nothing to confess except that he is running his business honestly in Tallinn and that all the Blackheads can vouch for him.'

'I don't doubt it,' murmured Melchior.

The Brotherhood of Blackheads was large and powerful. They were rich and getting steadily richer. The Blackheads were loved, and they did everything to be loved even more – they arranged splendid tournaments and other entertainments for the townsfolk.

'Listen,' shouted de Wrede, 'how long are you going to keep me here? And I don't need an apothecary. There's nothing wrong with me.'

'Oh, there isn't *now*,' remarked the Magistrate darkly, 'but let's see how things are when you've sat in that chair for a little while.' And Dorn's gaze fell on the straps that would shackle the prisoner to the chair.

'Are you threatening me?' whined de Wrede in response. 'But you can't threaten me. If I'm not accused of anything you can't keep me here. And no one has accused me of anything. I know the law.'

'But what if I charge you myself?' said the Magistrate suddenly, his lips twitching. Melchior knew this sign. Dorn was getting angry. Dorn had not forgiven de Wrede for the long hike into the forest beyond Reppen's Pastures, and he was not likely to do so in a hurry.

'Interesting. What are you going to charge me with? Have I overcharged someone in some deal? Then they were fools themselves. And I haven't gone against any Council ordinance, since I don't weave cloth myself and don't sell herring in the marketplace –'

Dorn cut him off. 'What if I charge you with witchcraft and tell the Bishop and the Dominicans? Then there will be a heavy court procedure and a big pyre built on the gallows hill.'

This hit home. De Wrede was so alarmed that he hit his head against the back of the chair and bit his lips.

'Have you swallowed your tongue now?' asked Dorn maliciously.

‘I haven’t taken part in any witchcraft in Tallinn,’ murmured de Wrede anxiously. ‘I don’t understand what you’re talking about.’

‘Ah, you don’t *understand* …’ jeered Dorn. ‘You were asking earlier why I had you brought here. I’ll tell you. I invited you here to show you a couple of interesting things.’

Dorn banged on the door of the torture chamber, and from it emerged a man who could be recognized from his red uniform as Wulf Bose, the town executioner. The man had in his hand a few spiked rings, skewers, hooks and a very terrifying-looking contraption with screws, shaped like a wood plane. He put them on the table in front of Dorn, bowed and went to the corner of the room.

‘Oh, what a lovely device,’ warbled Dorn with satisfaction. ‘I would ask you to stand up and take a look over by the door to the back room there. There’s an interesting wheel-shaped thing, and I can tell by the smell that the hot coals in the brazier are just about ready.’

‘Quite ready, sir,’ said Executioner Bose. ‘Red hot and scorching more painfully than hell.’

‘Go, go and have a look over by the door,’ urged Dorn. And as de Wrede stepped towards the door, looked over the threshold and then again at the Magistrate, even in the dim room it was clear to see that he had turned pale and gone weak in the knees. He was gasping for air as he spoke.

‘Wh-what do you w-want from me?’ whispered de Wrede. ‘I don’t practise witchcraft.’

‘You see, he’s still denying it,’ Dorn observed to Melchior. ‘Mr Bose, do you have a couple of hours free, or do you have to be somewhere?’

‘I’m completely at your disposal, sire,’ said Bose obligingly. ‘I don’t have any tasks anywhere. Besides, this wheel of ours wasn’t working so well last time it was used, so we fixed it, but we haven't had a chance to try it out since with the full weight of a man.'

'I haven't practised any witchcraft,' cried de Wrede in terror. 'I'm a merchant. I run my own business. I have certificates to prove it.'

'Have you been running your business in the woods beyond Reppen's Pastures?' asked Melchior suddenly and quietly.

De Wrede was petrified. His eyes bulged as if he had been hit hard in the stomach. He fumbled for the back of the chair, found it and collapsed into it. But he was a quick thinker and had a robust spirit, for the very next moment he declared, 'Reppen's Pastures are not on the town's lands. Whatever I did or didn't do there the town cannot charge me. Your authority doesn't reach there.'

'But my eyes do,' countered Dorn forcefully. 'And do you think that if I write to the Order and the Bishop that you've been going there for sorcery that they'll leave it at that?'

'Go ahead and write then,' replied de Wrede pluckily, 'if you have witnesses. I have witnesses.'

'What sort of witnesses?' demanded Melchior rapidly.

'Ones who will testify that on Sunday I spent the whole evening in the Blackheads' Guildhall.'

'Oh, but I didn't say I was thinking of Sunday evening,' declared Melchior with a quick wink.

'Now you've landed yourself in it,' shouted Dorn.

'I haven't done anything of the sort. I was *supposing* that you were talking about Sunday, and whatever happened outside of the town you can't charge me with.'

'I am charging you with desecrating consecrated graves in St Barbara's Churchyard,' said Melchior abruptly, 'and St Barbara's is on the town's lands. You have been cutting up corpses of the souls entrusted to God's care so that they may not appear before the face of Jesus as when they died, and you have thereby committed a heinous crime against the ordinances of the Bishop of Tallinn and the Council.'

'Exactly,' affirmed Dorn.

'I saw with my own eyes how you paid Tonnis and dismembered corpses for the purpose of sorcery on ground consecrated by the Bishop. The Magistrate can testify to this, as he saw it, too, and the Magistrate's word counts here in town. You won't find witnesses against his word; not a single Blackhead would dare to swear a lie against the Magistrate's testimony. Don't be a fool, de Wrede. Tonnis wouldn't last a minute in this torture chamber – not even the time it would take me to say the Lord's Prayer.'

Melchior said this clearly and surely, his gaze fixed on the Fleming's eyes, and he saw that de Wrede was broken. His head hung down, and his hands trembled.

'What do you want from me?' he asked in a cracked voice.

'The truth,' replied Melchior. 'No more and no less.'

'This damned town …' whispered the Fleming. 'I knew it, I knew –'

'Don't mumble,' barked Dorn. 'Speak clearly so I can hear. You see these contraptions on the floor, don't you?'

'And it will only be possible for the Magistrate to be merciful and Master Bose to test out the wheel on someone else if you tell the truth and you swear that it is the only truth. You will also tell us everything you wanted to know from Rinus Götzer in the tavern by the harbour, what you were doing at St Michael's Convent, why you rob graves in the town of Tallinn and what you want from that sorcerer Kibutze,' demanded Melchior.

De Wrede had to steady himself. He asked for something to drink, and Dorn had some small beer brought to him. He drank greedily, and the beer spilled onto his jacket as he drank from the tankard with shaking hands.

Then he looked straight ahead with a sad expression, shook his head and finally said in a broken voice, 'My father and uncles have a business in Antwerp that trades with Tallinn and Riga. We buy grain, wax and bearskins from here because we're not allowed to trade directly with Russia, and we sell cloth, salt, spices, paper and wine. We have friends and connections in this region, especially in Riga. My brother wasn't a merchant. He didn't go in for that sort of thing, and in Antwerp he joined the Guild of St Luke to become a painter.'

'Your brother's name was Gillis de Zwarte?' asked Melchior, and the Fleming raised his head in surprise.

'So you know then?'

'Answer,' thundered Dorn.

'Yes, that was my brother's name. In our family we use both de Zwarte and de Wrede, but I have reason to be afraid, so I haven't told anyone that Gillis was my brother.'

Gillis de Zwarte had been an apprentice painter at the Guild of St Luke in Antwerp, but he wasn't talented enough to become a master there and start painting for churches, so there would not have been enough work. Since his family had good connections in Riga, they managed to get him commissions from churches there. Once in Riga he wrote home that the earnings were miserable, and Livonia was far poorer than Burgundy, but he had made a name for himself. He spent two years in Riga, and when the work there was starting to dry up he was invited to Tallinn to paint frescoes on the walls of St Nicholas's and the Church of the Holy Ghost.

Gillis would have preferred to paint saints' life stories on the walls and nothing else. His few letters from Tallinn were sad; he was troubled by homesickness, and he complained that people in this country didn't understand art.

'We have our own painters,' interjected Dorn sternly. 'We don't need any Flemish flapdoodlers here.'

'That's just what I said,' said de Wrede, taking a sip of beer and continuing. 'Gillis wrote two letters from Tallinn. In the first he cursed the churches for how stingy and deceptive everyone involved was. They strike a contract for a humiliatingly low fee and then they start chiselling away at it some more, so you have to go to the Council to get justice. But he said he'd got commissions from a couple of aldermen and from a wealthy citizen who also wanted paintings for his houses. He was hoping to be finished by autumn and then come home, show off his certificates and thus perhaps get himself recognized as a master before the Guild of St Luke. He was an enterprising and enthusiastic boy, and he loved painting. Father didn't force him to be a merchant and let him do as his heart desired ...' De Wrede fell silent and took another sip of beer.

'He wrote two letters,' said Melchior. 'What was in the second?'

'His second was short and confused. He must have been drunk when he wrote it because he did have that fault of occasionally drinking too much. He wrote that his latest work was ready, he'd been paid well and he was looking for a ship so he could get home before the autumn storms. He wouldn't survive another dark autumn and winter in this town. He wrote that he'd seen a ghost risen from the dead, which now haunted him at night and that he had to flee from it so it wouldn't drive him mad and kill him. This letter came on our company's ship. He was supposed to have arrived home on the next one, but only a coffin turned up in Antwerp. There he lay, his head smashed in, and we buried him and wept and cursed this damned town.'

'Choose your words better,' snapped Dorn, but Melchior silenced him with a wave of his hand.

'That last letter. Do you still have it?'

'I have it here,' replied de Wrede, tapping his head with his finger. 'It was just as I told you. His work was finished, including the last job, he had been paid well and now he was starting to look for a ship that would sail him back to his beloved homeland before the autumn and the storms. "The autumns are so terrible and the winters even more horrible. Everything freezes. This is a damned town, and I've been forced to paint unholy marks. And I've seen a ghost, risen from the dead, and now it haunts my nights and won't let me shut my eyes in peace. I have to escape because otherwise I'll lose my reason. It will destroy me. It will kill me." Those were his words. The final line was in such jumbled writing that we couldn't read it.'

'And that was the letter which brought you to Tallinn?' said Melchior.

'My father and uncles sent me here. The men on the ship told us that he'd fallen at night in the harbour while drunk and been killed by the blow, and since he'd already paid for his passage they used his money to buy him a coffin and sent him home because there was no one to give the money back to. I was instructed to punish the guilty party and ...' De Wrede fell silent, coughed and groped for the tankard, which was almost empty. Melchior whispered to Dorn to have some ale brought in. The Magistrate looked doubtfully at Melchior but asked Master Bose to see if there was any ale in the antechamber because he was thirsty.

'So you came to avenge your brother? Because his head had been smashed in?'

'We were told that he had fallen in the harbour against a large rock, but we didn't believe it. His wound looked as if someone had hit him with something hard. And those words about the damned town, unholy marks and the ghost –'

'In the churches here it is the custom, and it is done by the command of the Bishop himself, for evil to drive out evil itself,' interrupted Melchior. 'Don't you know the Scriptures? The Mark of Triquetrum *has* to be painted on a church wall so that evil demons cannot torment Christian people.'

'What a country,' muttered de Wrede. 'But, yes, I had heard that there is still such a custom and that the bishops themselves insist that symbols of Satan are painted on church walls.'

'And the battered head?'

'My brother was slightly built. With his weight he would never have fallen hard enough to receive a wound like that. Somebody must have smashed his head in and taken his money. I was sent here to take revenge on his murderer, and, if he was murdered by a ghost, then I was ordered to conjure up that ghost.'

'What a country,' sighed Dorn sarcastically. 'You wouldn't believe that there are any Christians in Flanders.'

Bose brought the ale. Dorn drank much of it himself then passed it to Melchior, who took a swig before passing it on to de Wrede.

'So what was demanded from you?' he asked.

'My father said that many things weren't right about his son's death. Those unholy marks and the story of the ghost meant that someone had bewitched him. In our family there is ...' De Wrede fell silent, searching for the words. 'We've encountered things like this before,' he continued, 'and if someone had put a death curse on my brother then I had to find the culprit and have him cursed likewise. Father cut off Gillis's scalp – because it contains great power – and he gave it to me to bring with me.'

'And what did you do in Tallinn?'

'I did some business because business needed to be done. And I looked for that curse that killed my brother. I've never heard so many ghost stories in any town as there are here. I went among the Blackheads, and I listened. I made myself talk to everyone who had ever known my brother here. I searched for the curse, and I didn't find anything. I started doing other things, which –'

'At the Red Convent, as I've heard,' remarked Dorn with a sneer.

De Wrede blushed and continued rapidly, 'I was looking for a sorcerer who could help me. It took time, but I was finally led beyond Reppen's Pastures where one of them is supposed to live. He demanded parts of my brother's body, and I gave him the scalp. He demanded more body parts from me, and I went to St Barbara's Churchyard to find some.'

'So you *have* been desecrating the dead?'

'Yes, I have,' admitted de Wrede, 'but only because I was seeking the truth about my brother's death. That sorcerer demanded the foot of a virgin and a hanged man's sex organ and took a hell of a lot of money. Those first ones that I cut off at night were not good enough for him, and he sent me off for new ones. I did a deal with a gravedigger ... and I suppose you know the rest.'

'What did the sorcerer promise you?'

'That if my brother had died under a curse he would conjure up my brother's spirit and punish its bewitcher by making him die the same way. He boiled up those body parts, and the smell was so strong that I wanted to run away, and then he said that they were still the wrong ones, and I had to bring new ones and pay him even more silver and a keg of ale, at which I got angry and pushed him into his own cauldron.'

'Good gracious,' exclaimed Dorn, 'and, to begin with, you believed him?'

'That's what I was sent here for, to punish the guilty party because Tallinn Council would do nothing about it.'

'What were you doing at St Michael's Convent?' asked Melchior to silence Dorn.

'I went there because I heard one man in a tavern beyond the town wall saying that Master of the Tower Grote had fallen to his death, and he had an expression on his face as if he'd seen a ghost, and that Grote had been terribly frightened at the Apothecary's pharmacy when the Apothecary told him he looked like he'd seen a ghost.'

'You don't know who the man might have been who spoke about my pharmacy?' ventured Melchior, scarcely concealing a smirk. Dorn had a heavy coughing fit, and when it had passed he retorted that that chatterbox must have been a town guard.

'He probably was,' said de Wrede. 'Certainly someone in the service of the Town Council, but maybe I didn't see his face very clearly. At any rate, I understood from him that the Tower-Master had a wound on his forehead like my brother. It seemed a very strange coincidence to me, so I went there to ask more about it.'

'And what did you find out?' asked Melchior.

'Not much,' admitted the Fleming, 'actually nothing. He had fallen and died, and whether he was bewitched by someone or what he said about a ghost – nothing.'

'What do you know about the death of Master Laurentz Bruys?'

'He was some respected and pious merchant, wasn't he? He died a week or so ago, and his funeral was the other day. They held a remembrance for him at the Blackheads'. I didn't know him myself. We didn't do business with him.'

Melchior thought for a moment and exchanged a wordless glance with Dorn. If you read the words to him and frighten him a little, that'll be enough for me, said Dorn's look.

'And what other ghost stories have you heard in Tallinn?' asked Melchior.

'That on Rataskaevu Street there is a house that's haunted. My brother was working next door to it, at Mr Goswin's place, but I haven't managed to talk to him. He's an old and feeble man who keeps away from the world. And then he was painting for the Knight Kordt von Greyssenhagen, who also goes to the brothel, but I don't know any more about him … I have been to Pastor Witte's church services, the one whose house is haunted. He is also a very pious and diligent servant of God. I did hear that one of the whores at the Red Convent had once said that she'd also seen a ghost, but then she drowned in the well.'

'And you went to the Red Convent to make enquiries?'

'I have been there,' admitted de Wrede, 'and no one can blame me for that – even some councillors go there. Magdalena is supposed to have said that she saw a person risen from the dead. But it's not worth believing whores' stories; they're all liars, and they'll tell you anything as long as you open up your purse.' De Wrede's voice was indignant, even angry.

'And you swear that this is all God's truth, and you swear it in the names of all the saints?' asked Dorn.

'Yes, I do.'

'Then get out of my sight,' shouted Dorn, 'and keep in mind that I forbid you to go outside the town walls other than to the harbour, where you can go with all your belongings as fast as possible, in the name of St Victor. If I hear one single word more, just one, that you have been seen at St Barbara's Churchyard or beyond Reppen's Pastures, you're going straight to court and into the frying-pan.'

De Wrede got up from the chair, bowed and thanked the Magistrate, then made off in the direction of the street door as if he had a hundred demons at his heels. Executioner Bose shook his head sadly, collected his implements and retired to the torture chamber.

'So you think he was telling the truth?' asked Dorn after a while.

'He has boldness and enterprise,' declared Melchior, 'so his gullibility is all the more strange. He is prepared to pay a lot of money to a country quack, he associates with a whore, he believes all kinds of stories about ghosts, yet he appears to be a good Christian. I think you did the right thing letting him go for now. He has already punished that sorcerer, but whether he was telling the whole truth ... I don't know. He said something very interesting, which doesn't seem to fit with the rest, and that is something I have to think about.'

'If he lied to me, even a single word, then he will be the first Fleming to be drawn and quartered in Tallinn,' said Dorn. 'Yes, I swear it, in the name of the laws of Lübeck, the Council and St Victor.'

25

Melchior's Pharmacy, Rataskaevu Street
The Night Before 12 August

MELCHIOR'S FATHER had taught his son chess at one time, but he had forgotten what he'd learned. Ten years ago the Lay Brother Wunbaldus and Prior Eckell had unintentionally forced Melchior to relearn how to play. It was a reflection of life, every piece with its own significance, and if they are arranged properly on the board one could configure a situation that helps one to think through a difficult dilemma, see it objectively and often from an entirely different viewpoint. The blessed Prior Eckell had once done this, and it had helped Melchior to find his murderer. Chess helps you to create order in your thoughts. Chess tells you about life, like a star chart, but you have to look at it from the right angle.

Melchior couldn't sleep. He felt that the Wakenstede curse, which had crushed him at St Barbara's Churchyard, had not yet gone far enough away; it was still close at hand and looking for a fresh moment to attack when his spirit was at its weakest. He had slept only for a couple of hours, and outside the window it was pitch black. Groping with his hands, Melchior went down to the kitchen, lit a candle and drank from a clay bottle a strong drink that he had mixed to ward off the menace. It didn't ever really do much in the end, but it did help to keep a new wave of the curse at bay, at least for a while. Then, in the shop, he kneeled in front of the image of St Cosmas and prayed to be given a clear understanding so he could find the evil that had led to the deaths of all these people.

All these people … he said to himself. How many people?

The chessboard might provide an answer. He took the candle to the board and placed the pieces on it. Then he moved the figures on the board. He imagined a face for every white piece and arranged it as he believed it would confront the black. But when he finally looked at the arrangement he couldn't make any sense out of it; it was simply a confused mass where everything might mean anything, and there seemed to be no clear meaning. Angrily he pushed a few pieces away and set about rearranging the figures. He took the white king, saying that it was Master Bruys, and put it in the middle of the board. He set the black king against it and said that this was an evil fate, and then he put figures on both sides which he believed to be in the service of each side. The white queen was St Bridget and the black bishop Bruys's wicked son Thyl. The black castle represented the evil Unterrainer house. Around these he placed the other figures which seemed to be involved in the story, although there were still too many of them.

Too many.

Too much confusion, too much evil, too much black.

He cleared all the black figures off the board except the king and stopped to think.

Master Bruys stood opposite his evil fate and beside him only St Bridget.

Next to the white king he lifted a black knight and thought of it as Greyssenhagen. But in this game Greyssenhagen shouldn't be black; he should be on the same side as St Bridget. Or should he?

Even when he lifted the curse of the black castle, the Unterrainer house, he couldn't find a proper place for it. He didn't know how near to Master Bruys to place it. It didn't suit this game. He cast it aside.

And then he stared at the chessboard in surprise. All the White bishops and pawns now suddenly seemed to make more sense. He set about attacking them one by one with the black king and they collapsed. The board was too empty.

Now he cleared all the white pieces off the board except the king and put it opposite the white queen, the penitent, Master Goswin. Then he put the other black figures on to the board to threaten the white king. There was too much black on the board and too little white, and there still seemed to be no place for the Unterrainer house, as if he were solving some doctrinal issue invented by dogmatists which didn't actually exist at all in the Scriptures. Hinric had once told him there are scholars who see a need to interpret the Scriptures where there is nothing to interpret, and their invented problems exist only in their heads and nowhere else.

Were these murders only in his head, and was it just some tramp who was killed in front of the Unterrainer house? And were all these ghost stories also just in the head of a half-mad apothecary who, because of a scourge on his own family, saw an evil curse in everything?

Yet the figures seemed to have some invisible connection between them – too many links and, at the same time, too few. Too many had died. Some evil power seemed to be moving across the board against Melchior's will and clearing away the figures that he didn't want to see there.

Shadows, thought Melchior. The board is lacking in shadows and spirits. The things we don't see. Those we should be aware of.

Then he took up the white bishop thoughtfully, put it next to the white king and asked, 'Who are you?'

26

The Dominican Monastery
12 August, Morning

IT WAS WEDNESDAY, and Melchior had been invited, along with other respectable townsmen, to the Guildhall of the Great Guild where a reception was being held by the Bishop of Tallinn and at which Arend Goswin would announce his incorporation as one of the patrons of St Bridget's. The canons, the Toompea merchants, the Tallinn guilds and many more respected citizens would all be taking part. This would be a great occasion for the town, one which could reconcile the doubters to the idea of the convent; eventually this would have to happen, but it continued to face much opposition. Still it was a surprise to many that Master Goswin would that evening kiss the image of St Bridget, hand over a great part of his assets and take the place of Master Bruys.

That morning, however, Melchior found himself following the familiar road to the Dominican Monastery. He had to hope that Hinric had forgiven him for uncovering those old secrets – and giving rise to new riddles in the process. Hinric was a Dominican, body and soul, no matter how close a friend he was to Melchior – it was his Viru County blood, like Keterlyn's, full of strength and obstinacy. He arrived at the monastery after third prayers and mass, when the monks were setting about their daily tasks. Melchior tried to spot Brother Lodevic in the yard so that he could impart a few choice words about the incompatibility of the vow of abstinence with biscuit-gobbling, but he could not see the old man anywhere. Hinric, however, came rushing towards him from the garden, his eyebrows furrowed and his face grey.

'Melchior,' he said morosely, blinking rapidly. 'God knows I've always been glad to see you here, but lately I've been thinking a lot about all those sermons as to how a man's trust can be wickedly exploited.'

'My good friend,' Melchior said gently, 'please don't hold it against me.'

'My job is to show mercy and forgive. Sometimes, though, you make it very hard.' Hinric stopped and nodded towards the door that led to the southern ambulatory. 'The brothers are at their work just now. No one will disturb us there. I don't want many of them to see you just now. You have greatly disturbed the peace of the community.'

It was cool, quiet and dim in the processional ambulatory. Hinric sat down on a big stone bench and Melchior beside him.

'I don't have much time,' said the *cellarius*. 'Winter is coming, and I have to fetch firewood, I have to work out the cobblers' fees and write to a greedy man from the manor who has sent fewer eggs and less barley for our herrings than we agreed. What is this world coming to, when estate managers start cheating mendicant monks?'

'I visited Pastor Witte's home,' said Melchior, 'the Unterrainer house.'

'The house where … where Adelbert's corpse remains?' asked Hinric. 'Did you … find anything?'

'Maybe yes, maybe no. Have you come across the respected Pastor's sister Margelin?'

'I don't know her. Pastor Witte hasn't lived here all that long, and we haven't had much contact apart from the couple of times when he has complained to the Council that we preach too much and that we're stealing his congregation.'

'That woman seems to be a bit mad in the head,' opined Melchior.

Hinric shrugged. 'That's surely not why you came here.'

'Yes and no. I got the impression that Witte knows something about the house that he wants to conceal, and he's afraid that his sister will talk. She told me that Witte has certainly heard a ghost, although he himself denied it.'

'If the woman is insane she might think every squeak of the door is a ghost, but Witte is an educated man and a servant of God, so, of course, he will deny it.'

'I suppose so,' muttered Melchior. 'But tell me, friend, do you know anything about the Holy Virgin having once written a letter that the angels brought to the City of Rome?'

Hinric was taken aback and stared in surprise at the Apothecary. 'That is a very odd question,' he said.

'And what is meant by thirty-three and a half days of suffering after which the whole world will be saved?'

'This is heretical talk, Melchior,' said Hinric, shocked. 'The Pope himself has denounced this as evil and ordered flagellants to be punished. Even the Bishop of Tallinn has that letter.'

'Flagellants are the ones who scourge themselves with whips?'

'Flagellants are heretics because, even though our order regards whipping as a proper punishment for some wrongdoers, we have to condemn most severely those who overdo it. It's an old madness that breaks out now and again among Christians – I think there was a case a few years ago in Erfurt where a fanatic was put on trial for it. I'm sorry to say that there were even some Dominicans among those who went mad over the whip and the false gospel.'

'But they haven't been seen around these parts?'

'Luckily, no. You might think that this heresy had been rooted out, but time and again messages reach us that somewhere some Master has appeared and invited people to join the Brotherhood of the Cross. Then they walk through towns and along highways, whipping themselves and singing hymns. These poor wretches believe that the Holy Virgin really did write to Rome ordering people to flagellate themselves for thirty-three and a half days and repent of their sins, then Christ's blood would be joined with their own and the world would be saved. This is a tragic heresy, and the masters of some flagellants have gone even further. They have declared that consecrated priests are unnecessary, that there is no need for the sacrament. They demand that the churches cease their pastoral care and all sinners join their brotherhood … Melchior, why are you asking about this?'

Melchior considered and then said very slowly, 'I wouldn't want to cast aspersions on an honourable servant of God because of a madwoman, but I suppose I already have.'

Hinric took a long look at him and then said thoughtfully, 'If a person punishes himself with a whip but doesn't run naked through the streets screaming that only the Master's whip can redeem sins rather than indulgence and confession, then I see no harm in it.'

'And the flagellants said that the Master's whip redeems sins?'

'Yes, there were leaders who referred to themselves as Master, and some of them claimed they could work miracles. They beat their followers, and they beat them until some of them died. They said that a master could forgive sins and there was no need for a church. They insisted that their pilgrimages with flagellation had to last thirty-three and a half days. The Church cannot allow such heresy.'

'And who were these masters?'

'Self-appointed usurpers, heretics,' cried Hinric loudly, and his words echoed off the walls of the passageway. 'Everyone who entered their Brotherhood of the Cross had to swear loyalty to the Masters. The Masters drove their disciples out into the town squares and holy houses, ordered them to go bare-chested and confess their sins, and then the Master would whip them, and after that they would all take whips and give each other a thrashing. Anyone who's witnessed these things has burst out crying from sheer terror and disgust and run to their father confessor or to their council offices to complain, but there were even councillors among these flagellants. Flagellating madness spread like wildfire across the empire, breaking out now in the north, now in the south, and, although divine vigilance has put the fires out, the poison is already out of the bottle. You often hear of some man greedy for power and pain who gets pleasure from scourging bare flesh and concocts heresies to satisfy his own filthy passions, jabbering about angels and the Holy Virgin. And always, Melchior, they always have followers. In Danzig they say there was a tanner who suddenly called himself a Master, started whipping people, and the very next day he had a hundred people around him who congregated in front of a church and forgave each other's sins by whipping. That is a blasphemy against the one and only holy faith.'

'It certainly is,' affirmed Melchior. 'I wouldn't even know what to think of a town where the people ran into the square and started flogging themselves for thirty-three and a half days in a row.'

'In a town like that an apothecary might have a lot of work to do,' noted Hinric venomously, 'if he wasn't one of the floggers.'

'Apothecaries have been given much wit and understanding by St Cosmas and St Nicholas. Apothecaries aren't going to go mad in that way.'

'I'd rather you told me they'd been given cunning.'

'Well, it amounts to the same. You said something about those masters who get pleasure from beating naked flesh?'

'And I already regret saying that,' said Hinric sadly. 'I should have known that such matters are of interest to apothecaries.'

'So you have heard of such masters?'

'Yes, I've heard of them, and Prior Moninger even spoke of them in a sermon a year ago or so. There were sects of flagellants who demanded that men kept strictly away from women, putting their own flesh to death, but there were also those who took women into their sect and then beat and whipped them naked – but, Melchior, I'm not going to start telling you about the indecencies that arose from that.'

'I suppose I can imagine them,' sighed Melchior.

'And if you do that too eagerly you'll have to go to your own father confessor.'

'Certainly,' said Melchior quietly. He raised his eyes, let his gaze rove across the vault of the ambulatory and added, 'I'm confessing to you now, friend. I think that Cristian Unterrainer became one of the masters. Now, decades later, Gottschalk Witte and his sister Margelin are living in his house. They were once part of Unterrainer's brotherhood. Miss Margelin flogs the Pastor, and they get pleasure from this depravity. If this is sinful knowledge then pardon it and keep the secret of the confessional.'

Hinric whispered a quiet prayer. Then he made the sign of the cross over Melchior, and the Apothecary kissed his hand.

27

Goldsmith Casendorpe's Workshop, the Red Convent, the Town Hall and the Guildhall of the Great Guild

12 August, Noon to Evening

GOLDSMITH BURCKHARDT CASENDORPE had previously been the Chief Officer of the Kanuti Guild but had given up that post five years ago and now dedicated himself solely to his work. He was one of the most sought-after goldsmiths working in Tallinn, whose handiwork was owned by a number of bailiffs and vassals across Livonia and even further afield. He had a prickly relationship with Melchior. He respected the Apothecary greatly, but in ten years he had been unable to extract from him the secret of how a gold collar he had made, and which he had sold to the Commander of the Teutonic Order on Gotland, had found its way to the almshouse of the Church of the Holy Ghost. Melchior knew how it had happened – he must have – Casendorpe was sure of it, but Melchior was evasive. Maybe Casendorpe held him in even higher esteem because a man who can keep a secret is worth his weight in gold.

And no one knew the value of gold better than Casendorpe.

He was not surprised when Melchior looked in at the window of his premises on Kuninga Street and told him he didn't want to buy gold today, but, if the good smith would allow it, he'd like to have a couple of words with his apprentice Simon.

Casendorpe adjusted his spectacles and opined that he would allow that but not for very long because Simon was just now learning to engrave the words *me facit,* and so far it had come out wrong and he had to practise diligently. Soon the boy would be going to Münster for his journeyman years, and Casendorpe could not let his house suffer the shame of Simon engraving *me facit* badly.

'And may St Eligius spare me from making that mistake,' cried Melchior. 'I'll only be a moment. I just need to ask him something.'

Casendorpe commanded the boy to go out into the backyard and asked the Apothecary to join him there away from prying eyes.

'I don't suppose the boy has stolen anything?' he asked in a hushed voice. 'Or something worse?'

'Not at all. You don't have to worry about him, Goldsmith,' replied Melchior nonchalantly, hurrying through the gate to the yard.

Simon Schoeff was quite tall for his age, with tough bony hands and rough fingers, which were quite hard to imagine undertaking the fine work of a goldsmith. Yet Melchior knew that Casendorpe regarded him as a talented apprentice, and these must have been among his last days in Tallinn.

'Did you call for me, Apothecary?' asked Simon in a very low voice, which had none of the tone of the angelic voice that had once sung in St Nicholas's choir.

'Yes, Simon, I did call for you. I need to ask you something – actually two things – and I ask you to answer me honestly and truthfully.'

'If I can, I certainly shall,' answered Simon.

'That's good then. My first question is this. Do you like cardamom-flavoured sweets which melt in the mouth when you suck them?' And, so saying, Melchior fetched a whole handful of them from his breast pocket, popped one in his mouth and looked slyly straight at the boy.

Simon swallowed. It was a rare treat to be offered this kind of gentleman's confectionery, and he acknowledged it. 'Yes, very much, sir.'

'That's good,' said Melchior. 'This whole handful is yours if you answer my second question just as honestly. And the second question is, is it true that a few days ago you and the merchant's daughter Ursula Kogge heard a ghost on Rataskaevu Street?'

This was a harder question for Simon. He seemed to be a boy who would think carefully, but he wanted to answer the question too quickly and then bit his lip and gave it some thought.

'Answer boldly and honestly,' Melchior urged. 'I shan't say a word to Mr Kogge if you *were* out with his daughter that evening. Ha! It's not even worth mentioning. I simply want to know what happens on my street.'

'So you already know, Mr Apothecary?' responded Simon.

'I've been hearing women's market gossip, but I want to hear a *man's* story.'

Simon was still hesitating. He looked at the sweets, consulted with himself and scratched his armpit.

'What's being said in the marketplace?' he asked at length.

'In the market they are saying that Ursula heard a ghost – not a word is said about you. But I thought that Ursula would not have been out with anyone else that evening because you're the only person she likes to be with. That's obvious.'

Now Simon blushed, looked greedily once more at the sweets and said, 'Something sort of crackled there, like a rusty door or something …'

'Aha,' cried Melchior. 'And which day was that?'

'Monday of last week, the day after that terrible downpour.'

'Yes, Simon, go on.'

And Simon told him. They had been in the backyard of the Unterrainer house behind a large bush, and then they had been talking about ghosts, or rather Ursula had been. Then there was a mouldy stink as from a freshly opened grave. And then there was a noise which could not be made by a living person – it had the sound of a ghost from beyond the grave, and they ran. And perhaps – Simon wasn't sure of this – perhaps, before they fled, they had seen a white shape flashing in the dim light, but he couldn't swear that he saw it. 'Father has taught me that you may only speak the truth, that which you've seen with your own eyes. But if you don't know what you've seen, then it's better to be silent, I think,' he said.

'You should keep your father's teaching very carefully in mind,' said Melchior. 'Your father is a goldsmith, and he knows. But then, Simon, you said that you ran. Where did you run to?'

'We ran from in front of the old wall of the stables behind the houses and through the garden to the well and from there to St Nicholas's Churchyard.'

'But did you see anyone on the street or by the well or maybe in the churchyard?'

'No one. Only Ursula was with me.'

Oh, Melchior believed that. After such an escape the boy would hardly have eyes for anyone but Ursula. He pressed the sweets into Simon's palm and promised that if the boy had any dealings at the pharmacy before he left he could have anything required at half price.

After this Melchior had an errand in a part of town where he didn't venture every day. This was to the east of the Seppade Gate towards the Cattle Gate. There were still wooden shacks here, left over from earlier times, mixed with newer single-storey stone houses, and this was home to all kinds of poorer artisans, porters, ale- and water-carriers, sack-makers, joiners, rope-makers and other lower-class people. This was where tenant farmers escaped to from their estate landlords, and it was mostly Estonian spoken here. The street running along the wall was not paved with stones, and pedestrians had to step through slurry and mud. Pigs and goats were herded into the green scraps of garden left between the houses, a practice strictly forbidden by the Council. It was a shabby and notorious quarter, and if anyone within the town walls should want beer or a woman of pleasure late at night then this was where they had to come because it housed the only brothel within the walls.

Melchior stopped in front of the house known as the Red Convent and pondered the fact that in the forty years of his life he had got by without ever visiting a prostitute, but now, tracking down a ghost, he had to go into a brothel. Finally he took courage and opened the door, assuming that he probably didn't need to knock first.

The entrance hall was small and narrow. It seemed once to have been an ordinary domestic entrance, but now the walls were covered with shabby planks, and in this way the rooms were separated. From the street door a passage led straight to the back of the *diele,* where a staircase led up, evidently to rooms intended for slightly more elevated people. Melchior was greeted by a sneering old hag, who snapped, 'Look, Sire Apothecary has finally come to look over the girls.'

Gritting his teeth, Melchior searched for a penny in his purse, slammed it down in front of her and said that he was here on Council business, and if he wasn't told what he wanted to hear a terrible misfortune would befall this house.

'But no girl will open her mouth for that money,' laughed the hag. 'Nobody's put that down for ages. Anyone coming from the Council would know what kind of money has to be paid.'

Melchior laid another five pennies on the table and said, 'This money is all yours if you tell me about a prostitute called Magdalena. The one who drowned in a well in the spring.'

The hag stared greedily at the money and grumbled, 'She has died and met her Maker. What more is there to say? She took men to bed, she did her job honestly and didn't speak ill of anyone.'

'Before she died did she say anything about a ghost on Rataskaevu Street?' insisted Melchior, and, seeing how the hag was taken aback, he went further, 'You must remember if she talked about it. When and where did she see it? Did it happen just before she died?'

'That's not something for the Council to get involved in,' she asserted.

'Then nor are these pennies yours,' declared Melchior and gathered up the money.

'Stop there, Apothecary.' Greed flashed in the woman's eyes. 'Don't rush off now. I'll tell you what I know.'

'Then tell me and quickly because I don't like being in this house.'

'Oh, that's what all the great and rich and respectable gentlemen say, but sometimes they get hungry, too. Haven't I seen all sorts of burgomasters and merchants here, all those nice knights and their henchmen sent out to get women.'

'Don't you slander respectable people, and tell what you've got to tell,' yelled Melchior. 'What did Magdalena say about the ghost?'

'She didn't tell me anything. I heard from another woman that she'd seen a person risen from the dead – and a thing like that doesn't bode well – and that maybe her last hour was near.'

That's exactly what it meant, thought Melchior. 'And that was all?'

'I didn't hear any more.'

'Tell me about her,' demanded the Apothecary. 'What sort of woman was she? Was she a gossip?'

'But you've come too late, Mr Apothecary,' sneered the hag. 'If you want to know what sort of woman Magdalena was, sir, you should have come last spring.'

'Don't evade the question. Tell me.'

'She was a smart woman,' said the hag, suddenly growing serious. 'It's not easy for a woman to live in the world if she doesn't have anyone to feed and clothe her and she's been driven away from her Master's home. In this house she had clothes to wear and food on the table, and she'd saved enough money to go to the almshouse in her old age and not suffer for want of anything. That great merchant – and wasn't *he* buried like a saint? – he wasn't so holy and pious after all. He'd lived wildly in his younger days, even had a bastard child, but when he heard that Magdalena had taken a few men to bed for money he threw her out on the street. That's the sort of man *he* was, see. To the end of her days Magdalena never forgave him for that.'

'Did Magdalena say that Bruys had a bastard?' Melchior asked suddenly. A thought had suddenly entered his head, a mad thought, but it had slipped out again so quickly that he couldn't catch it.

'She didn't say anything, but I must have heard it somewhere.'

'Woman,' commanded Melchior, fumbling for a couple more pennies, 'if you know then speak, but if you don't keep silent. With whom did Master Bruys have a bastard?'

'I don't know her name, and many years have passed since someone said that he had a wife at home but kept sneaking around town after younger ones. I don't know any more than that. Now shall I look for a girl for you, Mr Apothecary?'

But Melchior left without saying goodbye. He hurried to the Town Hall troubled by dark thoughts. They forced him to believe something that he hadn't believed before, to regard as possible things that did not seem to come from this world where Christian people lived. But he well knew what horrors are committed during wartime or to demonstrate one's own power. He knew very well what hatred can do to a person.

He rushed up to the writing-room of the Town Hall where Clerk Johannes Blomendahl and his two assistants were working; one of their tasks was to fill in the daily legacy inventory, in which a note was made of all sales and purchases of houses, inheritances and encumbered transactions.

Clerk Blomendahl had, by Melchior's reckoning, been in his post for at least fifteen years. He was a fair-haired, lanky and slightly hunched man who also carried out notary's duties and wrote wills, contracts and other important documents for all the townspeople who wanted them. Whereas he might once have been a cheerful and jovial novice lawyer, now the job had made him into a taciturn and serious man, one who had never been seen drinking ale at the guilds and did not seem to be married either, although he was a town citizen with full rights and a member of the Great Guild.

'Melchior, what do you want?' he snapped as soon as the Apothecary stepped into the office, breathing heavily from climbing the many steps. 'I've got a lot of work to do.'

'Good health to you, too,' said Melchior, bowing. 'What do I want? I'd like to see the town's inventory.'

'You know very well that without Council permission –'

'Without Council permission it can't be shown, I know. But I have sworn the oath of an assistant magistrate, and I am a deponent witness for the town, and I have an urgent need to know what that book says about a particular house.'

'An alderman has to give permission. Otherwise you can't.'

'Would the permission of a magistrate be enough?'

'The permission of a magistrate *would* be enough were it in writing or stated here before me.'

'But is it acceptable if a magistrate gives that permission *after* the Clerk has read to me from the book, and this action will lead to a murdering evildoer being thrown into the prison tower and brought to justice?'

The Clerk had to consider. Ordinarily this would, of course, have sufficed, but he remembered that this had happened before. The Magistrate had ordered a reading from the town's record book to the Apothecary. And what Magistrate Dorn had already done several times before, maybe he should not have to do again. Furthermore, the Magistrate usually arrived full of irritation if he were obliged to climb up all those stairs to the office just below the roof.

'Which house do you want to know about?' Blomendahl then asked with a sigh. 'I'm not allowed to read it out or copy it out, but what I suppose I *can* do is look at what it says and then tell you "inadvertently" what I know. That I can do.'

'The Unterrainer house, where Pastor Witte now lives. Could you "inadvertently" tell me who has bequeathed and bought that house?'

It took some time because Blomendahl had to go into a back room, browse through old dusty scrolls, make several calculations and then commit numbers and names to memory. But when he came back Melchior heard that that house had been bought in 1347 in the name of Cristian Unterrainer from Colberg, who had, on arrival in Tallinn, extended it considerably. Seven years later it came into the ownership of one Jurgen Zeneberck, who had brought before the Council the deed of sale made by Unterrainer; it was certified by the Clerk of the town of Rostock and witnessed as due and correct by the Council.

'But who bought it there in the name of Unterrainer if not himself?'

'I just happen by chance to remember that I got the name of someone called Greisshacken from the inventory – or something like that,' replied the Clerk reluctantly, 'and then I think it said as a dowry for his daughter.'

'Greisshacken?' asked Melchior excitedly. 'Are you sure?'

'The Clerk at the time might have written that name differently, and every name is spelled in its own way in every town, you should know that,' Blomendahl pointed out. Then he sighed again, adding, 'Gretzhaycken and Groishagen are the other forms of the name, but a man with that name from the town of Colberg bought the house as a dowry for his daughter Hermecundke, that's what seems to be in the book.'

Suddenly one of Blomendahl's assistants raised his head and said, 'Mr Clerk, Mr Clerk, that is very like the name of the Knight

Kordt von Greyssenhagen. Isn't that why that Knight came here asking about the house?'

'What are you on about?' snapped Blomendahl testily.

'Well, that time he came here to report that he'd bought his stables and asked, by the way, who bought that house and what was written down about it, and I said we couldn't tell him without Mr Clerk's permission. And then he got angry. But that's the house that's supposed to be haunted.'

'Oh, I understand,' whispered Melchior.

'You should keep your mouth shut,' grumbled the Clerk, and his assistant buried himself back in his book.

'What else was there?' asked Melchior slyly.

'It said that Jurgen Zeneberck died in 1364. The house was occupied by his brother and then the latter's son Hartwig Zeneberck. In his will he had made his nephew his heir. He was living in Germany and didn't send a single letter to Tallinn. Then two years ago Pastor Gottschalk Witte turned up with a contract to show that he had bought the house from Zeneberck's relatives.'

Melchior thanked the Clerk politely and left. He only had time to drop home quickly to put on a formal coat and choose the most suitable hat for the evening – not a difficult choice as he had but two. During the day Master Goswin's housekeeper Annlin had visited the pharmacy bringing, on her Master's instructions, a bottle of malmsey. Melchior tasted it and found that ale was a drink more to his taste, but this wine, regarded as very delicious, could be used in mixing medicines – perhaps by boiling honey in it and adding wormwood juice. That would be a remedy for a number of diseases and was good to drink anyway.

Towards evening Melchior stepped over the threshold of the Guildhall of the Great Guild, which was located near Town Hall

Square and had been completed only a year and a half before; in fact, it was so new that it still smelled of paint and varnish, and the master builders were still finishing off the banisters and walls. The tall building was prominently visible from the eastern side of the Town Hall, and some were already calling it the Little Town Hall because the edifice was meant to announce to the world the wealth and importance of the town's merchants. Like the Town Hall the Great Guild building was a symbol of the town's freedom.

This evening's event, however, was special in several ways. Usually only the Great Guild itself gathered in the Great Guildhall, and that meant the Council, too, because the Council was the Great Guild and the Great Guild was the Council. Today however, members of the town's other guilds had been invited here, as had respected burghers of the town, the Bishop of Tallinn, vassals and canons ... But not all of them came. Apart from the Commander of the Order, who had fallen ill, the people of Toompea had come, but there were not so many men from the Lower Town. A new convent near Tallinn – and, what was more, a convent run according to the rules of a Swedish saint – which was starting to take *money* away from the town of Tallinn, well, it did have its detractors, but surely people understood that Master Goswin's investiture was just the first step, and it would be followed by others. Then the real battle would begin to see that the convent, now so feared by the town, became the property of the town and add to its power, fame and prestige. At some point, once it began to minister to the souls of the townspeople, Tallinn would have to start using the convent's facilities, and this would add to the importance of the town.

This evening, though, would commence with a banquet with musical accompaniment, all paid for by Master Goswin, and then there would be speeches by the canons and Greyssenhagen, speaking for the Knights of the Order. The Bishop of Tallinn would congratulate Master Goswin, who would kiss the image of St Bridget and sign the certificate, which would be witnessed by the aldermen, Greyssenhagen and the Bishop with their seals.

Melchior sat at the banqueting table between the merchant Kogge and Franck, an accountant, both of them a little glum but tucking into the food that was put before them – cod and perch, roast lamb with ginger and garlic, leg of goose, white bread and little peppered sausages. Melchior didn't feel particularly hungry, and it was not only his thoughts that were drawing him away from the food, but he felt he could sense the approach of the curse of the Wakenstedes, which it had not had enough at St Bridget's Churchyard and now demanded more. He was finding this quite a depressing occasion, and not even the Council's musicians could cheer him up with their playing. The concept of a new religious community was unfamiliar to the town, as was Master Goswin's accession to the place of his former enemy. Melchior noticed that Goswin ate little, too, hardly touching the dishes placed in front of him, his sad eyes roving over the Guildhall as if seeking forgiveness and understanding from the burghers. Dorn was there, and he was jolly enough because the meal was far from frugal, and Melchior even saw de Wrede at the Blackheads' table.

It happened later, after the banquet, when Greyssenhagen and Canon Albrecht had praised Master Goswin and the Bishop had congratulated him and called for prayers for him in the town's churches; it happened as Greyssenhagen was handing the clay image of St Bridget to Goswin for him to kiss. That moment lasted a long time. Greyssenhagen's hands were trembling, but Goswin's were firm as he took the figure. He kissed it, and a sigh of relief issued from the Knight's mouth, one that he seemed to want to suppress. It was a solemn and spiritual moment, and just then Melchior felt his knees faltering and his eyes starting to swim. The curse must have been nearby; it was announcing itself. Death and misery were close to Melchior, and at that moment he understood everything: evil and hatred, which are stronger than death. At that emotional moment, as Greyssenhagen handed Goswin the figure of St Bridget, yes, then he understood. Hatred can be stronger than death. It extends beyond the grave and poisons the souls of the living and annihilates the spirits of the dead.

Melchior had to clutch the edge of the table so as not to fall. No one noticed it. Everyone was looking at Goswin kissing the statue of St Bridget. He accepted the saint's call and promised to uphold her cause in his life. Greyssenhagen smiled broadly and candidly. He had won over a new ally in the town.

Afterwards ale and wine were brought to the tables. But Melchior stood by the wall. He was unable to sit, he was suffering, the pain had seized his body and a terrible realization had paralysed his consciousness. The guests took their tankards of ale, clinked them with Greyssenhagen and Goswin, bowed before the Bishop and kissed his hand. Among them he saw Pastor Witte. The Knight was drinking ale, his voice growing increasingly shrill; finally he sat down among the diners, as did Goswin silently after him.

'Apothecary,' cried Greyssenhagen from afar and pushed his way through to Melchior. 'You seem down this evening. Are you unhappy?'

'My thoughts are confused,' replied Melchior. 'I deeply respect St Bridget, but that's not why I've been invited here. Rather, because you asked, sir, how my hunt for the ghost was getting on.'

'The holiest acts are over now,' said Greyssenhagen gleefully. 'So, tell me now, because that really is why I invited you. For years

I've been hearing that my neighbour's house is haunted, although as a Christian I can't take that sort of story seriously. But now they say that the Apothecary of Tallinn himself is chasing the Rataskaevu Street Ghost.'

'I'm not *chasing* a ghost,' said Melchior quietly. 'The ghost is just a shadow of the past. It can't be hunted. At some time a woman died in that house, a woman called Ermegunde, but according to the family her maiden name might be –'

'I'm not interested in what the woman's name might have been,' interjected the Knight rapidly and rather sharply. 'I was just asking you, as a bit of fun, whose spirit might be seen there.'

'Oh, I don't think you asked just as a bit of fun, sir,' answered Melchior, but then he added loudly, so loudly that everybody nearby could hear, 'I've seen the ghost with my own eyes. The human mind is a strange thing. I saw something with my own eyes I thought had vanished from my memory. Only today did I understand from how deep in the memory a recollection can reappear before one. I have seen an apparition that I thought was dead, and now it really is dead, but when it should have been dead it wasn't dead at all. That is why my thoughts are confused, and I ought to go before the Council and tell them clearly but not today. Tomorrow, gentlemen, because it concerns Master Bruys's will. Tomorrow, because now I'm ill, the grave will have to be dug up. Yes.'

'He's had too much to drink,' someone shouted.

'The Apothecary can't get a clear word out of his mouth,' another voice joined in.

'I'm ill. Forgive me,' Melchior forced himself to say. The Wakenstede curse seemed to be overcoming him, as it often did when he felt hellish hatred, evil and killing around him.

He bowed awkwardly towards the Bishop and to Greyssenhagen, who stared at him in astonishment, and then he staggered away, supporting himself with his hand on the wall and seeking out the Magistrate with his eyes. Dorn caught up with him at the street door where the Guild's attendant was standing.

'In the name of St Victor, Melchior, what kind of a mad yarn have you been spinning?' demanded Dorn angrily. 'What ghost? What will? What grave to be dug up? Have you gone out of your mind?'

Melchior reeled out of the attendant's earshot and through the front door, then supported himself against the wall of a house and answered, panting, 'My head is clear and confused at the same time. I said what I had to say, and it's as true as it is false ...'

'Now you've gone completely off your rocker.'

'Listen to me,' said Melchior, seizing Dorn by the cape. 'You must come to my home as soon as the feast is over and the guests have gone. You must come quietly and without being seen. The door will be open – don't knock – but, most importantly, don't let anyone see you. No one.'

He said no more but stumbled and reeled back home.

28

Melchior's Pharmacy, Rataskaevu Street
12 August, Late Evening

FROM KETERLYN'S perspective Melchior could see that his wife would have a number of bones to pick with him – the shop had been busy over the past few days, yet he had hardly been at home at all – but as soon as Melchior stepped inside his wife understood that now was not the time for a telling-off. Melchior's face was pale, he could hardly stand and there was madness flashing in his eyes. Judging by all the signs the Wakenstede curse had afflicted him again.

'Darling,' called Melchior in a weakened voice. Keterlyn ran to him, and her husband embraced her. To Keterlyn Melchior seemed different from the other times that a wave of the curse had come over him. He wasn't usually like this, anxious, excited.

'Darling,' Melchior whispered in his wife's ear, 'don't ask any questions please. Take the children and go upstairs to sleep, to the attic, among the boxes of plants, and don't come down from there, don't come on any account, no matter what happens or whatever you hear. When it's all over I'll come to you myself.' And he kissed her.

No woman in the world would agree to a request like that. No woman would simply go without question, and nor did Keterlyn – but Melchior closed her mouth with a kiss.

'I'll manage,' he said. 'I'll drink some medicine, and I'll manage. Don't worry. But I'm expecting something, expecting someone, and you and the children should keep away. Go now, in the name of the Blessed Virgin.'

When Keterlyn had gone Melchior quickly poured himself the drink, to which he had added several ingredients that he wouldn't usually – dried snake's meat, toad's scales, a little drop of lily-of-the-valley wine, opium-poppy seeds and rose oil. He hoped it would help; it *had* to help. It was the most disgusting drink Melchior had ever drunk, but it *must* help.

Dorn came as it was getting dark and the townspeople were preparing for bed. The town guards came on to the streets and checked that no one was wandering around armed. Through the window one could see a faint candlelight. The front door was ajar, and a pale strip of light seeped on to the steps. Dorn cautiously pushed the door open and saw Melchior resting at the table, his head in his hands; there was a bottle of wine beside him and in front of him some half-completed writing.

'Hey, Melchior,' whispered Dorn. 'I am here now. Are you asleep?'

The Apothecary was startled, and he lifted his head. As he raised his face the Magistrate saw that his friend was dripping with sweat, and the earlier pallor had been replaced by a flush.

'Come in quickly,' whispered Melchior in reply. 'Don't shut the door. Leave it ajar.'

'Good heavens, you're sick, man,' responded Dorn, stepping softly inside. 'Will you please tell me what's going on?'

'You'll have to be patient. I can't tell you anything because I can't prove it. Be patient, and we'll get the evidence.'

'Evidence of what?'

'Quietly, Wentzel,' hissed Melchior. (Only very rarely did Melchior call the Magistrate by his first name. Dorn, however, as a Council official and a man older than Melchior, never called him by his surname.) 'Quietly,' repeated Melchior. 'We mustn't talk so we can be heard from the street. I made a space for you behind the curtain. Slip behind it and talk only in a whisper.'

Dorn mentally cursed his friend and looked at how the door leading to the back room had been pushed open and Melchior had hung a large cloth in front of it. There he found a chair and a candle stump, which barely flickered.

'Whose will were you rambling on about at the Guildhall?' insisted Dorn when he had finally sat down. 'Everybody thought you'd gone out of your mind. Who has died or hasn't died?'

'I won't tell you now. You wouldn't believe me,' said Melchior softly, almost inaudibly, in a trembling voice and breathing hard. 'This story, Wentzel, this story is a weird one. It's monstrous, it's horrible, and my soul cries with pain when I think of it. To believe it you first have to believe that a demon can come to earth, that Satan has stolen a person's soul and put only wickedness and hatred in its place.'

'You're making me shiver all over,' grumbled Dorn from behind the curtain.

'That's good. You should be afraid, because you're going to find something out that human understanding refuses to believe. You have a candle – read this and think, then blow out the candle. Be alert and very still.'

Melchior handed Dorn the torn sheet of paper on which he had been writing at the table. It had seven lines on it, written in the spidery hand of a sick man.

'What's this?' asked Dorn.

'These are a few keys. They'll give you the solution as it was given to me. If you work it out for yourself then I haven't accused anyone unfairly, and you'll know what we're expecting.'

Dorn muttered in vexation that he couldn't stand guessing games, but he read it anyway:

Foot chopped off tramp and why Bruys couldn't walk
Bruys sent Thyl to Germany
Bruys had a bastard child
Annlin's son Hanns is 41 years old
Goswin gave up trading in salt
De Zwarte had completed the portrait
There was very heavy rain on the day Grote and Bruys died

'This is a strange and confused story of yours,' declared Dorn, blowing out the candle as commanded. 'These facts are known, but this business of Bruys's bastard is such an old rumour ...'

'You think about it,' recommended Melchior.

Dorn considered, and for a long time silence reigned.

'You don't say a word here about that ghost and the Unterrainer house, so I don't understand what you're on about at all,' Dorn remarked at length.

'There's one more thing I can tell you that I didn't have time to write down. I visited the Red Convent, and I heard that Magdalena had said before she died that she *saw a person risen from the dead.* And that is what de Wrede had also heard her say, you remember? You see, that's the key to everything. But let's be wary now. I think the time is at hand when he should come.'

And again they were silent. Time passed. Evening was turning into night. Somewhere far away a dog barked on the street. The late-evening flies were circling around the fading candle flame.

Finally Melchior heard Dorn whispering, 'Melchior, explain to me. It was de Wrede who cut off the foot of that tramp, but what has that to do with Bruys, whose legs were infirm from the disease of old age, which the monks there in Mariazell –'

'Quiet now. I heard something.'

Melchior put his head on the table between his hands and remained quietly resting, just breathing. Dorn was amazed but stayed as quiet as a mouse. He made sure he could see around the curtain and watched the door and window. He did think he saw something, some shape flitting past the window … and then going back again. It might have been a town guard passing, but he couldn't be sure. After that nothing happened, all was silent and still. The candle on the table cast the last flickering splashes of light into the dim room. Dorn eyed the darkening window attentively. He directed all his attention on it, trying to penetrate the darkness, but still he couldn't see too well. The window was composed of small panes of glass and cames; the glass was dull and soiled and almost impossible to see through. Yet suddenly Dorn was taken aback; something appeared at the edge of the window. And then he saw, very slowly, very slowly, some blurred thing was moving from the wall to the middle of the glass pane. And when that something suddenly stopped Dorn realized that it was also hard to see inside from without. That something was a human eye, and it was cautiously examining the inside of the shop through the glass. And then, in a flash, it was gone. Dorn realized that he had been holding his breath.

Melchior, who was still sitting motionless, suddenly snored and so loudly that Dorn himself was frightened. Damn, he thought,

Melchior has fallen asleep, but then the Apothecary hissed almost inaudibly, 'Be ready.'

Dorn saw the door moving. A hand was pushing it open slowly, ready to withdraw at the first creak. But the heavy door did not creak. Dorn thought the door had always creaked. Had Melchior oiled it recently? The door was still moving, and now, in the darkness, he could see a shape appearing on the threshold. It moved as silently as the grave, cautiously and slowly, slipping halfway through the doorway. Dorn wasn't breathing. The shape must be an enemy, someone who had come with evil intentions, and now he began to understand Melchior's plan – in order to accuse this furtive stranger there had to be an accuser. He was that accuser, and Melchior was the bait. So Dorn didn't move but made himself ready.

The candle had almost gone out. The intruder was wearing a black cloak with a hood. Dorn wasn't sure that he could see well enough through the chink beside the curtain, but it seemed to be an expensive coat, fur even.

Melchior snored once more.

This was a signal to both the intruder and Dorn. The dark shape suddenly took a couple of very quick steps forward, and from under its front it pulled out something long and shiny. Dorn jumped out from behind the curtain at the same moment that the weapon flashed. The Apothecary had kept half an eye open, for he turned to evade the blow and rolled on to the floor. Yet the attacker was so agile that it managed to raise its arm for another blow as Dorn rushed up to it and shouted, 'In the name of the Council …' The assailant struck, and Melchior struck back, but Dorn was there. He pushed the figure away from Melchior, felt a cold-bladed weapon pulling across his jacket and heard a screech. The intruder screeched like a demon being drowned in holy water; it struggled against him, it scuffled, kicked and bit Dorn in the jaw, and then from the street behind the door came another cry.

'There's someone else,' shouted Dorn, pulling the screeching, writhing intruder to the floor.

'I know,' cried Melchior and jumped up to help Dorn. He forced the long, sharp knife from his enemy's grasp and threw it across the room.

Dorn hit the stranger in the chest with his fist and put his arm around the stranger's neck. Melchior grabbed the sputtering candle from the table with one hand and with the other pulled the hood back from the stranger's face.

They saw the face – distorted with hatred, insanity, burning with inhuman rage – of Annlin.

29

The Torture Chamber of the Council Prison

13 August, Noon

MASTER AREND GOSWIN'S servant Hainz had been stripped bare and fettered to the wall of the torture chamber in the Town Council's prison. He had been shackled to a frame, his legs strapped to a moving rack. With one hand Executioner Bose turned a handle that forced Hainz's legs further apart and with the other held a pole on the end of which was a scoopful of glowing coals that were positioned directly under Hainz's sagging testicles and penis.

Hainz was a big man with broad shoulders and tough muscles. His long grey hair fell down the sides of his head, and from his mouth seeped a bloody froth, caused by the spiked torture instrument – a poison spider – that had just been removed. When placed in the mouth and the person is tortured at the same time and he starts to scream with pain, the poison spider causes hellish agony.

Bose turned the spindle, and Hainz's legs bent into a gruesome position; the bones creaked and the blood vessels darkened.

Hainz screeched, 'The Master doesn't allow us to talk. No talking allowed to anybody.'

Hainz had at one time been a salt-carrier in Tallinn, and salt-carriers were all tough, strong men. They were mostly Estonians, but Hainz apparently came from somewhere around Lübeck and had ended up in Tallinn after being shipwrecked. Since then he had been afraid of the sea and had joined the Brotherhood of Porters and sworn the citizen's oath. The Council required all porters to swear the oath because such strong men were always needed, and doing so granted the porters citizens' rights. In return the town required that they bear arms in defence of the town, haul stones for building up the town wall, rescue people in the event of a fire ... That meant they had to live in the town and not beyond the town walls. Porters had to load loose cakes of salt from the small boats on to wagons and then lift them off again at the weighing-house. When the salt was milled, they stuffed it into bags and heaved it on to the scales; then they laid the bags out in the merchants' cellars or put them on carters' wagons and unloaded them at the merchants' houses. For years Hainz had been hauling Master Goswin's salt sacks, and Goswin had taken him on as his servant. By that time Hainz was married to Annlin, the daughter of a certified grain-measurer at the weighing-house.

'No talking about the salt-cellar. The Master won't allow it,' yelled Hainz. He was crying, and his tears mixed with the bloody saliva. Melchior was standing next to the Magistrate. He wasn't enjoying this scene, but he couldn't allow himself any sympathy for this man when he thought of the suffering that he had brought to others. God had not given Hainz much insight but still enough for him to understand what pain is, what torture is, what is right and what is wrong. Hainz, however, had chosen to follow darkness and failed to do the duty of a Christian. Melchior had seen his tears before, at sermons at both the Dominican Monastery and at St Nicholas's, yet this man had chosen to torture and kill innocent people. Yes, passion was at the root of it, because the man evidently desired his wife, even loved her in his own way, the basis of it being obedience to his Master, whose money fed and clothed him, kept him from hunger and protected him from cold. A woman's warm body and a warm room, herrings, bread and turnips, and for that you sell your blessed soul? Without even hating your victims or without caring anything for the pain you cause their many kinfolk?

'The Master doesn't allow talk,' screamed Hainz, yelping and floundering, which caused him even more pain. Wulf Bose scorched Hainz's dangling balls with a hot coal, and the man howled in agony, yelping, screaming and shrieking.

The door of the torture chamber opened, and the executioner's assistant pushed Annlin into the room. The woman was half-naked. She had been whipped, and her back and shoulders were covered in wheals. She was thrown to the floor, and there she lay for a while, panting. She looked wretched and feeble. Just yesterday, though, she had wanted to kill Melchior, and a person can feel no sympathy for one who has come to slit his throat with a knife. Then Annlin lifted herself up, her wrinkled face quite expressionless despite the humiliation, pain and hopelessness. There were wounds from whipping even on her sagging, tuberous breasts.

'Leave him alone,' said Annlin in an unexpectedly clear and assured voice. 'He won't tell you anything anyway as long as the Master won't allow it. You're just torturing him to death.'

'The Master won't allow talk. Mustn't talk about the salt-cellar,' yelled Hainz.

Bose took the tongs and stepped over to Annlin. Dorn raised a hand.

'Confess,' he commanded the woman.

'The Master won't allow …' Hainz's voice had weakened.

'Speak,' commanded Melchior. 'You won't get out of this chamber without confessing, and you know it. Did you kill the prostitute Magdalena, de Zwarte the painter and Master Grote of the Quad Dack Tower?'

And Annlin spoke. Hainz had gone to the whorehouse and waited there until Magdalena came. Hainz had given her money and said he wanted to fuck her and knew a secret place and told the woman to come with him. Magdalena came, and Hainz led her to the backyard of Master Goswin's house. There he grabbed the woman firmly by both arms, and Annlin held a pillow over her face until she choked. Later, towards evening, when it had got dark, they hauled the corpse to the well and pushed her in.

'The painter de Zwarte, you hit him on the head with a stone in the harbour, didn't you?' asked Dorn, as Executioner Bose raised a hot coal to Hainz's testicles again.

'Don't torture him,' cried Annlin. 'He won't tell you anything. Let me talk ... Yes, I hit him on the head with a rock. It was I, but I did it on orders. That painter was a liar and didn't keep to his word. Hainz grabbed him as he was going for a piss, and I struck –'

'You would have killed him anyway,' said Melchior, 'regardless of whether he promised to keep quiet or not. From the moment he started painting he was condemned, but you couldn't kill him before he went to the harbour. And then you took his money as well.'

'What use is money to a dead man? Yes, of course, I took his purse. It was our money. It was the price of obedience.'

'And Grote? How did you kill him?'

It had been difficult and required a lot of adjustments. Annlin had gone to the evening sermon at St Michael's, where she had been known since she had taken Dorothea to join the holy sisters. After the sermon she had concealed herself behind the bathhouse and stayed there until the evening. Hainz had been waiting on the street on the south side of the nunnery. When Grote came to the tower and it was getting dark, Annlin opened the small gate and let Hainz in. He had quietly run around the perimeter and gone into the area between the two walls. Then Annlin had called the Tower-Master by name; she had called several times in a loud voice. As his wife was doing this Hainz crept up the steps, and, seeing that Grote was going out of the tower, he ran along the walkway through the second storey of the tower and pushed Grote over. The Tower-Master's bones did indeed break as he fell, but he didn't die. Annlin took away the torch that had dropped from the Tower-Master's hand as he fell, stepped up to him, raised the torch to his face and saw that the man recognized her. His face was pale with terror, and he was blabbering something about a ghost. Annlin struck him on the head with a rock.

'A rock on the head,' repeated Melchior softly. 'And, of course, you took the torch with you. Grote wouldn't have gone on to the wall in the dark, but no torch was found with the corpse.'

'It was a good torch,' said Annlin.

'And the weapon you chose to kill me with was a dagger …' Melchior had been spared a knife attack, but Dorn had suffered a slight wound to the wrist, and raising a knife against a magistrate was a very serious crime indeed.

'The Master thought that if the poison didn't work … just in case,' said Annlin.

'You mustn't speak. The Master won't allow it,' howled Hainz.

'What poison was it?' demanded Melchior.

'I don't know. The Master gave me a bottle and ordered me to take it because the Apothecary was snooping around too much and asking dangerous questions and would soon work this business out. And when he came to the Guildhall in the evening, he said that the Apothecary already knew too much and wanted to dig open the grave and that in the morning he would go to the Council to complain. The poison must have been too weak and old and didn't work … So since the Apothecary didn't die he would come to kill him.'

Melchior recoiled in horror. He had only just escaped the knife attack and could never have anticipated that the old woman was so quick and nimble.

'And that poor unfortunate, did you kill him, too?'

'No, the Master did. It was the Master himself … I didn't kill him … The Master stuck him with a knife, that same knife, the Master killed …'

30

St Michael's Convent, the Brewery Tavern
15 August, Towards Evening

BETWEEN THE CONVENT walls it was always quieter and more peaceful, even when the town was buzzing with sensation and everyone was asking each other the news. Everyone had heard something, everyone knew something and that it was startling, weird and incredible, and if anyone knew the whole truth it would be the Magistrate or the Apothecary. They said the Council had Master Goswin taken to a prison cell in the in the Bremen Tower. Just think – Master Goswin, a member of the Great Guild. The town was swarming and seething, and the Magistrate and Melchior had to get away to be by themselves and drink a few tankards of ale in peace at the Cistercians' taproom. Brother Hinric had come with them.

But even in the nuns' tavern there was a smith as well as a servant of a canon, who just happened to be there and who offered to buy the Magistrate a drink if they could hear a bit of gossip. They had managed to shoo Lay Sister Gude away, but she continued to prick up her ears to eavesdrop on what Melchior was saying.

Melchior, Dorn and Hinric were sitting at the rear table of the tavern, and through the window they could see the Quad Dack

Tower. They were drinking the nuns' mint beer, which Hinric regarded as a very good brew. They sat in silence, waiting, and only when they had already drunk one tankard did the Knight Kordt von Greyssenhagen arrive in his splendid red hat. The Knight had been to quiz Melchior the previous day about the ghost and Bruys's will and what hypocrisy the Apothecary had witnessed at the Guildhall of the Great Guild, but Melchior had asked him to wait a day or so to collect his thoughts and ... recover.

'Gentlemen,' said Melchior finally in a slightly tremulous voice. 'I am going to tell you a couple of peculiar tales, and I admit that without ale I wouldn't be able to get them past my lips. In the year of Our Lord 1349 there lived in Tallinn a merchant named Cristian Unterrainer, who was a wicked and evil man. He had a wife, Ermegunde, but we have to believe that Unterrainer didn't live with his wife in order and decency and wanted physical pleasure only from torture. Now, this woman's maiden name was something like Greyssenhagen, and she was from the town of Colberg, but the Knight himself can tell us more about that presently.' Greyssenhagen nodded sorrowfully. 'At the same time, seventy years ago, an indecent young monk, Adelbert, came to Tallinn. He would go through the town with his alms-basket, and we can't say who seduced whom, but it is clear that he started visiting Ermegunde and that they enjoyed sinful love. However, in a small town nothing goes unnoticed, and stories reached the monastery. The Prior, Helmich, was a mild-mannered man, and he did not punish Adelbert as he should have. Instead of whipping him he only admonished Adelbert, but passion in the young monk was stronger than his oath of chastity. He was a young man, full of life, and he couldn't give up Ermegunde's love. Passion is sweet and sin even sweeter, so one day he returned to her house when he thought her husband wasn't at home. Unterrainer, however, came upon them, and his revenge was terrible.

'That man was not an ordinary human. He was a monster. He shut his wife and the monk in the cellar, bound them and then tortured and whipped his wife for several days until she died. By law he could have dragged his wife through the town and shamed her in front of the people, but that wasn't enough for him. He forced Adelbert to look on as he tortured and starved her.' Melchior was silent for a moment, took a recuperative draught of ale and carried on, his eyes dull and dark. 'Next, gentlemen, it seems to me that after his wife was dead Unterrainer threatened the monk and forced him to choose. Either he would immure Adelbert alive with his wife's corpse or let the monk go free – but only after Adelbert had defiled his wife's corpse while Unterrainer watched.'

Hinric hung his head but nodded silently. Greyssenhagen's face was as dark as a storm cloud.

'By St Victor,' murmured Dorn. 'Do you know that for sure?'

'I can't know for sure, but I can assume so.'

'But what Unterrainer demanded from the monk,' asked Dorn, 'did he do it?'

'A few days later he arrived back at the monastery, troubled and confused,' said Melchior. 'So, yes, he did. Maybe several times. He wanted to avoid being buried alive. Maybe, gentlemen, maybe Unterrainer cut the foetus of the child that had been fertilized in sin from Ermegunde's body, but I don't know. And Unterrainer kept his word. He let the monk go free because he believed he would never talk about it.'

'But it could have been so,' whispered Dorn, looking at the Knight, who remained silent. 'They might have had a child.'

Melchior shook his head, swallowed and continued. 'Unterrainer was wrong. Adelbert talked about his sin to the Prior and then he put his own hand to it. He castrated himself. He himself chopped off what had led him into temptation and horror. He could no longer live with the knowledge of what he had done with his penis ... He could no longer feel that thing every day as part of his own body, remember it, call it to mind, live again through what he had done. But his body was too worn out. He'd lost too much blood, and he died.

'Prior Helmich was supposed to have Adelbert buried in unconsecrated ground as a suicide, but he didn't. As I said, he was a man with a pliant nature, but he was also cunning. He didn't want too many bad rumours getting out about the monastery. He had managed to conceal how Adelbert died, and he came up with a clever plan. He let a closed coffin be buried and pretended that Adelbert was in it, having died of a disease. The coffin was empty. The real corpse, I think, he had dragged away by a couple of reliable lay brothers through the little eastern gate and thrown into a hole somewhere under a bush. He couldn't have Adelbert buried on consecrated soil like an honest Christian and give him the sacrament, but neither could he allow the townspeople to know about an indecent brother living in the community. Adelbert's seeming death and burial on monastery land stopped the talk, and it was almost forgotten.

'Unterrainer, however, did immure his wife's corpse in the cellar and left Tallinn. After a few years, though, the Council had the wall pulled down, and the woman's corpse was discovered. This gave rise to rumours, and since then the Unterrainer house has been said to be haunted. But in Colberg Unterrainer sold his house to one Jurgen Zeneberck who started trading in this town. The house belonged to Zeneberck's heirs for a time, then stood empty until finally Gottschalk Witte bought it when he became a pastor in Tallinn. Since the pastor is in the habit of having himself whipped, anyone on the street could hear his wailings, and that would give extra impetus to the rumours that it was haunted.

'I must say one more thing about Witte so that you understand everything, but this has to stay between ourselves. I think Witte didn't buy that house by chance, but he wanted to settle there. I think Witte had come across Unterrainer at some point, because Unterrainer became a Master of Flagellants in Germany. He invited others around him and flayed them because that was the only way he could feel virile pleasure, and young Gottschalk Witte and his sister Margelin must have been disciples. Unterrainer told them what had happened in the house and how he had once flayed sinners there. I can only guess that for Witte and Margelin this was the ideal place for penitence. They sought Unterrainer's heir and bought the house from him so they could come to Tallinn ... Maybe this was a way to escape because their secret had perhaps got out somehow, and that would be thought heretical. In any case, Witte has himself whipped, and I don't want to think or guess any more beyond that. And it's not of any great importance either, because this is where the story of the Unterrainer house ends and another story begins.'

'What happened behind the monastery walls can stay there,' said Dorn. 'How do you know all this, though? That's what I don't understand.'

'Brother Lodevic told me some of it – Prior Helmich had used the story as a lesson. There were holes in this tale, though, because all the gossip said something about castration. Something had leaked out of the monastery somehow, and gossip like that has great power – there's no smoke without fire, as they say. The townsfolk had to remember what sort of person Unterrainer was, and I couldn't understand how the business of castration had attached itself to Adelbert's story and why. I didn't believe that Unterrainer would have dared to raise his hand against a reverend brother and shed his blood. And I thought about that poor tramp whose corpse was found in front of the Unterrainer house, and I admit that I thought all sorts of mad things, but I had to know. If that monk really was buried in the Dominican cemetery then … Anyway, Adelbert couldn't have already been castrated when he arrived back at the monastery because Helmich couldn't have kept that under wraps. I had to know, and I asked to have that grave dug up. The grave was empty, so I thought he had to have killed himself. The rest I guessed.'

'Prior Moninger knew,' said Hinric. 'It was entered in the scroll that is passed down from one prior to the next and which other eyes don't see. The story is that Adelbert knew he was dying and asked permission from the Prior to be castrated before he died because he didn't dare, with that appendage with which he'd committed the most grievous sin, to hope for resurrection. What sort of sin it was, the Prior doesn't write, but Adelbert didn't want to go to the other world in that physical form. He didn't want to appear before Christ with that sinful organ. The Prior couldn't castrate him, but he let Adelbert do it himself, so he felt guilty about his death.'

'So did that monk really … with that woman's corpse …?' Dorn fell silent, looking inquisitively at Hinric.

'It was written that Adelbert had confessed his sins, and the most grievous one was that he'd been forced to defile a corpse, and for that he would never find redemption,' said Hinric quietly.

'But now I think the esteemed Knight wants to tell us something,' said Melchior. 'He has found out the truth about the

Unterrainer house, which was one reason why he bought a house in the Lower Town, I think. But now he will soon hear about the ghost.'

'Yes, I'll tell you,' said Greyssenhagen. 'It's not a long story. Ermegunde was my great-aunt. My grandfather, who held a Junker estate in Pomerania in the service of the Order, had eight children, five daughters and three sons. He married the daughters off to other Junkers, but Ermegunde didn't have children, and her husband was killed fighting the Poles. No one wanted to woo the barren Ermegunde, but a merchant from Colberg promised to take her because he didn't want children anyway. He also demanded a dowry, and Grandfather helped him, with his own money, to buy a house in Tallinn. Only when the merchant had set off with Ermegunde did my grandfather hear that the man was a flagellant with followers. They all sang psalms and paraded around and whipped one another until the blood flowed. But by then it was too late. Unterrainer had left with his wife. I have to say that it wasn't at all usual in Pomerania for a Junker's daughter to be given in marriage to a townsman, but Ermegunde didn't want to be forced into her only other option in life, to go into a convent. A few years later word reached my grandfather that Ermegunde, who was already over thirty by then, was finally expecting a child. The next messages didn't arrive for years, and they said that Unterrainer had long since departed from Tallinn and that Ermegunde's corpse had been found immured in his cellar. No one knew anything about the infant.'

'Jesus,' cried Dorn. 'So what happened to the child?'

'I don't think we'll ever know,' said Melchior, 'and maybe it's best that way. And I don't *want* to know any more details because what I have to tell you now is quite difficult enough as it is.'

'No,' said Greyssenhagen, 'I don't suppose we'll ever know. That story is told in my family, and when fate brought me to the Tallinn area I started to hear about a haunted house where Ermegunde had once lived – and I wanted to know. I bought the house next door, but I didn't find out anything further, only rumours and women's gossip, until one day I heard that the apothecary on my street was hunting the Rataskaevu Street Ghost. I'm afraid I don't have anything more to tell you.'

'And that is enough,' said Melchior. 'May the Lord God himself decide on the guilt of those unfortunates. Adelbert's and Ermegunde's terrible fate actually has no connection with what happened next door to Unterrainer's house a few decades later. Let it teach us that we mustn't believe any old gossip about the supernatural, and yet we tend to do that too readily. Above all, let it be a lesson to me because at first I didn't see the most important element. All three who died – de Zwarte, Magdalena and Grote – had said that they'd seen a ghost, but none said that they'd seen the ghost of a *woman*. None of them actually said that they'd seen the ghost of a woman in the Unterrainer house, or whatever it was that was supposed to haunt it. Nor did anybody say that they had seen the ghost of a monk. Actually they were talking about something quite different. Hinric, what did Grote say to you? Do you remember his words?'

'He'd seen a ghost at the end of Rataskaevu Street who came to bring him a message from the realm of the dead, saying "May Heaven have mercy on Bruys."'

'Exactly,' said Melchior, 'but for *which* Bruys was he asking mercy? And let's recall de Zwarte's exact words in the letter he sent home. De Zwarte wrote that in Tallinn he *saw* a ghost risen from the dead and now it was haunting him day and night. But

Magdalena had said that she saw *a person risen from the dead.* What I mean is that actually nobody said anything about a ghost or the Unterrainer house. It was my own interpretation that bound these things together – and thank heavens it did because the wrong path led me on to the right path. When I finally saw it, everything was so clear and simple – I had been making the story unnecessarily complicated. Gentlemen, what is a ghost? What does a person regard as a ghost? I suppose it is when they see an apparition of a dead person – something unearthly, something supernatural. But wouldn't we also, when we meet a person of flesh and blood whom we knew for certain is dead, say we'd seen a ghost? That's what Grote and Magdalena saw, and Magdalena said it quite precisely, too. She had seen a *person risen* from the dead. She had seen someone who should have been dead. So, once I started to see all these things clearly, when I finally put aside all the silly gossip and thought only about what we actually knew then –'

'Then they saw a person whom they thought was dead and couldn't believe it,' Hinric interjected.

'Because that person looked dead. That individual no longer had a human face,' said Melchior, 'so they couldn't believe they were seeing a living person. Gentlemen, I will now tell you the story of Laurentz Bruys and Arend Goswin, who once came to this town as friends, full of hope and zest for life, but ended up as the most terrible of enemies. It's a terrible story and will remain a nightmare during my sleepless nights for a long time.'

They all sipped their ale, and Melchior continued. 'Bruys's and Goswin's businesses flourished in Tallinn. They made good money out of salt, but they weren't granted family happiness. In the year of Our Lord 1394, of the seven children in Bruys's family, only his son Thyl was still alive because God had called the other children to him. Arend Goswin's three sons had died in childhood, and his wife died giving birth to a daughter, Dorothea. The child grew into a marvellously beautiful maid, but her mind was feeble – in fact, she was regarded as an imbecile. Goswin loved her unreservedly, the only one of his blood who had survived, and the girl should have come here to the Sisters of St Michael as a nun as she was unlikely to be married because of her feeble-mindedness. Yet Dorothea was the most admired girl in the town, and Thyl Bruys lured her somewhere to a secluded place beyond the town and deflowered her – so they say. Evidently this didn't happen violently, but at first the girl simply didn't understand what was being done to her. Later, in her own way, she came to understand it. She thought she was now filthy, that she was a whore, that she couldn't appear that way before Christ and St Michael. She drowned herself, and as a suicide no church would bury her in the sanctified way. It was a catastrophic blow to Goswin, as it would be to any father for his only flesh and blood to perish in that way.

'Goswin demanded revenge, but there was no way to bring Thyl to justice. Dorothea didn't die a virgin, but neither did she die by Thyl Bruys's hand. There were no witnesses that Thyl had taken Dorothea by force, and the nuns couldn't find signs of violence on Dorothea's body. In Goswin's eyes, though, Thyl was guilty – maybe before God Thyl would be found guilty, too – but Goswin couldn't demand punishment for Thyl before the court. Dorothea had drowned herself. So Goswin demanded justice from his old friend Laurentz Bruys. Bruys was a fair-minded man. He agreed that Thyl should be punished because he must have known very well what sort of a son he had. But he was *his* son. He offered Goswin money, he left Thyl without an inheritance, but that wasn't enough for Goswin. Goswin demanded more. He demanded what no father would do to a son. He demanded Thyl's death because he was blinded by his grief and rage. He rejected Bruys's money and said that only blood was a just punishment. Bruys was horrified by this demand; suddenly he saw a monster before him instead of a friend. Then Goswin demanded Thyl's castration, and, of course, Bruys would not agree to that either – and that was another reason Bruys sent his son into exile in Germany. He sent him away because in Tallinn Goswin would have killed him or paid someone to kill him. When Bruys eventually received the news of Thyl's death he said that even the Lord God can't give sanctuary to those who don't want to find sanctuary. He had sent Thyl into exile so that his son wouldn't fall victim to Goswin's revenge, but that was all he offered Goswin in compensation, and they became sworn enemies.'

'All this was twenty-five years ago,' said Dorn with a sigh. 'They say that time heals all wounds – but not those that a person brings upon himself.'

'Punishing Bruys became Goswin's sole aim in life – and that is where the just desire for revenge turned evil. Goswin was even more angered by the fact that the following year another son was born into Bruys's family. God seemed to be making a fool of him. So he then decided that if he couldn't punish the culprit he would punish the innocent because Dorothea had also died an innocent. In fact, this began to seem more just to him – Bruys had to suffer the same pain that he had suffered. Bruys had to feel pain for the suffering of the innocent. What satisfaction would there be for Goswin if the culprit died? The innocent had to suffer, and the innocent were Bruys, his wife and their young son Johan. Only that would be justice.'

'So Annlin told us,' said Dorn mournfully. 'She had to be tortured with the tongs, but she did tell us.'

'Goswin thought up a cunning plan, one of the wickedest that a person in the grip of evil and blind hatred could devise,' continued Melchior. 'He knew that Bruys had a bastard son. He had been born several years before Johan when Thyl was still in Tallinn. It must have been some silly bit of mischief, in some village beyond the town, where Bruys sometimes had to go on business. Bruys didn't acknowledge the child, and why should he if, after disowning and exiling Thyl, another son had been born to him? He wanted nothing to do with the other son, who meant nothing to him, because not having been born in lawful marriage the boy would never have become his heir or a citizen of the town. But Goswin knew about him. He had the boy found and bided his time. That time arrived when Johan was twelve years old. Now I have to tell you about a physical flaw in Laurentz Bruys, one he passed on to his progeny. On Laurentz Bruys's left foot there were six toes, and his sons had them, too.

'Magistrate, Sir Knight, Brother Hinric, you have to talk to people. Even when they have every intention of lying to you they aren't always lying. Some grain of truth always slips into their story. No lie is so enduring that it can be perpetuated for ever. A lie has to be believable, and so an enduring lie is never a complete lie. Annlin was lying to me about that night when the tramp was killed on Rataskaevu Street, but she slipped in some truth about her son. Goswin was lying to me about his penitence and injustice towards Bruys. He was playing games with me, but he couldn't check himself completely, and at one point he called Thyl Bruys a bastard. At first I thought he was just swearing, but then it occurred to me that Goswin might have meant it literally, *expressis verbis,* and I thought for a second that maybe Thyl was *the* bastard, but no. There were six toes on Laurentz Bruys's left foot and six toes on Thyl's as well. And so had the bastard son and Johan. Nature, or God, plays such a cruel joke on people that flaws are passed on from father to son – and shouldn't I, of all people, know that?

'It was my dear Keterlyn who pointed out that the same things had been done to the tramp's corpse as to Bruys – he couldn't talk, he couldn't have children and, instead of the sixth toe, he had the whole foot cut off. I should have seen the truth straight away, but I was blinded by an apothecary's thinking. I thought that somehow someone needed that foot. And when we found de Wrede cutting up corpses I believed that it was he who had removed the tramp's foot. How stupid I was.'

'Was that foot actually cut off by Goswin?' asked Hinric.

'Goswin ordered it to be done,' declared Melchior, 'but Hainz did it, and not because Goswin needed it but so that no one would see it. Six toes is quite a rare deformity, and if anyone had noticed it the story would certainly have spread, someone would have realized that that poor creature had to be Laurentz Bruys's son.'

'He was his son, his bastard son?' asked Greyssenhagen.

Melchior shook his head, drank some beer and thought for a bit. 'It isn't easy for me to talk about this,' he said. 'This horror took place on Rataskaevu Street, near my home.'

'No one was allowed to know it,' muttered Dorn. 'Bruys and Goswin seemed to have agreed to pretend that the old hatchet had been buried.'

'So that tramp wasn't his bastard?' Hinric asked.

'No,' said Melchior, taking a deep breath, 'he wasn't. Twelve years ago Goswin put his plan into action. He waited for the right moment. He was patient and tenacious. Hainz and Annlin ambushed Bruys's bastard one evening outside town, lured him into town and took him to Bruys's storehouse. At that time Johan was alone there in the granary. Hainz throttled Bruys's bastard and knocked Johan unconscious. Then Annlin set fire to the store. The fire was a terrible thing. There were many more wooden buildings around then, it was a confused situation, people milling around everywhere, and the fire spread. Then they led the half-conscious Johan away. I don't even know the name of that bastard son, but I suppose the court attendant will find the woman who went to Bruys's funeral – who, I would guess, was the mother of that boy. The bastard was so badly burned in the fire that he could only be identified by the sixth toe, and Bruys had no reason to doubt that it was the corpse of his son. Johan had died, and Bruys's wife died of grief days later. After that Bruys dedicated his life to pious causes. God had punished him, and now he had to seek his peace with God, and so, finally, he became one of the patrons of St Bridget's and a man who was called a saint in his own lifetime.'

'If a person dies in a fire, then the body is usually found curled up,' said Dorn.

'Exactly,' said Melchior, 'but Mathyes told me that Johan's corpse was lying straight. No one understood the significance of that, for there was no reason to doubt. Johan was alone in the granary, and there he died. But the corpse of a person burned alive is usually rolled up into a ball, as that person tried desperately to ward off the fire until their very last breath.'

'And they took Johan to Goswin?' asked Hinric.

'Goswin put him in the salt-cellar. He shackled the boy there and gave up trading in salt. He cut out the boy's tongue so that he wouldn't scream; he cut off his sex organ because then a prisoner is more tame. He made Johan his slave, torturing and humiliating him, but he kept him alive. Twelve years. Can you imagine that

Goswin kept him like a dog in the cellar and took pleasure in every moment? He kept him in chains, had him brought to him while he had breakfast, forced him to beg for scraps of food, whipped him, let him wallow in his own faeces. Annlin and Hainz took care of him, buying ointments for his wounds to keep him alive. Goswin had them collect medicine from *me*. They bought the ointments for his wounds, and I found traces of that ointment on Johan's body. If wounds are smeared with my salve the skin remains slightly yellow for a few months.'

'But how could Goswin force two Christians to commit such crimes?' Tears were appearing in Hinric's eyes. 'Was it money?'

'Oh no,' said Melchior. 'When I had swept from my thoughts all the connections with the Unterrainer house, when I saw the story clearly and simply … When I realized that the murderer could only go into hiding in some nearby house because he had nowhere else to go – Simon and Ursula were in the yard of the Unterrainer house that evening, and they thought they heard a ghost and saw some indistinct shape – I thought about the Goswin, Witte and Greyssenhagen houses. Yes, esteemed sir, I even thought that that corpse might have been some tenant of yours or a victim of Witte's whipping or one of Annlin's relatives from the country … And then I recalled Annlin's words – she has a son in Tartu named Hanns who is forty-one years old. The idea came to me in the brothel when the old hag was talking about Bruys's bastard son, and then it all became so clear, so terrible, and everything fell into place at once: the hacked-off foot, the fact that Goswin gave up the salt trade, supposedly out of blindness, and even the contradiction that de Zwarte had written home that his last work in Tallinn was finished and he had been paid well.'

'He hadn't been paid well,' remarked Dorn. 'Everyone thought he was a bad painter – and, anyway, how is that Flemish dauber mixed up in all this?'

'And what's the significance of Hanns being forty-one years old?' asked Hinric.

'If you calculate, then you'll work out that Hanns was born in 1378,' replied Melchior, 'and Dorothea drowned herself when she was seventeen.'

Mathematics had never been Dorn's strong suit, but Hinric was good at reckoning. 'That means that there can't have been more than a year between the births of Dorothea and Hanns,' said the Dominican.

'A few months,' declared Melchior.

'So what does that signify?' demanded Dorn. 'The horrible old hag didn't talk about that under torture.'

'I understand,' whispered Hinric. 'Now I understand.'

'Goswin's wife died giving birth to Dorothea,' said Melchior, 'and someone had to suckle the girl. Annlin's son was born a little later, so Annlin suckled Goswin's daughter. They grew up in the same house. They were like brother and sister – to Annlin, Dorothea *was* her daughter.'

'That is why she, too, hated Thyl to the depths of her soul,' sighed Hinric. 'Dorothea was just like her own child, and Hainz would do anything that Annlin and Master Goswin commanded.'

'But now the business of that damn Fleming?' Dorn insisted. 'What portrait? I couldn't understand what the old woman was wailing about while Bose was pinching her with the tongs.'

'I also commissioned him to paint a picture,' remarked Greyssenhagen. 'The picture was finished, but … I don't know … so far I've never hung it up. It's not quite my likeness.'

'Goswin had Annlin buy a great deal of medicine for wounds and aches this winter because Johan was at the point of death,' Melchior explained further. 'They did make him well, but in the meantime Goswin was starting to fear that the boy might not survive. He paid de Zwarte to paint a portrait of him because he might need it when his prisoner died. It was a poor substitute but at least some consolation for Goswin, who had been awaiting his revenge for so long. He forced de Wrede to keep quiet and paid him very well, demanding that the painter should not tell anyone what he had to do, and Goswin told everyone in town that the portrait was of him. This explains why de Zwarte said that Tallinn was an accursed town and he'd seen a ghost ... Poor tormented Johan no longer looked like a living person. It was hard to guess his age because his face had shrunk from the darkness and the poor diet. De Zwarte didn't dare to put into words exactly what he had done ... but he was in desperate need of the money. He couldn't go home poor and a failure, and Goswin paid him handsomely. De Zwarte wrote home that his works were finished, *even the last one, and he was paid well.* In Goswin's house, though, there are no paintings, and Goswin told me that he'd thrown the painter out, straight to the harbour, and the portrait hadn't been completed. Of course, Goswin would never let de Zwarte leave Tallinn. If he had seen Johan and been ordered to paint him, that was his death sentence.'

'What about Magdalena and Grote?' asked Hinric.

'Hainz is thick in the head,' explained Dorn. 'He must have left the cellar open and Johan unchained, and the boy escaped. He bumped into Magdalena in front of the house, and Magdalena had lived in Bruys's house along with Johan.'

'Magdalena didn't tell Bruys because Bruys had cast her out,' continued Melchior, 'but she did tell other women, even though she didn't understand what exactly it was she had seen. She supposed that she'd encountered a person risen from the dead. Why was Grote killed? Because Bruys was dying, and Goswin was in a hurry. Bruys went to Marienthal on 1 August, and Goswin wanted to take Johan there that same night in a cart. But Johan was able to break free and escape when they tried to haul him on to the cart. Not far, it's true, but he remembered the way home. He had got no further than the corner of Rataskaevu Street and Lai Street when Hainz and Annlin got hold of him and dragged him back to the cellar. But Grote the Tower-Master saw him while he was drunk and started to think he'd seen a ghost. He babbled on about it in the taverns and at the monastery. Goswin got to hear and ordered him killed. I can imagine that poor Grote, who was quite stunned by the sight of Johan, thought that Annlin, approaching him in the dim light at the moment of his death, must have been a ghost, and that's why he looked so startled. Besides, Annlin must have smelled quite bad if she'd been cleaning the prisoner's faeces out of the confined salt-cellar all day. There was a dead tomcat next to Grote's corpse, too, which also stank, and that must have added to the effect that caused Grote to think that Annlin was a ghost. And he was half-blind in one eye.

'But that evening when Johan got out Goswin no longer had time to convey him to Marienthal. The town gates were already shut. He had to wait for the next evening, but there was heavy rain that day. In that weather he wouldn't have been able to make the trip. The cart would have got stuck in the mud, and it would have attracted too much attention if it left town in that weather. Then Bruys died that same day. Because of the rain it wasn't possible to send a message from Marienthal to town, and news of Bruys's death reached town only on 3 August. This was a dreadful blow to Goswin. His entire plan had collapsed, his revenge and the only pleasure he had to look forward to in life had crumbled to dust. He was maddened with rage and desperation. He went to Johan and attacked him with a knife. There was no more reason to keep him alive. Goswin ordered the corpse to be taken out of town on a cart and buried in the forest. But Johan wasn't dead. He must still have had some desperate will to live, so he was able to get out one final time with three wounds on his body. But this effort robbed him of his last strength. Hainz and Annlin caught him in front of the house, but the town guards saw them. The guards rushed to the spot, Annlin and Hainz ran back into the house, but Johan died there and then. He had no more strength left in him.'

Melchior was silent for a moment, and his eyes clouded over.

Hinric shook his head and whispered something in Latin.

'For twelve years Goswin kept him in a torture chamber,' Melchior said quietly. 'Can you imagine what that boy had to go through? That was the time when he was growing from a boy into a man; his tongue was cut out and his sex organ cut off, but he still had to remember who he was, who his parents were and where his home was. Goswin told him why he was keeping him alive and what sort of death he should die.'

'And he was very good at hiding his hatred under a mask of sorrow,' noted Greyssenhagen. 'There was a time when I thought that someone might have helped Bruys to die – when someone rich, and who has plenty of enemies, dies it's not at all unusual for that to happen. And it was I who invited Goswin to be a patron in place of Bruys because I had noticed that he had never said anything against the convent. I could never in my life have guessed that it was all just hypocrisy and for some horrible revenge.'

Melchior nodded. 'It was supposed to be Goswin's final and actual revenge. He was biding his time, and fate seemed at last to be on his side. Bruys built a prayer house attached to St Bridget's Convent. It was placed in a secluded corner at the back of the convent's land, and this suited Goswin very well. Gentlemen, this revenge of his – this was the moment he was living and breathing for, it was to be a perfect masterstroke, a work of art ...' Melchior swallowed and continued, 'Before Bruys died, Goswin wanted to take Johan before him and say, "Look, you didn't want to punish the culprit, so now you have to punish the innocent, because only then will you understand the torment I had to feel when my only daughter died. Here is your son, whom you thought was dead and buried – but, look, he's alive. All these years he's been chained in my cellar, wallowing there like a castrated dog in his own shit and begging me for scraps of food that I spat out in front of him. Now take this dagger and do what I asked when your son killed my daughter. Now you can choose again, but this choice will be harder. Stab your own son through his throat, release him from his torment and die in the knowledge that you killed your own son by your own hand, or die in the knowledge that your son will stay in my cellar to the end of his life to suffer torment."

'That was supposed to be Goswin's revenge, and he held that moment sacred. Bruys had lost the power of speech, and Goswin was not afraid that he would be able to say anything about it. But when Bruys died it seemed to Goswin that all his dreams had collapsed, but fate gave him one more chance. He was invited to be a patron of St Bridget's, and he accepted. He gave the convent his assets because he wanted to obliterate Bruys's legacy from the memory of Tallinn. He didn't want to continue the man's venture; he wanted to snuff it out, so that, even in a hundred years' time, when his gravestone was laid in the floor of St Bridget's they would speak of Arend Goswin as a founder of that convent but no one would remember Laurentz Bruys. When Greyssenhagen handed Goswin the image of St Bridget to kiss, I understood that. It was written on Goswin's face, all his hatred and his hope that he would blot out any memory of Bruys for ever …'

All of them went quiet for a while, no doubt thinking about poor Johan. Melchior knew that he would never be sure exactly how much of Johan's reasoning power had been left, but he feared that the boy hadn't lost it completely. He was afraid that the boy remembered, remembered all of the twelve years, all the pain and torment, oppression and hopelessness. His mind could certainly not be clear, no one's would be, yet if he'd been given a few more moments of life, to draw one more breath, maybe he would have managed to say who he was and that he had fled from his imprisonment.

'Tomorrow the Council will discuss what will become of Master Bruys's will,' added Dorn with a sigh. 'It's a complicated story, because Johan outlived him. Johan should have inherited.'

'And de Wrede is bringing a lawsuit for the killing of his brother,' added Melchior. 'If anyone kills on a master's orders, that master is just as guilty, I say. Goswin is now writing letters to all the religious communities in Livonia and elsewhere asking to be given asylum as a penitent, but the Council –'

'The Council wants to prosecute him,' said Dorn. 'Annlin is to be buried alive and Hainz left on the rack to die, but Goswin …'

'They'll order him to go on a pilgrimage and then into a monastery,' whispered Melchior.

'Hainz is a citizen of the town and is allowed to testify against his Master. Maybe the Council will send Goswin on a pilgrimage for killing and enslaving Johan, but for him to have ordered the fire in the town ... for that he would have to be drawn and quartered,' declared Dorn, 'but that decision is in the hands of the burgomasters.'

'I would sentence him to being immured alive in the salt-cellar,' said Melchior, 'and leave him some water and bread and a dagger as well. Let him choose the kind of death he would prefer.'

Ursula and Simon had run back again to their hiding-place. Here, between the old wall of the stables and the bush in the backyard of the Unterrainer house no one could stumble upon them as they said goodbye to one another. In two days Simon was to board a ship to travel to Münster. They were no longer afraid. There had never been any ghost in the Unterrainer house, only the sounds made by that poor troubled Johan Bruys in Goswin's cellar. Everyone in the town now knew about that.

Arend Goswin had died a week before, right there in front of the court, just as he had dropped to his knees to beg for mercy. He had died of humiliation and shame. People would throw excrement on his grave.

But Ursula and Simon had to say farewell. May all the saints bear witness, they didn't want to do it. They kissed – they now knew how to kiss. It was sweet, but the pain was all the greater. They barely spoke, for words no longer meant anything.

Ursula was the first to get up and say that now she had to leave. She didn't want Simon to see her tears.

Simon remained leaning against the wall, watching, with a broken heart, as the girl set off at a run. Suddenly a light breeze seemed to seize Ursula's hair. The girl stopped and looked around, alarmed. Yet there she was, the wind ruffling her hair, and it seemed to Simon that Ursula was listening to something. It only lasted a moment.

Then the girl turned around and asked Simon, 'Did you hear it, too?'

'No, I didn't hear anything.'

Ursula smiled sadly. 'She blessed me in the name of St Michael. She said that you'll marry me, but I have to be patient and determined.'

'Who did?' asked Simon. 'Who blessed you?'

'She said her name was Dorothea,' called Ursula softly, glancing back at the boy for a moment and then running off.

Simon gazed after her for a long time.

And then he felt as if, through the dusk of evening and the cool haze, a warmth were glowing around him and someone had taken his heart between hot hands and whispered in his ear words of love and hope.

But maybe it only seemed that way to him.

ALSO AVAILABLE FROM
PUSHKIN VERTIGO

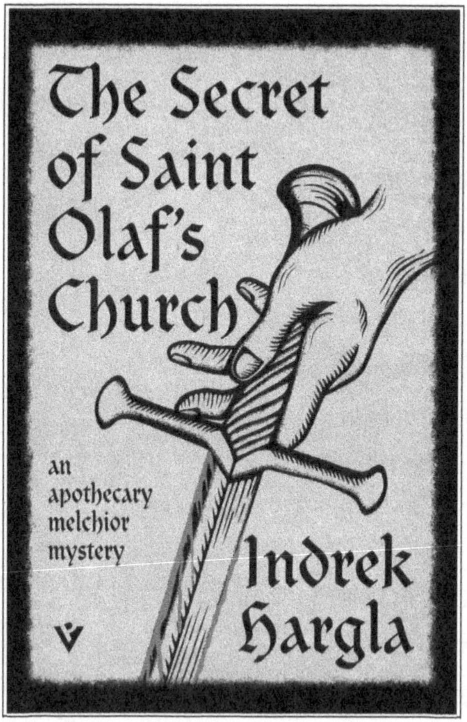

'Richly detailed and vividly imagined'

Crime Reads

AVAILABLE AND COMING SOON FROM PUSHKIN VERTIGO

Jonathan Ames

You Were Never Really Here
A Man Named Doll
The Wheel of Doll

Simone Campos

Nothing Can Hurt You Now

Zijin Chen

Bad Kids

Maxine Mei-Fung Chung

The Eighth Girl

Candas Jane Dorsey

The Adventures of Isabel
What's the Matter with Mary Jane?

Margot Douaihy

Scorched Grace

Joey Hartstone

The Local

Seraina Kobler

Deep Dark Blue

Elizabeth Little

Pretty as a Picture

Jack Lutz

London in Black

Steven Maxwell

All Was Lost

Callum McSorley

Squeaky Clean

Louise Mey

The Second Woman

John Kåre Raake

The Ice

RV Raman

A Will to Kill
Grave Intentions
Praying Mantis

Paula Rodríguez

Urgent Matters

Nilanjana Roy

Black River

John Vercher

Three-Fifths
After the Lights Go Out

Emma Viskic

Resurrection Bay
And Fire Came Down
Darkness for Light
Those Who Perish

Yulia Yakovleva

Punishment of a Hunter
Death of the Red Rider